Honeysuckle Lane

LULU MOORE

Cover Design by Ink and Laurel

Map Design by Ink and Laurel

Editing by Making Manuscripts

Copy editing by Editing4Indies

Proof reading by Julia Griffis

Interior Formatting by Cleo Moran/Devoted Pages

this one is for those on the verge of giving up hope.

don't.

Valentine Nook
Oxfordshire est. 1511
Cupid's Arrow
The Beanery
Hendricks's Vet
Valentine High Street
The One True Love
Alex's Cottage
Honeysuckle Lane
The Valentine Nook Fountain
Cricket Pitch

Rose Garden
Burlington Hall
Blackberry
Farm Yard
Stable Yard
Sunday & Thunder
Hamish, Maud & Dolly
Miles's Cottage
Bluebell Cottage
Burlington Gates
Park

Prologue

Hendricks

Six years ago – age 21

"Hen?"

At the sound of knocking, I turn to find my brother Alex standing at my car window. My eyes meet his, serious and concerned, just like the expression written all over his face as he opens the door.

"What are you doing?"

Swiping a hand under my nose, I open my mouth to speak, but I can't bring myself to tell him because then it'll be real. It's too awful. I don't even know the words to use.

"Hey, you're shaking." Alex gently places his arm around my shoulders and pulls me out of the car. "Come on, come inside. You can tell me what's wrong."

It's only then I realize I'm outside of his cottage, because I have no memory of getting here. Two hours ago, I was in London having a conversation I never expected when I woke up this morning. Autopilot kicked in soon after, bringing me back to the village I grew up in.

Valentine Nook, my favorite place in the whole

world.

Alex guides me up the path and inside. We go straight into the kitchen, where he pushes me into a chair. Switching on the kettle, he sets about making cups of tea and places the biscuit jar on the table. Inside, I find a packet of chocolate Digestives. I take two out and stuff them both in my mouth.

I haven't been to Alex's in a while, and it always amazes me how neat and tidy he is. Even without his housekeeper, everything would still be immaculate. Everything would have its place.

It's not a word you could use to describe the cottage where Miles and I live.

It's clean, thanks to the same housekeeper we share, but it's only tidy for approximately an hour after she's left. My study books and veterinary texts are spread out on the kitchen table because that's where I like to revise. The rest of the kitchen is treated as an overflow of the mudroom, where Miles dumps any broken piece of horse tack or polo mallet that he plans to fix but never does.

It's currently going through the longest tidy stretch it's ever had. That's only because Miles has been playing polo in Argentina for the past month, and I'm in London at the Royal Veterinary College four days a week. I'm halfway through my third year of a five-year course, and once I graduate, I'll be a vet in Valentine Nook—something I've dreamed about since I was ten years old.

Assuming I've not completely fucked things up.

Alex puts a steaming cup of tea in front of me and sits down. Easing a Digestive out, he dunks it in his own cup and bites into it. He watches me while he chews and swallows, then takes a long sip. When he leans back, arms crossed, I know my time is up.

"Right. What's happened?"

Thumping sets off behind my eyes, a pressure from the million thoughts running around and around my mind. I open my mouth to begin, only to close it again.

Fuck. Fuck. *Fuck.*

"Hen, it can't be that bad . . . Is it school? Have you failed your course?" He frowns, like that's the only thing I could have ruined. But he couldn't possibly understand.

Six years older than me, Alex has always been sensible, for want of a better word. Cautious is more accurate. Controlled.

If I'd been a little more controlled, I wouldn't be in this mess, one Alex would *never* find himself in. Alex, along with Lando, my eldest brother, has always been too focused on work to find time for anything else.

They're a team, but where Lando has been busy running Burlington since he was eighteen, Alex is working to build overseas operations. Together, they're the leaders of the next generation of our family, while Miles and I have been given the freedom to forge our own paths.

And the second we were old enough, we took that freedom and sprinted, much to their chagrin. But we were born without the weight of responsibilities our older brothers have, and—as we learned very early—Miles and I are also blessed with the ability to work hard *and* party hard.

When we're not partying, Miles channels his energy into becoming the best polo player in the world, while I study my arse off so that I can take over the Valentine Nook Veterinary Practice.

Lando and Alex run the world their way. Miles and I *play* in the world our way.

We have the uncanny ability to get out of any situation virtually unscathed.

Or we did. *I* did.

I shake my head. "Do you remember when you were in London a couple of months ago, and the four of us went out?"

It takes him a second to recall. "Annabel's?"

"Yes." I nod. "And I hooked up with that girl. Sienna?"

His mouth rolls because I could be talking about anyone. He stopped paying attention to my social life a long time ago. "I didn't know that was her name. But okay—"

"I've seen her a couple of times since." I pick up another biscuit out of habit, only to put it back down. I have no appetite. "She's pregnant."

The cup of tea stops halfway to Alex's lips, and he slowly places it back on the table. "And it's yours?"

Swallowing the resurfacing lump in my throat, I nod. "Apparently so."

He says nothing more and rubs along his brow.

Since our father died when Miles and I were young, Lando and Alex have taken on his role, especially as we've gotten older.

Eight and six years older than us, respectively, they're a fine balancing act. Lando's less tolerant than Alex. He's too focused on building Burlington to put up with the mountain of shit Miles and I get up to. Therefore, Alex is the one we usually go to as a first port of call when we need bailing out—literally, in Miles's case, last summer.

But I have no idea how Alex will react to this latest news.

His fingers slowly scratch along his stubbled chin, back and forth. I know he's thinking about how our father would have dealt with this.

By the time he asks, "Have you spoken to Miles?" the anxiety of waiting for his reaction almost has me in tears.

I shake my head. Even though it's nearly lunchtime in Buenos Aires, there's no way Miles will be up. "He's still asleep."

"And this girl? Did you talk to her about what she wanted to do?"

Sienna's determined expression flashes in my eyes, and I nod once. "She wants to keep it."

I don't add that she already shared her financial demands and expectations, or the one thing I'm trying not to think about—that she got pregnant on purpose. There were two of us there, and I thought we were always careful.

Fuck. What a mess.

"You know you need a paternity test."

"Yes." My face drops in my hands, but Alex stands and pulls me into a hug, cradling my head while I sob on his shoulder.

It's not the first time he's comforted me like this, and it won't be the last, so he lets me cry until I'm ready to stop.

"It's going to be okay, Hen. We'll figure it out. Let me call Lando, and we'll drive to Burlington to find Mum too. May as well tell them both at the same time."

I sniff hard, and my sigh is so deep it makes my stomach convulse. I only just make it to the kitchen sink before I throw up. I haven't eaten since last night, so all my stomach contains is the acid that's steadily built up since I walked into the coffee shop. It burns my throat, my eyes sting, and I don't stop until Alex stands behind me holding a glass of water.

I knock it back in one go, only to vomit it all up again.

It takes another five minutes of resting my head against the cool marble of the sink before I feel anything close to normal, though I suspect *normal* isn't something I'll get to experience for a while.

When I finally stand straight, Alex stares at me, his face twisted with worry.

"I'm fine, really." I swipe a hand across my mouth, hoping he doesn't catch the lie. "I need to run back to the cottage. Can you wait ten minutes?"

He nods. "I'll let Lando know we're coming."

Leaving my car outside Alex's, I walk the half mile down Honeysuckle Lane to Rosehip Cottage, where Miles and I live. I've spent the best part of today either in my car or sitting in a London coffee shop. Fresh country air is what I need. While I'm not putting too much pressure on it, a couple of deep lungfuls is all it takes to dial down the anxiety by at least twenty-five percent.

I even manage a small wave to Mrs. Winston, walking on the other side of the road. But I pass too quickly for her to stop me for a chat, and as I'm nearing the fountain, I hear my name and look up.

There she is.

The one person I want to see most in the world right now, besides Miles.

Story MacIntosh.

My best friend since I was six. My permanent sunny day, whatever the weather.

Her entire face lights up. For a second, my day rights itself. The anxiety curdling my bones subsides, and I completely forget how fucked my life is.

Wrapping her arms around me, she squeezes me tight, and just like always, I rest my chin on her head. It's been something I've done since my growth spurt at thirteen because she stayed the same height. The scent of her shampoo floats under my nose.

It's all I can do not to bury my nose in her thick mop of chocolate-brown hair to calm my racing heart.

It's been less than twenty-four hours since I last saw her, but it feels like forever. My world is not the same as it was yesterday.

I wish I could go back to last night, when the two of us snuggled under the blanket on the sofa, watching our Monday night movie with a bowl of popcorn. It's a ritual we started the summer we were thirteen, and we've continued it every Monday we could. But with us both being away at university, yesterday was the first Monday movie night we'd had in forever.

Even though we speak every day, we hadn't both been back in Valentine Nook at the same time for a couple of months, so I couldn't fucking wait to see her.

Everything was set up the way all our Monday movie nights are. I'd bought her favorite popcorn, ordered two pizzas—pineapple for me, spicy pepperoni for her—and the movie we'd been waiting to watch together was ready on pause.

It was the same as always, but better somehow. The two of us together again, finally. We'd barely watched the movie because we'd been talking too much, and when it came time to leave, I hadn't wanted her to go. I always struggled leaving Story, but last night it was different.

Last night, I finally felt things shifting into their rightful place. Our time had arrived, and we would get our chance.

"I thought you had to be in school today," she says, stepping back, though her fingers stay looped in mine.

"I did. I *was*. I came back."

"Oh amazing, lucky me." She grins wide, and her fading summer freckles spread across her nose. "I was going to call you . . . I want to talk, actually . . ." She pauses, and her head tilts as she regards me with an expert eye. Only Miles knows me better than Story does. "Hen, are you okay?"

I shake my head. "Not really."

She can tell by my face that whatever's bothering me is nothing to joke about because that's what she'd normally do. Make a joke.

"What is it? What's happened?"

I push my fingers through my hair. I've already told Alex. I've said it out loud, yet telling Story is infinitely harder.

My eyes find a spot in the distance, past the fountain and into the field where the Aberdeen Angus bulls are grazing. I know, in the field beyond, are this year's calves, all growing nicely. My throat is suddenly dry.

"There's a girl I hooked up with—"

I don't imagine how the grip of Story's hand on mine loosens.

Her voice is weirdly high-pitched when she replies,

"You've been hooking up with someone? I didn't know that."

"Yeah, not often, just a couple of times. Alex and Miles were in London a few months ago, and we went out—" If I tell her my brothers were there, maybe it'll feel less like my fault.

And Story will be less annoyed, because I know she'll be annoyed.

"A few *months*?"

I know why she's mad. I never told her. But the one thing Story and I never talk about is the girls I hook up with—or, in her case, the guys.

If we don't talk about it, we can pretend it doesn't happen. An unwritten rule that started in our mid-teens.

Plus, I haven't seen Story in person since I met Sienna.

"She called me this morning on my way into class. I went to meet her after . . ." I stop talking, and my eyes find the bulls again. I can't look at her. Fuck. "She's pregnant."

Normally, when I'm having a bad day, Story envelops me in her usual sweetness, and that instantly relaxes me. But I know that's not going to happen this time.

"Pregnant?"

I pinch the bridge of my nose. I can barely believe it. No matter how many times I say it, it doesn't feel real. "Seven weeks."

"Seven weeks?" Her voice is so quiet I barely hear it. "What are you going to do?"

"I don't know." I shake my head. "She wants to keep it—"

"Are you in a relationship with her?"

"No." The word is almost shouted, and I shake my head so hard my brain rattles. "No. It's always been casual. We don't talk much outside of when we all go out. But now . . . I don't know. I guess I have to see what the paternity test says."

I don't know anything.

The sum of my conversation with Sienna was being told she was pregnant before she left me to meet her friends. And *left me* in the coffee shop with nothing but my dumbfounded thoughts and the bill.

Fuck. Fuck. Fuck. I'm going to be a dad. I'll have to put my studies on hold. I'll have to move away from Valentine Nook. I never wanted to live in London full-time, but I guess I don't have a choice now.

I'm so deep in my thoughts that I don't notice Story hasn't said anything for a while. But when I look up, she's crying.

"Stor?" I reach for her hand, but she jumps away before I can.

"How could you do this?"

"What?"

"How could you be so stupid?"

"Story—"

"Last night . . . I thought, *finally* maybe . . . and now . . ." She pauses, snatching a tear away as it falls. "No. I'm not doing this. You know what? It's me. I'm the stupid one . . . You are *never* going to change. You and Miles . . . It's always going to be like this. Forever—"

"What? What does that mean? What is always going to be like this? What aren't you doing?"

"When are you going to grow up?"

"Excuse me?" I snap, but I'm not entirely sure she's talking to me. Or *about* me. Or maybe she's talking to herself.

"No, excuse *me*."

"Story?"

She holds her hand up, and I stay silent. Tears spill down her cheeks and drip off the hard set of her jaw. I can't recall ever seeing Story as angry as she is right now. And she can get mad, but not like this—cheeks blazing while murdering me painfully in her mind.

"Why are you mad?"

"Why am I mad? Why am I *mad*?" Her voice gets higher-pitched. Her eyes narrow, and her lip curls in a snarl. If looks could kill, I'd be dead a thousand times over, reduced to nothing more than a chalk outline. "Fuck you, Hendricks. Figure it out for yourself."

My stomach twists, and I'm too stunned to move. My body is frozen in shock. I forget all about why I'm standing here in the first place, why I'm not in London right now, and why I've spent most of the day stewing in my own anxiety, because my best friend shoots me one last withering look before storming off.

"Stor . . . Story!" I call after her right before she disappears around the bend in the road.

Picking up my phone, I dial her number only for it to ring once and get sent to voicemail.

What the hell just happened?

I'm about to run after her when Lando drives toward the fountain. He spots me and pulls up.

"Alex just called me."

The engine's still running as he jumps out and wraps his arms around me.

And just like that, my present smacks me in the face, and for the second time in fifteen minutes, I sob into my big brother's shoulder.

"Come on, let's go back to Burlington, and we'll figure it out."

I tell him everything on the way, getting the practice in before I break the news to my mother.

Truthfully, that should have been the worst of it, but I'm numb as I repeat my predicament. I'm barely listening to a word she says, because all I can think about is Story and the devastated look on her face.

Once my mother is done, I call Story again, only to be sent to voicemail *again*.

> **HENDRICKS**: Story, please pick up the phone. I'm freaking out, and I need you. I need my best friend.

I try her two more times.

> **HENDRICKS:** Stor, I don't know what I've done to make you so mad, but please talk to me. Call me back.

She never called. And I lasted thirty-six hours until I cracked and went in search of her.

Only I was too late.

1

Story

Miss MacIntosh.

Ms. MacIntosh.

Sophie.

I step back, pick up the eraser, and wipe away my name.

Then wipe away Ms. MacIntosh. Not sure what I'm trying to prove to a bunch of five- and six-year-olds. Miss MacIntosh, it is.

Then I scrub it all off and start again, writing *Good morning, welcome back. My name is Miss MacIntosh.* I turn to face the room.

The classroom looks as good as I can get it.

Bare walls have been replaced with posters of the alphabet and numbers. Colored paper chains stretch across the ceiling, giving the impression we're inside a Big Top. I'm certainly no interior designer, but anything's better than beige.

If I were still in Australia, I would have been much more prepared for the beginning of term. I like to start planning the return from each break a few months out, but to put it bluntly, the end of last year went to shit, and

I've done my best with the tools I had.

Now here I am in the classroom I never thought I'd return to while I try to muster up the enthusiasm my soon-to-be pupils deserve. But I'll be damned if my enthusiasm isn't being shoved out to make space for memories I don't want—namely, of sitting in the desk second row from the front, my six-year-old hand in the air, desperate to answer a question.

This time, I don't let the memory take hold. Instead, I jump up, shake out my arms, my body, and finally, my head, hoping it might shock some sense into me.

Maybe this morning won't be so bad, and my anxiety is giving me a rough ride just for the hell of it.

"Knock, knock. *Hellooo.*"

I turn to the door of the classroom to see a head peering around it. A blond head, belonging to a very smiley woman around my age. Her smile is so wide I'm tempted to ask what she's taken, and if she can give me the name of her dealer.

"Hey there." I do my best to match her fervor as she walks in, though it's more bounce than walk.

"Hi. Hi. Sorry to barge in before the morning chaos begins. I couldn't make the meeting yesterday, so I wanted to introduce myself. I heard you just moved here from Australia. Wow." She sets down two full coffee mugs, both bearing the Valentine Prep School crest, and taps a glossy red fingernail on her name badge, which reads Miss C. Scott, next to a matching red apple. "I'm Celeste. I teach the other reception class with you. I brought you a coffee—" Her eyes catch the paper chains roped across the ceiling. "And *wow*, I love what you've done with the place."

Ah, Celeste Scott. My teaching buddy, as Mrs.

Benson, the headmistress, referred to her. *Perhaps wow is her word of the day*. I mentally scold myself for being such a miserable bitch.

I'm in a situation entirely of my own making. I have no one to blame but myself. Taking a deep breath, I force my smile to reach my eyes.

"Thank you so much, just what I need." I hold my hand out. "It's great to meet you. I'm Sophie."

Sophie MacIntosh. Former Valentine Prep pupil. Master fucker-upper.

But she knocks my hand out of the way and yanks me into a hug. "None of that. We're a team now."

"Ooh, okay," I barely manage to squeak out as she squeezes me, and to my surprise, I find myself laughing. It's easier than crying, I guess.

"And honestly, you being here is saving me, big time. Running two classes last term was hard work." She rolls her eyes. I can't tell whether it's overly dramatic or if that's just who Celeste is. "And I don't want to speak ill of the dead, but Dave really left us in the S. H. I. T." She mouths each letter she spells out.

The news is enough to shake me out of my funk. "He *died*?"

She shakes her head, throwing it back with a laugh she digs from deep in her diaphragm. "No. But he'll wish he did if I ever get my hands on him."

My shoulders slump. Not because I'm disappointed he's not dead, but I was expecting a better story. "What happened?"

"Decided teaching wasn't for him and just didn't come in one day. Left on a round-the-world trip with a girl he'd met on Tinder the month before."

My mouth drops, because I get the impression that's the reaction Celeste is after. I don't share that I once pulled a similar stunt because the less I think about that, the less my stomach feels like it's shredding itself from the inside out.

Instead, I borrow her word of the day. "Wow."

"I know." Her lips purse. "Anyway, aside from saying hello, I came to bring you this. It was left on my desk, but it's for you."

She pulls a clear blue folder from under her arm and waves it. I stare at it, then gingerly ease it from her fingers. I double down on every single prayer I've ever said, which admittedly isn't many, but the cause of seventy-five percent of my anxiety is inside that folder.

Come to think of it, it might be closer to ninety, and I really want it to go away.

"Thanks, I was wondering if I was going to get this."

"Yes, just the curriculum for the term and your class list." She grins, not noticing how my entire body has stiffened. "Sorry, you should have had it yesterday."

I pull out the top sheet where sixteen names are written in alphabetical order. Checking it twice, I let out a sigh of relief that feels more like an exorcism because I don't see any name I recognize. God is clearly sweeter on me than I originally thought.

For one blissful second, I think this might all turn out okay.

But Celeste is peering over my shoulder. "Oh, fudge. That's not yours. Sorry . . ." With a giggle, she snatches up the folder and rushes out the door, returning thirty seconds later waving another clear blue folder. "This one's for you."

The churning in my stomach starts up again, and

for the second time, I pull out a list of names. This time, I don't need to scan down it because it's right there at the top.

Maxwell Angus William Burlington.

This was a mistake. I shouldn't be here. I can't do it.

If I let out a groan, Celeste doesn't seem to notice because she's pulled a pen from her pocket and is placing a red dot next to a couple of the names.

"Watch out for the parents of these ones. They're difficult. Constantly complaining about something," she tuts. "Spend their entire life on the phone, then wonder why their child is acting out at home. Nothing you ever do is right—"

I nod silently. But she's not done.

"And this one likes to eat crayons . . . this one's mum is having an affair with this one's dad . . ." She sucks in her cheek and peers around to check no one's listening even though we're in a classroom by ourselves. "I realize I'm being terribly indiscreet on your first day, but"—she taps against the name I don't want to look at—"his dad . . . well, you'll find out for yourself."

Celeste fans herself while I'm wondering where the bin is so I can throw up.

"A glimpse of him every morning is a really great start to the day." She giggles.

Why? Why did I think I could get away with this?

All I planned to do was visit for Christmas break. Slip into Valentine Nook, spend time at my parents' place, then leave without being spotted. I've done it before. I could do it again.

But luck was not on my side this time. Dumb or otherwise.

In fact, ever since I stepped foot in the village this year, things have gone from bad to worse. First, my dad broke his leg, then my mum got the flu, and because my stupid brother spent stupid Christmas with his stupid girlfriend, I was left to hold everything together. I had to run the farm and man the Christmas tree stand.

Which is when the shit really hit the fan.

I can still feel Hendricks's anger from the afternoon he turned up. And I deserved it. I deserved every bit of his wrath. I'm nothing but a coward who runs from her problems instead of dealing with them head-on.

I could barely make out the usual piercing blue of his eyes, narrowed at me from underneath a baseball cap. He was so angry that for a split second, I thought it was Miles glaring at me.

"But he doesn't always do drop-off, so a lot of mums leave disappointed."

Oh God, she's still talking.

"Sorry, who are you talking about?" I ask, though I don't know why. I *know.*

"Hendricks Burlington. The Burlingtons are an extremely important family around here. Max is in your class. Sweet boy." She picks up her coffee and sips while perched on the edge of a desk in the front row. I guess we're going to be talking, then. I suppose that's better than stewing in my own vortex of bad decisions that led me up to this point. "So where did you teach before you arrived at Valentine Prep?"

"Australia. A private school in Sydney." I smile, thankful for the change of subject. I take a sip of my own coffee and almost gag. My usual coffee comes with a side of six spoons of sugar, something I rarely tell people because I'm never in the mood to hear the judgmental gasps of *six*. "Mmm."

"The coffee machine in the staff room is top-notch. It's a fight to get to it in the morning."

I lift my mug to her and pretend to take another sip. "Then thank you for risking your life for me."

She knocks her mug against mine and laughs. "You're welcome. We have to look out for each other. I'll take you around the village when you're settled in. Why did you leave Australia?"

She slips it in so casually at the end that I barely notice.

Only when my brain catches up do I realize I need to come up with a decent answer that doesn't raise further questions. Because telling her the full truth is going to lead me down a path I don't want to venture down. She's only just veered off the topic of Hendricks and the Burlingtons. If I tell her I grew up in Valentine Nook, we'll go straight back. I definitely don't want to undo all the work I've done to block him from my mind.

It's already unraveling far too quickly.

In the end, I go with half the truth. "My boyfriend and I broke up earlier last year, and it coincided with my teaching contract ending. So I came to England to spend time with my family and had to stay longer than I planned. This job came up unexpectedly."

"*Dave*." Celeste tuts, and her brows drop before she smiles broadly. "I'm sorry to hear that. His loss is our gain, though."

I nod, and my mouth rolls in. "Just one of those things."

"Well . . ." Her eyes flick up to the clock on the wall. It's followed by her wriggling off the desk to land on the floor with a little jump. "I'm single too, so we can have some girl fun. But I must finish getting prepped before the bell rings and the doors open. Holler if you need anything, and I'll meet you at breaktime for a full debrief."

I flash her a genuine smile. Celeste is as vibrant and raring to go for the school term as I always used to be. I love teaching. It's been my dream as long as I can remember, but being back in Valentine Nook is messing with my head.

The truth is I just need to stay here until my dad is back on his feet, then I'll be gone *again.*

I can leave this place and all the memories behind. Celeste can add me to her shit list next to Dave.

"Thanks. I'll come and find you."

"Good luck." She waves and leaves with a parting comment. "I love your skirt, by the way. Very pretty. Gorgeous color."

My eyes drop to the ankle-length lilac satin I'd spotted in the dress shop the other day and bought on a whim. I haven't worn this color in years. It was one I used to wear to some degree most days, usually on my nails or with a hair tie. A pair of knickers that no one ever saw except me.

It's been hanging on the front of my wardrobe ever since, while I stared at it, trying to summon the happiness this particular color used to make me feel. I only decided to wear it five minutes before I left the house this morning, only to pull it on over a navy cable-knit jumper and boots.

Stupid. I'm being stupid.

The bell startles me enough that I spill my coffee on the floor. I don't have time to remember my nerves because the next couple of minutes are spent rushing around, wiping it up with paper towels, and double-checking that all the desks are straight. On each one, I leave a packet of newly sharpened pencils and a colored eraser.

Finally, before I can think about it any further and talk myself into doing another runner, I open the door and brace myself for the arrival of the boy I once loved with my whole heart.

2

Hendricks

Age 6

"Mummy. Mummy. Mummy."

From the back seat, I see her eyes appear in the mirror. "Yes, Miles?"

"Are you sure Hendricks and I aren't in the same class this year?"

His shaky voice means he's trying hard not to cry. Reaching out, I grab his hand and hold it tight. I'm secretly nervous about us being split up too, but I don't want to show him because he gets upset.

"No, sweetheart, you're not. But you're right across the hall from each other. You're the distance that my bedroom is from your bedroom. It's so close. You're still in the same year, and you'll still be together, but this will give you the chance to make more friends."

"But we're not sitting next to each other?"

"No, but you know who you can sit next to? Lucas. Or Emily. Or Jack."

Miles relaxes next to me, like when we stroke the dogs' bellies, and they roll over. Jack is our friend from kindergarten. The three of us always play together during school break, and this summer holiday, he was allowed to have a sleepover, and we made a tent in our bedroom. Alex brought us hot chocolates, and we stayed up too late.

I'm happy for a second because Miles is happy, but then I realize if Jack's in Miles's class, he's not in mine.

"Mummy, I thought Jack was in my class."

"No, darling, he's in Miles's class."

The little bubbles in my tummy start fizzing again. Miles squeezes my hand because he knows that I'm getting more nervous now. When one of us is sad, we can tell, even if we don't say it.

I'm not as upset as Miles about us not being together, but this is our first year in the big school, and not all our friends will be there.

Mummy parks her car, and we undo the buckle on our car seats so we can jump out when she opens the back door. After we take our school bags from her, we each take one of her hands and walk toward our classroom.

"Look, there's Jack," shouts Miles, dragging us forward quicker.

"Go and say hello to him," Mummy says, letting go of his hand so he can run off.

I'm glad he's happy again, but when Mummy kneels and puts her arms around me, I feel like I'm going to cry. I want to hug her and breathe in the flowers she always smells like, but I don't. We're in the big school now, and Lando said you're not supposed to cry in big school.

"You know who I think is in your class? Samuel."

I smile even though I don't really like Samuel. I saw

him chase a cat once. “Okay.”

“And when I come to collect you after school, you can tell me all about your first day. You’ll see Miles at break and lunch, and you’ll do all your sports together. And when you come home, you’ll be able to tell each other about your days.”

The bubbles in my tummy go away a little bit, and I smile at her.

“Come on, let’s go meet your new teacher.”

“Hen, Hen. Mummy,” shouts Miles, this time pulling Jack over toward us. I see his mum standing by the main entrance. Her hand is raised in the air, and Mummy waves back at her. “Mummy, Jack invited Hendricks and me over for supper.”

I forget about being nervous. I love going to Jack’s house. He’s got a cool tree house in his garden that we made into a den this summer. I look up at Mummy. “Please, can we go?”

“Yes, maybe, let’s all get inside first. We don’t want to be late on our first day.”

I take her hand again, though Miles and Jack run back over to his mum.

There are so many children here this morning, more than when we were in kindergarten last year, and we all look the same in gray blazers with red stripes. Alex helped us tie our ties. He and Lando don’t go back to boarding school for a couple of days, and when they do, it’ll just be me, Miles, and Clementine, our baby sister.

Burlington will be quiet again, except for the dogs. Mummy says Miles and I make enough noise for everyone.

We walk into the main hall and down a long corridor decorated with colored posters. They make me feel happy and nervous at the same time. Miles and Jack are already standing outside a door, and I can see the teachers pointing everyone toward the school pegs and lockers.

"Hen, Hen, this is your class. That's where you put your coat. It's next to mine." Miles points, then spins around to face one of the doors. "And I'm in there. We're so close."

"Cool." I take off my bag and put it on the peg. There's a picture of a cow underneath my name. Miles has a pony on his.

We *are* close, and when I say goodbye to Miles and then Mummy, I'm not sad anymore.

My teacher, Mrs. Benson, tells me to find the desk with my name on it. It's right in the middle of the classroom, and sitting next to me is a girl I haven't seen before. She wasn't in my kindergarten class, so maybe she's new. Her dark hair is in a long braid that looks like Zeus's, my daddy's horse, and it's tied at the bottom with a ribbon.

She turns her whole body toward mine when I sit down.

"Hello. I'm Sophie," she says. "What's your name?"

"Hendricks."

"When's your birthday? Mine is the fifth of February. I'll be seven."

That means she's older than me. "I'll be seven in May."

"What's your favorite color?"

"Blue," I answer even though it's a fib.

"My favorite color is green. It's the color of dragons and grass and magic."

I frown. "Magic?"

"Yes."

"Magic doesn't have a color. It's not real."

"It is real. And it's green."

"How do you know magic is green?"

"What other color would it be?" She shrugs, and I don't reply because I don't know. I'll ask Lando when I get home. He always knows everything.

"I saw a dragon once. He was walking down the road."

"No, you didn't."

"I did. He was wearing a top hat and carrying a red briefcase. He said good morning to me as he passed."

I stare at her, just like Lando stares sometimes when he's annoyed. There's no way she's seen a dragon. They're not real. And even if they are real, they don't wear clothes.

She's fibbing, then I remember I fibbed. So instead of arguing with her, I say, "Actually, blue isn't my favorite color."

"What is then?"

I pause. "Purple. But light purple, not dark purple."

"That's not purple." She giggles in that annoying way girls do. "It's *lilac*."

"Lilac," I repeat. Huh.

"Why?"

"Why what?"

"Why is it your favorite color?"

My face scrunches up. Maybe I should ask her why she's asking so many questions, but it probably wouldn't be kind, and I don't want to upset her.

"Because," I begin, "it's the color of the flowers my mummy grows in the garden, and they make her happy."

I don't say the lilac flowers are what makes Mummy happy *since my daddy died*. I always see her smile when she smells them. And when she's smiling, it means she's not crying.

Sophie's eyes narrow at me, and she taps her chin like my granny does when she thinks. "Hmm. Do you want to be my friend?"

Mrs. Benson's telling everyone to settle down and face forward. But Sophie's waiting for an answer, her face wide like one of the dogs when they're waiting for a biscuit.

So before I do as I'm asked, I nod to Sophie and say, "Okay."

3

Hendricks

Miles sits at the kitchen table with a mug of coffee in his hand. It's the first indication that today won't go as planned.

Which is to say as quickly as possible and without drama.

Miles is rarely awake before breakfast. There's only one reason he's here, and it's me. He thinks I'm falling apart.

I stand in the doorway, arms crossed over my chest, while I wait. He looks up at me and shrugs, daring me to prove him wrong.

For fuck's sake. I'm fine. *Fine.*

So what if the woman I've been in love with before I ever realized has returned after a six-year absence?

So what if I have no idea why she's back or for how long? Or the reason she left in the first place, beyond wild guesses pulled from the depths of my soul in the middle of the night.

So what if she's returned looking nothing like the Story I remember?

That my head's in a spin because of it. Or the weeks

I've spent poring over the thousands of photos I still have of her—of *us*—just to check. Because what if she's exactly the same, and I forgot?

But I am *fine*, whatever Miles believes to the contrary.

He's only here for moral support because he thinks I'm taking Max for the first day of term. Which is great and all, but he's wasted his time. He got out of bed for nothing.

"Birgitta's taking Max," I tell Miles after a minute of unspoken dialogue. "But I appreciate it."

"Hen—"

I walk over to the coffee laid out for breakfast and pour myself a cup. I've been up for three hours already. This is my fourth, but I'm going to need it. While the household was still asleep, I stood at the window, watching the darkness and debating what to do.

Then I went about the day as normal, waking my son and making his breakfast.

"I have an early surgery."

"Do you?"

"Yes."

"What is it?"

"A feline hysterectomy," I reply with as much confidence as that sentence allows.

I'm not going to tell him that it was originally scheduled for this afternoon or that it wasn't even *my* surgery, but while I stood at the window, I stole it and bumped up the time. He can guess because I don't normally deal with small animals. Beyond my weekly surgery hours, I specialize in large and farm animals.

In fact, it's been months since I performed a cat spaying.

Miles's eyes roll, and he picks up his coffee. I know exactly what he's thinking. That I'm a pussy, and he's correct.

I am.

Max's school bag is laid out on the kitchen island, and I set about packing it up with his freshly washed and folded sports kit, a change of uniform in the very likely event he gets the one he's wearing all dirty before home time, his holiday homework, school books, pencil case, and his water bottle.

Though before I do any of that, I rescue a glitter-covered snail I find crawling along the bottom and put it outside. Maybe it'll crawl back to the disco where it's clearly been.

"You'll have to get it over with sometime."

I shake my head and grab an apple from the fruit bowl to cut up. "No, I don't. I never have to get it over with. Birgitta can do drop-offs and pickups forever. And if not her, then Mum or Clementine. Alex and Haven said they'd do it too. And you, apparently."

He shakes his head slowly. "No. I'm going to be by your side or nothing."

"What does that mean?"

"I'm not doing your dirty work." He scratches through his beard, but I'm not expecting him to give up the subject. Miles is like a dog with a bone. "On second thought, do you want me to take Max? Story won't know the difference, and I can sort things out once and for all."

I scoff loudly, and a smile is momentarily raised. We both know that's not true. Story was one of the very few people who could always tell us apart at first sight.

"You never know, maybe Australia has addled her

brain. I *am* better looking now. The years haven't treated you well, big brother."

I launch an apple at his head, only for him to catch it and bite down with a smirk.

"Fuck off."

"Then I guess it's down to you."

Zipping up Max's bag, I leave it by the door and pull out the chair next to Miles, slumping into it with a deep sigh.

"I don't want to see her, Milo. I *can't* see her."

Miles leans forward in his chair. His elbow falls on the table, and his body twists so he's as close to me as he can get without us touching.

I glance up at my twin, my mirror image, and the other half of me. When I hurt, he hurts, and vice versa. Story leaving might have broken my heart, but it broke him too. Just differently.

Miles picked me up after she vanished.

Miles helped me wade through my desolation and unravel my feelings for Story, the friend I loved, with Story, the girl I was *in love* with.

Miles was the one who helped me get through Sienna's pregnancy and my first year of being a father.

He was there when I cried all night because I couldn't cope and didn't understand how Sienna could be such a godawful mother.

It was Miles who saved me and kept me sane.

Miles carries as much anger as I do.

He knows that when I say I don't want to see Story, I mean it.

But he also knows that I *need* to see her.

Deep down, I know it too.

"What's the point? She's probably going to fuck off again in a month. It was just a shock."

"She's here for more than a month, Hen. Her contract runs to the end of the school year."

My eyes widen to the point they sting. I shouldn't be surprised he knows this because Miles can usually get whatever information he's after. But I'm surprised he hasn't already told me, because the guy cannot keep a secret.

"How do you know?"

"There's a girl I've slept with in the admin office. She told me." He shrugs. "And that takes us up to July. You can't avoid Story for six months."

"Wanna bet?" I grumble even though I know I can't. Not in Valentine Nook, where everyone's in everyone else's business.

Not to mention, as the village vet, I spend my time treating animals, including the cows on Story's dad's farm. Everyone knows Story, and everyone knows how close we were as children, then as teenagers. I'm amazed no one spotted me at the Christmas tree stand. Even more so, no one's asked how I feel about her returning.

They probably would if I hadn't been avoiding the village.

I'd heard she'd returned and barely lasted a week before I stormed over there. I shouldn't have done it, but I had to see her.

I wanted to know if the girl who'd left me without another word could return just as silently. I didn't want to believe it, but she'd been there all the same, in the dimming December daylight.

Same but so different.

Her freckles were still there, scattered across the nose she always complained was too big, no matter how many times I assured her it was the perfect size. Her full mouth, even pursed, was exactly as I remembered it—soft, with its thin silvery scar from the time she split her top lip open.

But it was her eyes—that distinctive shade of pale brown—I can't get out of my mind, as they found mine. Weary, defensive, a little sad. Enough that I had to clench my fists to stop myself from wrapping my arms around her. And her hair . . . it might have been mostly hidden under a beanie, but I could see it was now too short to braid like she used to. Or fasten in a ponytail that swung with each of her strides.

Instead, dark strands curled against her collar, brushing her hardened jaw.

Did it still smell like the shampoo she always used? The one I used to love burying my nose in. Like summer and autumn all at the same time.

I didn't dare get close enough to find out.

"Hen, we'll get it over with together."

My eyes close in defeat, only for the sound of rapid footsteps to stop me from descending into complete panic, because ten seconds later, my son sprints into the kitchen. He's mostly dressed and whipping his tie in the air like a lasso, followed by Dolly, Hamish, and Maud.

It's the reality check I need.

"DADDY! DADDY—"

Dark brown curls bounce on his head with every step, his stocky little legs powering him across the wide Cotswold stone tiles on the kitchen floor. He's my mini-me in every way, except for his nose. The rounded, button end comes straight from his mother.

And his volume comes more from Miles than me.

Regardless of his energy and noise levels, there's also an inherent sweetness to him that makes me so proud to be his father. He's kind to everything and everyone, with an unmatched curiosity that makes me want to learn more just so I have more to teach.

"Daddy, can you tie my tie please?" he asks, chucking it at me. He climbs into my lap before I get a chance to reply and peers over my shoulder. "What's Uncle Miles doing here?"

Miles raises an eyebrow. "A good question, Maxy. The answer is, I'm taking you to school."

Max's eyes slice to mine, constantly inquisitive yet bordering on suspicious. Nothing gets past this child. "Are you not coming to school with me?"

Fuck. Fuck. Fuck.

I'm always so firm in my convictions until Max looks at me with his Burlington blue eyes and the pout Miles taught him. Rockets have launched slower than the time it took him to learn that particular expression can get him almost anything.

"Of course he is," Miles answers before I can. "We're both going."

"Even Birgitta?"

As he says her name, Max's nanny walks into the kitchen.

Tall, lithe, blonde. Always clad in some kind of Lycra. Typically Swedish, objectively beautiful. As usual, her eyes fall on Miles before anyone else, only he's now nose deep scrolling on his phone, probably liking Instagram pictures of Lando and Holiday on the red carpet—his latest achievement is getting the hashtag #hotduke to go viral.

After he slept with Max's previous nanny and she quit when he didn't want a repeat, he's been banned from being within twenty feet of anyone else without supervision, so he finds it easier to ignore her.

Unfortunately for him, she's excellent with Max. And Max loves her. So for now, she's staying as his nanny. I don't have time to initiate someone new. Not to mention the impossible feat of finding a nanny who doesn't want to sleep with Miles.

"Even Birgitta what?"

"You're coming to school with me, and Daddy, and Uncle Miles," Max shouts because it's his only volume. "We're all going."

Birgitta looks at me for confirmation because it's not what I told her this morning when I went to wake Max up. That she'd need to do pickup and drop-off until further notice. Until I caved.

It's the God's honest truth. I thought I'd last longer than one day.

"Yes," I reply reluctantly. Miles is right. I can't avoid Story forever, no matter how much I want to. But if I have to be wildly uncomfortable, then so does Miles. Therefore, Birgitta is coming with us. I turn back to my son. "Now stop wriggling and sit still so I can do your tie, or we're going to be late."

Easing his collar up, I fasten his top button and loop the tie around his neck. I have vague memories of my father doing the same to me, but it was Alex who taught me how to tie one for myself.

Max's eyes are on me as I cross the thicker end over the narrow part, loop it around, and thread it through the knot. He knows exactly what I'm doing, and if I get it wrong, he'll call me out on it. It's the mirror he gets confused in front of, but soon, he'll be tying his own tie, so I want to savor these moments for as long as possible.

Once I'm done, I tuck it inside his school jumper—gray with red piping—just like the rest of his uniform, the same all five of us wore, and lift him off my lap.

"Did you brush your teeth after breakfast?"

Max's face screws up. "Um . . ."

"Go brush them, and I'll meet you by the front door."

"Oh-*kay*," he groans dramatically with a well-practiced eye roll, but he rushes off with Birgitta following close.

My cheeks puff out on a long exhale.

Miles picks up my phone and passes it to me. "You need to cancel your cat thing."

I snatch it out of his hand with a tut.

"C'mon, it won't be that bad. What did Story always say?"

A hazy memory flashes in my brain, and I huff a laugh. Everything was a story for her. A chance to build up experiences she could look back on. Nothing ever went wrong because she wouldn't allow it. She'd just change the direction and say, "More fuel for the plot, Hen," then add a wink that always made me laugh.

"I'm not sure this is a plot." Plots aren't supposed to feel like someone's reached into your chest and ripped your heart out.

"Of course it is." He slings his arm around me. "Come on, let's get it over with."

Clemmie's heading down the corridor toward the kitchen when we walk out. She's still in her pajamas and looks barely awake.

"Are you off to school already?" she asks, rubbing her eyes.

"Yup."

Her gaze darts to Miles and widens. We all know Story is Max's new teacher. I'm just glad my mother's still in Switzerland with her girlfriends, because I literally wouldn't hear the end of it. I'm surprised she's not called already this morning.

"Oh. Okay, good luck then."

I'm about to say thanks, but my sister crosses her arms over her chest and pops a hip. Her eyes drop down to my feet, and by the time they arrive back up to the baseball cap I'm pulling on, her lip's quivering.

"What?"

"Nothing. You look good, is all." She leans in and takes a long sniff. "Smell good too."

I'd like to think I don't care in the slightest what I look and smell like on this particular morning, but based on how my tummy flips slightly, that would be a lie. Instead, I grumble, "Thanks."

One of the Burlington staff has the car ready for us as we walk into the cold, and Max is already in his seat, with Birgitta next to him. It's been a while since I had an entourage for the school drop-off, but I slip into the driver's seat.

Max is waiting for me to catch his eye in the rearview mirror. "Ready?"

"Ready, Daddy. Music, please."

Switching on his favorite tune—a clean version of "It Was A Good Day" by Ice Cube . . . Miles's influence, *obviously*—we make our way out of the Burlington

Estate, and so begins the journey to school.

I drive in silent contemplation while Max and Miles rap along with impressive accuracy. When the song finishes, we start again, only this time without singing but with questions. Max asks when he can next ride Chester, Miles's favorite polo pony, followed by Max listing all ponies in order of his preference, which can change daily. He then quizzes Miles on the rules of polo and the new handicap rankings, which take effect at the beginning of each January.

Ten goal is the best and rarest. There are currently only nine ten-goal players in the world, ninety-five percent of which are Argentinian. Miles was a ten but dropped following a nasty accident a couple of years ago. He's just gone back up to nine and plans to be ten by the summer. Something Max is very supportive of.

If I could bet money on him following Miles into polo, I would.

He's as talented as Miles was at his age.

"Thunder and Sunday are out. Have we got any polos? Can we stop?" he shouts, followed by, "Can we go to Foxleigh tonight? Can we see the baby goats?" It all comes out in one long, breathless sentence. A stream of unpunctuated words.

I find his eyes in the rearview mirror. "Sorry, buddy. No to all the questions. We don't have time, but I'll bring polos this afternoon so we can stop on the way home. It'll be too late for the goats, but we'll see them at the weekend, deal? And we'll go to Foxleigh then too. You have a swimming lesson tonight."

"Okay," he replies, content with my answer because it means he'll have something to look forward to. Plus, he's too busy waving at Thunder. So I slow down at the fence for him to gallop along with us, with Sunday doing his best to keep up.

As we pass through the main gates, Miles turns around to face Max. "Maxy, what are you most excited about for school this term?"

"Um . . . break time."

Miles grins. "I used to like break time too—"

"I have a new teacher—"

"I've heard."

The conversation continues, and the car eats up the road.

We pass fields and fields I know intimately, worked by farmers I've known since I was Max's age, locals walking their dogs, cows I've helped birth, and horses I know by name. It's everything I inherently love about living here, but this morning, I barely notice.

My heart pounds harder with each mile because it's somehow only now dawned on me that this will be the first time Story has met Max. The first time she'll have seen him, if you don't include the photos I sent when he was born, which she never acknowledged. She never acknowledged anything I shared, and after a few years of radio silence, I finally gave up.

Aside from the interaction at the Christmas tree stand, we haven't spoken in over six years. Since the day she left me at the fountain after I told her about Sienna being pregnant.

I wonder if she'll see me in Max. See the boy I was when we first met.

"We're here!" Max squeals, banging on the window as his best friend crosses the path ahead of us. "There's Owen. OWEN."

"Max, we need to get out of the car before we start shouting. Remember your inside voice," reminds Birgitta for what's likely the thousandth time as she unbuckles his car seat.

But even after they're both unbuckled, they stay there. And I remain in my seat because I'm not ready.

"Hendricks, the child locks are on. You need to let us out," she says eventually in that tight, Scandinavian accent, which makes everything sound like disapproval.

"Right. Sorry," I reply with a groan, flicking the latch so she can open her door and let Max out.

"You okay?"

Twisting in my seat, I find Miles staring at me.

"What if she gives him a hard time because he reminds her of me? Maybe I should have requested a class change—"

"She wouldn't—"

"You don't know that."

"I do, and so do you. Even though it pains me to say this, she's not *that* much of a dick." He snatches up a baseball cap from the floor that he likely left in here the last time and slips it on. "Let's get this over with. I'll hold your hand if you want."

A laugh snorts out of me, loosening a little of the tension in my chest at the same time.

Max runs ahead with Birgitta while she tries to put his blazer on, leaving me to gather up his school bag, sports bag, and the rest of the paraphernalia that children need for the start of the term.

I soon lose sight of them in the sea of pupils and parents fresh from Christmas break, all making their way through the gates. Some I recognize from school, though most I know because they've brought their dog/cat/rabbit, etc. into the practice.

"D'you remember our first day here?" Miles asks quietly. "I really didn't want to be apart from you."

"Only until you found out all our friends were in your class."

"Yeah." He chuckles.

Up ahead, Max comes back into sight only to disappear around the corner toward the reception building, where his classroom is, dragging Birgitta by the hand. In contrast, each footstep of mine is increasingly slow and sludgy like I'm walking through mud. My insides become knotted, and my eyes are on stalks as I scan for the first sighting.

It doesn't happen until Miles and I turn the corner, and all it takes is a flash of lilac to realize she's standing in the entrance to Max's classroom. Regardless of how many flowers of the same name my mother fills the house with—the long, woody stalks and delicate petals in varying shades of purple—it's a color I'll forever associate with Story.

Her smile burns into my brain, beaming out at the children arriving, and I pause in my stride to watch her entire face light with happiness as she greets each one with a warm "good morning," taking time to introduce herself to her pupil first, then to the parent.

This is the Story I remember. The one who was desperate to become a teacher, the one who practiced her morning greeting in front of the mirror and wrote her name over and over in her notebook for the day when she'd write it on the board. I'm so proud of her for achieving exactly what she wanted, even if I wasn't a part of it.

Even if I didn't get to see how she arrived here.

Her hair bobs along her shoulders—I *knew* she'd cut it—something she swore she'd never do. But it suits her.

And suddenly, I realize I don't know this person.

She's a stranger yet familiar. A stranger in a cloak of memories.

She was the one person I could tell anything to, and now, I don't know how to talk to her. Don't know where to begin. There's so much I want to say that it would take weeks and weeks.

And now is definitely not the time.

I'm stuck in place as I watch Max reach her, still holding Birgitta's hand, and I know the second he tells her his name. Her body stiffens, her smile freezes, and her big liquid-chocolate eyes dart around until they find mine.

My chest stalls. Six years of bottled-up anger and a heart mended together with Band-Aids. It's like my confrontation a few weeks ago never happened. That *this moment* right here is the first time we've seen each other since the fountain.

Neither of us blinks. Parents and kids flit around us. Her gaze holds mine as we assess the changes between us that time has brought on. The broken pieces of our hearts, the corners of our souls that we knew better than our own but no longer do. We stay there for what feels like hours but is, at most, seconds.

We stay until Miles brushes against me, and her focus flicks to him. I don't need to look at him to know he's glaring because I see it all play out on Story's face. The way her eyes narrowed like they always did when he pissed her off before turning away to a parent calling her name and another child to greet.

We walk inside, and I hang up Max's bag on his peg, put his sports kit in his locker, and ride the wave of flashbacks to my first day with Story sitting next to me.

I smile at all the parents I know and nod knowingly at a couple of the dads dropping off their kids on their way to work. The ones I occasionally meet for a beer or commiserate with on the really tough parenting days. Everyone else, I keep my distance from, because Max sprints back to me.

"Bye, Daddy."

I kneel, kiss him, and run my hands through his thick curls. My mini-me. The other half of my soul. My life. "I love you, bud. Have a good day. See you later."

Wrapping his hands around my neck, he says, "Have a good day, too. Don't be sad that I'm back in school, okay?"

It's enough to form a lump in my throat, but I smile anyway and kiss him again. "I'll try not to."

"Good." He grins, and it's fucking heartbreaking.

I know Story's eyes are on me. I can feel them. But when Max runs back to the classroom, and I look up, she's not there.

I hate it.

And I hate that her absence has been the story of my life for the past six years.

4

Story

Age 8

"Sophie, come on. We don't have long . . ."

Annabel stands by the door of the changing room, waving at me to hurry up while I hop about, trying to pull on my outdoor shoes. They're the ones we only wear for break time. I don't know why.

Once I'm done, I run toward her and the treasure map she's waving in my face.

"Where are you going?" asks Mary, pointing at the map in Annabel's hand. "What's that?"

"A secret treasure map for school," Annabel replies.

Mary's mouth opens into a perfect circle. "Where did you get that from?"

"Sophie and I drew it."

"So it's not a *real* treasure map?"

"Sure it is," I say, pulling the door open. "We're going on an adventure with it. Do you want to come?"

Mary looks nervously toward Mrs. Stevens, our art teacher. She's such a goody-goody and always needs permission for everything. But my granny always says it's better to ask for forgiveness than permission, which I think means you have more adventures if you don't ask.

And we're not doing anything naughty, anyway.

Last week, Mrs. Stevens set the task of creating something based on an object she gave us, and today, we had to finish it. Annabel and I were given a pirate's hook, just like in *Peter Pan*. I saw that Hendricks was given a shell, and I think he and Miles painted a beach.

We always have to go in pairs, and Annabel and I were together.

We have art with the other Year 3 class, so Hendricks pairs with Miles, or sometimes he pairs with Jack or Thomas. But never me. Never me in any of our shared classes because the boys all stick together. And the girls stick together.

I don't mind, though, because I get to sit next to him for the rest of the day since our desks are together in our classroom.

When we get back, he'll tell me what he did on break, which is usually playing with a ball or talking about horses with Miles. It's so boring, but when Hendricks is done, I tell him all about the adventures the girls had during break, and I like it when he listens to my stories because he always smiles.

Sometimes I wake up in the morning and think about what my story for Hendricks will be for the day.

I already know that today's will be good.

"Come on, Mary." I hold the door open, waiting for her to make a decision. "Let's make a treasure hunt."

"Okay, I'm coming," she finally replies.

"Follow me," I whisper, and lead the three of us outside over to the far side of the playground, near the bushes.

If you time it right, you can sneak behind the mound on the edge while the teacher isn't looking, and then no one can see you.

I come here a lot. When you lie back, you can see the sky stretching out for miles and the airplanes crisscrossing over. I always wonder where they're going, and what the people in them are doing.

On the other side of the mound are the rugby pitches, but no one is out there right now, so it's like we're hiding. And beyond the rugby pitches are the fields, which lead onto Honeysuckle Lane, and *way* beyond that is my dad's dairy farm.

The three of us slump against the soft grass, and I turn to make sure no one has spotted us. But all I see is Mrs. Stevens drinking her coffee. Before I look at Annabel and Mary again, I quickly try to find Hendricks. He's running around with Miles, Jack, and Thomas.

"I don't think we're allowed to be here. We're going to get into trouble."

Twisting around, I lie next to Annabel. "No, we're not. No one can see us."

Mary doesn't look like she believes me, but she doesn't say anything. Instead, she watches Annabel smoothing out the map. "Why do you have this?"

"Because Mrs. Stevens gave us a pirate hook. And pirates have maps because they hide treasure. So we made a treasure map for the school. We can leave the map lying around, and someone might pick it up and think there's treasure hidden in school."

"But why would there be treasure? Wouldn't

someone have found it already?"

Annabel tuts as I say, "You have to use your imagination."

Reaching into my pocket, I pull out a drawstring bag that I found in my dad's office and tip out the contents. There's a big silver coin I took from under my brother's bed, some jewels from the craft table I had at my last birthday party, and a pink lip balm.

"We're going to hide this." I grin.

Mary's eyes widen. I can't tell if she's excited or scared.

Annabel looks away, and I know she's getting annoyed. I like Mary, but we don't play together much because she's not very good at pretending. She doesn't have an "active imagination" as my granny calls it.

Not like me. I love making up stories.

"How will people find it?"

"With the map. We'll leave clues."

"Where are we hiding it, then?"

"Here." Annabel points at the map where she drew a big X. It's beneath the giant conker tree. "We'll put it in the little hole at the bottom of the trunk."

Mary sits up and peers over the mound. I know she's looking at the tree on the other side of the playground.

"I guess it'll be safe there. But what happens once we've left it?"

"Then we leave clues around the school and see if anyone finds them."

"But how will we know?"

Stuffing my hand back into my pocket, I pull out a tube of glitter, also left over from my birthday. "Let's empty this into the pouch as a trap. Anyone who opens it will be covered in glitter."

Mary giggles, which means she's finally on our side. "So we start with the tree and work backward."

I nod. "Yes."

We all twist around again and lie flat on our bellies.

Mary points at the conker tree. "So we have to run over to there?"

"Yes."

Annabel peers over the edge of the mound. "Mrs. Stevens is talking to Billy Cross, so she's not looking this way."

"Okay, let's go. But we have to be careful not to get caught. Don't talk to anyone."

One at a time, we walk over the mound and head for the conker tree. Years one, two, and three are on the playground, so it's easy for us to get there without anyone seeing, but we don't stop until the branches hide us.

I'm concentrating so hard that I don't even look for Hendricks.

Annabel runs to the trunk and bends down, wiping away all the leaves in the way. "Here's the hole."

Handing over the pouch, I let her push it inside.

"Now what?" asks Mary.

"Now we have to lay clues."

"Where are we leaving the first one?"

I'm thinking about it when the bell rings, which signals the end of break time, and has us all groaning in annoyance. Although it also gives me time to think about the clues we need to make.

The three of us stand.

"Let's go back before we get in trouble," says Mary, the goody-goody once more.

Annabel passes me the map, and I fold it carefully and slide it into my pocket.

I kind of want to keep playing with our treasure map, but I also don't mind going back to our classrooms because it means I'll see Hendricks again.

5

Story

It's eerily quiet when I take my coffee out onto the patio. The air is damp from the storm last night, and it's still dark, though the navy sky is lightening in the distance.

Fog rolls down the hills, gradually turning a deep burnt orange when it hits the horizon.

In lieu of switching on the patio heaters, I grab another couple of blankets from inside, plus all the outdoor cushions, and get cozy.

Oxford, our family golden retriever, plods outside, and I lift him onto the bench to join me. Plumping the cushions around us, I wrap us both in more blankets, and his head rests on my thigh.

It takes me back to when he was a tiny puppy and used to curl up in my lap while I revised for my GCSEs. His tail never stopped wagging, even when I was lamenting quadratic equations and struggling with my Latin verbs—neither of which I have ever used since.

Ten years later and his wag is still there, though not quite as energetic. His enthusiasm, however, sparkles in his eyes.

My one worry every time I returned home was that

he wouldn't remember me, but the second I walked through the front door, he bounced over and covered me in kisses. It was the same greeting whether I returned from the shops or was coming home from university for the weekend.

Oxford was the one I found it hardest to leave when I went to Australia. His fur mopped up my tears the day I decided to go. Tears from leaving Hendricks by the fountain. Tears from leaving a life I thought I would have.

He lets out a loud, contented groan as I stroke through his silky fur and sip my coffee. It's followed by a deep sigh I feel in my bones.

"I know, Oxie. I know," I groan back.

He sighs again, his own way of communication.

"Exactly. What am I doing here? What am I doing, full stop?"

A lump forms in my throat, but I swallow it down with another long sip of my coffee, then take a breath that finishes in a wide yawn.

"I really need to sort my life out."

I can't even blame it on the jet lag because that disappeared a couple of weeks ago. This tiredness is purely self-inflicted. It's more than five days of sleepless nights that I thought would get better as the week went on, but it hasn't.

This tiredness is evidence of a losing battle with myself to get over the boy I met when I was six. It's one I'd pushed so deep down that I almost convinced myself it didn't exist. But my mind has been playing tricks on me.

I thought I was fine.

I thought I could do this.

Every day, I've regurgitated an old memory I once swallowed as a bitter pill because every day, I've had to look at a carbon copy of my childhood best friend and try to act like it hasn't affected me. My heart has finally reached its capacity for lies and can't take any more.

Day one, I gave myself grace. I was doing okay. Better than okay under the circumstances.

I was thankful Celeste had warned me about the morning drop-off because it gave me a couple of extra minutes to prepare. I'd seen Hendricks once since I'd returned to Valentine Nook, and I could do it again. But that first time had been a blur, distorted by a torrent of emotions at a reunion after a necessary and brutally painful absence. It hadn't been enough to commit him to memory.

The second time was.

When I left, Hendricks was a man on the verge of becoming an adult. He was strong and broad, but his muscles still had that gangly quality.

Not anymore.

Six years and Hendricks has turned into an absolute rig.

Even under his thick jumper and body warmer, it was obvious there's a strength to him that's come from more than just lifting weights at the gym. Hendricks has grown into his size and his width, and if the craning of my neck was anything to go by, his height. He's taller than I remember, much taller.

Under my brief assessment, the only thing I could see that hasn't changed was his nose. Long, strong Roman with the bump down the middle from the time he broke it playing rugby, but it has still somehow remained perfectly symmetrical with the rest of his face.

The bump offset the prettiness of his clear blue eyes, long lashes, and full mouth.

Pretty was not a word you could use now.

Where he'd always been fresh-faced, now a thick layer of dark brown scruff covered his jaw and hid the dimples he used to flash at any opportunity, much to my annoyance. He and Miles both. A hard-set mouth replaced the smile I loved so much.

Fun, sweet teenage Hendricks had owned my heart and broken it, but this guy . . . this guy? This guy could demolish it.

This guy had me slack-jawed to a mortifying degree, and the longer he held my gaze, the longer I felt like I was being stripped bare until he could see every single piece of me. Even the pieces I always kept hidden from him.

The longer we stared, the quicker everything I'd blocked out came rushing back.

But in typical Miles fashion, he ruined the moment. Or saved me. I've yet to decide. Because if my heartbeat stalled when it saw Hendricks, it gave up altogether when I realized the impossibly beautiful blond woman holding the hand of a familiar-looking little boy was with him.

By day two, the shock had worn off.

But when the school bell rang for the start of the day, and the blonde brought Max to school without Hendricks, sadness took over.

Sadness turned to an anger I thought I'd moved on from already. It turns out I was just sticking a Band-Aid over a bullet wound that reopened exactly a year ago, and I've spent the week riding the stages of grief. The first four, anyway.

I can't see myself accepting this situation any time soon, just like I refused to six years ago. This time, it's infinitely harder.

Avoiding Hendricks is one thing, but I'm spending all day with his mini-me—Maxwell Burlington—who, I'm loath to admit, is the cutest kid I've ever come across.

He's exactly like Hendricks was at his age, and it's impossible to see anything else. I've tried.

Every mannerism, every smile, even his handwriting, big and round, belong to Hendricks. The eye rolls I've caught a couple of times are all Miles, however.

I've tried to laugh through it. When Celeste asks me if I'm okay, I've brushed it off as new-term tiredness.

The supply closet off my classroom has become a place to cry without being seen when the ache in my chest becomes too overwhelming to hold it in.

Max is a part of Hendricks's life I know nothing about. He's a living, breathing reminder of why I ran away.

Max is proof that I left Hendricks standing alone by the fountain. Proof we lived the past six years without sharing every single detail like we used to. Without sharing anything.

Hendricks moved on, and I only *thought* I did.

Our combined worlds stopped spinning that day.

We went our separate ways, and up to a week ago, I had only heard snippets of how his life continued without me. My mum would share an update on the Burlingtons that I pretended not to listen to or show no interest in, when, in reality, I was salivating over every morsel.

One thing she failed to mention was *the blonde.* Max's mother, I'm assuming. Stepmother, perhaps.

I don't know why I'm surprised, because Hendricks always did the right thing. Growing up without a father left a huge hole for him, I know that much. He said she wanted to keep the baby, and he would have done everything he could to make it work with her.

I haven't asked anyone for confirmation. Not my mum, not Celeste. I don't know if my heart can take any more disappointment if I make it real.

My first kiss wasn't with Hendricks.

Neither was the first time I had sex.

But I always held on to the hope that we were somehow waiting for each other, and the humiliation of it burns. Of course, Hendricks isn't single. When has he ever been? Why would he be?

The blonde has the future I always thought I'd have. If that wasn't cruel enough, I'll be reminded as such every Monday to Friday during term time until my contract finishes. I'm counting down the days.

I groan again. "What a fucking mess."

Oxford lifts his head as he hears footsteps coming toward the back door, and my mum appears with a coffee in one hand and a plate piled high with an entire loaf's worth of toast and marmalade in the other.

"You're up early."

My stomach rumbles as the scents of toast, hot butter, and citrussy sugar hit my nose, and I pick up a slice. "Couldn't sleep."

After I shift along the bench to make space, she sits down next to me. The warmth of her body provides extra protection against the nip of the morning.

"Are you okay, love? You've been quiet this week."

"I'm fine, Mum. Just tired," I reply, ignoring the urge to cry. Maybe I'm getting my period.

"Probably the weather. Not like the wall-to-wall sunshine Sydney has right now."

"No." I shake my head. "Not quite."

"We should have come to visit you this Christmas. It would have been less dramatic."

I manage to laugh with her and pass my crust to Oxford. He gently takes it between his lips and chews noisily, then snuffles up to me for the next piece.

"How's Dad this morning?" It might be early, but I know he's been awake for hours.

Mum rolls her eyes and lets out a sigh. "He's fine. Grumbling away already, but I've taken him tea and toast. Now I get to enjoy some peace and quiet."

I chuckle through another bite. My dad was in the hospital for a week when he broke his leg. It was pinned in two places, and I truly believe the doctors were glad to see the back of him when we picked him up. My dad is not one of those people who are good at sitting still. Therefore, any type of forced recouperation is as painful for those around the patient as it is for the patient themselves.

If he could have it his way, he'd have been out on the farm using his crutches the next day. Only after a stern warning from the specialist that he would walk with a cane for the rest of his life if he didn't recover properly has kept him from leaving the house every day except to attend his physio sessions. As it is, my mum and I have driven him up to the farmyard most afternoons just so he can check it's being managed properly.

And therein lies the problem with being a militant

control freak who doesn't trust anyone to do a job as well as they do it themselves. His problem became my problem when my mum begged me to stay in Valentine Nook and help. Probably because she didn't want to deal with his grumpiness by herself, and I don't blame her.

But the reasons I agreed had nothing to do with my parents.

"He'll be back on his feet soon. It's only been six weeks. He has four left to go before the pins are out, then he can start walking properly."

She blows on her coffee and takes a long sip. "Thank God for that day. I'm so grateful you were able to stay and help out, love."

I drop my head on her shoulder. "You're welcome."

The blanket slips from around me, and I pull it back up. The sun has fully breached the horizon now, and we sit in silence listening to the sound of the birds waking up and Oxford's soft snoring.

"Are you going to talk to me about what happened with you and Noah?"

My stomach plummets. It was only a matter of time before she asked. I open my mouth to reply, though I really have no idea where to start, so it's a saving grace that a loud rustling in the bushes distracts us. Oxford lets out a low growl followed by a halfhearted bark as a goat appears through the hedge halfway down the garden and trots up to where we're sitting. It stands there, staring at us, until my mum hands over a slice of toast with marmalade.

Now I understand why she made enough to feed a family of six.

"Mum! I can't believe you're still feeding Churchill!"

"He comes every Saturday," she says by way of explanation.

"Don't let Dad catch you. He's still pissed from seven years ago when Churchill stripped half the apple orchard."

She hands over another piece to the patiently waiting goat. "What he doesn't know won't hurt him."

"Valentine Nook villagers single-handedly keep Churchill alive and thriving." I grin with a shake of my head. "He'll leave here and go to someone else who'll feed him a second breakfast."

She strokes down his face. "That's okay. He knows who loves him best."

Deciding Churchill has had enough, I take the final piece of toast and bite into it. "It's whoever feeds him last, Mum."

My mum lets out a *pfft*, only for Churchill to turn around and leap over the side gate into the field next door. Oxford stands, spins until he's closer to her than me, and drops down again. His head rests on her lap this time, as if saying, "Don't forget that I love *you* best."

Raising my arms, I stretch to momentarily ease the stiffness and tension in my body. The fog has almost disappeared, leaving behind a cloudless and beautiful day, if freezing cold.

I might have grown up on a farm, but I've become accustomed to beginning my days with a surf, and I miss the heat of the sun I left behind. I've barely moved my body since I came back, and coupled with the anxiety I've been stockpiling like it's going out of fashion, it's high time I did.

Plus, I have very little else to do after checking on the cows. A small crew of farm staff rotates the cows every morning for the daily milking. They're all perfectly capable of running the place without my father, but I know if I don't go, he'll only insist on going down there himself.

Throwing off the blankets and braving the chill, I stand. "I'm going to go for a run over to the dairy. Do you want me to pass the bakery on the way home?"

"Yes, please. And I won't say no to a box of flapjacks either."

"You got it," I reply with a laugh because she already knew it was happening.

The flapjacks from The Beanery are more addictive than crack. I tried for years to get the recipe out of Claudia, but she won't give it up.

I manage to dress in enough workout gear to keep me warm without restricting blood flow, although being cold just motivates me to run faster. As long as I don't get frostbite, I'll be okay, and ten minutes later, after returning for a beanie, my feet are pounding down the winding lane to my parents' dairy farm. In the summer, we can leave through the gate in the garden, but it's too muddy in the winter. And I hate mud.

The scent of manure circles the air, and I breathe it in willingly. It's a smell that will forever remind me of being home, of being in Valentine Nook, and of the memories that inevitably follow. Hendricks, running through fields of long grass and sunflowers, sharing cold bottles of beer by the waterfall with Annabel and Mary while we watched the boys jump off the highest rock and hit the bottom. I'd hide behind the safety net of my sunglasses so no one could see me watching Hendricks. And later, when he'd go off with Ella Cartwright, or Millie Jones, or Zoe Glasston, no one could see the hurt I'd ignored for years.

What made it worse was that I knew that none of those girls cared about Hendricks. They just wanted to get with a twin, and it didn't matter which one because they couldn't tell the difference.

Not me. Miles annoyed me at the best of times, and the rest I'd be on the verge of inciting violence. Hendricks was the only one I wanted.

Deep in my thoughts, I arrive at the farm just as I hit my stride. I'm greeted with mooing and hooves clopping across the farmyard to the milking stall. Pete, my dad's farm manager, is guiding the Ayrshires with their chestnut and white markings through the gate, with the help of a couple of younger farmhands. I haven't seen him since before the Christmas holidays because I've so far managed to visit when he's been busy elsewhere.

I'm tempted to turn around, but as the last cow passes through, he spots me and waves. "A'right, how's it going?"

Swiping a bead of sweat from the end of my nose, I wave back. "Good, just coming to check you're okay."

I add an eye roll, which he interprets exactly how it's meant to be. *My dad* needs to be told all is well. Daily.

"Tell him we're doin' fine and missing him."

I snort, followed by a dribble of snot that I wipe away as quickly as I can. Damn this cold weather and my runny nose.

"I doubt that, but I'll tell him anyway."

His eyes flick to where the cows are being lined up in the milking barn, checking the guys are okay before striding over to meet me. It's not that I don't want to speak to him. I just don't really want to get into a conversation because I know how it will end.

"Still here, then," he says, stopping just shy of being

too close.

"Yup." I rub my hands together, making it clear I'm cold and won't be sticking around. "Until Dad's back on his feet."

"Tomorrow, if he's got anything to do with it." He pulls his phone from his pocket and waves it. "Most messages from one person I've ever had in my life."

I laugh, genuinely, because I can only imagine how much my dad's trying to do from the comfort of an armchair while his leg is resting at ninety degrees. When the laughter dies down, Pete is staring at me.

"Seeing as you're still here, how 'bout we catch up over a drink? It's been a while."

Yup. As predicted, and I work hard on keeping my cringe to myself.

A couple of years older than me, Pete's worked for my dad since he was sixteen. Once or twice through the haze of too much alcohol, I've thought he was hot, with his floppy hair and permanently ruddy cheeks, maybe even ended up with his tongue down my throat, but it never went any further, and not since I was seventeen.

Ten years ago.

I've changed in that time. I've learned I can't run from my feelings.

I can't hide behind someone else. I can't agree to marry another person, no matter how much I care for them, in the hopes they can erase any memories I don't seem to be able to forget. Because the ugly truth is my heart has only ever belonged to one person.

Until I deal with *that*, I won't be going for drinks with anyone.

But it's too early to get into a conversation about

the state of my love life, so I just say, "Sure," and thumb behind me. "I should leave you in peace and get going before my muscles seize up."

Pete nods. "Always happy to be interrupted by you, Story."

I let out an awkward chuckle and try not to grimace. I haven't been *Story* for six years. It's a name I've grown to hate. A name too reminiscent of painful memories.

"It's ah . . . Sophie. I don't go by Story anymore. But yes, probably see you tomorrow."

"I'll be here, *Sophie*."

Sprinting out of the yard, I'm almost home when I remember I'm supposed to go to the bakery and take a left turn. It takes me a minute to realize the tightening in my chest isn't from running too fast, but because I'm heading down the lane that leads past Hendricks and Miles's cottage. I don't even know if they still live here. Do they still live together now that Hendricks is with the blonde?

I can't imagine she'd want to live with Miles. And I doubt Miles would ever live with a woman, even one in a relationship with his brother.

Oh *God.*

What if they're there now? What if they come out when I pass?

For a second, I hop about on my feet, deciding what to do. I could turn back and cut across the field, but I hate the mud more than I hate the idea of bumping into Hendricks. So instead of slowing down, I sprint, narrowing my eyes to the point I can only see a tiny shard of the road in front. If I can't see the cottage, then logic dictates that the cottage or anyone in it can't see me.

I'm still sprinting by the time I reach the fountain and only slow down when I run into the crowds already shopping on Valentine High Street, and maneuver so I'm swallowed into the throng. It's the first time I take a full breath.

There's a freedom to being hidden by strangers, and it's both overwhelming and exhilarating. I'm a spy on the run, even if it's only from my own overactive imagination. But I learned a long time ago that my mind is always overactive when it comes to Hendricks.

My thoughts are swirling enough that I don't notice the group in front of me veer into a store. I only take a couple of steps alone when I hear someone calling my name and spin around.

Agatha Chase wears a pinched look of frustration, standing on the pavement outside *Agatha Chase's Love Emporium*, dressed in her customary deep purple and black. Swathes of fabric billow around her, and she either doesn't notice the people pushing past her to get inside or she doesn't care enough to move.

"Oh, hey, Agatha." I hug her before I realize what I'm doing.

Her bracelets jangle against my ear as she grips my shoulders and pulls me back. "*Finally*, Story. I was expecting to see you months ago. Oh well, better late than never."

I'd forgotten how little sense she makes. I concluded long ago that it's in her delivery. Sometimes she's wistful, giving the impression she's working on a different plane of existence than the rest of us, and sometimes—like right now—she's forceful to the point where all you can do is nod politely in agreement.

And people lap it up. Outside of the Burlingtons,

she's probably one of the wealthiest members of the village because of the many love potions and spells she makes. She's living proof that love is a money-spinner.

Especially with her three-for-the-price-of-two deals.

I bought one once.

I was seventeen and desperate. But I followed the instructions and brewed it up at midnight on the next full moon. I had to write a list of everything I wished for—Hendricks—and burn it, then drop the ashes into the brew I was making and drink it under the power of a moonbeam.

It didn't work.

In fact, it had the opposite effect because that weekend I saw Hendricks snogging Olivia Cussions in The Cupid's Arrow.

I didn't buy another one, and when I told Agatha it hadn't worked, she said I hadn't wanted it enough. And that's when I knew she was a fraud. I'd never wanted anything more than Hendricks.

But I'm not going to get into it now. I need to buy bread and flapjacks, then get the hell home. "I guess."

"Don't worry, it won't be much longer."

"What won't?"

Before I can stop her, she places a hand over my heart, millimeters away from touching me. I'd say it was weird, but that's Agatha. All she'll be able to detect is my heart still hammering away from sprinting down the lane.

"The heaviness will lift soon, Story. Hang in there."

I don't have the energy to tell her it won't. The heaviness is a part of me. It has been for a long time.

It's there twenty-four seven, and if I happen to forget,

it will always remind me.

Like the day Noah proposed.

"Cool. Thanks, Agatha."

"Have faith," she calls behind her as she turns and walks back into the store with a "come and see me for a reading."

In hindsight, I can totally blame her for what happened next. If it hadn't been for her, I wouldn't have been distracted enough that I wasn't paying attention to where I was going.

I wouldn't have walked straight into the thick, broad—very solid—chest of the guy I've been unsuccessfully trying to avoid as though my life depended on it.

At this point, I'm living on borrowed time.

"God, I'm so sor—"

"Story."

My mouth opens, then closes. So much for sprinting past the cottage.

It seems Hendricks is struck down by the same dumb affliction I am, and we stand there like goldfish until the silence is broken by a screeched "Daddy" followed by "Miss MacIntosh."

I peer down at Max, who's run at full speed out of the bakery, waving a paper bag in the air, and into Hendricks, who grunts upon impact.

I want to believe it hurt a lot more than he's letting on. I crouch down until I'm face to face with his mini-me.

"Hi, Max, how's it going?"

"Good, Claudia gave me a flapjack."

"Wow, lucky you. I love flapjacks."

"Me too. So does my daddy. It's our favorite."

I know Hendricks is staring at me, seeing how I'll react, and it takes all my strength to keep a neutral expression and reply, "Is that right?"

"Yes, we come down every Saturday to get here early."

"Well, looks like you were in luck. I hope you saved me some."

"It's okay. Claudia put another batch in the oven." His whole face lights up as he tells me, his head wobbling enough that a big curl flops onto his forehead. It's almost painful to look at him.

"What else do you have planned once you've eaten all the flapjacks?"

"We're going to Foxleigh Park. I have a lesson with Uncle Miles. He plays polo, you know."

"I did know that, yes."

In the corner of my eye, I see Hendricks pushing his hands into his pockets. I try to spot a wedding ring, but all I catch is the flash of gold from his large signet ring. The one that all the Burlingtons wear, stamped with the Valentine Nook coat of arms.

There's only so much I can take under the weight of Hendricks's gaze, and I stand back up so that once again we're staring and waiting for the other to speak first—goldfish state.

And I want to say something, but I just have no idea where to begin.

I have the feeling it's the same for him.

Two things happen then.

Max realizes he's forgotten something in The Beanery and runs back inside. And my eyes spy a woman emerging from a store on the other side of the street. She may as well have a spotlight on her for how much she's illuminated through a sea of January beige drabness.

Seriously, who looks that glamorous on a Saturday morning?

"How've you—" Hendricks begins as I say, "Well . . . hope the three of you have a wonderful weekend. Must dash."

His brows drop. "Three?"

"You, Max, your . . . wife?" I take a step back. I do not want to be here when she arrives.

Deep lines form across Hendricks's brow. "I don't have a wife."

"Girlfriend then. The *blonde*," I snap before I can stop myself.

Regret kicks in before the sentence has even left my mouth, but my pride is too thick to allow me to take it back. It feels like six years ago when Hendricks told me he'd not only been *seeing* someone for a few months, but that she'd also fallen pregnant.

He turns around to where my gaze keeps bouncing, and when his eyes return to mine, he's confused.

No, not confused. *Angry*.

"You don't know what you're talking about."

Might as well keep digging this hole. Maybe I'll dig all the way back to Australia.

"I know exactly what I'm talking about." I actually *don't*.

"Quit while you're ahead, Stor."

My teeth grit. "My name is *Sophie.*"

"Not to me."

"Then do me a favor and don't talk to me again." God, I'm such a child.

His blue eyes bore into me, even through angry slits. "Fine. It would be my pleasure."

"Fine."

"*Fine.*"

The blonde is about five feet away when I turn on my heel and sprint off, dodging through the crowds until I'm around the corner and safely out of sight.

And later, when my mum asks what happened to the bread, I lie and tell her I'm trying to avoid gluten.

6

Hendricks

My eyes stay trained on Story attempting to disappear around a couple of people who've come out of a store on the other side of the high street. If it's on my account, it's pointless.

I could find her anywhere, anytime. Her ponytail no longer swings behind her, replaced by blunt edges bobbing along her shoulder, but the way she holds herself with hard-set shoulders, a straight spine, and a determined stride . . . I'd recognize her anywhere. My mind flashes back to the day I told her Sienna was pregnant, and I watched her storm away.

But if Story's angry with me—still, again, *now*—it's nothing on the anger I feel.

"Was that Max's teacher?"

Tearing my eyes away from where my ex-best friend has finally vanished around the corner, I turn to Birgitta and nod. "Yeah."

"She looked mad."

"Yup."

"Why?"

I shrug and shake my head, because I don't have an

answer.

"I didn't know you were coming into the village. I could have collected what you needed."

"It's your day off," I reply mindlessly, my eyes back on the corner of The One True Love. The last spot Story was visible.

I wonder how far she's gotten.

I'm so tempted to go after her. I want to run her down and shake some sense into her because she's clearly lost her mind.

"I'm always happy to do whatever you need."

My eyes flick back to Birgitta, and it's then that a piercing pain hits me right between them before turning into a dull throb.

I know what people think when they realize Birgitta is my nanny. It's what Story clearly thinks. Nothing more than a fucking cliché. That *I'm* a cliché. Not to mention how insulting it is for Birgitta.

Normally, people's opinions are the least of my concerns, but they're not holding it against me like Story is. And that brief thirty-second interaction has my blood boiling way more than it should on a frosty Saturday morning, because all it does is remind me of when she left England last time.

"Thanks, but you enjoy your weekend."

She can't have gotten far. Even at the speed she was sprinting, I could catch up to her or at least see where she was.

Fuck it.

"Actually, on second thought, could you give me a minute? Max is in the store. Would you mind waiting for him?"

Birgitta's lips purse in slight confusion, and I'm not surprised. It's her day off and I rarely ask her to work on a Saturday. Even if it's only for a few minutes. It's how I keep the boundaries in check.

"Sure."

I take off, calling, "Thanks," as I dodge a couple of Labradors on leads and hope Story hasn't taken a shortcut through the fields. Though given the rain this week, it's going to be muddy, and Story hates the mud.

After a couple of near misses where shoppers flock out of a store right as I run past, and ignoring Mrs. Winston calling my name, my memory proves correct. I round the corner and find her slumped against the fence halfway up the road by Miles's cottage, head in her hands.

It stops me dead because even from where I'm standing forty yards away, I can tell she's crying, shoulders jerking softly as she sobs, and my anger vanishes.

Since Max came along, my ability to withstand other people's tears has diminished by one thousand percent. Not that I ever particularly cared for it, but now I just have this inherent need to fix the cause. Except this time, the cause is me, and it's a problem I'd like to get to the bottom of once and for all.

Her head jerks up at the sound of a stone being kicked, her big, slightly bloodshot, brown eyes flaring as she spots me.

"I'm not in the mood," she snaps, drawing a sleeve under her nose and then wiping her eyes.

"You're certainly very irritable since you returned to Valentine Nook," I remark, working hard to keep my tone even so that my annoyance doesn't return. "But I don't give a shit, Stor."

"My name is Sophie," she grits out.

"I haven't called you Sophie since we were ten."

She lets out a deep sigh, takes one sniff, and stares right at me. "What are you doing, Hendricks? Why have you followed me?"

"Why d'you think?"

"I have no idea what you do or don't do, Hendricks. Or the reasons behind your actions. I never have."

Her gaze is still locked onto mine, jaw working side to side. My mind spins with every conversation I've had with myself, every conclusion I came up with as to why she left, and it all boils down to the day I found out Sienna was pregnant. Miles calls it jealousy, and maybe he's right, but I never believed it was as simple as that.

One thing neither of us has ever been able to wrap our heads around is how she vanished with no explanation. Especially me. I might have fucked things up to begin with, but she fucked things up worse. I'd just found out my life was about to drastically change and she left me.

I'd needed my best friend.

Cutting me out the way she did was nothing short of callous. It would have been easier to deal with if she'd died.

My heart never fully mended.

"Well, that makes two of us." I cross my arms over my chest. "Why are you crying?"

"Because I wish I'd never come back. I wish I'd never agreed to stay and help. I wish I'd never taken that job. I wish . . ."

She catches herself before the words leave her

mouth, but I know what they are. She wishes she'd never seen me.

I can't deny that it doesn't hurt. It does. Not quite reaching into my chest and ripping my heart out, like she'd done before, but close.

And really, how dare she? Does she think she's sparing my feelings after what she put me through?

"Don't feel you have to stop on my account. Please, do continue."

Her jaw juts and clenches, then her shoulders drop. "It just would have been easier, that's all. We both know it."

"I know nothing, clearly, so feel free to enlighten me. What would have been easier, Story? Come on, use your words." I know I'm taunting her, but I don't care.

She throws her arms up. "Not knowing how you are. Not seeing how your life is. Not . . ."

Her eyes drop, and everything she wants to say but hasn't is left hanging in the air, along with her wrong conclusion about Birgitta. I know that's what she's thinking because she's practically snarling at me now.

If it wasn't so sad, it would be funny.

Miles always believed Story was in love with me, but I've never had his confidence. Moving our relationship out of anything other than friendship proved harder than it sounds. Believe me, I tried.

I only know how *I* felt back then. How I feel now. That after six years, seeing her can still add an extra *thud thud thud* to my heartbeat. But even the dance against my rib cage isn't enough to make me forget the pain.

My life changed in more ways than one on that day.

"You're pissed at me? No, Story, you don't get to be

pissed at me. You don't get to vanish for six years with no explanation and act like it's not okay that I have a life."

"I'M PISSED AT ME."

I step back, giving her space in case she explodes—a likely scenario given the color of her face. But she takes a deep breath, and her skin returns to her usual rosy pink.

"I'm pissed at me." It's quieter, smaller even, but no less impactful.

"Why, Stor? Tell me, I want to know. I deserve to know."

Her nostrils flare as she shakes her head. "It doesn't matter. I don't want to talk about it, and it's in the past. But truly, Hendricks, I know you have a life, a family. You're a vet like you always wanted to be, and . . . I'm happy for you."

I'd believe her if it wasn't for the sad smile on her face. I'm very tempted to let her stew, but my conscience gets the better of me.

"Not that you deserve it nor do I have to explain myself, but Birgitta is Max's nanny. She's neither my wife nor my girlfriend. And no, I haven't fucked her."

I have to admit the look of utter shock and embarrassment on Story's face is one I'm enjoying. Story is rarely wrong.

Now that I have the floor, I'm debating whether to continue, but I honestly don't know where to begin.

In front of me is the girl I used to share everything with, every secret, every good and bad day. But now I live a life she's not part of, one that took me to hell and back, and it's going to take more than a snatched five minutes on a Saturday morning to fill her in. Even with

Birgitta watching Max for me.

She's still staring at me, wearing the same expression she always did when her brain was running in circles. It's not the first time I've wished I could literally read her mind.

But as is the case when you're a single parent, reality smacks you in the face at the most inopportune times. The ringtone I have assigned for Birgitta buzzes in my pocket and I'm reminded of my priorities.

"Hey, sorry I'll . . ." My voice cuts off as I take in the sound of my son wailing down the phone. "I'm on my way now."

My gaze hasn't left Story even though hers is fixed back on the ground. My gut twists with all the things I want to say to her. Instead, I leave with the only ones I can find.

"Sorry, I have to go. I'll see you around, Stor."

I sprint off without looking back, retracing my footsteps until I spot Birgitta outside The Beanery where I left her. Only she's sitting on the pavement, cradling Max, one hand on his head, the other on his nose, trying to stem the blood pouring down his face.

"Da-da-daddy," he wails as he sees me, his tiny chest heaving with wracking sobs as he holds his arms out to me.

"Oh buddy, what happened?" I ask.

"He ran out of the store and tripped, landing on his nose. The bleeding is slowing down." Birgitta pulls back a paper napkin, and immediately another flow of blood pours from his nose.

It's made worse because he's crying so hard, and the blood, tears, and snot all mix. Taking a clean napkin from a pile next to Birgitta, I hold it to his nose and scoop him out of her arms into mine.

"It's okay, Maxy. We'll go to the surgery and get you all patched up, okay?"

He tries to nod, but I'm holding his nose, so all he lets out is a little grunt and a sniffle. My chest lurches from how brave he's trying to be.

As I stand, I see Birgitta's pale, beige hoodie is covered in blood. "I'm so sorry. Tell me where it came from, and I'll get another one ordered for you."

But she brushes me off with a wave of her hand. "Don't worry about it. It happens. I should have caught him, but he came running out so fast."

I throw her a smile because I know exactly what she means. While it's admittedly on the worst end of his usual injuries, this isn't the first accident Max has had. It won't be the last. He's a child who prefers sprinting as his mode of transport.

"C'mon, bud, let's go," I whisper to him. I turn to Birgitta and add, "See you back at the house."

"Bye, Maxy."

He gives a weak lift of his arm and drops his head on my shoulder. I carry him across the road and down the other side of the street until we reach The Valentine Vet, the surgery I took on as mine two years ago. It's where I've wanted to work since I was ten years old.

Open Monday to Saturday for appointments, and Sundays for emergencies, there's a small team of dedicated vets and vet nurses. Though I'm mostly out visiting the yards, seeing horses and farm animals, I still keep an office here that I use twice a week for a drop-in surgery, which is always busy. It's good for community relations, and truthfully, I enjoy seeing the bunnies and hamsters just as much as birthing a cow.

When I push the door open with my feet, Glenda, my receptionist, who I inherited along with the rest of the staff, greets me. I honestly couldn't run the place without her.

"Hendricks, we weren't expecting . . . oh, *OH* . . . Max, what happened?"

"Collided with the pavement. I'm just going to patch him up," I tell her, marching quickly through to my office without acknowledging anyone sitting in the waiting room.

"Okay, Maxy, I'm going to set you on the bed," I say and carefully deposit him on the cold metal surface.

The blood has finally clotted when I remove the napkin, and on first observation, I suspect the blood all over his face makes it look like a far worse injury than it actually is. His nose still appears straight, if a little bruised. With three brothers, I have enough experience to recognize a broken nose.

I go about fetching antibacterial wipes and cotton strips, then fill a small bowl with warm water. I'm not a doctor, so there aren't the usual implements one would normally find there. If it's truly broken, we'll have to make another trip.

"The bleeding has stopped, buddy, so I'm going to clean your face up, and we'll make sure it doesn't start again."

Max gives one sad nod as I get to work. "You know, I fell over once when I was a few years older than you, and I broke my arm. It hurt so much . . ."

Max nods again and tries to sniff, but it's clearly painful, given the tears that well in his big blue eyes.

"And Auntie Clemmie always used to bang into something. Not to mention Uncle Miles fell off his pony so many times when he was younger. He still does—"

"He was in hospital?"

I nod. It's not that Max would remember what happened because he was too little, but we've talked about it enough that he knows Miles was in hospital after a nasty accident. "He sure was. That was so scary."

Scary is an understatement.

A couple of years ago, during a polo match between England and America, Miles almost died from a dangerous collision. He was placed in an induced coma for twenty-four hours to reduce the swelling in his brain, and I never left his bedside.

Miles, being Miles, made a full recovery, in no small part helped by the army of doctors and nurses who flocked around him, attending to his every need.

It took six months before the doctors would sign him off to ride again, and another six months of hard rehab and training to get him back to the level he had been at. For the past year, Miles has been more focused and determined than I've ever seen him. I'm certain heads will roll if he's not back up to ten in the summer.

Santiago Torres, the American player who caused the accident, was banned from playing polo for two years.

"Did Uncle Miles cry?"

I nod, remembering how I held him while he sobbed on my shoulder after the surgeon told him he'd be in rehab for months. "Yes, he did."

"Did you cry when you fell over?"

"I also cried, yes."

"Who made you feel better?"

My memory flits back to the time he's referring

to, playing in the fields above Honeysuckle Lane and rolling down the hill. It's where we always met up. Racing each other until our lungs were bursting, sweat dripped down our backs, and we cried laughing.

"Probably Granny," I reply, picking up a fresh cloth and taking a second pass of Max's face.

I gently clean around his nose and stuff two cotton balls into his nostrils to ensure it's fully clotted. He winces when I run my finger down the bridge, squeezing gently along the cartilage, but I stand in my assessment.

"It's not broken, bud. Just a little bruising."

"Does that mean we can get a hot chocolate?"

Suppressing a smile, I keep my nod as solemn as his tone. "I think we can manage a hot chocolate."

"And another flapjack?"

"You got it."

Tidying my office up as quickly as possible, and wiping us both as clean as we're going to get under the circumstances, we leave as we arrived. Quickly.

And once Max is holding a hot chocolate along with a flapjack, which he dunks inside, it's like nothing happened.

I wish I could be so easily placated.

What a morning. Between Story and Max, I feel like I've already been through an entire day, and it's barely ten o'clock.

This is me. Hendricks Burlington.

Dad. Mum. Doctor. Nurse.

As much as I'd like to think my life is together, it's not.

I've not had a full night's sleep since Story came

back. I might have wished for her return every day for the past six years, but it doesn't matter. Max is my priority. It's him and me in this life together. My brave little boy, wearing his hot chocolate mustache, is doing his best to eat a flapjack with two cotton balls stuffed up his nose while his eyelashes still hold the remnants of tears.

The reality is, I'm not free to open my heart up to anyone. Let alone with someone who hates my guts. Someone who could very well leave again.

I miss my friend, but I've missed her for so long that it's almost intrinsic. I know what to do with missing her, and right now, my hands are full enough. Too full to change anything.

I have neither the time nor the ability to fix something I don't know can be fixed.

Therefore, as much as I don't want to, maybe it's better that we keep our distance.

7

Hendricks

Age 10

"You want to roll all the way down to the bottom?"

"Yup."

I peer over the ledge of the flat expanse of grass we're sitting on. The bottom is waaay down below. So far down that Honeysuckle Lane looks like a narrow path, the sheep are fluffy white balls of cotton wool, and the tractor in the distance is smaller than my Lego. I can see the fountain on Valentine High Street and The One True Love, but it's all so tiny.

"It's so far."

"You think we can't do it?"

I shake my head. "No. I dunno. We won't get all the way down."

"We will. I've done it already."

Sophie's eyes are as wide as her grin, and it makes me frown. Sometimes I can't tell whether she's making up a story or telling the truth.

"You have not."

"I have."

"When?"

"Last week."

I peer back down the slope. Maybe it's not as steep as it seems even though looking at it is making bubbles pop in my belly. But if Sophie's done it, it can't be that bad.

"Did you get sick?"

Her long braids flick around when she shakes her head, and I notice the ends of them are tied with bands in my favorite color. "Only a bit dizzy."

"How long did it take?"

She shrugs. "Maybe fifteen minutes. I had to keep stopping."

Whoa. Fifteen. It would easily take us twice that to get back up to the top.

"How did you get home after?"

Sophie's smile grows across her face. "Walked, silly."

I peer down to the bottom again and back to Sophie. She's as excited as I've ever seen her, and if this is what she wants to do, then I want to do it too. Even though I'd be just as happy sitting here with her for the rest of the afternoon. Normally, when it's just the two of us, I listen to the latest story she's made up, but today, we've been telling secrets.

Hers is that she hates working on the farm with her dad, and mine is that I heard Lando crying about being nervous to take over Burlington. He's eighteen now, and everywhere we can see belongs to him. Even the hill Sophie wants to roll down.

"I don't think he wants to be in charge of people."

"I love being in charge of people," Sophie replies, even though I already knew that. At school, she's always the one to put her hand up for group leader when we have to do activities.

"I don't." My nose scrunches up as I think about it. "I only want to help animals. I want to work at the vets."

Rolling back onto the grass, she jumps up and holds her hand out to me. "Come on, we're doing this. More fuel for the plot."

I don't know what that means, but I go with it anyway and let her pull me to standing. "Okay, fine."

She points down the hill. "You have to stay on this side because the other is more bumpy, and it stops halfway."

I nod. "Okay."

Following her lead, I line my feet up with the edge of the grass where it drops down. On second glance, it's not as steep as I thought, but the bottom is really far away.

"I'll go first, so you can follow me," she says, lying flat on her belly and easing herself down.

She doesn't roll very far. She also didn't stick to the left side and ends up in the middle, plus her braids keep getting stuck under her shoulders.

Rocking forward gets her moving again, and she giggles the whole way. It's so fun listening to her that I forget I'm supposed to be rolling down too, until she gets stuck again and waves up at me.

"Hen, come on."

Getting into position, I manage to make it all the way to where Sophie is waiting and laughing her head off.

"You have to stretch your arms out like you're Superman. It makes you go faster," she tells me, lying down again. "Are you ready?"

I peer down to the bottom again. It doesn't seem any nearer, and this next bit of the hill looks way bumpier than the one we just rolled down. But I don't say that out loud, especially because Sophie's staring at me.

I lie down flat behind her. "Ready."

She goes first again, and I follow. I was right about it being steeper and bumpier than the first. I'm not sure I like it, but Sophie's laugh gets louder with each roll. When I reach the bottom, she's still lying down, and I bump into her.

"That was the best one I've done so far." She turns to me on the grass. Her cheeks are pink, and her smile almost reaches each ear. "C'mon, let's do it again."

"Okay." I grin back. There are twigs in her hair, both of us are covered in grass and mud stains from the ground, and I know we rolled over some sheep poo, but I have to admit that it was really fun.

It's not so fun walking back up to the top.

"This is much higher than it seemed when we were going down." I puff.

"I know," she groans, scrambling up a particularly hilly bit.

"Let's do it from here," I suggest when we reach halfway. "The roll will still be as good."

Her eyes move to the top of the hill. "Yeah, okay. Great idea."

But instead of lying out, she just sits. "It's really pretty here, isn't it?"

My eyes glance over the valley. I mean, I guess. It's just fields of grass and trees, which is kind of boring. But I can see the Burlington herds of cattle, and I can see a couple of ponies trotting down the lane with their riders, and I do love animals. One of my favorite things to do is go out with Lando on the four-wheelers and check on them.

So I smile at her and say, "Yes."

"I love our adventures." Her shoulder pushes against mine, and I nudge her back.

"Me too."

"Come on. We're not done."

Sophie starts first again. "Don't forget to stretch your arms," she shouts back, because she knows I did forget.

I should stop rolling, but instead, I push my arms out and keep going. It's when they're fully stretched that my left arm suddenly hurts so much I scream. The pain makes me jerk and twist on the hill, enough that I roll again, right over where it's hurting. By the time I manage to stop myself, I know I'm crying. I can't help it.

Sophie's way in front of me, almost to the bottom. I try to move, because maybe I can walk down the hill, but it hurts too much, so I stay where I am and sit down. I'm trying so hard to keep still because even crying hurts my arm. The jerking movement as I catch my breath makes it feel like I'm being stabbed.

When she finally gets to the bottom and stands up, she turns to find me. When I don't return her wave, she looks confused. And when I still don't move, she's worried enough that she comes back up to find me.

"Hendricks . . ." she puffs. "Are you okay? What happened?"

"I hurt my arm when I stretched out." I let out a big sob, and it's so painful I squeeze it to my body tighter, but that hurts too. Everything hurts.

I just want to go home to my mum.

Sophie kneels opposite me and stares at my arm. She doesn't even blink. "Can you move?"

I nod. Doing my best to wipe away a fresh set of tears. "Yes, but it hurts."

"Do you think you broke it?"

When I try to shrug, fresh pain shoots down my arm. "I don't know."

She looks up the hill and then down, then back at me. "When my brother broke his arm, the doctor said he shouldn't move it at all. I think it's too steep to go up because we had to use our hands sometimes, remember, but we can go down, and I'll help you. Then we can call my mum to get us."

"Okay." I sniff.

Scooching to sit beside me, I feel her arm gently cup my shoulder. "I'm so sorry, Hendricks."

"It's not your fault—"

"It was my idea."

"I could have said no."

Her arm drops from my shoulder. "Do you need help getting up?"

"No, I think I can do it."

Sophie helps me anyway. She doesn't pull my arm, but she grabs my T-shirt when I try to stand and nearly fall over.

"Oww, ouch. *Owww.*"

"Let's try to walk, and if it's too steep, we can shuffle on our bottoms," she says.

My arm hurts too much to think of a better idea, so I nod and follow her when she carefully steps forward.

The pain in my arm is getting bigger, and it now feels like a drum is banging loudly inside my body, making my entire arm shake.

We go slowly. Every step I take is careful, with Sophie holding me so I don't fall. She doesn't stop talking the whole way, which is good because the pain in my arm is too much for me to speak. Sometimes it's too much for me to listen. I hear words like dragons, witches, and magic, and know she's making up one of her stories.

It takes us much longer to walk down the hill than it did to roll, but when we finally reach Honeysuckle Lane, I realize her stories have stopped the pain from getting worse.

"I really want my mum."

Sophie's hand slips into my good one. "I know, we're going to call her."

"Thank you."

Luckily, the cow gate is open. Otherwise, I'd have had to climb over it. We walk onto Honeysuckle Lane and follow the curve of the road up into Valentine Nook until we reach the fountain.

"Why did we stop?"

"I'm thinking who we ask first."

"First for what?"

"To borrow a phone."

I don't reply. I'm trying not to panic, and I don't want to make Sophie feel bad by telling her I don't feel so good. But I really don't. And then she screeches, "Eddie."

When I look up, he's walking toward us. Eddie is the landlord of The One True Love. He has a big mustache and always looks grumpy, but we like him because he always sneaks us a glass of Coke and a packet of crisps.

"What are you two doing? Up to no good, again?" he grumbles, but he's also smiling, and when he winks, we know he's not being serious. But then he sees that I'm crying. "What's happened? Hendricks, you don't look so good."

"Hendricks is hurt. We need to call his mum."

"What did you do?"

"We were rolling down the hill."

"What hill?"

Sophie turns around and points. "The one on Honeysuckle Lane."

Eddie's lips disappear into his thick mustache. "You were rolling down the hill? From the *top*?"

Sophie nods. "And Hendricks's arm got caught—"

I sniff loudly. I know there are still tears running down my cheeks. I can feel them.

"Okay, get inside, you two. Hendricks, I'll call yer mum."

We follow him into the pub, past all the people sitting outside enjoying the sunshine, and over to the big squashy chairs by the fire. It's not lit during the summer, and it's super quiet inside, so no one's staring at us.

"Stay put. I'll be back in a minute," he grumbles, though it sounds less grumbly than usual.

When he returns five minutes later, he's holding two glasses of Coke and two packets of crisps. One plain for Sophie, and the salt-and-vinegar kind for me.

"Thank you."

"Yer mum is on her way," he says, pulling over a spare chair and sitting down. "Now you want to tell me what you think you were doing?"

Sophie shrugs and takes a big gulp of her drink. "We just thought it would be fun. And I've done it lots. We both did it once to the bottom before Hendricks hurt himself."

Eddie shakes his head in the way grown-ups do when they're disappointed. And I can tell Sophie feels bad because her eyes aren't sparkling like they do when she's happy.

"It wasn't your fault."

She doesn't reply because that's when my mum rushes in, followed by Miles. She's moving so quickly she almost passes us by, but the second she sees me, I start crying again. Miles pushes between Sophie and me, until he's hugging me too.

"I knew something was wrong." He sniffs.

"Oh darling, what happened?"

Sophie answers because I'm crying too much. "He hurt his arm when we were playing on the hill. It might be broken."

She nods. "Okay, we're going to get you to the doctor. Sophie, where's your mummy?"

"I called her too, Your Grace," Eddie replies. "She's coming. She can wait with me while you get Hendricks fixed up."

"Thank you, Eddie."

Miles stands and takes my good hand to help me. When I turn around, Sophie's crying too, and I feel so bad because it was an accident, but I know she thinks it's her fault.

"Mummy, Sophie helped me all the way down. She didn't let me fall. And she told me stories, and we got down safely because of her."

Sophie's lips rise in a small smile, and I feel a little better. I hate seeing her cry even though I've seen her cry loads.

"More stories, eh? Why doesn't that surprise me?" adds Eddie. "As you're quite the storyteller, you can tell me some while we wait for your mum to arrive."

When we get to the doctor's, he tells me my arm is broken, and I have to go to the hospital so they can fix it in surgery. Miles and Mummy were both given an extra bed next to mine because I have to stay overnight. In the morning, I'm allowed to have jelly and ice cream for breakfast, which Miles has too.

When I get my cast put on, Sophie is allowed to come over and visit, and she's the first one to sign it after Miles.

Sophie The Storyteller to the Rescue.

8

Story

A tin of biscuits is shoved under my nose. "Chocolate Digestive?"

Looking up, I find a colleague I've met precisely zero times before, though I think he teaches a class two years above me. I shake my head, offering a polite smile, and go back to peering around the room.

This is only the second staff meeting I've been in since I arrived at Valentine Prep, and the first where everyone's in attendance, including the six teachers in the sports department, all in one corner dressed head to toe in PE kit, acting like they own the place.

It's not a huge school—with fewer than five hundred pupils from kindergarten to thirteen—but you wouldn't know it, given how many of us are here. With everyone talking at once, it's impossible to hear what one single person is saying.

My brief time here has been so busy that I've barely met anyone properly, and any spare moments I have had were spent catching up on what I should have done earlier in the day. I always loved school, and I wanted to be a teacher as long as I could remember, but no one warned you about the admin. The hours spent poring over spreadsheets and reports, adhering to the curriculum.

If they had, I would have seriously considered my life choices.

According to my watch, we're already five minutes late starting this meeting, and I briefly question whether I can make a quick cup of coffee. However, it would involve navigating around the group hovering possessively in front of it—most of whom look like they don't need any more caffeine and would fight anyone who said otherwise.

After a brief deliberation with myself, I decide to leave them to it. School starts early enough. If you're going to add an extra thirty minutes to the start of the day, everyone deserves all the caffeine they can get, and I'm not the only one stifling a yawn. That is, until a cloud of perfume wakes me up, and thoughts of coffee leave as my lungs fight for what's left of the oxygen in the room.

Mrs. Benson, the headmistress, marches in wearing a skirt covered in flowers so bright that several people wince.

"Good morning, good morning, everyone," she calls out, with a singsong voice that grates down my spine.

Next to me, Celeste replies, "Good morning, Mrs. Benson," like we're in morning assembly, though I can't tell if the chuckle she adds at the end is sarcastic or not.

"How is everyone this lovely Monday morning?"

Based on the grunts echoing around the room, I'd say not many people think this morning is particularly lovely. It's also raining, so "lovely" is debatable, and it's *Monday*, but I stop myself before my eyes roll, and button down my annoyance.

Truthfully, I'm annoyed that I'm annoyed. I used to

be like that—cheery, bright, and excited to begin the day with a room full of eager learners. And now, I have no idea what I'm doing.

Unless what I'm doing is having a midlife crisis. That would make sense.

"Sounds like good weekends were had by all," Mrs. Benson continues, adding a hearty chortle to her tone.

I lean into Celeste. "Does this happen every Monday?"

She nods. "But there were discussions on moving it to either midweek or Friday afternoon."

I balk, and my neck cranes. "*Friday afternoon*?"

"It was quickly shot down."

I can't tell from Celeste's pursed lips whether she thought a Friday afternoon / after-school meeting was a good idea or not, but I know that if teachers in England are anything like the teachers in Australia, Mrs. Benson would have a riot on her hands if anything got between the last class at the end of the week and a trip to the pub. Or in the case of my Sydneysider teachers, a surf.

By the time you hit 4 p.m. on a Friday, you'd be lucky if you found one single human—teacher or pupil—left in school. Five minutes later and the faculty would be lining up at the nearest bar for something to take the edge off their week. Looking after a class of high-spirited children for eight hours a day tends to require a stiff drink or a good wave.

Sadly, it would make no difference to me whether the meeting was on a Friday afternoon, Monday morning, or anywhere in between. My edge will be present regardless. It isn't restricted to a particular day and hasn't come from my class. It's already set in. And I *think* it's here to stay.

Personally, I'd pick the Monday morning time slot and get into work early because it beats staying in bed, staring at the ceiling, for another hour. And why are you staring at the ceiling, Story, you ask? Well, because annoyingly, my brain won't shut off. Because I don't know what to do about this situation I'm in.

Because I *can't stop thinking* about Hendricks.

Like right now when all I can picture is the look on his face right before he told me the blonde was his nanny. Thick dark brows drawn down with an expression that combined weariness with a little of the arrogance I always associated with Miles. Because Hendricks knew that I was jealous but couldn't decide whether to be annoyed or flattered.

He's not the only one confused, though my feelings are being tossed between sadness and humiliation. On the plus side, it's helped me move into the acceptance stage of grief. My name is Story MacIntosh, and I accept that I fucked things up.

The slightly—okay, *a lot*—less mature side of me is saying that I can stop there. I don't need to address things any further with Hendricks.

We (kind of) made our peace the other day—we agreed not to talk—but honestly, even if we can be cordial in our acknowledgments of one another when and if our paths cross, then that's all we need. In fact, we don't have to spend time together. Maybe I can insist that the blonde—*his nanny*—drop Max off in the mornings.

As a result, my day won't spiral because I won't be thinking about him and the blonde making blonde babies, and I can finally move on with my life.

As soon as this meeting finishes, anyway.

Mrs. Benson has given up shushing people and is loudly clapping her hands together.

"Now, first order of business, the beginning of term. We'll remind parents that they can't leave their car engines running or block the road if they're bringing their child to the classroom. If you're a teacher on duty in the drop-off zone, please keep an eye out for this behavior. We already had warnings from the village council. We don't need any more."

Next to me, Celeste mumbles something under her breath.

Will the blonde or Hendricks drop Max off this morning? Perhaps I can share my suggestion with them. The more I think about it, the more sensible I feel it'll be for all parties.

"Second, after much back and forth, the trees on the far edge of the sports fields will be out of bounds from next month onward. The roots are causing damage, and we've decided to have them chopped down—"

"The big horse chestnut tree?" I blurt before I can stop myself.

"Yes, Sophie, that's correct," she says, beaming at me, once she's recovered from being annoyed at the interruption. "We were going to do new joiners at the end of the meeting, but as it's only you, let me introduce you all to Sophie MacIntosh, the new reception form interim teacher taking over for David Burton. Or rather, welcome back."

Next to me, Celeste tuts. Dave's still on her shit list. Or S. H. I. T. list. Thankfully she doesn't pick up on Mrs. Benson's comment about welcoming me back.

A round of grunted hellos echo around the room, and I offer a small wave, while simultaneously trying to sink into my chair to disappear as my mind wanders back to the tree I used to love sitting under. I wonder what happened to that map . . .

"As I was saying, the tree will be repurposed into benches for the sports fields, to sit and watch the games. And that area will become an adventure playground course. So all in all, a positive turn of events, wouldn't you say?" Mrs. Benson shuffles the pile of papers in her hand. I don't know if she's waiting for everyone to agree with her, or if she's stopped for a dramatic pause. But no one says anything, so she continues, "And then we have our general admin of term dates, lost property, and if any of your students need to visit the school nurse, please ensure a classroom assistant accompanies them." She peers around the room and removes her spectacles. "Now . . ."

Next to me, Celeste sits ramrod straight. In hindsight, I should have paid attention, but I'm still thinking about the tree being cut down and *repurposed*. All those times I spent sitting under its shade and it will just be gone . . .

"Sophie and I will volunteer."

My head spins so fast in Celeste's direction that my neck snaps, and pain spears across my shoulder. "Ouch, fuck."

I glare at Celeste, whose hand is raised in the air.

Mrs. Benson claps again. "Wonderful. I'll let the committee know. The first meeting is tonight. Thank you, ladies. And that, everyone, concludes business. Have a wonderful week, and my door is always open if you need me."

A wave of relieved groans surrounds me, along with a fresh waft of perfume and the chaos of screeching chair legs and hurried steps, as everyone moves back and rushes to the coffee machine for one last top-up before the bell rings. I, however, am trying to figure out what I've just been signed up for.

"You okay?"

I squeeze along my shoulder, trying to ease the tightness in the muscle. "I twinged my neck."

"Ooh, painful. Do you want to go to the nurse and get some painkillers?"

I'm tempted, but say, "No. I want you to tell me what you just signed me up for."

Celeste's face lights up in a way that makes me nervous, and she jumps from her chair. "Come on, let's get coffee, and I'll tell you all about it. It's so much fun."

I'll reserve judgment on the fun until I know exactly what it's supposed to be, but I get up anyway, and we make ourselves a coffee.

"So," Celeste begins, flicking a small packet of sugar between her fingers. I wait patiently for her to rip it open, pour it in, and stir with one of those wooden sticks. I wait so long I'm almost ready to shake the answer out of her. "Every February in Valentine Nook, the village committee hosts the Valentine Festival. It takes place over the weekend near Valentine's Day. The reception pupils give a little concert, and there's lots of fun and games. It's a *big* deal." She pins me with an intense look.

The Valentine Festival. How had I forgotten we're about to enter the busiest time of year in Valentine Nook?

"Okay . . . what's that got to do with us? We have to do the concert?"

If I'm being honest, a concert for a bunch of five- and six-year-olds is always a cute time, even if it is a bit like herding cats. But seeing their little faces as they sing their hearts out cracks even the stoniest of souls, and I can cope with a Valentine concert. You never know, it might bring some life back to mine.

"No, we do that anyway. I volunteered us to be on the committee." She grins, like I'd be nothing other than ecstatic.

To be clear, I'm not.

The concert is one thing. Being a member of the committee is quite another.

I remember one year when my mum volunteered. As the weeks closed in on the fourteenth of February, we saw less and less of her. By the time the big day came around, she looked like she'd been awake for thirty-six hours, powered by sugar and wine. When my dad presented her his Valentine card, she threatened to divorce him.

At any time of year, Valentine Nook is a hive of activity—random marriage proposals, maneuvering around the constant queues outside Agatha's store, the couples walking around starry-eyed . . .

But during February . . . it's love on steroids, and most definitely not for the weak.

It's hard to get excited about love when your heart and soul are currently in a state of apathy. In fact, if you cut me open right now, you'd probably find my organs to be less pink and more gray turning to black.

Maybe I can call in sick.

I don't want to be reminded that I'm alone, and I definitely don't want to be part of the committee that prides itself on hosting the best festivals in England and possibly Europe.

Celeste is still talking, and I'm nodding politely, but my mind is running a million miles an hour.

"It's so much fun. I didn't grow up around here, but I did come to the festival once when I was a teenager. My friends and I spent the whole time in the queue for love potions." She's speaking so loudly that a couple of colleagues walking past stare at her. "Half the money raised goes toward the upkeep of the village, the other half goes to the local children's cancer hospital. Last year we made over twenty thousand pounds."

"That sounds good," I say, because it's the only positive thing I can manage.

"Yes, and I thought we would have fun. It's also good to take your mind off your boyfriend—"

"Hendricks isn't my boyfriend," I snap defensively, making Celeste giggle.

"Hendricks? Hendricks Burlington?" She giggles more. Seriously, she giggles way too much, especially for a Monday morning. "No, silly. Your boyfriend in Australia?"

Oh my God. *Oh my God.* I blink hard. How did I forget? "Noah. *Right.* Yes. We broke up."

"Yes, *and* so this would be the perfect opportunity to move on, maybe find someone new . . ." She elbows me. "And I'll keep your little crush on Hendricks Burlington a secret. Don't worry, we've all got one. It's a club."

I stop walking. This needs to be nipped in the bud right now. I don't care who's crushing on him because *obviously* everyone is crushing on him.

"Celeste, I do not have a crush on Hendricks Burlington."

Not sure why I think I can convince her, seeing as I've never been able to convince myself.

She holds her hand up in defense. "I'm only teasing because obviously that would be so awkward. Plus, he's mine," she adds with a wink, clearly not letting this go.

"You can have him," I snap. Except I want to know what she thinks is going to be awkward even though something's telling me not to ask. But I can't help myself. "Why?"

"Because he's chair of the committee this year. So you'll be spending a lot of time together over the next month."

I knew I'd regret asking.

Hendricks Burlington, chair of the Valentine Festival committee? Of course he fucking is.

I glance out of the window, catching the remnants of my plan to move on with my life floating away on the breeze. Spending a lot of time with Hendricks was not part of that.

Fuck Monday. Fuck my life.

9

Hendricks

"Easy, boy. You're okay. You'll feel better soon."

Chester's big hooves paw at the concrete yard floor, and he snorts his disapproval.

Stroking down the white blaze on his face and along his soft, whiskery muzzle, I lift it gently so I can check his gums. He cracked a back tooth a couple of weeks ago, and we decided to remove it, which seems simple enough. But when you're dealing with half a ton of animal, things become slightly more complicated, and it requires said horse to be fully tranquilized.

As a result, he's been on stable rest and a limited diet since, something he's been increasingly irritable about. Even the five-star service Miles gives all his ponies—including daily equine massage—doesn't seem to have helped his temperament.

"You're such a brave boy," Miles coos, stroking down his neck. "Uncle Hendricks will be done soon."

Chester's ears move from almost flat to perked upright.

I feel along his jawline for swelling or any abscesses that may have developed during his recovery, but don't find anything of note.

"Okay, we can sign you off," I say, pulling off my rubber gloves and patting him down. "He can go back to exercise, but you need to watch around the bit. It might take a little time for him to adjust—"

"Hear that, sweetheart? We can be a pair again." Miles smacks a kiss to Chester's muzzle.

"And stop giving him lemon sherbets."

The pout Miles gives me is identical to the one Max pulled this morning before school when I told him he needed to brush his teeth. "But he loves them. They're his treat at the end of the day."

"Milo, c'mon, no lemon sherbets. He needs to learn to like apples. Or better yet, carrots." I point at the huge bucket of carrots by the main doors to the stables. It's topped up every day and is there for all the horses to be given one whenever they want. "See. Not to mention he's supposed to be an athlete."

Miles gently fits a halter around Chester's muzzle. "Uncle Hendricks sure is grumpy today."

I refuse to take the bait. It's exactly what Miles wants. I bide my time instead and pack up my surgery bag.

"He can stay on the anti-inflammatories for another few days, but I'll lower the dose. Let me know if he has any issues. Just gentle exercise for the next week, a bit of stick and balling, nothing strenuous around his mouth."

"Got it." Miles salutes me and kisses Chester again. "Hear that, Chessy? We can do some exercise."

Chester nudges him in response, and whickers loudly while he drags his hoof along the concrete floor of the stable block, telling us both that he's raring to go. Four large heads poke out of the end stables nearer the far doors, all nosy enough to see what the commotion is, and they stay there because if someone is walking down the central path, then it's likely they'll be given a carrot or three.

Grabbing a handful from the bucket, I snap a couple in half and hand them out as we pass.

"So are you going to tell me what happened with Story the other day?"

Wiping a saliva-covered hand on my jeans, I hand over another carrot. This time to Clover, one of Miles's newer ponies. She's incredibly speedy, not to mention fearless. And Miles has never failed to score while riding her.

"There's nothing to tell."

"I think there is."

The sigh I let out is deep. Enough that Miles knows Story coming back to Valentine Nook is messing with my head more than I ever expected.

"I saw her, we had a quick chat, then Max fell over and I left to bandage him up. That is literally the entirety of what happened."

"Did you take Max to school today?" he presses.

"Yes—"

"And—"

"It was fine. Same as it is every day."

The last carrot goes to Soldier, a sturdy Welsh cob who never seems to tire, hence the name. He's so gentle when he takes it, and I stand there, stroking his muzzle and trying not to think about how I caught Story watching me this morning at drop-off.

But I agreed not to talk to her, therefore I didn't. She never said anything about not looking at her, however. I tried to concentrate on Max, and only Max, but every couple of seconds I'd be drawn to where she was standing, only to catch her brown eyes flicking in the opposite direction.

It happened enough that when her back was to me, I used the opportunity to kiss Max goodbye and slip away with a final glance and a wide grin.

Returning to the car, I sat there for a full ten minutes while I tried to make sense of the thoughts turning my brain into a vortex. When I didn't get very far, I came here hoping that Miles would help me, but now that he's asking, I don't want to talk about it. I don't want to talk about Story full stop. It only makes everything more confusing than it already is.

Reaching around Chester, his hand claps the back of my neck and squeezes gently. "The offer still stands if you want me to do drop-off."

"I know." I nod, but the problem is I *want* to take Max to school because I want to see Story.

I want to see her as much as I don't.

"She's still in love with you, Hen. It's obvious."

I stay silent. I don't even know where to begin in response, and Miles knows it. He wasn't expecting me to reply. He just wanted to remind me. To jolt me into admitting I feel the same.

"Let's go out for a drink tonight. In fact . . ." Miles stops Chester walking. His brow arches sharply, a sure-fire way to know he's plotting something. "Let's go to London, blow off some steam. Give you something else to think about."

I'm tempted. More tempted than I've been in a long time.

Since Max came along and my partying was curbed overnight, I choose my nights out carefully and wisely.

If you don't count our family's New Year trip to Aspen, it's been months since I've had a night free to do what I want, and a morning when I haven't inevitably woken to a five-year-old snoring next to me.

Outside of Miles dragging me into the city like he's trying to now, my sex life is nonexistent. I've never had a girlfriend, I've never introduced Max to anyone, and that's how I plan to keep it until he's old enough to understand. Until I've met someone worthy of introducing him to. He's already had one woman leave him who was supposed to stay forever. I'm not planning on any more.

I've never been able to prove Max's mother is the devil incarnate, but why else would her name—SIENNA—be flashing on my screen right as I'm thinking of her? It was EVIL BITCH for a long time, thanks to Miles, but now that Max is learning to read, I thought it should be something a little more suitable for the woman who birthed him. Even if it's true. Because as much as I hate her, she gave me Max, and for that, I will always be grateful.

My twin, however, is much less compassionate. The second he sees my phone screen, his mouth drops.

"What the fuck does she want?"

We stare at it in my hand, both of us willing it to stop.

"Why's she calling? When did you last hear from her?"

I shrug because I can't actually remember. "A few months ago. She wanted money to invest in that Ayahuasca retreat."

"It should be studied how she manages to blow through so much cash." Miles snarls, adding something under his breath that sounds a lot like "Gold digging bitch."

It's possible Miles hates her more than I do. Because Miles was with me when I was going through it all, when I was living on autopilot, trying to figure out what to do, how I was going to be a good father. But even before Max was born, it was clear I was trying to make it work with a woman I didn't like very much.

It's one thing to spend time together between the hours of 1 a.m. and 4 a.m., when talking isn't really the priority. It's another being forced into an inescapable situation.

I should have paid more attention to the fact she wasn't particularly interested in being pregnant, beyond the shopping and the pregnancy clothes she could model on Instagram all day. That the only affection she ever showed me was when it was benefiting a post.

Because Sienna refused to move to Valentine Nook, my time was split between Oxfordshire and London, driving the two hours back and forth. Exhaustion didn't take long to set in, especially on the days I had to be at the practice or had a full day of school.

I hired a nanny to help us both. Me, so I could continue studying for my veterinary exams, and for Sienna so she didn't feel too overwhelmed. I'd come home desperate to see my son, and Sienna would be desperate to go out to the newest club or bar, using my name to get in.

But it wasn't enough.

The final straw was her shipping Max and the nanny off to Burlington when he was nine months old so that she could go to Ibiza for a week.

The custody solicitors had drafted up terms by the

time she returned home.

Miles comforted me while I sobbed long into the night after a grueling day of school and taking care of Max while he battled through teething or his first cold, wondering how I would do this alone. He was next to me as I read through the latest round of demands from Sienna's solicitors—a bunch of cut-throat city guys who sniffed out big money from a hundred yards away.

In the end, I gave her whatever she wanted, as long as I had Max full-time, no contest. She got a flat in central London, a monthly stipend, and a settlement figure.

For the first year, I didn't hear a word from her. She never checked in, didn't wish Max a happy birthday, no presents, nothing.

When Max was eighteen months old, she called to ask for a larger monthly allowance. When I said no, she threatened to take Max, knowing full well the law favors mothers in any custody situation. So we drafted new terms, and she got more.

It's become a pattern, one I've unwittingly allowed because she knows that she has me between a rock and a hard place. I can afford whatever settlement she wants, and she knows I'll pay it to keep Max. Since I've had full custody, and she's seen him a handful of times during supervised visits.

It's what keeps my stress levels running higher than my doctor would like because I never know when the call will come. I just know it'll happen at some point.

Miles is still looking at me, and I suddenly want to forget everything. Forget my life. Forget the mess I'm in. Between Sienna and Story, blowing off some steam is exactly what I need.

"You know what, I'm in. If we leave after I put Max to bed, then I'll only miss breakfast and drop-off tomorrow."

"Done. Let's go to Five Hertford Street, that pretty server works there on a Monday and I still haven't persuaded her to sleep with me."

I roll my eyes. "Fine by me."

He pulls his phone out. "I'll get our table reserved."

"Cool." As I slip mine back in my pocket, the phone lights up with the missed call and Sienna's name. "God, I fucking hate her."

"Hate who?"

Miles's and my heads snap up at the sound of the voice. We find Alex walking toward us with his baby daughter strapped to his chest. He only found out a couple of months ago that he was a father to a six-week-old, and he came around to the idea of being a father much quicker and more adeptly than I did.

It probably helped that he was already desperately in love with her mother having met her the year before in Aspen, where we'd gone to escape the chaos of Lando's almost-wedding.

When Haven turned up with Everly, Alex jumped into action, and now it's almost impossible to imagine a time when he wasn't a father. Even without confirmation, I know he was responsible for dressing her in that polar bear snowsuit because he loves it. It must run in the family because I was the same.

Before Max was old enough to choose his own clothes obviously. Now if I suggest something for him to wear, he argues against it on principle. Thank God he has to wear a school uniform because otherwise he'd wear his Spider-Man costume seventy-five percent of the time.

"Hey, Al. What are you doing here?" Miles says.

"Can't I pop over to my youngest brother's yard to show my daughter his polo ponies?"

"No argument from me. I'm all for starting them young."

"Where's Haven?" I pull Alex into a hug, while taking care not to crush Everly. I drop a kiss on her head instead.

"She's not feeling too good."

Miles, being Miles, immediately pulls the neck of his jumper up to cover his mouth. "What's she sick with? I can't get sick, Al. I have a tournament next weekend, and Chester's just been given the sign-off."

"Milo, I said *light exercise*."

Alex rolls his eyes. "It's not contagious, but I'll let her know you were sympathizing."

"How d'you know she's not contagious? Has she seen Oliver?"

"No—"

"Then—"

"Oh, for fuck's sake. She's pregnant."

Alex pauses, his eyes flicking from Miles to me and back as a huge grin spreads across his face. He may have rendered Miles speechless, which is something nearly everyone attempts but rarely succeeds.

My arm is still holding Alex's shoulder, and without thinking I yank him into another hug. "Congratulations. Fuck. That's amazing news. Does Mum know?"

He shakes his head. "We haven't told anyone yet. We wanted to wait another few weeks. I'd say keep it to yourself, but now Milo knows . . ."

The implication is clear, not to mention valid, regardless of Miles's expression of objection. Miles cannot keep a secret if his life depended on it.

I snort a laugh. "Do you know what you're having?"

"No, she's only just at six weeks. We have to wait a bit longer."

"Max will want a boy." My son was the least impressed Burlington when Alex's daughter turned up. The initial excitement of having a cousin wore off quickly when he discovered it was a girl.

"He'll have to wait like the rest of us."

My grin widens. "I'm so happy for you both. It's really wonderful news."

I can feel his happiness as he glances down at the bundle on his chest. "Me too. I missed the whole of Haven's pregnancy with Everly, and now I get to be part of this." His sigh is profound. "Anyway, what are you two doing?"

"Chester had his checkup." Miles runs his palm along Chester's face. "He was such a brave boy, weren't you, darling?"

Alex grins and turns to me. "Hen, how are you doing? Have you seen Story yet?"

Miles snorts, even though he's still focused on Chester. "You could say that."

And he wonders why we think he's got a big mouth.

"Yes, I've seen her, but I don't have anything to report. It is what it is." I shrug.

I can feel their eyes on me, just in case I have more to add. I don't. Not right now, and this time Miles stays quiet.

"Al, we're heading to London to blow off steam, so Hendricks can forget all about Story. Come with us."

"No offense, but there's nothing I want to do less than go out with you two." He laughs at Miles, louder when his face drops with a huff.

"I do take offense."

"What about the duke?"

"Nope. Lando's still in the States." Miles's eyes widen with a shit-stirring twinkle I know well. "But I did get hashtag hot duke trending on Instagram."

Alex laughs loudly. "You're lucky he's six thousand miles away."

"Only for another week, because they're coming back for BAFTA."

"Excellent, another black-tie event he'll have to look good for." Miles rubs his hands together, making Alex laugh enough that Everly stirs.

I'm also laughing enough that none of us immediately notice my phone ringing again. For a second I'm expecting to see Sienna's name flash across the screen, but it's a local number I don't recognize and for that I have to pick up. With Max I don't have the luxury of not answering a call when he's not with me.

It's not about Max. And it's not Sienna either. Though arguably no more welcome a call.

"Hendricks. Just calling to remind you about the meeting tonight."

Mrs. Winston. One of the senior residents of Valentine Nook, owner of Churchill the ever-escaping goat, and one of the village busybodies. She's loud enough that both my brothers can hear her speaking, and they stop messing around to stare at me with a grin.

They know a call from Mrs. Winston always involves something we'd rather not do.

Granted, I'm not the most organized, but I would have remembered a meeting in the diary if I had one. Especially because I rarely make evening plans as ascertained when Miles asked me to go to London.

"Hello to you too, Mrs. Winston. I'm afraid I have to ask you to jog my memory—"

"The Valentine Fair. You're chairing the committee."

Alex snorts loudly, and Miles is grinning so wide I kick him, only he moves out of the way before I make contact.

Valentine Nook hosts festivals throughout the year. They're good for business, tourism, and funding the upkeep of the village. My father started them, and they're a tradition Lando kept on when he took over. For some reason, Lando likes for one member of the Burlington family to lead each committee. There's enough for us to take in turns, and I'd completely forgotten (or perhaps blocked out) that my turn was coming up.

The Valentine Fair is the biggest of the year—love on steroids—and now I'm leading the charge. Because I don't date, Valentine's Day normally passes me by relatively unnoticed, but now the thought of being surrounded by saccharinely happy people for the next month is enough to give me hives.

I should never have picked up the phone.

Taking it away from my ear, I hiss to Miles and Alex, "I'll pay either of you two to do it instead."

They're too busy smirking at each other to answer, and Mrs. Winston is still squawking down the phone.

"Hendricks . . . you there?"

"Yes, sorry, Mrs. Winston."

She takes it as confirmation that I hadn't forgotten. "Wonderful. See you in the village hall at eight o'clock sharp." And promptly hangs up before I can reply, or object *or* tell her I can't make it.

Fuck's sake.

I turn to my identical twin, who already knows what I'm about to ask.

"No—"

"Milo, please—"

"No—"

"I can't face the Valentine committee. No one will know the difference."

"I love you, Hen, but no. I did it last year, and that was bad enough. They spent an entire month trying to convince me to settle down with one of their daughters. I don't know why Lando insists we do the fair committees, especially when he hates them. Besides, I'm going to London. I have a date with the pretty server."

"You're still going? Even though I can't?"

"Yup."

"Al?"

"No way, I'm running the summer."

"I'll swap my next two with you."

But Alex shakes his head, so I try Miles again. "You still haven't paid me back for the time I had to take Olivia Kenwood out because you double booked yourself."

"That was ten years ago, and I think I have. Not to mention you had sex with her—"

"Yeah, but she thought I was you! She kept moaning *your* name."

His hands grip my shoulders. “Hen, you’re going to have to pull on your big boy trousers and go. Sorry, bud. Besides, it’s for charity.”

Ten minutes ago, I was looking forward to a night out. Now I have to spend the next month at the beck and call of the village busybodies.

I’ll say this—if anyone of them even tries to set me up on a date, I’m resigning.

10

Story

"Sorry, sorry! Have you been waiting long?"

The answer is debatable.

If compared to say standing in line at Sydney Airport customs while desperate to get out of the airport as quickly as possible—one time it took three hours—then no, I haven't.

But if you agree to meet someone ten minutes before the start of an event and you actually arrive closer to an hour earlier—so early the lights in the hall haven't been switched on yet—then yes, I have.

However, no one except me needs to know that.

I'll take it to the grave that I got here almost an hour before I needed to because I didn't want to arrive after Hendricks. And knowing Hendricks as I do—or used to—he will be right on time. If I'm already seated with a group, he may not notice me right away. Hide in plain sight, perhaps. I dunno, it seemed like a good idea at the time.

"No, not long at all."

"Oh good," Celeste says, shaking her mittens off and rubbing her hands together. She begins to unravel the giant scarf. I thought I didn't like the cold, but she's more wool-covered mummy than woman. "It's freezing. C'mon, let's get inside and have a coffee before everyone else gets here. Why are you so dressed up? Have you had your hair done?"

I wonder if she's trying to defrost her jaw with all the questions, but she's staring at me clearly waiting for an answer. I peer down at my jeans and trainers, the camel-colored knit jumper that somehow makes my eyes seem even lighter brown, and my hair super shiny. I don't know how, it just does.

"Am I?" I reply, as nonchalantly as possible.

I haven't had my hair done the way she means, but I did rush home, slap on a hair mask, a face mask, and lie in the bath for an hour while I tried to quash my anxiety. Because obviously, the idea of being in a room with Hendricks Burlington for however long this meeting is going to be had me close to losing my mind.

If I'm going to spend the evening in his company, I'm determined to look good while doing so. However, looking like I've dressed up totally defeats the point. I should have worn a different jumper, and I now regret going with the lipstick *and* the cat's eye. One or the other, Story. One or the other.

"You look like you've spent the day at the spa. And I know you didn't because I saw you four hours ago." She laughs and heads into the village hall. "Oh, we're the first ones. They must have left the lights on."

The lights are on because I switched them on. No one else had arrived, and I came back out into the cold to wait for Celeste in the spot we agreed to meet. Maybe I should tone down the makeup.

"I had to check on the cows, so I changed."

She stops on her march over to . . . I'm not sure exactly, because there's nothing here. It's not been set up. There are no chairs, no coffee, nothing.

"Cows? What cows?"

"Um . . ." *Shit*. This is what happens when you don't pay attention to the lies piling up. Not that I've lied per se, I just haven't yet told Celeste that I'm a local. *A Valentiner*. Not that she asked where I lived. She just assumed I was only here because of the job. And I never corrected her. "My parents' cows. On their farm, on the other side of the village."

"Your parents live here? In Valentine Nook?"

I nod and offer a sheepish smile. "Yup."

"How long for?"

"My whole life, and longer. It was my grandad's farm. But my mum is from Gloucestershire."

"You never said—"

"Didn't I?"

"No." The curtness of her response tells me we both know that I didn't tell her.

Guilt creeps into my gut, unwanted, as guilt tends to be.

I like Celeste. In the week I've known her, I've discovered she's kind and generous, if a little over enthusiastic, and I feel bad that she thinks I've deceived her in some way. On the other hand, I'm not opening up my private business to someone I've only just met.

Especially one who seems to have a crush on Hendricks.

"Sorry, I thought I had. Yes, I grew up in Valentine Nook. My parents have the dairy farm over the hill on Honeysuckle Lane, but I've been in Australia for the past six years, as you know."

She rolls her mouth together until her lips purse. "So I guess you'll know everyone here, then."

"I don't know who's coming. I didn't even know about the meeting until this morning, remember," I reply, and it's true. I don't. Except Hendricks. But that doesn't seem to satisfy Celeste.

She huffs and walks over to the far wall, where I didn't notice a pile of chairs stacked up. "I suppose we should set up the hall for the meeting, but perhaps you know that already."

Her back's to me, so she doesn't see my hefty eye roll. "Actually, no, I haven't. My mum was on the Valentine committee one year, but swore she'd never do it again."

Celeste doesn't join in my laughing, and I honestly don't know what she's so annoyed about. But I have other shit to worry about than trying to placate her, so we place the chairs in silence. By the time Mrs. Winston walks in, followed by Eddie carrying six bottles of wine and two dozen plastic cups, we're almost done.

"Oh girls, well done. Thank you. This is so helpful of you," she coos, only to promptly rearrange everything.

"Bloody hell, Story MacIntosh as I live and breathe."

Jesus. I'm never going to be Sophie in Valentine Nook.

Celeste, who's still ignoring me, turns around looking even more annoyed. "Story? What story?"

"It's an old nickname I *never* use." My eyes roll again, while I relieve Eddie of the wine and cups. "I saw you last month. I delivered the Christmas tree to the pub."

He taps a stubby finger to his forehead. "So you did. So you did. But what are you doing here? Thought you'd gone back to the land of giant spiders and kangaroos."

"Not yet." My eyes slice to Celeste, who's hovering a couple of meters away, desperate to be included. "Eddie, can I introduce you to Celeste, my colleague . . . *friend* . . . we work together at Valentine Prep. We're representing the school for the committee."

Celeste beams at him, a smile I see her use on parents every morning.

"Hello," he grunts before the weight of his focus is back on me. "You're working at the school? You're staying? When were you going to tell me?"

"I'm telling you now."

"Glad I'm not the only one discovering things this evening," Celeste adds, though I note the tone is less hostile than it was five minutes ago. Maybe I'm forgiven.

"Keeping secrets from you too, is she?" grumbles Eddie, at which Celeste giggles. "Is this 'cause of your dad? How is he?"

"Yes. And he's fine. He'll be back on his feet soon—"

"So you're not staying?"

"What is this? The Spanish Inquisition?"

"I just want to know if I need to stock up on whiskey. Does *everyone* know you're back for good?"

Oh okay, I see where this is going. His raised brows and beady eyes peering at me over his bifocals don't need interpreting.

Eddie was the only one I ever spoke to about Hendricks. Not that I said much of anything at all, but on the occasional and brief visits I made home over the years, Eddie was the only one I ever dared to ask how Hendricks was doing. He'd reply with his usual gruff, "Fine," which could have been interpreted in a dozen different ways, but I took it as Hendricks having a great life, loving being a father, a husband, a successful vet . . . whatever.

In hindsight, my translation skills aren't all they're cracked up to be. Though I was correct about his love of being a father. Just from a week of casual observation at morning drop-off, the way Hendricks is with Max is enough to warm even the coldest hearts.

"Yup." I nod, turning to the table to lay out the wine and glasses, and pick up one of the bottles to open. Alcohol will be needed to get through the next hour or three if no one can interrupt Mrs. Winston. Although caffeine isn't out of the question. "Is anyone bringing coffee?"

"Me."

The deep baritone zips down my spine. Goosebumps spread across my skin like tentacles, wrapping themselves around me until I can't breathe. I put down the bottle of wine I'm trying to open, while Eddie swiftly snatches the corkscrew from my other hand.

I brace myself. For what, I'm not entirely sure. This isn't the same as drop-off surrounded by two dozen other people. And when I turn around, I have my answer. It's the dark slash of brow under his baseball cap as he frowns, disappointed that I'm here too.

"What are you doing here?"

Summoning the deepest breath possible, I flare my nostrils only to get a noseful of Hendricks and that leathery rich, mossy scent that follows him around. The one that sets off a tranche of memories and an erratic heartbeat. "Let's just get through this without arguing, please."

"I don't plan to argue, and that didn't answer my

question. Are you on the Valentine committee?"

"Why else would I be here?"

His eyes narrow, and his head tilts a fraction of a degree. I don't know whether he's going to answer my question or if he thinks it was rhetorical. I'm not so sure myself, but as I stare back, his smile grows until it's stretching from ear to ear.

"I see your mood hasn't improved since the weekend."

The proximity to Hendricks becomes too much for Celeste as she thrusts an outstretched hand between us, and drowns out the sarcastic retort I have on the tip of my tongue.

"Lord Burlington, hel-*lo*. We've not formally met. Celeste Scott. I teach the other reception class at Valentine Prep. Max is an exceptional child and a real asset to the school."

I know Hendricks is used to people blowing smoke up his arse. They've done it his whole life, yet it still doesn't seem to tire him because he just smiles and says, "Thank you, I'm rather partial to him myself."

"Oh, ha ha, yes. I'm sure." She guffaws loud enough that even Eddie's mustache twitches with amusement. "Well, it's wonderful to have you here. We're all very excited to have you lead the committee."

Blue eyes slide to mine. "*All*?"

I shrug, indifferent, but Celeste doesn't notice. "Yes, all of us."

"Then it's wonderful to be here." He clasps her palm. I know he's lying. I know he'd rather be anywhere else. "Reception seems to be in excellent hands this year."

For a split second, I wonder if Miles and Hendricks

have swapped. Because this guy with his baseball cap and toothy smile, stubble short enough that I can see his dimples pull in as he bats his eyelashes while Celeste preens, is too smooth for his own good.

It's nauseating.

But then he winks at me.

And with that one singular gesture, I'm taken right back to being a teenager. To being best friends. To watching girls fawn around him while I stood on the sidelines. But no amount of fawning would get them anywhere because both Hendricks and Miles were adamant they never wanted a girlfriend.

I was the only commitment Hendricks ever made. Me and our friendship. I was the one he called at the end of the day.

Our friendship made me special, and no one could ever compete. Girls were jealous, and sometimes girls were mean, or they'd try to use me to get to him. But it didn't matter, because I knew it wouldn't get them anywhere.

Until that day by the fountain.

He made a lifelong commitment to someone who wasn't me. In a second, jealousy ate me up and spat me out. My heart shattered beyond repair. For as long as I could remember, I was hopelessly in love with a boy who never saw me. My entire being was entwined with him, and it unraveled faster than I could comprehend.

Because I found out, in that moment, *his* whole life was not and never would be entwined with mine.

I'm suddenly too beaten to stand here and listen to them talk. I hate it. I hate that I'm not over him. I hate that he still has this effect on me after years apart. Even when I tried moving on with Noah.

Without saying another word, I turn my back and make my way over to the chairs, already filling up. Mrs. Winston is fussing around, greeting everyone who enters—Claudia from the bakery, the couple who run the bed and breakfast, and a few faces I don't know. And then there's Agatha Chase wearing an extra billowy dress under a long scarlet cape.

It's Agatha I make eye contact with, and when she pats the empty chair beside her, I sigh in defeat and take it.

"Story, dear. Good evening."

I don't bother to correct her, there are too many people here who've known me as Story, and it would take the rest of my depleted energy.

"How's it going, Agatha?"

"Splendid. Splendid." Her voice is deeper and more throaty than usual. "Are you ready for the full moon tomorrow?"

"Um..." I'm trying to listen to her, but I'm too focused on not paying attention to where Eddie, Hendricks, and Celeste are all laughing by the table, where the wine is now opened and poured. I watch people maneuver around them to get to the drinks, but they're oblivious to it through their own amusement. "I didn't realize it was a full moon."

"Don't you feel it in the air, Story? The energy around us is electric. You *must* feel it."

I shake my head. "I'm sorry, Agatha."

"Oh dear, it's more dire than I thought. I'm hosting a full moon bath tomorrow evening with my sisters in magic, come and join us."

"I—"

I'm vaguely aware of her moving next to me, rustling around in the meters and meters of fabric her dress must take up, until she clasps my hand tight in hers. It's so tight it almost bites into me.

"Keep this close to you, Story. It will help you open up. But you must come and see me. I can't help you if you don't come."

When she lets go, I find a small, rough pink rock in my hand.

"Rose quartz. It will clear the blockage around your heart."

"You make me sound constipated."

"And this . . ." She ignores me, pressing a small vial into my palm. "I want you to rub onto your pillow every night before you sleep."

"What is it?"

"A potion of my own making. It will help."

"Is this what the apothecary gave Romeo?" I smile weakly at my pathetic joke. "Thanks, Agatha. I appreciate it."

"You're welcome. It won't be much longer," she replies, and I get the impression she's about to add something, only for her mouth to close, and she turns away.

"Charming," I mutter. But a second later, I understand why.

"Anyone sitting here? No? Good. I'll take it, then." It all comes out in one long sentence, and he doesn't bother waiting for me to answer before sitting down. "You rushed off without taking a drink. I didn't know which you wanted, so I brought you both."

I'm staring at Hendricks and the two cups he has

thrust toward me. One in each hand—a coffee and a cup of wine so full to the brim I don't know how he's not spilled it. I know there are at least three other people in this room staring too—Eddie, Celeste, and Agatha. Although Agatha is close enough to eavesdrop, so she doesn't need to stare.

"You brought me a drink?"

"Two, actually."

"Why?"

"I told you. I didn't know which one you wanted."

"What are you drinking, then?"

"Whichever one you don't."

"Okay." I'm still eyeing him, waiting for the catch. I don't know why he's suddenly being so nice when I've been nothing but a total brat. But I reach for the wine because no one ever gets my coffee order correct, and only by slurping the top do I not spill it. "Thank you."

His head bobs, and his throat works as he swallows. Air? Relief? Something at least. "You're welcome."

"Could you have poured any more in here?" I ask, taking another gulp, but as I do, he places the other cup on the floor.

Removing his jacket I'm treated again to a heady waft of Hendricks, and I do my best to hold my breath while he settles into a seat too small for his shoulders and stretches out his long legs. I wait for him to pick the coffee back up, but it stays on the floor as he leans back, his thick bicep resting against my arm.

"What are you doing? I thought you were drinking whatever I didn't."

"Yes. But I'm not drinking that coffee. It's got enough sugar in it to induce a diabetic coma."

I blink hard. "You put sugar in it?"

"Yes." He arches a thick, dark brow at me. "Or have you stopped taking six spoonfuls of sugar in your coffee?"

It takes all my effort to hold my mouth straight and not betray any hint of the surprise and excitement bubbling inside me that he remembered. Even when he says it like *six spoonfuls of sugar*.

"No, I haven't."

"Then I won't be drinking it."

"But you said you'd drink what I didn't."

"That's true. I lied."

I don't know why his honesty is so amusing to me, but coupled with the disgust on his face, it is. So I hold out my wine to him, more out of curiosity to see what he'll do. Whether he'll shake his head or take it.

His gaze drops low enough that I can no longer see his bright blue eyes I can still summon whenever I close mine. Whenever the moment is needed. I know I don't imagine the crackle of static when his fingertips brush over mine, and he eases the plastic wine cup from my hand.

There's no hesitation as he lifts it to his lips. My stare is contemplating as he holds it and takes a large sip before handing it back to me. "Thank you."

"You're welcome."

I know my cheeks are heating, and they're almost bright pink, I just don't know why. But something about the way he's still staring at me intensely forces me to look away.

An hour ago, I was equal parts dread and excitement at the thought of seeing Hendricks, and now we're sharing a cup of wine.

"Order, order," Mrs. Winston shouts at a volume I never expected from her. "Thank you all for coming. It's so wonderful to have a varied group of Valentine Nook volunteers this year—"

"Volunteers? More like strong-armed—" Hendricks mutters.

"And thank you to Hendricks, Lord Burlington, for chairing this year's Valentine Fair—"

Hendricks, being Hendricks, hits her with his best smile. "I'm excited to be part of it—"

"We have a month to get prepared, and the village ready with decorations. The posters are going up this week, and we want to ensure we have lots of fun new ideas to add to our usual host of activities. Let's get the meeting started, shall we?" She waits until all you can hear is the wind whistling outside. "Excellent. Now, Agatha, would you like to begin?"

Agatha rises gracefully to her feet. "Thank you, Eunice, and may the moon bless all of you and our plans this wondrous evening." Her stare is so intense as she peers around the room at everyone that a couple of people shrink into their chairs. Though Eddie, next to Celeste, looks like he's already fallen asleep. "Over the next month, my emporium will be busy brewing additional Valentine love potions to meet demand, though, as we have done previously, it's only available on a first-come, first-served basis. The store will be opening at sunrise to offer readings for the enlightened, and I will be calling on my sisters in magic for help in spell work for those who really need it."

Agatha turns and aims the last part of her sentence at me, to which I scowl and take a glug of wine so large

I almost choke. Thankfully, no one hears over the small round of applause and rustling of material as Agatha sits down.

"Thank you, Agatha. That all sounds wonderful," Mrs. Winston says, beaming. "Eddie, can you update everyone on what you have planned for The One True Love? Chris from The Cupid's Arrow couldn't make it tonight, unfortunately, but they will be hosting a weekend of poetry readings—"

Eddie jolts awake after a nudge in the ribs from Celeste.

"We have speed dating on the evening of Valentine's Day. Singles only allowed, and we're brewing"—he grins at Agatha—"some Valentine's cocktails."

"Lovely, lovely."

Claudia goes next with her plans for The Beanery, covering everything from decorations to valentine bakes. She's followed by the couple who run the Valentine Nook bed and breakfast—a charming little place which is always booked out six months in advance. Celeste announces the Valentine Prep Reception Choir, and Mr. Jones—representing the Post Office—reminds us all that valentine cards can be dropped into the special post box being erected at the end of the month.

And so the meeting continues, all the while Hendricks and I share our cup of wine. His fingers brush mine every time he takes it and I know people notice. I don't imagine their eyes on us, wondering what the hell's going on because even I'm unsure, when finally, we move onto the decorations.

Valentine Nook is always the best dressed village, but for Valentine's Day it's taken up several notches. There won't be an inch of Valentine High Street undressed.

It's a love fest, and frankly, exhausting just listening to it. But Mrs. Winston's not done, pen at the ready in case something needs to be added to the minutes.

"Does anyone have anything more to add, any activities the fair would benefit from? Remember, no idea is too small."

The wine has dulled my wits. I'm too caught up in the tips of Hendricks's fingers brushing mine. I'm too slow to object before Hendricks offers up words I hoped I'd never hear again.

"Let's bring back the kissing booth."

11

Story

Age 13

"I'm so excited."

"Me too."

"Who do you want to kiss?"

"A twin, of course."

"Which one?"

"I don't care."

My neck is sore from going back and forth between Annabel and Mary, watching them each apply almost an entire tube of lip gloss. Mary's lips must be so sticky by now that whomever she ends up snogging today will have a hard time *unsticking* themselves.

I've also applied gloss, but one swipe only. Okay, maybe two.

"I thought you wanted to kiss Sam Pelling."

Annabel scrunches her face, and her eyes meet mine in the mirror's reflection. She's so pretty. Her hair used to be darker, but now has blond bits around the front, which she swears are still from the sun last summer, though Mary said she dyed it. Not like mine, which is dark brown. No matter how many times I beg my mum, she won't let me change it. It's so dull.

"No. I changed my mind."

"Why?"

"Because we see Sam Pelling every day at school, and he's kind of boring. And we only get to see the twins during half term and the holidays. Until next year, that is." Her eyebrows wiggle at me.

My fist clenches around the lip balm in my hand, enough that the top shoots off and squirts across the room. *Shit.* Grabbing a jumper I left on my bedroom floor last night, I rub at the pink glitter, praying it doesn't stain, then slump back.

Hendricks and Miles, along with Jack, Lucas, and a few other boys in our class, left Valentine Prep to attend Wellington for their senior school. They only come back now for a weekend during each half term plus the holidays. At the end of this year, Annabel will also go to Wellington, like her sister did, but Mary and I will stay in Valentine Nook and go to the senior school here. We're all splitting up.

I'm sad about it, but what makes me sadder is that since last summer, Annabel has decided she likes the twins. Both of them. And even though I've never ever said to her I like Hendricks, she knows. So does Mary. In September, she'll see them every day. And I won't.

I stare at the drawer in my desk where I've hidden all the letters Hendricks has written me since he's been away. Wellington makes all their pupils write one a week, and I know he alternates between writing to his mum and writing to me. Only my mum knows that Hendricks and I write to each other because she's the one who collects the mail. I don't know why I keep it a secret since we text all the time and he's on my Snapchat.

But our letters are different. Even though we don't

share anything exciting, it feels like something only we share. I update him on how school is boring and that Mrs. Benson is now the deputy head and so bossy. I told him I can run up the hill at Honeysuckle Lane in thirteen minutes. He didn't believe me, so we're doing it together when he next comes home. I've told him about the new cows my dad bought, and how Lando came over to see them the other day. My dad said he's been doing a good job since he took over the village.

If I have time, or the week's been particularly boring, I write him a short story.

Then I always sign off with "Love, your best friend, Story."

Hendricks always signs off as "Hendricks."

I haven't seen him since Christmas, but his last letter arrived yesterday saying he was excited to be coming home. His mum just got a new litter of puppies so he's going to invite me over to name them, and I can't wait. But what really has my belly doing flip-flops is his text this morning asking if I'll be at the kissing booth.

It's the Valentine's Day Fair, and all Annabel, Mary, and I have been talking about for the past month. Plus the rest of the girls in school. I told Hendricks about it, and he told Miles, who told all the boys. Someone put it in the ideas box for the fair, though no one will admit who it was. And it was printed, so we couldn't even tell from the handwriting.

The girls in the year above us designed it to look like a lemonade stand in the shape of a heart where you'd kiss a boy you liked, but after a couple of parents complained, it was scrapped.

Instead of kissing, it was decided we'd link the booth with the local pet shelter to encourage pet adoption.

Everyone except Annabel loved that idea even more. Each pupil in our class is taking a turn to look after the booth and introduce visitors to the dogs where they can have a picture, and hopefully adopt a needy dog or donate money.

Officially, it's an adoption drive, but unofficially, Annabel's using it to organize her own event, which involves the alley behind The One True Love.

"Have you been practicing on your hand like I showed you?"

"Yeah, but it's weird." Mary nods, pulling a face at the same time. "I don't know why I need to bother."

"You don't know what's going to happen later, do you?" Annabel waggles her eyebrows again, and I wish she'd stop it. She's been annoying me a lot recently. Ever since she got boobs, she's acting like she's better than Mary and me. "Someone will want to take you down the alley," she adds with a hair flick.

Mary's wide-eyed, like she's never heard anything so exciting. "And that's when you're kissing a twin? Properly."

"Yup. I bet they're so experienced too. I heard they've been kissing loads of girls since they got to Wellington. Valentine Nook is so boring." It's like neither of the twins gets to decide for themselves. She then stands up and turns to me, one hand on her hip. I'm still sitting on the floor against the bed, so I have to crane to look up at her. "God, Story, when are you going to admit it?"

"Admit what?"

"That you like Hendricks."

"Wh . . . *what*? What? We're just friends—"

"You've liked him since we were little kids. C'mon, we're not stupid," she snaps. "Don't you trust us?"

"Hendricks is my friend," I repeat. "Of course I like him."

"That's not what I meant."

My shoulders jerk up. I don't know why I'm so reluctant to tell them. It just feels like something I need to think about a lot more because I don't know when it became different. That *liking* Hendricks changed from being friends and hanging out on Honeysuckle Lane to wondering how it would feel to kiss him. And ever since the kissing booth was announced, I've been keeping my fingers crossed that today will be the day I find out, because Annabel's unofficial booth isn't the worst idea for having your first kiss.

I just wish she'd shut up about it.

"I don't know if I like him."

The gloss on her lips catches the light as she purses them. So sticky. "So you don't care if I kiss him, then?"

Urgh. God. I glance at Mary, who's trying to look like she doesn't care about this conversation but is equally as interested in the answer as Annabel.

My jaw clenches so hard I wonder if Mr. Dobbs, my orthodontist, will be able to tell, and through gritted teeth, I say, "If you could limit your kissing to Miles, I would appreciate it."

Immediately, she drops down, and the pursed lip is replaced by a wide smile as she pulls me into a hug so tight I squeak. "You got it."

Valentine Nook is as pink and red as I've ever

seen it before. Hearts hang from the archway, and even more hang from each lamppost, looped across the road. Every window is decorated with cherubs and love hearts, poems and paper chains. It's so pretty. It's so busy.

"It's so *pink.*" Mary points out the obvious as we pass by Agatha Chase's and the queue that stretches down the high street. "Do you guys want to go get a potion?"

"No, I'm not waiting in *that.* We can get one any day of the week," Annabel says, dodging someone dressed in a giant Cupid's outfit, handing out love hearts. "Besides, we don't need a potion."

I wish I had her confidence. Annabel is the most confident person I know. Even though I'm confident a lot of the time, I'm not when it comes to boys. I make a mental note to come back when the queue is shorter and Annabel's not with me.

"Do you know when the twins are arriving? I mean, all the boys?"

I shake my head. "No, I guess sometime around lunch?"

"What time is your kissing slot?"

"Eleven. How much money do you think we'll raise?"

"All day?"

"Yeah. Ten thousand?"

"We're not raising ten thousand pounds, Annabel." Mary laughs. "There aren't enough of us, not to mention it's mathematically impossible. We're charging a pound per dog. There aren't going to be ten thousand kisses, and there aren't *ten thousand* dogs."

"Well, whatever, we're still raising a good amount."

Annabel pouts, smacking away the love hearts thrust in her face by another passing Cupid.

It's not just Cupid.

I see someone dressed as an ancient love scholar, on one knee, proposing to a very embarrassed lady. Her boyfriend doesn't look too happy either. There are giant fluffy hearts pushing their way through the crowd too.

"Story. Stor . . . Wait up."

It feels like everything happens in slow motion as I whirl around at the sound of my name.

There he is. It's been six weeks since I last saw Hendricks, and his hair has grown so much. Curls flop over his forehead, and he's *tall*. Way taller than he was at Christmas. His legs are so long, and he must be a whole head bigger than me now. He could probably rest his head on mine when he hugs me, but I'm not hugging Hendricks while people are around.

He's wearing that goofy smile he does sometimes, the one I always tease him about because it's so lopsided. I can feel mine stretching so wide that my cheeks hurt, and my chest flutters as my heart pounds harder. That is, until I realize Annabel and Mary are watching me, so I pull it back, and my cheeks turn red instead.

"Hey."

He stops right in front of me. "Hey, hey, guys."

Annabel points at him. "Hendricks twin, right?" Like she could tell the difference if he hadn't made it obvious he wasn't Miles.

"Yup." He nods, but he's looking straight at me. "What are you up to?"

I don't know why I'm so shy around Hendricks all of a sudden, because he literally knows more about me than any other person. I talk to him as much as I talk to Annabel and Mary, more probably, and it would be weird if I weren't happy to see him. But not spending so much time together makes it more obvious how different he is right now. The same, but different. Whereas I don't think I've changed at all. I'm definitely the same height, for one.

"Not much."

"Just wanted to find out what time your dog thing is."

"Are you coming?" Annabel interrupts before I get the chance to reply.

"Think so. I want to come and see the dogs."

"Cool. Make sure you bring Miles."

"I'm at eleven," I tell him, ignoring Annabel.

He thumbs behind him, narrowly missing a Cupid. "I'll find my brother and the boys. We'll try to make it."

I want to ask him if he wants me to reserve a space, so he can come up to the counter, but instead, I say, "See you later."

He jogs off through the crowds, and as he disappears, a smile reappears on my face. I feel ridiculously happy. Pushing my arms through Annabel's and Mary's, I link us together. "C'mon, let's go see the booth."

Like everything else in the village today, the booth is covered in big red hearts. It's set halfway down the high street, outside The Beanery, from where the smell of sugar is floating into the air.

There's a long queue of people, some of whom I know from school, some I've never seen before. A couple of much younger boys hold their mum's hands, and, from the sounds of it, the girl standing behind the pink-and-red-striped counter, holding a wire-haired terrier, is their sister.

"This is so cute. Do you think any have been adopted yet?"

"I hope so," Mary replies. "I wish my mum would let me get a dog."

"Is that Sam Pelling?" Annabel asks, pointing at the front of the queue. "Yeah, it is. Sam! Sam!"

He turns around and waves.

Sam is the last person in the queue before I take my spot at the counter. I get to hold a little pitbull / Labrador mix puppy whose tail is so waggy that his whole body vibrates. He's got one white patch over his eye, and the rest of him is dark gray. I decide to name him Patch even though his name tag says William.

He's adorable, and the first person to come up to the counter is a lady a bit younger than my mum. She takes one look at him and decides to adopt him on the spot. She doesn't even want a picture with him. So I introduce her to the adoption staff at the shelter, and they take her to sign papers.

When I get back to Annabel and Mary after my turn is over, Hendricks is there too.

"Are you already done?"

I nod. "Yes, my dog got adopted, though, so that's cool."

Hendricks's face drops. "I wish I'd seen it. I'm sorry I missed it."

"That's okay." I shrug, and I'm not that disappointed, seeing as I didn't have to do much, so he didn't miss anything.

"Hey, guys, hey, Twin," Sam greets as he walks

toward us, pointing over his shoulder. "Annabel's dog seems to be enjoying himself."

The four of us turn around to see Annabel standing arms crossed, looking annoyed, while her dog tries to hump the chair she's supposed to be sitting on. Mary snorts a laugh before she can catch it.

"It's Hendricks, by the way, Sam."

Sam looks at me, then looks at Hendricks. "Oh, sorry."

"No worries. Used to it," Hendricks replies, but grins at me.

Literally no one can tell them apart, and ever since we were in junior school, if there was no way to identify them, they were always addressed as Twin. *Hey, Twin, see ya, Twin.* Sometimes I wonder if people are blind. It always amuses Hendricks how annoyed I get.

They stand there, neither saying anything else. I know Hendricks doesn't like Sam much, but Sam stayed at school here instead of leaving for Wellington, so I got to know him a bit better. And I like him. He's nice, and he's always making us laugh.

"Anyway, I need to go and find my mum," Sam groans. "I said I'd look after my little sister for a couple of hours."

"Sure, no worries."

"Bye, guys. See you later, Story."

There are murmurs of "bye" except from Hendricks, who's frowning at me.

"What?"

"Why's he calling you Story?"

I shrug. "I dunno. Everyone does."

"But that's my name for you," he grumbles. At least I think that's what he says because Annabel grabs my arm so hard I flinch.

"Ouch. What was that for?"

She doesn't reply, only stares, unblinking, but a second later I find out anyway.

"Hey, Annabel, how's it going?"

She flicks her hair so violently over her shoulder that it hits Mary. "Hey, Miles, good. You?"

"Good." He grins, which Annabel seems to take as a sign that he likes her, given the way her eyes widen and her lashes flutter. More so when he slings an arm around his brother's shoulder, and as usual, Hendricks has to step away from me. Miles is so annoying. "Hen, c'mon. I've been looking for you. We need to go find Jack."

"Cool, I'm coming now." Hendricks smiles at me, making his dimples show. "Catch you later, Stor. Okay? I'll come and get you. Sorry I missed your slot, but I'll take you to see the puppies at Burlington. They're amazing."

"Sure." I smile and give a small wave. "See you later."

Once they're out of earshot, Annabel moans and flops onto Mary. "God, he's so fit."

I roll my eyes.

"C'mon, you have to admit Miles is fit, seeing as you fancy his *identical* twin."

"No, they look different to me. Miles is . . ." I try to find the words, but all I can come up with is "Arrogant. Hendricks is kind. It makes them look different."

"Whatever, they're both fit to me. Anyway"—she pulls out her lip gloss and reapplies it, followed by her phone—"ohmigod. Miles wants to meet me by the fountain now. Do I look okay?"

"Yes, you look very pretty." I nod truthfully while she straightens her top and runs fingers through her hair.

"Okay, thanks. Wish me luck."

"Where's Hendricks?" Mary asks when Annabel runs off.

I shrug. "Don't know. Do you want to go and get a hot chocolate? Claudia might still have some flapjacks left."

"Yes, let's go."

Neither of us speaks as we walk over to The Beanery. I'm sure Mary's wondering the same thing as me, which is how Annabel is doing. I'm also wondering if I'll ever get the chance to kiss Hendricks. Or at least see what it's like. Wet maybe. Soft.

"Annabel will be able to tell us what we do with our tongue," mumbles Mary with a mouth full of flapjack and sits down on the bench outside.

"Yeah, good point." I nod, blowing the steam away from my hot chocolate before I sip, returning to our silent contemplations.

We've barely finished our drinks when Annabel returns. It's like she has cartoon stars circling her head.

"Well?" Mary's eyes are wider than I've ever seen them. "How was it?"

She should be given an award for how dramatic her sigh is. "Amazing. Miles is the best kisser."

I don't bother asking how she knows that seeing as he's the *only* person she kissed. I'm also a bit confused because I can see Miles straight ahead of *me*, and he's with Lauren MacCauley. His arm is around her, and he doesn't look like he's been kissing anyone other than her. Certainly not in the past half an hour. But I turn to where Annabel is now staring wistfully.

My heart drops to my belly before I fully figure out what's happened.

The rest of the boys are all clustered in a circle by the fountain, including the one Annabel's staring at, hand pushing through his curls. But it's not Miles.

The boy who's been making out with my friend for the past fifteen minutes is Hendricks. *My* boy.

12

Hendricks

"Daddy, who's your valentine? Daddy?"

I crank one eyelid expecting to see a glimmer of morning light, but I see nothing. It's pitch-black.

"*Daddy*?"

It's when I open both and shift back slightly that I can make out the silhouette of my son lying inches away from me on the pillow. "Max, why are you out of bed? It's not morning yet."

It's definitely not morning. My words barely croak out of me.

"I know, but I've been thinking," he continues, like it isn't the middle of the night, though I actually have no idea what time it is. "Who is your valentine? I don't have a valentine."

Turning to my side, I scoop my son up and twist us both around until he's snuggled against me. "You're my valentine, Maxy. Now go to sleep, and we'll talk about it more in the morning."

Heaviness overtakes me again. My eyelids close, and I think I've won him over because he stays silent. He relaxes into my arms, and his breath settles down enough that my own steadies, and I'm right there, on the verge of sleep again.

"Daddy?"

I jolt from the faint whisper. "Shhh, Maxy, sleep."

"Just one more question."

"What is it?"

"Did you have a valentine before I was born?"

I kiss the top of his head, breathe in the soft, sweet scent of his shampoo, and calm my heart before it starts racing.

"Just one."

"Who was it?"

"It was a long time ago, Maxy. She was my friend, and I kept it a secret. Let's sleep now, please. We have a busy day tomorrow." Holding him tight to my chest, I whisper, "I love you beyond the hills."

"Love you beyond the hills, Daddy."

Satisfied that he has the answer he was looking for, it takes seconds for Max to fall asleep again. I'm not so lucky this time around. Twice, I hear the grandfather clock in the great hall chime the hour as I lie there thinking about Story. Old memories resurface. I replay every interaction we've had since she returned.

I go over our conversation at the town hall meeting a couple of days ago.

Suggesting the kissing booth was stupid. Reckless. Pointless. And given the look on Story's face when I did, it was hurtful.

What did I think it would achieve? What did I want it to achieve?

Between the calls from Sienna that morning and the

surprise of seeing Story later, my head was not entirely screwed on. But being *that* close to her—enough so I could make out each lash framing her big brown eyes and the fast-fading freckles scattered across her nose and breathe in the soft, earthy scent that always surrounded her—did something to me.

When I watched her slump down next to Agatha, there was a defeat to her I hadn't seen in a very long time. I intrinsically knew I was the cause. I wanted the fire to return, the spark of annoyance that flashed across her face when she turned around and found me standing in front of her holding the urn, the one that she was struggling to bite back. When I sat next to her later, pulling the stunt with the coffee and wine was nothing more than an attempt to remind her I still knew her better than most people.

But when she looked at me, scanning my face in confusion, all I could think about was the pain of her leaving and how I would feel if she left again.

And so when Max wakes up, full of his usual beans, I'm incredibly groggy and in dire need of caffeine and more sleep.

It doesn't help that he's singing at the top of his lungs. I wouldn't mind so much, but he inherited my inability to hold a note, and I can't even tell what it's supposed to be. Neither could the dogs, by all accounts, given that all three of them walked out the moment he began.

"Hendricks, you want me to drop Max again this morning?" Birgitta's head pops around the doorframe of Max's bedroom while I'm laying out his school uniform, as Max climbs up the side of his bunkbed wearing his Spider-Man costume.

Some mornings are just . . .

"Yes, thanks." I'm heading over to the farmyard to check on the pregnant heifers, but not until ten, so I can squeeze in another hour or so of sleep if I'm lucky. But on the other hand, I haven't been to the school all week . . . "Actually, no. I'll do it. Can you take over here?"

"Sure." She marches in, authoritative. Way more than I can summon this morning. "Max's breakfast is ready downstairs. Let's hurry up and get dressed so we can eat . . . His bag is packed, and there's a clean uniform on the side too."

The gratitude I have this morning is nothing short of immense. I have more than most people, more help than most people, and I still find it hard to cope. I don't know how single parents manage.

"Thank you. I'll see you downstairs. Max . . ." But he's not listening, so I slip out and hear him yell, "Birgitta, watch this." It's followed by a thud, and I *know* he's jumped from the top of his bunk—something he's not allowed to do.

I wait for the sound of crying—*anything*—but nothing comes except a stern warning from Birgitta not to do it again, so I rush back to my room and jump in the shower.

"You look nice. Smell good too." Clementine smirks as she passes me on her way into the kitchen, twenty minutes later.

It's the smirk that stops me from responding. There's an implication there I don't appreciate, much less want to acknowledge.

"Max, hurry up. We can't be late this morning," I yell, hoping that he's somewhere close by, but who knows. He inhaled his porridge and ran off. I pray he's not back in his Spider-Man costume, or we *will* be late.

"Boo!"

Dropping the bags, I clasp my hands to my chest and feign surprise at my son peering from behind the stone pillar in the great hall. "Oh! You got me."

It's a move that never fails to have him doubled over with laughter. I'm not even sure at this point whether he realizes I'm mostly playing along, but I do know that he usually only plays hide-and-seek when I'm distracted. It's his way of getting my full attention.

"I got you, Daddy."

"You did, bud. Now get in the car, please."

"Daddy, do you think we should get a puppy to keep Hamish, Maud, and Dolly company?"

The aforementioned dogs are all sitting by the front door, not giving off the slightest impression they want more company.

"They look fine to me, Maxy. C'mon, *car*—"

"They told me this morning they would like another puppy."

"Did they now?" I reply, scooping Max up because otherwise we'll be here all day.

Tossing his bags in the boot, I strap him in and slip into the driver's seat. I nearly weep when I see Birgitta's left me coffee in the cup holder.

"Okay, ready?"

"Ready, Daddy."

"Music?" I peer at him through the rearview mirror, expecting a thumbs-up, but he shakes his head instead.

"Actually, not right now."

We slip out of the driveway and along the winding road heading out of Burlington, past the fields with

Thunder and Sunday. Max is uncharacteristically quiet, and I'm about to ask him if everything's okay.

"Daddy?"

"Yes, bud?"

"How do you pick a valentine?"

I'd forgotten about our middle-of-the-night conversation. I'd ask him where it's coming from, but I know they started rehearsals for the Valentine concert, so they're obviously talking about it in school. From the sounds of it, they're talking a lot.

"Um, well, you think about someone you really like and go from there."

"What if I really like two people? Or three?"

"Three?" My eyes flick up to the rearview mirror again. Perhaps Max is taking after Miles more than I realized.

"I don't want anyone to be left out." He shrugs, breaking my heart in the process.

"That's very kind of you. If that's the case, you can have as many valentines as you like."

"Should I keep it a secret like you did?"

Reaching the Burlington gates, a large tractor approaches, and I wait to let it pass before pulling out. I also use it as an opportunity to distract Max because I don't want to get into a conversation about secret valentines. I don't even want to think about them.

"Look, Maxy. Say hi to Frank."

Max lowers the back window and waves frantically at the tractor driver. "HI, FRANK." He acknowledges Max with a salute.

There's another thirty seconds of silence.

"Daddy, why did you keep your valentine a secret?"

I should have stayed in bed. "Because . . . I wasn't sure I wanted anyone to know."

"Did Uncle Miles know?"

"I think Uncle Miles guessed."

"Can I guess?"

"Maybe later, bud."

Max returns to peering out of the window again, past the herd of Aberdeen Angus bulls, past the fountain, past Uncle Alex's house, to which we both wave and shout hello, until finally we reach the school and get into the long queue of cars at drop-off.

"I think I'm going to keep one of mine a secret. And one of mine not a secret," Max announces as I unbuckle him.

"That's a good idea. You can do whatever you want."

He jumps out, loops his arms through the straps of his school bag I'm holding, and takes my hand. We fall in line with other parents and his classmates and play the usual dance of head nods and acknowledgments while I dodge the mothers who like to linger a little too long until we turn the corner, and Story is standing there.

"Good morning, Max."

"Good morning, Miss MacIntosh."

"Good morning, Hendricks."

Suddenly, I'm parched, desperate for water.

She's so pretty. No, that's too basic. Stunning. Beautiful. Luminescent.

Every time I see her, I have to reconcile that this woman, currently dressed for business in a crisp, fitted white shirt, navy trousers, and a blazer hugging her in all the right places, with glossy, blunt ends tucked behind each ear, is the one I used to chase through the fields behind her house. Roll down the hill with. Sneak to the fountain after dark to swim and drink beer with. Watch movies under the blanket with.

But this morning, it's the full mouth painted red that renders me speechless. All I can think about is kissing it off. Fuck everything else.

"Hendricks?"

Clearing my throat, I blink away the stirrings of lust and haze of fantasies about what I'd do with that mouth. "Sorry."

She frowns. "Are you okay?"

"I am." I nod.

She's still frowning but turns to Max. "How are you this morning?"

"Very well, thank you. I'm deciding on my valentine."

"Oh well, that's exciting to hear, and we have our singing to practice today. Two new songs—"

"My daddy has a secret valentine."

Fuck.

How did I not predict this would happen? Kill me now. Perhaps the look Story is shooting my way will do it for me.

I glance down, half expecting to see a chalk outline of my body.

"I'm sure he does." Story smiles, though it's miles away from her eyes.

"He asked me who my valentine was . . ." I begin, though totally unsure where I'm going with it. It's stopped by Story's hand.

"You don't have to explain."

"I—"

"Seriously, *don't*."

"Right. Okay." I finger-gun the door, which is quite possibly the worst part of my entire morning. "We're going to head inside. C'mon, Maxy, let's hang your bag up."

Thankfully, I don't have to go through the awkwardness of saying goodbye to Story because once I've been through the process of getting Max into his classroom, I'm caught by one of the dads who asks me to go for a beer one evening. By that time, Story is in and leading the charge.

When I get back to the car, my phone is flashing through the car window. *Sienna*. That she keeps ringing is making me increasingly nervous, and I need a game plan to stop it. I dial the only person I know who could help.

"Morning, Arthur, it's Hendricks." I greet our family solicitor. He's the one who drew up the various offers and settlements for Sienna to accept. He's dealt with every legal aspect of Max's birth and future.

"Hendricks, how are you? To what do I owe this call?"

I get straight to the point. "Have you heard from Sienna's solicitors in the past few weeks? Or Sienna?"

"Max's mother?"

"Yes."

"No. Should I have?"

My head falls back against the headrest. "I don't know. She's been calling me."

"About what?"

"I don't know. I haven't answered."

His silence says the obvious way to find out would be to answer. But I don't want to speak to her, and Arthur knows that.

"I'll let the office know to be on alert. If anything comes in, I'll call you immediately."

"Thank you." I go to hang up, then stop. "Wait, Arthur. She can't take Max, can she? Legally?" Even saying the words out loud makes me feel sick. Panicky. Lightheaded.

"No. You have full custody. But . . . if she decides she wants to fight that. Well—"

"Got it." If she decides to fight, that's a different matter. "Thanks."

"I'll let you know."

This much is true. I'll tear the earth apart before I let anyone take Max from me. He is my son, born to a mother who abandoned him for the pursuit of fuck-knows-what and a payday. She will never be part of his life. I will not have him suffer because of my mistake.

My grip tightens around the steering wheel while I try to figure out what to do.

The school entrance has emptied. All the 4x4s have gone, and it's quiet when I make my way back into the main school building. This time, I turn left toward the administration offices and the head's study.

Which is when this morning's total and utter shitshow is cemented.

13

Story

"Miss MacIntosh?"

The voice is deeper than one I'm used to calling me Miss MacIntosh, but it's needed over a classroom of rowdy children who are yet to settle in their seats.

Mrs. Benson, the headmistress, peers around the doorframe. Her presence, however, has no effect on the class. They're still too young to realize Mrs. Benson is in charge and commands a level of respect plus a healthy dose of fear that I still carry from my school days here.

I clap my hands together, at least giving my boss the pretense I have some kind of control.

"Class, let's find our seats, please." It's my schoolteacher voice. I keep it gentle but firm, though some mornings are harder than others. "Seats, everyone, please. Put away the games and let's tidy up. Once we're done, let's say good morning to our guest, Mrs. Benson."

By my estimation, it's a good three minutes until everyone's settled, by which point Mrs. Benson stands leaning against the doorframe, beaming at anyone who looks at her.

"Good morning, Mrs. Benson."

"Good morning, R1 class. How wonderful. What a lovely beginning to my day. I've come to borrow Miss MacIntosh for a moment. I hope you don't mind."

"Are you bringing her back?" asks Tilly, a small girl with blond ringlets who's already designated herself as class leader.

"I am, of course." Mrs. Benson's smile widens, and she chuckles heartily, making her sound a little like Father Christmas. "Miss MacIntosh, if you wouldn't mind."

"Not at all." I glance at Katie, my classroom assistant. "Could you . . .?"

But she's already standing by the desk.

"Everything okay?" I ask once I'm standing in the corridor.

Aside from the initial interview, when I think she was too desperate to fill the role to delve much into why I was taking it, and the staff meetings, I haven't had much face time with Mrs. Benson. It's alarming how little she's changed since I left Valentine Prep nearly fourteen years ago. Still the same haircut, still the same beady eyes peering over her glasses, and still the same penchant for drowning herself in insanely sweet perfumes.

"Yes, yes, but let's go to my study, shall we? Talk in private."

I can't help it. The idea that a teacher wants to talk to me alone will forever and always fill me with anxiety. That I'm about to get a dressing down for something I've done wrong. I've never been able to shake it, and I'm racking my brain the entire way we walk—brusquely, obvs—while Mrs. Benson talks and I pretend to listen.

I'm none the wiser when we get there, but at least

leaving the door open is somewhat of a positive sign that I'm not about to get a massive bollocking. I only came here twice as a student—once after the Valentine Fair following the incident with Annabel and Mary, and once when I was made head of my schoolhouse.

Nothing's changed. Same wide mahogany desk, same huge arched windows looking out onto the playing fields, and beyond that the bank I used to escape to at breaktimes, the horse chestnut tree . . .

"Now," Mrs. Benson begins, steepling her fingers together as she leans across the desk, "how are you finding things here? Coming up on three weeks now. It must be odd to be back."

"How am I . . ." There's no way she pulled me out of class for a chat about whether I'm enjoying my job. "It's good. Great. I'm . . . it's lovely to be back. Good to see what's changed. What hasn't."

"Yes, I'm sure."

My mouth rolls together, and my hands ram between my thighs to stop the jittering.

"Anyway, I wanted to discuss your contract. You're signed until July, and I wanted to understand your plans for returning to Australia. If you are, in fact, returning, or if you would consider extending your contract for a year or so."

My brows shoot up. Wow. Okay.

"You're offering me a long-term job?"

"Yes, you've been doing great work since you began. I know it's only been a short time, but Miss Scott sings your praises, and I can tell the children are very happy in your care."

Well, I wasn't expecting that. I also don't expect the lump in my throat or the stinging in my eyes that I need to bite back. Staying here wasn't a long-term plan, but I don't have one either. I never did.

Then I think about Hendricks. Aside from my family, he's the one thing keeping me here and, ironically, the only thing that would make me leave.

There's no denying things between us have been fairly shit at best, even during the committee meeting the other night—although that veered more into awkward territory. We've become strangers who barely know what to say to each other.

I think about the secret valentine Max mentioned, which brushed over me at the time, but do I really want to be here if Hendricks is in a romantic relationship with someone else? When I thought the blonde was his wife, I would have quite happily locked myself in my bedroom and never left.

If I stay, can our relationship be fixed? What would it look like?

"Thank you," I say eventually. "That's lovely to hear."

"And how's your father?"

I laugh. "Back on his feet. Thankfully, he's having rehab. Though he's a little unsteady, it's hard to keep him away from the cows." I know full well that by the time my contract is up here, he'll be back running the place like nothing happened.

"What about Australia? Do you have plans to return?"

"Yes. I do."

It's the truth. All my things are there, and I was only planning a two-week visit. I'm lucky the landlord in my apartment building can keep an eye on things, but no matter what happens here, I'll still need to go back at some point. Even if only to pack.

"I see, and when will that be?"

I nod. "I'm going back to Australia at Easter, my flight's early April."

"Right. Well . . ." Mrs. Benson's eyes leave mine, and she focuses on something over my shoulder.

Turning around, I see what she's looking at. Or rather who. My spine straightens. Whatever has happened in the forty minutes since I saw Hendricks, he's riled. I have the strangest feeling he was glaring at me before I turned around, and though he acknowledges me with barely more than a flick of his gaze, I'm certain it narrows as it passes.

"Ah, Hendricks. Hello. How can I help?"

"Sorry to interrupt, but could I have a word, please? It's important."

"Of course, we were finishing up," she simpers, and I guess that's my cue to stand. Her eyes flick from Hendricks to me. "Must be strange for you to have Sophie back, teaching young Max. Not that long ago, it was the two of you together in the classroom."

"Long enough," Hendricks snaps, which I feel is directly aimed at me.

What's his problem? Surely, he can't be annoyed about Max's secret valentine remark. If anyone should be annoyed, it's me, and I've decided not to be.

I've decided to be the bigger person.

My guess is he's not waiting for a response, so I take it upon myself to make everyone—*me*—more comfortable and go back to my classroom.

"Miss MacIntosh, have a think about what I said, please."

"I shall do. Thank you." I smile, taking one last

glance at Hendricks, who's now glaring at me. "Bye, Hendricks."

"Story."

I don't even get to eavesdrop on their conversation because the moment I'm out in the hallway, he slams the door behind me.

In true fashion, I find it virtually impossible to concentrate for the rest of the day. My thoughts flip-flop between the task at hand—practicing the songs for the Valentine Fair, and it's going to take *a lot* of practice—wondering whether I should accept the longer contract and stay at Valentine Prep for the next year—my position varies in accordance with how many tears are being shed at any one time—and Hendricks.

Thought one is manageable. Thoughts two and three are less so, yet innately tied together. Six years ago, I left for Australia to get away from everything Valentine Nook, everything Hendricks. I didn't plan to stay six years. I didn't plan much at all, but I did, and I found a life there. I found a boyfriend and then a fiancé, albeit the wrong one, but a fiancé nonetheless.

More importantly, I found myself. At some point. Kind of. At least, I found someone separate from the girl whose life revolved around Hendricks Burlington. The few times I returned to Valentine Nook, up to and including the last one, I came for myself, not him.

And I might still be in love with Hendricks, but I'm not lost in him.

By the end of the day, I know I can make a decision without my feelings clouding my judgment.

I stay at school later than usual, but tomorrow is Friday, and I want to prepare for the following week. With the Valentine committee getting into full swing, there's a lot to do. By the time I leave, it's started to rain, and rain clouds completely obscure the full moon.

"Well, the weather certainly isn't a reason to stay," I grumble to myself, thinking about the thirty-degree temperatures in Sydney right now.

I'd also planned to run home this evening, which was me being full of good intentions this morning, but it's so cold. I moan about it all the way through getting changed, packing my bag, and lacing up my trainers. I thought I might be able to talk myself out of it because I couldn't recall packing my high-visibility vest, but it's there at the bottom of the pile of running clothes.

It takes five minutes of trudging along the lane away from the school before I find any kind of rhythm, and another mile of cursing what a stupid idea it was to run in the pitch-black and rain, before I begin enjoying myself. Something about the coldness of the air kicks you up the arse and breathes a little more life into you.

But as I turn the corner, I pick up a sound that fills me with dread.

A noise, bleating, but frantic, deeper almost.

"Hello?"

There it is again. Crying. Whatever's making the noise is in pain. My heart is already racing from my run, but that noise causes it to beat harder. This is exactly how horror movies begin. In the dark lane, alone, with rain.

But I clearly have no sense of self-preservation when I pull out my phone and switch on the torch to follow the sound. Especially when I end up in the ditch on the opposite side of the lane.

The bleating gets louder, enough that I know it's an animal of some kind. Not distinguished enough that I can tell what it is or whether I want to get close enough to find out. But as my eyes adjust to the dark and torchlight I see where it's coming from.

Shit.

"Churchill?"

The whites of his eyes bulge in his mud-covered face, and whatever he's struggling against is making it worse. He's not getting anywhere.

All thoughts of being murdered vanish as I scramble down the bank, slipping quicker than expected thanks to the rain switching from drizzle to downpour, and rush to him as quickly as I can. Thick squelchy mud sucks me in like quicksand, along with one of my trainers.

"Shit and fuck."

Trying not to scare Churchill so he doesn't hurt himself more, I approach him as calmly as possible.

"Hey, Churchy, it's okay." I don't know if he remembers me—and in all honesty, given the amount of toast I've fed him recently, I'd be insulted if he didn't—but his struggling seems to slow once I'm close enough to stroke him. "Shhhh. It's going to be okay."

His head pokes through the hedge, and his body appears to be in the field on the other side, but it's hard to tell. Taking the torch and peering down, it's nearly impossible with all the rain hammering my face, but as I crouch, I think I can make out barbed wire looped around his foot and back leg. There's so much of it I can't tell where it begins or ends. But given the amount of blood pouring down him, I'd say it was a lot.

"Oh buddy, how've you gotten yourself into this

mess?" His cry in response nearly sets me off too, especially when his head leans into my hand as I stroke him. "It's okay. I'm going to help you."

It doesn't take my long-forgotten girl guide skills to figure things out.

I need something to cut the barbed wire, I need enough muscle to lift a fifty-kilo goat, and I need a car.

But mostly, because I know I can't do this alone, I need a vet.

I pray I have enough cell reception to google the number for Valentine Nook vets, and when I do, I add another, hoping it'll be my lucky night and someone else will answer.

But it's not, and they don't.

14

Hendricks

"Are you sure that's what you heard?"

"Yes. She was talking to Benson. She's leaving at Easter. Back to Australia."

I knew this would happen. I don't even know when, over the past few weeks, I'd convinced myself it wouldn't. Story is leaving again.

"But I thought she was staying until the end of the school year." Miles picks out a piece of cucumber from the salad and tosses it in his mouth. "That's what Clare said."

"Your intel is wrong."

"It's not wrong."

"Milo. I heard her with my own ears. She's going back to Australia at Easter."

"Why were you up at Benson's office anyway?" Lando interrupts before Miles and I start arguing again.

I take a deep breath, then another, but they're ineffective. What I want is a drink, a large glass of vodka, tequila, or whiskey. Anything. But I'm on call. Therefore, I'm drinking sparkling water. Just how my fucking day is going. I barely drink anyway, but on the one night I really need something to take the edge off, I have to abstain.

My teeth crunch together as I grit out the word. "Sienna."

Lando looks from me to Miles and back. I can't bring myself to continue. I'm too furiously swiping bread around my bowl of bolognaise and stuffing it into my mouth. If my mouth is full, then maybe it'll give me a second to calm down before I punch a hole in the wall. Or cry.

"Sienna's been calling him. We don't know why. Hen called Arthur this morning, and Arthur's not heard from her or the solicitors. He was seeing Benson because he wanted to warn the school in case Sienna showed up—"

"What? Is that likely?"

"Who knows. I don't even know if she's aware which school Max attends."

They both turn to me, and I shake my head.

"She doesn't even know what he looks like." Miles shrugs, and there's so much sadness in it.

"What did Benson say?"

"The school is secure. You can't get into any of the buildings without a code anyway. No one's going to hand over a child to a stranger—" The words, the insinuation . . . it's too awful to think about, and I squeeze my eyes shut before the tears fall. "But they're being extra vigilant."

"Okay. Do you want security there?"

I shake my head. "No, I don't want Max to be affected in any way. I'll find out what she wants when she calls again. Or she'll call Arthur. Or I'll call her once I can calm down."

"Maybe she wants more money?"

"No, it's not that. Whenever she's wanted money before, it's always gone through Arthur. This is about Max. I know it."

Lando places his arm around me and pulls me into his side. After today, and the fitful sleep I had last night, I'm weary, and the hold I have on my emotions weakens enough that the tears leak out.

"Hen, nothing will happen to Max. Nothing. I promise you that."

It's words I needed to hear. He's so firm, his tone so serious that I believe him. "Thanks, Lan."

"Ahhh, isn't this lovely?" drawls Alex, walking into the kitchen. Only when I sit up and wipe my eyes does his smile drop. "What's happened? I was only gone five minutes."

"Sienna," I snarl, scooping another helping of spaghetti into my bowl.

Alex pauses on his way to sitting down. "What's she done now?"

One thing I really love and appreciate about my siblings is the murderous expression each of them have when her name is mentioned. I also love how none of them push me to talk about her.

Lando shakes his head and says, "Long story, catch you up later."

"How's Everly?"

My dilemma is forgotten, and a smile stretches across Alex's face. It's one I'm familiar with, one I had when Max was a baby. Still have.

"Asleep, thankfully. Her blanket had tangled."

Miles picks up the bottle of wine and tops up Alex's glass. "And the girls were worried we wouldn't be able to cope on our own."

My brothers and I are having a boys' night at Burlington. Good wine (I'm not enjoying), homemade pasta and bolognaise, two children soundly asleep despite how loudly the rain is crashing against the windows. Clementine, our mother, and Haven are all staying in London tonight with Holiday, Lando's girlfriend, who's filming on a celebrity talk show to promote her new movie. Therefore, we decided to take the opportunity to hang out ourselves. Nothing to do with it being Alex's first entire night *on his own* with Everly, or why he's decided to sleep at Burlington tonight instead of his own place.

Lando has been traveling with Holiday over the past few months, and we haven't seen as much of him as usual, so we used the girls' absence as an opportunity to catch up. It hasn't been the four of us together for months, and with the busyness of everyone's lives, it's easy to forget how much we miss it.

"So what else is news?" Lando sips his wine. "How's the committee going?"

I roll my eyes at his smug expression. He hates the committees, we all do, yet he insists on them *and* takes great pleasure in how infuriating we all find them. Until the time comes for his turn, then he doesn't stop complaining.

A loud snort from Miles says everything. "I can't believe you suggested the kissing booth. That is so lame. What're you planning to do with it? Make out with Story for real this time?"

Alex's fork stops halfway to his mouth. "Wait, what?"

"I don't know why I suggested it. I'm an idiot." I stare at my twin. "I was thinking about how you fucked it up that day. You know they haven't had the booth since?"

"I did no such thing. And if I remember, which I do, I was the one who got punched in the nose. It wasn't my fault that I tripped into the stand and broke it. That girl had clearly been taking boxing lessons," he replies, twirling his fork around the spaghetti and shoving it in his mouth.

Alex and Lando are wearing identical expressions of amusement. It was the first time a girl had ever punched Miles. It wasn't the last.

"And anyway," he continues, with a sip of wine, "I'd been trying to get with Lauren MacCauley forever. Plus, you owed me. You lost the last game of Burlington Snaps. It was your dare."

"I didn't know Annabel Stenson was expecting us to make out—"

"Neither did I—"

"I thought I was just asking her on a date for you, when she launched herself on me. Story didn't speak to me for a month."

"That's because she was in love with you. Still is."

"I'm *not* getting into this again," I snap, all my annoyance and frustration from everything that's happened in the past twelve hours resurfacing.

I still remember that day at the fair as the first time I'd ever properly been angry with Miles.

"I don't know how you've not been punched more, Milo." Alex chuckles.

Miles's response is a drawled, "I know when to dodge."

Lando holds his hands up. “Sorry, just to rewind because I wasn’t really listening before, but you and Story? You’re friends again?”

“There is no me and Story,” I say as firmly as I can. Not sure it’s firm enough for me to believe it, though, but it’s worth a try. “We’re not friends again. She’s Max’s teacher. That’s it.”

“Then why the booth—”

“They’re both on the Valentine committee,” Miles explains, using a tone he usually only reserves for Max. “Hendricks got too caught up reminiscing about old times and had a lapse in judgment.”

“Ah. Got it—”

I’m glad someone does because I sure don’t, and whatever Lando is about to say next is interrupted by my phone ringing.

“If that’s Sienna—”

“It’s not, it’s the surgery.” I cut Miles off mid-snarl and answer, “Hendricks Burlington.”

“Hendricks?”

I recognize her voice immediately even though I’m confused why she’d be on the end of the line patched through from the vets. “Story?”

All three of my brothers sit up straighter. Miles practically leans across the table in a bid to hear what she’s saying.

“You have to come . . . Churchill . . . stuck . . . rain . . .”

They’re the only words I hear through the patchy signal we suffer from in the depths of the countryside. The panic in her voice stays consistent, though.

I stand so quickly that my chair is only stopped from clattering to the floor by Lando’s quick reflexes. “Story?

Where are you?"

"Honeysuckle . . . La—"

"I'll be there in ten minutes. Sit tight."

Three sets of eyes and concerned faces stare up at me. "I don't know what's happened, but it didn't sound good. I think she said something about Churchill—"

"That bloody goat."

Alex is looking toward the back doors leading out onto the lawns. The floodlights do a good job of illuminating how hideous the weather is. "She can't be out in this, surely."

I snatch up a set of car keys, along with my surgery kit. "Dunno, but I'm going to find out."

"Want one of us to come with you?"

"No, I'll call if I need anything. If Max wakes up, just tell him I'm at work. He shouldn't, though."

"Take one of the estate Land Rovers, then you have the walkie-talkies in case there's no signal."

I wave the keys I'm already holding and grab my thickest raincoat. "Way ahead of you."

If the weather looked bad from the warmth of the kitchen, it's nothing compared to what greets me as I speed down the Burlington driveway and out onto the lane. The windscreen wipers are no match for the incessant sheet of water.

Racing around the fountain, Valentine High Street is empty. From the looks of it, everyone's taking refuge in The One True Love. Slowing down as I hit Honeysuckle Lane, I realize that I have no idea *where* Story might be. Or what car she drives. Even crawling along at ten miles an hour, I don't spot any vehicle stopped. When I hit the end of the lane, I turn around to look again.

This time, a flash of reflective material catches my eye from deep in the ditch at the side of the road. *Story?*

What the actual fuck?

I slam the brakes so hard the car almost hydroplanes to a stop, and I'm out of the door and sliding down the bank before I turn the engine off.

One look at me, and her face crumples. "Hen . . . Oh *God.* Thank you—"

"Are you insane? Are you hurt? What the hell are you doing here, Story? Someone could have hit you."

She doesn't answer. She just moves out of the way and behind her is Churchill.

He gives a halfhearted struggle against whatever's trapping him as I step forward. Even through the rain, making it nearly impossible to see clearly, it's obvious he's in a lot of pain. "Oh buddy, what've you done?"

"He's caught up in barbed wire. There's so much of it, Hen." She opens her hands, and all I can see in the light from the car is her palm covered in bloody scratches. "I tried to loosen it, but I couldn't."

Her face is streaked with black mascara. The red lipstick from earlier is gone, and her hair is plastered to her head as the rain drips down her cheeks. She's looking so forlorn, I forget all about how mad I've been at her today. I need to focus on the task at hand: freeing Churchill. Once that's done, then I can figure out the rest.

It's impossible to stop myself from swiping away one of her tears, however. "We'll get him out. Don't worry."

Scrambling back up to the car, I do a quick scan for what I need, grab my vet bag, and toss the walkie-talkie to Story. "Message through to Lando, tell him I need him here and to bring bolt cutters and a chainsaw."

Opening my bag, I pull out a foil blanket, which I wrap around as much of Churchill as I can to keep him warm. He might be somewhat listless, but his eyes still bulge when I pull out a needle and a vial of ketamine, measuring out enough to take the pain away but keep him conscious.

"Don't worry, Churchy. It'll make you feel better, and you'll be back to stealing apples in no time."

He barely makes a sound as I slip it into his right foreleg.

"Stor, come and stand next to him. I haven't given him enough to knock him out, but he's going to be really dopey in a minute, and I don't want him to fall."

Scooching closer, she hands over the walkie-talkie. "Lando's on his way."

"Thank you," I say, as she gets into position, and I realize how much she's shivering. She's barely wearing anything at all besides Lycra. "Story, where are your clothes?" My eyes scan down her body, following the line of her curves all the way to her— "*Where's your other trainer*?"

"In the mud somewhere." She hugs him as he leans against her, eyes flickering closed. "I ran home from work, and I heard him crying."

"Jesus, you're going to get hypothermia."

I don't know why I'm snapping, but for fuck's sake, her lack of self-preservation is astounding. Not to mention her clothes are so clinging and wet I can see everything far too clearly, even in the dark. She's too close and all of it—the swell of her breasts, the hard points of her nipples, her firm, tight arse—feels taunting.

Moving her out of the way, I take position next to

Churchill instead.

"In the car, you'll find another foil blanket, a jumper, some rain trousers, clean socks, and a couple of pairs of wellies. One will fit you, as Clemmie always leaves hers lying around. Go get dry."

"I'm fine."

"You're *not.* And I need to keep an eye on Churchill, not worry about you. Go get dry."

Through the rain and the glow of the headlights, I catch her scowl. "I didn't realize I was such an inconvenience."

I watch her scramble back up the bank, instantly regretting being so harsh. "What a mess, Churchy. What a mess."

The angle of the car on the road means I can't see anything, but I turn my back anyway to give her privacy. I don't want to think about her changing in the car, practically naked. Thankfully, by the time she's done, Lando has pulled up.

"Glorious evening." He's brandishing a chainsaw in one hand and cutters in the other like he's in a horror movie. Holiday's influence is rubbing off. "Trust this fucking goat to get stuck on the night it decides to drop a year's worth of rain."

"Yeah." I roll my eyes. "It's bad, though. He's stuck in barbed wire."

Lando's expression turns thunderous. There's not an inch of Burlington land he doesn't know and isn't aware of.

"Where the fuck's that come from? There shouldn't be barbed wire anywhere near here."

I shake my head. "No idea. But we need to get him

out."

"What do you need me to do?"

"He's sedated, and I think we need to chainsaw around the hedge, then I can see how bad he's caught."

"Got it." He steps forward, then turns to Story. "Can you move both the cars so the lights are facing here? Block the lane if you have to."

"Sure."

"Also, hi, nice to see you back in Valentine Nook, Story."

I want to add, "Not for long," but I bite my tongue.

With more light, it's easier to assess the situation, which isn't great, but not as dire as I originally thought. The first kick of the chainsaw, however, causes Churchill to panic enough to deepen his wounds, so I get another dose of ketamine until he's knocked out, and it makes things much easier.

In total it takes twenty minutes to free Churchill.

I cut the barbed wire where it's tangled in the branches, but I can't remove it from his legs without causing more damage.

Lando and I work together quickly, while Story stays next to Churchill soothing him. I should tell her it's pointless because he's unconscious, but truthfully the muffled whisper in his ear is soothing me too. I can't hear what she's saying but every time I glance at her, I'm transfixed watching her mouth move.

Full lips, still slightly pink . . . *fuck*, the things I want to do to it.

"Hen?" Lando's holding his hand out, and I know I haven't heard a word he's said. Based on the smirk he's sporting, he's fully aware why. "Pass me the cutters, then

I think we might be able to move."

The hardest part of the entire operation is getting him up the rainy, muddy slope, until Miles arrives with one of Max's old sleds and we hoist him into the back of the car.

"This is not how I expected my evening to go." Miles slams the Land Rover shut. "Poor Churchy, I hope he's going to be okay."

"I think he will, but I need to get him back now."

"Did anyone call Mrs. Winston?" Story's stopped shivering, but she's back to being wet and muddy like the rest of us. "I can if you want."

I nod. "Yes, thank you. Tell her he'll be at the surgery. Lando or Miles can drop you home."

"No, I want to come with you, if that's okay. I want to make sure Churchill is sound."

From the corner of my eye, I see Miles's brow raise, and he glances at Lando.

"Um, it might be a while—"

"That's okay. I didn't have plans anyway."

"All right then." I sweep my hand in front of me, gesturing her toward the passenger door, and turn back to my brothers. "I'll see you both later."

"Catch you at home. Hot Duke and I are getting the hell out of here."

I hear Lando mutter something along the lines of, "You're such a dick," and Story's already at the passenger side, so she doesn't notice that Miles doesn't acknowledge her. Though I doubt she'd care.

We drive in silence to the clinic, where the overnight nurse meets us at the door, and the three of us carry Churchill into the operating room. One thing's for sure, he's going on a restricted diet when he's out of here. His days of stripping every fruit tree in the village are over.

I thought Story would wait in the reception area, it was the only reason I agreed she could come because her in the operating room is nothing less than a distraction. But after we both get dry, the nurse offers her a scrub gown and she takes it.

"If you're going to stay, make yourself useful. In the drawer behind you are cotton swabs, razors, and antiseptic lotion. I'll cut the wires, and you can shave around the wound and clean it so I can see what needs stitching."

She nods. "Okay."

We get to work. I focus on Churchill. I cut, and she cleans. And we do it all in silence. Too silently.

Distractingly silent.

Story's close enough that every so often her hair flops back from behind her ear and falls into my face. Blood, mud, and metal mingle with a faint floral perfume. My eyes find hers too often and look away too quickly.

Her mouth is inches from mine, and I concentrate on counting the barbs in the wire instead.

"You're not an inconvenience to me, Story," I say at some point while dropping another couple of inches of wire into the trash. It clatters against the metal.

Her hand stills and it's the only way I know she's heard me.

"This wound looks deep," she observes a couple of minutes later.

I peer over. "Get a fresh swab and leave it on. I'll stitch it."

She does as I ask and continues with her role. Every

so often, she whispers something to Churchill and strokes his face, just like she did in the trench.

"What are you saying to him?" I ask, after the fourth or fifth time.

"That he's in the best hands, and you're going to fix everything."

The room suddenly feels too hot.

"Did you speak to Mrs. Winston?"

"No, she wasn't answering. I'll keep trying."

In total, I estimate I removed three meters of barbed wire from around Churchill's hind quarters, though I don't know how he managed to get himself so tangled up. I only needed to stitch seven of the wounds, as the rest were only big scratches. And we do fix everything, the two of us.

Afterward, we wheel him through to the recovery room, leaving him in one of the crates usually reserved for the really large dogs.

"I'm glad I called you," Story says, standing up after dropping a final kiss on Churchill's head.

"Technically, you called the practice."

Her lips roll together, teeth catching the bottom one. "I don't have your number."

"Still the same one. It hasn't changed."

She looks away and shrugs, which says it all. A knife pushed further into my chest. Confirmation that she completely erased me from her life.

"Funny. I still know yours by heart." It's not funny at all.

Her shoulders drop, eyes still glued to a spot on the floor. She looks as defeated as she did at the committee meeting, a point in time that feels so much longer ago than a few days. I'm thoroughly exhausted, enough that I don't immediately hear her.

"What?"

"I'm *sorry*."

I blink. "Sorry? What for?"

When she looks at me, it's not rain pouring down her face. "For everything. For leaving. For coming back. *Everything*."

There are no windows in here, and the harsh overhead light seems to be today's metaphor for putting a spotlight on everything we don't want to see. An operating room isn't where I wanted to have this conversation. I'm not ready. But then again, I doubt I'll ever be.

My sigh is deep, almost painful, and I carefully lean against the wall. If I'm here and she's over there, I can't do anything I'll regret.

"When you disappeared, it was like a part of me died."

She opens her mouth to speak, but I hold up my hand to stop her. If I don't say it now, I'm going to make myself sick reliving the memories.

"I was going through the most profoundly confusing and terrifying moment in my life, and I missed you so acutely that it turned to grief. And the worst part is that I still don't know why you left."

Bloodshot eyes twitch, and her jaw hardens. "You really don't know?"

I shake my head.

She stares at me long enough I wonder if she's expecting me to figure it out, but I've tried and gotten nowhere.

"You're not the only one who was grieving, Hen. You're not the only one who lost a part of themselves that day." She swipes a hand across her eyes, smearing tears into what's left of her mascara. I want to laugh because I know that if *she knows* she's done it, she'd be horrified, but all I can think about is how beautiful she looks.

Instead, I frown, confused. "What does that mean?"

Her head drops, then she throws her arms in the air, like she can't decide whether she's sad or mad. "It means that everything I thought I knew about our future was wrong. That I'd spent all our teenage years being hopelessly in love with you, watching you with other girls, waiting until we finally got our moment, our *timing.* And then you tell me you got a girl you'd been seeing pregnant, someone I didn't even know about, and I knew we'd never have it."

She's breathless, her chest juddering as she tries to compose herself.

I'm speechless but also *not.*

It's one thing to suspect, but quite another to be validated.

Hearing the words I'd wondered about—the confirmation of what Miles has been drilling into me for so long—jolts something inside me, and a switch flips in my brain.

Our moment, our timing. Something we'd never been able to get quite right, but I was the last to fuck up. My nails scrape along my scalp, tugging the ends of my hair.

What a fucking mess.

"Fuck. Stor—"

"I had to get out of Valentine Nook. I had to get away from you. Was it mature? Probably not. But it's done now."

Done now? Just like that. An act so simple and easy to move on from.

I push away from the wall. Four heartbeats and I'm in front of her, so close she has to crane her neck to find me.

"Do you know how much I missed you? Do you have any idea the hole you left in my life? One day you were there, the next you were gone. Not even a text or a phone call. Every message I sent you went unanswered—"

Creases mar her forehead. "What messages—"

"Three years I wrote to you. Every day after you left, wondering where you were—" Memories of watching my phone, waiting for it to beep with a response, are so visceral that I choke out the rest of my words. "Then every week, month. It took three years of my own stubbornness before I realized you were never going to reply. That you were gone. *Dead.*"

"Hen . . ." she sobs, tears streaming down her face. "No."

Anger hits me in waves at how stupid we've been. At how different our futures would be if we hadn't fucked things up. "I'm never going to regret my son, Story. Do I regret the way he came into the world? Yes. Do I regret my actions around then? Also, yes. It gutted me. I was only a child when I lost my dad, and I don't know if I truly understood what grief was back then. But when you left? It felt like the worst thing that's ever happened to me. I loved you so much, and you vanished into thin air."

A gasp is followed by a soft hand circling my wrist. "I

never got any messages, Hendricks. Please believe me."

"It doesn't matter now." I shake my head. "It's done. And for what it's worth, I'm sorry. I'm sorry for everything too."

"I'm here now." She lifts my hand to her face, pressing my palm to her cheek. My fingers curl around her nape, and I feel her pulse hammering beneath the surface of her skin. "I'm here, Hendricks. *I'm here.*"

Her face is so small in my hands. I can't remember if it was always that way or if I've never held her like this. She sniffs hard, tears stream faster than I can wipe them away, and then my thumb brushes across her mouth. That *fucking* mouth.

Minus the goat and the drama, this is the moment I've thought about for six years. Story MacIntosh here with me, again.

Pushing through her damp hair forces her head back, and against my better judgment, I find her eyes again.

"Hen . . . Hendricks, what are you doing?"

"What I've been waiting to do for a long time." My mouth dips to hers.

Her eyes close, but mine stay wide open. I don't want to miss a second of something I've dreamed about for so long. That I finally get to experience her lips on mine.

Except that's the moment Churchill stirs in his bed, letting out a confused bleat.

Fuck.

And for the second time, my first kiss with Story is interrupted.

15

Hendricks

Age 16

Kicking open the door to Miles's room, I flop on his bed.

"Milo?"

A face half covered in shaving cream appears around his bathroom door. Just like our older brothers, we inherited our dad's thick beard. It's such a pain to shave, though, so we usually don't bother during the holidays.

"What's up?"

"Mum wants you."

"Why?"

I shrug, and he disappears back inside the bathroom, and the sound of running water starts up.

"Why are you shaving?"

"Official photos for the England Under 21s are being taken before the first match."

His beard isn't the only thing Miles inherited from our father. He also got his skills on the polo field. Better, even, according to some who used to watch Dad play. I remember hours spent on the sidelines every weekend during the summer when Miles would run around with his polo mallet, shouting commentary as he followed the match.

All four of us can play and have done so since we learned to ride, but Miles is obsessed. And the only one who can play like our father. He'd have been so proud to see him selected to play for the England Under 21s during this summer.

I'm proud. We all are. The only dampener is that Dad won't be there to see it.

So I'm thankful he can't see me grimace. "I thought it was next week."

"Nope. Today, we've got to be at Foxleigh by twelve, and then the match is at three. You're coming with Mum, Clemmie, and Al, right? Lando's at the boring lunch thing beforehand, probably poncing about, but he'll find you after."

"Yeah. Course."

Fuck, fuck, fuck, and bollocks. I'd completely forgotten. I had plans this afternoon, important ones.

"Unless you want to go to the lunch?" He walks out, patting his face dry with a towel on his way to his closet, which he tosses at me, and I promptly drop on the floor.

"Nope." Couldn't think of anything worse, frankly.

Hanging out with a load of stuffy Londoners who like to pretend they live in the country and being pawed at by mothers who want me to meet their daughters. *No thanks*. Not to mention that if Miles is playing, he won't be at lunch, which means I won't have a buffer. He deals with shit like that much better than I do.

Plus, I now have to rearrange my day.

"D'you know Sam Pelling . . .?" I call out. I hear him opening and closing drawers, hangers being flung along the rack. It's haphazard and erratic. Two things Miles isn't. "Milo?"

"What?" he says, walking out wearing only a pair of boxers and holding up two shirts. "Which one?"

I point at the one in his right hand. "That's mine."

"Wondered why I like it." A grin spreads on his face. He tosses the other shirt back into his closet and pulls mine over his head. "It can be my lucky charm today."

I frown. Miles doesn't usually need or want luck for anything. "Are you okay?"

"Yeah. Why?"

"Milo . . ."

He's tugging on a pair of jodhpurs and stops halfway. "I miss Dad. I wish he were here today."

"Me too." Ten years. We've now had four more years without our dad than we had with him, and yet we still feel the loss so acutely. I glance at the photo Miles has on his dresser, the one of him and Dad sitting on Zeus, my dad's old horse. Miles is three and holding a mallet. "You know what he'd say, don't you?"

"Yeah. Strong wrist, elbows in, bump hard." He grins, reciting the three rules my dad always said were the key to being a good polo player.

"Just remember them, and he'll be with you."

He nods, then taps the photo on the dresser and walks back into the closet. "What did you ask me before—"

"When?"

"Just now?"

Even though it was only two minutes ago, I don't seem to remember, and when I do, I wonder how I forgot. "D'you know Sam Pelling?"

"From prep school?"

I nod.

"Yeah, why?"

My teeth sink into the skin on the side of my thumb. Now that I've started down this line, I almost don't want to finish. I should just forget about it. Pretend it's not true. Ignore it.

"Hen? What?"

Miles and I might be identical twins and run in the same core circles of friends we've had since we were younger, but Miles's is much wider than mine. He's on the polo team, which always attracts lots of people. I spend my spare time on the farm or, when I'm at school, in the biology department labs.

"Have you heard anything about him and Story?"

"Nope. Why?"

"I think they're seeing each other," I say, which is based on nothing but a hunch and the fact that he likes every single one of her Instagram posts.

Last week, he commented with a chicken emoji. Like what the fuck is that supposed to mean?

A fucking chicken, on a stack of books next to her bed.

"Why don't you just ask her?"

"We don't talk about stuff like that."

"Why not?"

"I don't know, we just don't. She has her life at school here, and we're at Wellington." It's been that way ever since the Valentine Fair three years ago. Since Annabel kissed me because she thought I was Miles.

"So Story doesn't know about you and Katie Singh?"

I shake my head. "There's nothing to tell."

"You had sex with her all summer term."

I shrug. "Yeah but we're not seeing each other or anything. She knows I'm not interested in having a girlfriend at school."

"Then maybe that's what Story is doing. She's not telling you anything because there's nothing to tell, and she doesn't want a boyfriend."

"You think?"

Miles's eyes meet mine through the mirror. He's been standing in front of it, trying to get his hair in that messy way he always does. Messier than I like mine, but mostly because I can't be bothered taking the time Miles does. Sometimes it's weird being an identical twin because you don't need a mirror. You can just look at them and decide whether something is good or not.

"Hen, you know what I think when it comes to Story."

I roll my eyes and pull my phone out of my pocket. Yes, I know exactly what Miles thinks.

He still blames her for Annabel Stenson punching him in the face after she thought she'd been snogging *him*, when in fact he was with Lauren MacCauley.

In his defense, and having been the one who actually snogged Annabel Stenson, it wouldn't have happened if Annabel hadn't launched herself at me. And it lasted twenty seconds max, enough time for me to get over the shock of it.

The worst part was hurting Story, because I'd really

wanted to kiss Story that day. It took me a month to get her to talk to me, and the valentine I had for her is still in my desk drawer.

"Can you just find out if she's seeing that dickhead? Like, for real?"

He nods because, as much as he doesn't like Story, he'll do anything for me. "Yes, I'll ask around Foxleigh, but you know who might know? Clem."

My head snaps up to his. "Yes. You're fucking right. Where is she?"

"Fuck knows." Miles shakes his head, standing in front of me. "I look okay, right?"

"You look good. Shit hair, though." I grin, adding a punch at the same time. "I need to find Clem, and don't forget Mum wants you."

HENDRICKS: Where are you?

HENDRICKS: Need a favor. Do u know Sam Pelling?

I wait for the dot dot dots, but they don't come. God, she's annoying. She's literally glued to her phone, and the one time I need her, she's vanished.

Miles has already rushed ahead of me, yelling, "Mum," as he tries to find her. While he's doing that, I refigure my day because I planned to spend it with Story.

HENDRICKS: Meet me on the hill in 30?

STORYTELLER: Sure thing. See you there, Henny.

I wanted to spend the afternoon hanging out on the hill, maybe go swimming, and get some drinks. Now I'll be at the polo, and Story won't come with me because she doesn't like Miles. But I *have* to be at the polo, and this isn't a situation where I can use Miles to be in two places at once.

He's in the kitchen when I eventually make it downstairs, though annoyingly, I haven't found my sister.

"Is Clemmie here?"

"Nope."

"Fuck. Okay, I'm taking Sprite for a walk. Tell Mum I'll be back soon. If you see Clem, tell her to check her messages." I pull him into the biggest hug I can. "I love you. You're going to be amazing today, Milo. I'll be cheering you so fucking loud." I shove my hand into my pocket and pull out a lemon sherbet. "Frankie can have this if he scores."

Miles glances down at his palm. "Why've you got lemon sherbets in your pocket?"

"No clue," I reply, whistling for Sprite, my Labrador. "And don't forget, strong wrist, elbows in, bump hard."

I make it in thirty, and Story's sitting, waiting for me.

In all fairness, she lives way closer to the hill than I do, which is why I brought the four-wheeler with me. Because the less time it takes to travel back, the longer I get to spend with Story.

Sprite rushes up to her, hurling himself on her hard enough that she falls on the ground. The pale purple sundress she's wearing lifts up to her thighs as her feet kick in the air. I pause, watching her squeal and playfully shove Sprite aside while he covers her in kisses. I wish I could do the same.

"Sprite, leave her alone." I laugh, pulling a ball from my pocket, and throw it as far as I can so we get at least thirty seconds alone while he fetches it and sprints back.

As I wander over and she pulls her dress down, her legs seem so long that I wonder if she's gotten taller, which makes me sad because then she won't fit under my chin. Holding my hand out, I pull her up to standing and tuck her into me.

"Oh thank God."

"What?"

"You're still short."

She reels back and slaps me hard on the arm—hard for her, anyway—which only makes me laugh more, and it gives me the chance to properly look at her.

Even though we talk every day, we don't spend as much time together as we used to. Today's the first time I've seen her in a few months—since I was last home for the weekend. I wonder if I look different to her in the way she looks different to me. It always feels like I spend the first five minutes wondering what's changed.

Today her face is tanned, there's a thick line of freckles along her forehead, and her dark brown hair looks like it's been dipped in bronze.

Even her eyes seem lighter. Milk chocolate instead of plain.

And when I shove her gently with my shoulder and say, "I missed you," her cheeks turn ever so slightly pink. It's always like this with us in person, ten seconds of coyness while we check we're still the same.

Still Hendricks and Story.

Still best friends.

"Missed you too, Hen."

I drop onto the blanket next to her, in the spot she's patting. The scent of flower meadows invades my next inhale. It's exactly how the Bluebell woods are at Burlington in the height of spring, but they're done for this year, so it can't be that. "What am I smelling?"

Story pulls her long ponytail around and holds it out to me. "I got a new shampoo."

My nose brushes against her cheek as I lean in and breathe deep. "Nice."

"Thanks," she says, flicking it back over her shoulder, but she stays close.

Sprite returns with the ball and drops it for me to toss again. "Are you nervous about exam results?"

She shakes her head. "Not really? I worked hard enough, except in science. I hate that."

"What? Science is the best." I gasp, shoving her again even though I know she only said it to get a reaction in that casual, flirty way she does.

And I'll give her all the reactions she wants.

"Not all of us can be brainiacs in that department, you know." She laughs, though it's more a snort than a laugh. Whatever it is, it's a noise unique to Story and always has me laughing harder. "We're not all Mr. Straight As."

"Hey, I won't be a vet without them."

"I know." She grins, leaning back on her elbows.

The movement has the hem of her dress rising up her thighs again, and I force myself to look away. "Proud of you, Henny. You're going to be the best vet."

"Thanks. And you're going to be the best teacher. Benson the ballbreaker, part two."

"As if." This time, she attempts to kick me, and it shifts her body enough that her fingers settle against mine. They glue me in position. No matter how uncomfortable I am right now, I'm not moving.

"How's Miles feeling?"

"You know Miles. He doesn't care about anything except polo. I'm not sure he's done any revision." I laugh, even though he's going to get into serious trouble if he doesn't pass. The exams we took at the beginning of summer determined which subjects we could take in senior year and where we would go to university.

The reason I've been working so hard is that I only want to be a vet and study at the Royal Veterinary School in London.

"D'you want to go to the waterfall today?"

Again, I want to scream to the heavens with frustration but instead reply, "I can't. Miles has his first match with England today. I have to be at Foxleigh Park by three." Fuck, fuck, *fuck*. "Why don't you come? It'll be fun."

But as predicted, she shakes her head. "No thanks, but we have all summer to hang out."

The disappointment vanishes slightly. "Yeah?"

"Yeah, let's go to the waterfall tomorrow. It's going to be a scorcher."

Spending the day at the waterfall is the best idea she's ever had.

"Does that mean you plan to wear your tiniest bikini?" My eyes fall to her mouth as it purses. "That blue one you put on Instagram?"

"Maybe. Have to wait and see, won't you?"

My brow rises. Fuck, she looked incredible. Standing by the pool, book in hand and boobs high and round, pushed together from the way her hand was shielding her face from the sun. It never occurred to me I was a boobs guy until I saw hers. "That was a hot one, Stor."

I love the way her cheeks flush whenever I pay her a compliment. She's so fucking pretty. I wish we could stay here all day, all night, *all* summer. Just her and me.

"Yeah?"

"Yes. It's a plan. You, me, the bikini, and the waterfall."

"Didn't realize you liked that bikini so much."

"Oh, yeah."

Except then I remember fucking Sam Pelling liked it. A peach, the cherries, and a tongue, like he's such a knob he can't even spell out words. I was so annoyed that I offered to play one-on-one with Miles, and he bumped me so hard I fell off.

My only consolation was that when I checked it later, the comment had been deleted. It's what made me think they might be seeing each other. That, and because I know he's always liked her.

Sprite drops the ball in Story's lap, and she throws it, but it goes five meters, if that.

"Pathetic. Guess we're working on your throwing arm this summer too."

Leaning over, she squeezes my bicep, but it could quite as easily be my dick for the effect it has. "So I can have guns like this?"

Sitting tall, I flex them at her. All the hours I spent in the school gym this year are now paid in full.

"Impressive." Her head drops on my shoulder. "I do miss you, Hen. I wish we weren't so far away from each other during term time."

"Me too, but we have all summer to be together. And now we're going into sixth form, I can come home more. Plus, once I'm seventeen, I'll have my car."

I hope she gets what I'm trying to say. That I like her and want to spend all the time I have with her.

"That would be cool, and I can come and visit you at Wellington too." Lying down, she props herself up with her elbow facing me, and I follow. Sprite decides he's had enough chasing the ball and lies at our feet. "Let's make a plan. We're sixteen now. Our exams are done, we have no obligations whatsoever." She reaches out and hooks her little finger around mine. "We need to make this summer count."

Her ponytail flops over her shoulder. Taking hold of the end, I run it between my fingers and move it back, watching her lashes flutter against her cheeks. Her attention darts between my eyes and my lips, and it's a movement I mirror. *No*, that's a lie. I'm not looking at her eyes because I can't stop staring at her lips.

She's not wearing any of that shiny stuff I usually hate, mostly because it tastes weird, and I get covered in it too.

No, she's just natural and perfect. She's Story.

Her finger releases mine but only travels as far as my belt loop, hooking into that instead. It's slight, but I swear she tugs me toward her. My pulse races, and blood rushes straight to my dick.

"We will definitely make this summer count. I promise, Stor."

"Can't break your promises, Hen."

We're so close I'd only have to shift an inch or two and my mouth would be on hers.

Is this really about to happen? It's a moment I've been thinking about since Annabel Stenson ruined everything three years ago.

"I would never—"

My phone lets out a series of pings that are impossible to ignore.

"Why's your message tone so loud?" She laughs, but her hand moves to my hip.

"It must have knocked in my pocket. Hang on. I'll turn it off," I say, rolling back only enough that I can extract it.

Scanning them, I quickly pray it's nothing important. There are a dozen messages from Miles, but the last one is from my sister.

CLEMMIE: Yeah, think that's the guy I saw sucking face with Story last weekend ✌️

16

Story

"This is a stupid idea, Story."

"I know, Story, but I'm not sure what else to do."

"Screams desperation if you ask me, Story."

"Shut *up*, Story. I didn't ask you."

"It's just going to be the same situation as before."

"No, it's not."

"We'll see."

As conversations I've had with myself go, it's not the best. I've also never done it while carrying a basket of apples. But here we are. I just really wish Glenda hadn't witnessed it.

"Are you coming in, dear?"

I wave at her from across the high street, wishing she weren't quite so loud and there weren't quite so many people between us. "In a minute, Glenda."

"Hendricks isn't here if that's what you're worried about."

For fuck's sake, does everyone here already know my business? I bet it was that bloody nurse on Thursday night who told everyone.

I don't want to count how many pairs of eyes just looked at me, likely nudged each other, and debated on whether I was a pathetic loser. Jury's still out on that one for me. I mean, what's that saying? "If he wanted to, he would."

And Hendricks might have given off all the vibes of wanting to kiss me, but whether he did is another matter. *He didn't.* And while I'd like to say it's the first time that's happened, it isn't.

I thought he might call, seeing as *"he knows my number by heart,"* but he didn't do that either, and it's been two days. I know being interrupted by a goat technically isn't his fault, and Churchill needed more painkillers, *blah, blah, blah,* but he never tried to kiss me again. Not once Churchill was asleep, and not at all during the journey home when he dropped me at my door.

And when he snapped, "*I know where you live, Story,*" after I mistakenly attempted to give him directions, I put the near kiss down to the heightened emotions brought on by an early evening goat rescue.

"*Doesn't explain what he said to you, though, does it, Story?*"

"No, Story, it doesn't. Which is why you're standing outside the vets, Glenda waving you in, and with half of Valentine Nook staring at you as she does."

"*Then get a move on.*"

"Urgh. Fine."

Pulling up my big girl knickers, I dodge a couple of shoppers and run up the steps to the vet before anyone else can see me.

"Hello, dear. How're you doing?"

I heave the basket onto the countertop and put on

my best cheery face, like it's perfectly normal for me to visit the vets on a Saturday. "Not bad, thank you, Glenda. How are you?"

"Smashing. Absolutely smashing, and so lovely to have you back. Bet your mum and dad are pleased. How is your dad?"

I think back to this morning and my dad yelling, "Where's my bloody crutch?"

My mum walked out because she'd had enough, muttering, "You better hope you don't find it because I'm going to knock you around the head."

"Oh, he's on the mend. Been down at the yard a lot—"

"Yer mum left me a couple of pints of milk yesterday. Will you thank her for me?"

"I will do."

"Now, how can I help you? Heard you had a dramatic evening on Thursday?"

I nod, smile, and chuckle, just as Glenda is doing. "Just a little. These are for the patient if he's still here," I add, patting the apples. I don't actually know he's here, because while I want to see him, they're a pretense to come for who I really want to see.

I am so lame.

"He is. It was best we keep him here to stop him from tearing his stitches by running around the village. You know, Eunice can't keep him in his stable because he always escapes."

"Can I go see him?"

"I'm sure he'll be delighted." She grins. "Go through the back theater to the recovery room, and he's there. Maybe don't give him the whole basket, though, dear."

"Don't worry. Just a couple." I wink. "And . . . *er*, there's no one else here?"

She shakes her head. "Nope."

"Cool. Won't be long then."

Churchill looks about as pleased to see me as a goat can possibly look wearing a pair of striped pajamas.

I forgot we put him in them, but after he woke up, Hendricks said it would keep him calm if he woke again.

"Hi, darling." I grab a couple of apples from the basket and leave the rest on the side, then walk over to the little enclosure we made for him.

I thought he might still be a bit dopey, but after he jumps up from his—very comfortable, I might add—bed and tries to butt me, I decide he isn't. And seeing as it's a more playful butt than anything aggressive, I also decide he knows exactly who I am—namely, his savior.

"You're welcome, Churchy. And I brought you something to cheer you up." I hold out the apple, which he immediately snatches and gobbles down. "Think we need to work on our manners."

They're no better the second time around. I hold out a third. "Gentle, this time." But then the door swings open, startling him enough that he snatches it and nearly takes my fingers off in the process. "Ouch. Fuck. Sorry, Glenda, just teaching Churchill some manners."

It's not Glenda.

Hendricks smirks, a barely there lip quiver that makes my heart stumble. "You're trying to teach a goat manners?"

Passing the last apple to Churchill, I push up off my knees and stand in front of Hendricks. Me short, him tall. "Manners are important."

"They are." He steps back and leans against the smooth metal countertop running around the room. Now we're separated by a table.

"What's that?" I point at the trainer in his hand.

The trainer identical to the one I lost in the mud on Thursday. The trainer that wasn't there on Friday, or this morning when I went to look for it.

"I found it on the way home—"

"It's clean—"

"I had it washed."

He places it on the table between us, and I pick it up to smell it. I know, *weird.* But it's clean, and Hendricks *washed* it. Or he instructed one of the Burlington staff, but same dif.

And then I remember all the clothes Hendricks lent me, which are still at my place. Including his jumper, the one I haven't been sleeping in because it doesn't smell like him. Definitely not.

"Shit, I should have brought your things back too—"

"You can bring them another time."

"Okay." I nod, and I wait.

Wait for him to say something, but he doesn't do anything except stand there looking like cashmere was invented for him, all blue eyes and full lips, thick curls and dark stubble. It's ridiculous.

The first time Hendricks and I nearly kissed, he pulled back and left me so abruptly. I didn't hear from him again for a week and when I did, it wasn't the same. The summer I was hoping might happen fell flat on its arse. We never talked about what happened.

The only times we visited the waterfall that summer were with groups of friends, where I'd watch him go off with every girl who wasn't me.

I should have called him out then, but I didn't.

Not this time. I'm older—*debatably*—more mature, and I've already lost everything I was once terrified of losing.

"So. Are we going to talk about Thursday night?"

He pushes his hands deep into his pockets. "Sure. What do you want to talk about?"

I know he knows me better than to think I'm going to back down from this conversation, but jeez, not even meeting me halfway. Okay then.

I start with a lighthearted, "We nearly kissed . . ."

For a split second, there's a flicker of something in his eyes. "Yup."

"And then we were interrupted."

He nods. "We were."

"Are we going to pick up where we left off?"

Every cell in my body tenses. My breath is stuck somewhere between my lungs and my mouth.

Eventually, his head shakes softly. My stomach drops, and it feels like every organ falls into the empty space it left behind.

"I told you so."

"Shut the fuck *up*, Story."

"I'm sorry." He almost whispers to himself. "I can't."

"Can't? What does that mean? Can't or don't want to?" It comes out way snarlier than I mean it.

His eyes bounce between mine, confused almost, but whatever emotion it is vanishes the next time I blink. "It's not a good idea. Too complicated. I have too much going on in my life right now."

My jaw clenches. "*Complicated*? Seems pretty simple to me. What about everything you said?"

"Stor . . ." His tone is so anguished, I almost feel sorry for him. "I shouldn't have done it. I shouldn't have kissed you."

"*Almost*."

"Yes, almost. I'm sorry."

The disappointment is tangible. So is my frustration, even as I try to take breaths to stay calm, but it all comes rushing back—the humiliation, the embarrassment, the desolation of unrequited love.

"I cannot *believe* you're doing this again."

The anguish vanishes. "What is that supposed to mean?"

"It means this isn't the first time," I snap, but we may as well get to the bottom of everything while I'm here. "Was it too 'complicated' then?"

"Then? *When*?"

"The first time you almost kissed me. On the hill, when you took off and barely said goodbye, and practically ignored me for the rest of the summer. I want to know what happened."

His brows become a dark slash on his face. "Stor, stop it—"

"No, I want to know." I'm *this* close to stamping my foot. "I deserve to know why you—"

"Clemmie told me she saw you making out with Sam Pelling—"

I balk, because what the actual fuck? "*What*?"

"That dickhead. Sam Pelling."

"I know who you're talking about. And he's not a

dickhead. And I never snog . . ." I pause as an eleven-year-old memory barrels into me. *Well, shit.*

Hendricks's eyes narrow, his behavior justified. "Yes?"

I'd completely forgotten about that night. Sam and I used to fool around in sixth form, nothing serious, but I'd totally blanked that anything had happened before then. And by that point, after a summer of watching Hendricks with other girls, I'd resigned myself to the fact that we would never happen.

Now I learn we're nothing but a product of bad communication and insecurity, and that perhaps I'm fifty percent responsible for this situation.

My shoulders drop, and the frustration is replaced by contrition.

"Okay, there's a *small* chance I *might* have snogged him that summer." I squash my fingers together. That's how small the chance is. Although it's accurate, so not *that* small. "There was a bunch of us drinking after our final exams. We played spin the bottle . . ."

Hendricks's jaw is so tight I can make out the divots from him clenching. I can almost hear his heart pounding as he weighs up the decisions he made eleven years ago. He stares at me. Stares and stares and *stares*, until, "Fuck!"

I don't move, watching as he paces back and forth across a room not built for pacing, given it only takes him five steps before he has to turn around again.

"Um . . . just for clarity, are you mad I snogged Sam Pelling? Or mad that we didn't . . ." I gesture back and forth between us.

"Both. Fuck. *Fuck.* Story, this is fucked up. *We* are fucked up—"

I scoff. "I mean, that's a bit extreme—"

"No, it's not." He shakes his head, slumping back. Dejected.

"Hen, two days ago you told me you loved me."

"I did love you, Story. I do. That's the problem." His fists ball against his forehead, and when he looks at me, all I see is enough sorrow that my heart cracks. "I meant what I said the other night. When you left, it was like you died. I can't do that again, and I'm not willing to."

Oh my God. How am I back here? How is it fourteen years ago, eleven, six? His eyes find a point somewhere on the wall, looking at anything but me, standing here in disbelief.

I glance down at a wet sensation and find Churchill licking my hand. It's so gentle it overwhelms me. I'm tired, I'm emotional, I'm *humiliated* and before I can stop it, I'm choked by a sob.

Immediately, I'm engulfed in cashmere and the delicious masculine scent of the countryside and everything I associate with Hendricks. I let him hold me as I cry, his chin on my head like it always used to be when we hugged, and the most ridiculous thought pops into my head. *I will never know what Hendricks's lips feel like against mine.*

I cry harder.

"I'm sorry, Stor. I'm *so* sorry," he whispers, his breath hot against my head. "But my son takes priority over everything. I have to concentrate on being the best dad I can be, and I can't think straight when you're around. I'm not bringing someone into his life who's going to leave again. It doesn't matter how much I want you, how much I love you. Have always loved you, Stor. I'm not the same person you left here, and I need to get used to you being here for now . . . until you leave again. Friends is all I can offer you."

His lips press against my temple. The hope I had this morning that perhaps, *finally*, our time has come is dashed.

And the worst part is, he's not wrong.

17

Hendricks

"Hendricks? . . . *Hendricks*?"

I'm brought back to the present by a severe nudge in the ribs from my brother.

"Ouch, what the fuck was that for?" I grunt. His chin jerks toward the center of the room, where I discover a set of beady eyes staring at me. "Mrs. Winston, I apologize. If you could repeat that—"

"I was saying the equipment and components for the kissing booth you suggested will be delivered here this week, so you'll need to collect it and assemble it—"

"And by assemble, you mean—"

Her eyes narrow. She's looking at me like I'm a spoiled brat who's never built anything, which I'm not, and I have. What I don't have, however, is any recollection that I agreed to this.

"It comes with instructions, don't worry. I'm sure you and Story will manage just fine together. Nothing like a little teamwork." She chuckles, and it takes all the self-control I have not to snarl at her. "And this was your idea."

I peer over at Story, who's looking far too innocent

for my liking. More innocent than I've ever seen her before, that's for sure. "Come on, Hen, what's the harm with a little teamwork between *friends*?"

Okay, maybe I deserved that. "No harm, Stor. I can build whatever needs to be built."

"*We* can build . . ."

"Right." I glance at Mrs. Winston. "Anything you need, *we* can handle."

She claps her hands. "Excellent. And I take it you've been making arrangements with the shelter this week too?"

"The shelter?" Did I miss a meeting this week? Because that's how it feels.

"The dog shelter in Oxford. Or are we using another charity for the kissing booth? That is how it was used previously, correct?"

Next to me, Miles coughs, which sounds an awful lot like "*Story.*"

Ignoring him, I nod vigorously and add the cheeriest chuckle I can manage. "Yes. Yes. Again, I apologize. I was a little confused there for a moment. The shelter has been contacted, and they're on board. We plan to have a good adoption drive for Valentine's."

"Excellent, excellent," she crows, then moves to the next point on the agenda and a new victim.

Miles leans into me. "Did you really contact the shelter?"

"I will have by the end of the day," I mutter back.

"By the way, if you wanted to play it cool, you're doing a shit job."

"I'm not trying to play it cool. I'm not trying to do anything."

He scoffs, uncrosses, then recrosses his legs. "Sure. If you say so."

I'm not going to argue with him, because I'm really not. Yes, maybe I am a little distracted, but I have a lot on my mind right now, and not just the image of Story sobbing in my arms, or the feeling of her body fitting perfectly against mine again after so long.

I'm proud of the way we've behaved like adults this week. Adults who are friends. I've said hello to her twice this week when I've dropped Max off at school, and that's what friends do.

It's neither here nor there that she's sitting opposite me right now, directly in my eyeline. Obviously, she's the one person I'd be looking at the most. If Agatha Chase was sitting there instead of the other side of Miles—which explains why Miles is so close to me, he's almost on my lap—I'd be looking at Agatha.

I'd be watching Agatha laugh softly at her seatmate, the other reception teacher who introduced herself last week. It would be Agatha quietly tucking her hair back, only for hairs to escape again. It would be the curve of Agatha's throat I'd see as she sipped from her glass.

It would be Agatha I'd be acutely aware of, *not* she who captures my attention to the point I miss everything being said.

"Am I an idiot?" I sigh hard.

"You're going to need to be more specific, Hen."

I side-eye Miles. "Why are you here again?"

"I came for a drink. I didn't know you were having a meeting. But as I'm here, I can remind you all that the charity polo match is the weekend after next."

I nod. This one I have actually remembered, because I'm playing. Miles, Lando, Alex, and me against the visiting team, usually made up of high-profile professionals Miles has corralled. We host one twice a year at Foxleigh Park, and the Valentine match is usually seen as the kickoff to the early social calendar. Therefore, it's always well attended and raises several thousand pounds.

It's a lot of fun, and by the end of the day, everyone's either drunk on love or lots of champagne, though usually both. It leads to excellent donations.

"And then one last item on the agenda, which I'm assuming is why you're here, Miles." She looks at Miles, then me, then back at Miles, who puts his hand up.

"It's me, Mrs. Winston. The better-looking one, remember?"

Across from me, Story rolls her eyes, and everyone else laughs politely—they've all been victims of Miles's joke at least a dozen times. Maybe not Celeste, however, who seems to think it's the funniest thing she's ever heard.

"Yes, quite, thank you." He winks at her, and flushed cheeks replace the laughter. Story's eyes roll even harder. "Anyway, I'm taking the opportunity to remind you that it's the Valentine Polo Match in two weeks. Tickets will be on sale here, in The One True Love, at The Cupid's Arrow, and The Beanery. Please encourage everyone you know to come, so I don't have to don my ponies in pink ribbons for nothing."

"Wonderful, wonderful." Mrs. Winston claps, cheery and excited as ever while everyone else looks like they're losing the will to live and can only be revived with a strong drink. "We shall certainly all be there. Now, if that's everything, then I bid you adieu. It's going to be a wonderful event this year."

There's the usual cacophony of chairs being pushed back, feet thumping on the floor, and a rush for everyone to get to the bar as quickly as possible.

I could certainly do with a drink myself.

Miles stands, and I follow. "Bar?"

"Lead the way."

"Hey, Hen—"

Spinning around, I find Story standing behind me. "Hi, Story."

She turns to my brother. She's not so petty as he is that she'll totally ignore him standing next to me. "Miles."

"Story." He shoots her a withering look and promptly walks off, leaving us alone for the first time since she cried in my arms.

"Still annoyed about Annabel, I see." She tuts. But as she focuses on me, the bravado from earlier in the meeting seems to vanish the longer she pushes nonexistent loose strands behind both ears, repeatedly smoothing her hair down. "So we're building the booth?"

"That's what it sounds like."

Around us, people are still shuffling out to the bar, holding their own conversations, shifting the furniture back, and she's watching them until her shoulders drop. "Look, I can do this by myself if you'd rather not—"

"No, no," I say, firmly. "It was my idea. I'll see this through."

Her eyes scan mine, checking if I'm serious. If I really want to spend time with her and whether I think it's a good idea. She won't find the answer, because I don't know myself.

Eventually, she responds, "Okay then. I'll check when it's arriving and let you know."

"Sounds good." I smile. "I'll look forward to it."

Very adult. Very mature. I wonder if I should hold my hand out to shake hers, then decide it's a step too far.

"See you in the morning, Hen."

"See you in the morning, Stor."

She walks out of the pub, ignoring Miles standing at the bar, and never looks back. I know because my eyes don't leave her until she's out of sight. Then my head drops, and I question every decision I've ever made.

I am an idiot. There is no doubt.

"Hen, what are you drinking?" Miles yells through the gap between the bar separating the front of the pub with the back.

I want a double scotch, but I go with Guinness instead. Picking up the final couple of chairs, I move them back to where they came from and join him by the bar. I get there right as my drink is placed down.

"Well, that was fun."

"Was it?"

He nods. "Yes, I particularly liked the part where you were squirming in your seat about having to spend the day with Story—"

"I want to spend the day with her."

"I know you do. That's why you were squirming." His smile reaches from ear to ear. "Your plan to be 'friends' with the woman you're in love with will crash faster than Max when he's had too much sugar. If you ask me—"

"I didn't ask you," I snap, ignoring the air quotes.

"She's leaving, so being anything other than friends is pointless."

"Maybe see what Agatha thinks," Miles says loudly at the moment she walks past us.

"Milo, for fuck's sake," I grumble as she turns around, brow raised.

She peers at Miles over the top of her large, black-rimmed glasses. "Yes, Miles. What do you need? Aside from enlightening."

I bark out a laugh. Agatha never fails to crack me up, especially when it has to do with Miles. She's the only one I know who can legitimately wind him up, and I love how haughty she gets with him.

"Don't you worry about me, Agatha." He winks, though his voice is tight. "Just curious if you're sensing anything about Hendricks."

Her mouth purses, and she clicks her tongue. "Like I said to Story, it's not long now." Her eyes slide to Miles. "Nor for you, alarmingly. But you must be careful."

Miles's eyes widen, his shock is almost amusing. Like me, he has no idea what she's talking about, though people rarely do, but I'm not planning to get into a conversation about it either.

I go with, "Thanks, Agatha." To which she nods deeply and walks away. Miles scowls until she's across the other side of the pub.

"Why do you let her get under your skin?"

He shakes his head. "I don't think so. No one gets under my skin."

My brow arches. "What about the girl in Aspen?"

Miles takes a long sip of his pint and swipes a hand across his mouth. "What about her?"

During our New Year's trip to Aspen, Miles was very nearly run over by a woman galloping on a pony while yelling at Miles for being an arsehole. After he tracked her down at the stables, an argument followed. He declared that she was the most obnoxious person he'd ever met and stormed off.

Most people would have let it go, but not Miles.

In all the years I've known him, he's never been *this* interested in a woman. I already know her polo stats—handicap, where she played, and where she'll be playing next season. It's the only woman anyone has ever known Miles to show the slightest interest in.

"I'd say she's set up camp under there." I tap a finger on his chest.

He rolls his eyes. "She hasn't. But"—he stops and leans in—"I found out who she's been working with."

"Who?"

His eyes flash, devilish. "Torres."

I gasp, followed by a splutter as too much of my Guinness ends up in my windpipe. "What the hell?"

A smirk I'm very familiar with creeps on his face. The beginnings of a plan. "Yup."

"Miles, don't do anything stupid. He nearly killed you before—"

"I'm aware, Hen." A muscle twitches in his jaw, the one that shows up in me when I'm under stress.

"Milo—"

"Don't worry," he says, like it's that simple. Because I know that no matter what, I'll go along with whatever plot he cooks up. No questions asked.

We stare at each other, silently conversing. Me begging him to be careful, him laughing until an interruption comes along, and we both peer down to find Mrs. Winston.

"Hendricks, I must say again, thank you so much for rescuing my Churchy."

"You're welcome. I'm happy he's on the mend. And thank you for all the shortbread you dropped off this week. But it was Story who found him, Mrs. Winston."

"I know, and Churchill's thanked her too." She sips at a pint of Guinness, leaving an inch of foam on her top lip as she smiles. "I must say, it's nice to see you two together again. I remember the pair of you running around the village—"

Miles's arm slings around my shoulder, stopping one of the worst village gossips mid-sentence. "We're all happy Churchill's still with us, Mrs. W. And we shall look forward to a long summer of him stealing everyone's apples."

"Ah, yes. He is a naughty boy." Her head falls back in amusement, and her eyes dart. "Oh, there's Agatha. Must have a word . . ."

"Thanks." I grin once she's out of earshot.

"You're welcome." He knocks the rest of his drink back, places the glass on the bar, and slaps his stomach. "Let's get out of here. I'm starving."

"Right behind you."

We try to be quick, but it takes a couple of minutes of pushing through the crowds, saying goodbye, listening and smiling to "Something I must tell you," all the while I'm looking around for Story in case she decided to come back in. When we finally get outside, I wish we hadn't.

"Hey! Miles, Hendricks. How're you doing? Long time no see."

We both turn to find a man walking toward us, hand outstretched, vaguely familiar. It's not until he steps under the streetlights that his face fully comes into view.

"Pelling," Miles greets, taking his hand and grinning at me so wide I'm tempted to punch him. "Shit, haven't seen you in—"

"Nine years."

"Must be. How are you?"

"Good, good. Can't complain. Working in the city, small hedge fund, you know how it is." He grins, and I refrain from telling him I don't.

I'm a vet. I hate the city.

"What are you doing here?" I ask, trying to keep the horror from my voice. Horror and suspicion. Like he says, nine years. In nine years, I have never once seen Sam Pelling in Valentine Nook, but now Story has returned . . .

"My parents still live in the area, so I pop down regularly. Usually catch up with some of the old VP crew while I'm here. Anyone who's around—"

"Really?"

"Yup." He nods. "You should come join us."

"Thanks, we'd love to." Miles grabs my shoulder, squeezing it so hard I wince. "But not tonight. We're needed elsewhere. Definitely another time though, mate."

"Great. Look forward to it." He salutes and walks into the pub we've just left. It's the only reason I don't take after him because I know Story isn't in there.

I take a minute, stuck on the spot as my brain whirrs. I know Miles is staring at me, waiting.

"Don't say it."

But obviously, he does. “Still think staying ‘friends’ with Story is a good idea?”

18

Story

Hell is working construction with Hendricks Burlington.

"It doesn't go there, Hen." I point at the very clearly labeled instructions where end A is supposed to be placed. "See?"

He waves the curved piece of plywood at me. "Stor, it says that A goes into B."

"But you have to attach these wiggly things first." I open my hand, revealing said wiggly things, which I'd been holding on to for him. "Otherwise, it doesn't slot properly."

He tuts, lets out a big huff, and snatches them from my palm. Armed with a screwdriver and an Allen key, he tries again. Unsuccessfully.

"Seriously, how can you stitch up a wound on an injured animal and not figure out basic assembly instructions? It's like you've never put IKEA flatpack together before." I'm joking, though the way he glares at me makes me think I've touched a nerve. And I know Burlington Hall is filled with priceless antiques, but he went to university. Students live off IKEA furniture.

"These aren't instructions." He whips up the paper and waves it at me. "They're drawings and not very good ones. And I have no idea what it is, but I know this *isn't* IKEA. There isn't even the correct number of wiggly bits."

My lips roll together. I so desperately want to laugh at how annoyed he is, mostly because he's used to excelling at everything. "Okay, I concede, not enough wiggly bits. Can't we just get one of the Burlington staff to do it? You must have a carpenter on call."

He peers over at me, though he's bending over the instructions so he's more looking up. His brows drop. "There aren't Burlington carpenters. Besides, that's cheating. But"—he pulls out his phone—"I can get some better tools sent over."

"Using your powers for good." I sit back against the wall and grab one of the beers I brought—something told me I'd need them—and wave it toward the wood scattered all over the floor of the village hall. The scene for today's debacle. There's also a length of red fabric that I can't figure out. "Where d'you think she got this all from anyway?"

"Mrs. Winston's House of Crap," he grumbles, only to burst out laughing a second later and slump next to me. "Reinforcements will be here in twenty minutes."

"Thank God."

We sit there in silence, both of us drinking quietly. "I've never put IKEA furniture together. I've never been to IKEA."

My entire body twists toward his. "What? How is that possible?"

He shrugs. "Why would I have gone?"

"To experience the meatballs, buy a Billy bookcase,

coat hangers . . ." I hold a finger up for each one. "What about all the kids' storage? That's invaluable. I've always used it in my classrooms. You can't get better anywhere else."

"I didn't realize you were so passionate about IKEA." He laughs.

"But what about when you were at university?"

"I lived in Eaton Square, remember?" he shoots back, mentioning his family's London house, which is about as far away from student accommodation as one could get.

"But what about when Max was born?"

"All the furniture for his room came already assembled."

"Of course, it did—"

"My mum organized it. Plus, I wasn't really in the best frame of mind to be spending hours in IKEA . . ." His sentence peters off, and he leans back again.

The silence returns, only this time the air feels heavier. We've veered into territory I'm not familiar with because I left. I don't know the person Hendricks became after that day. Over the years, I wondered. I thought about him more than I didn't, likely at some point every day.

I'd think about him with a kid, a girlfriend, as a husband. Maybe another kid, a couple of dogs . . . I'd think about him in the life I always imagined for myself. The one I'd go to in the depths of the night or the height of the day, dreaming about what could be. Lamenting what wasn't.

He doesn't live the reality I thought he would. Even with everything he has and all the resources at his disposal, it's vastly different. Smaller, almost. Calmer.

Even without him saying so, I know his world revolves around Max, and I wouldn't expect anything different.

"What happened?" I ask when the silence becomes too much for my brain to cope. "Max never mentions his mother. He talks about you, Miles, your mum, Clementine, *Birgitta*—" Even though I made peace with her being the nanny, I still choke over her name.

Hendricks doesn't notice. Shreds of the beer label pile on the floor where he's peeled it off and dropped.

"He never sees her. He has no contact with her, and since he was eighteen months old, he's only met her a handful of times. I doubt he'd recognize her."

My mouth opens and closes and opens again. His sadness is tangible, wrapping around the two of us like a weighted blanket. It's truly awful.

"I . . ."

"Yes. It's hard to imagine a woman deserting her baby like that. But motherhood wasn't for her, just the payoff from me."

"What does that mean?"

"I have sole custody of Max, and in return, she receives a very generous monthly stipend—" He lets out one bitter huff.

I gasp. "You pay her for a child she doesn't look after?"

"There's no alternative. She knows I can afford it, and I'd pay a thousand times over if it meant I'd keep Max with me."

"Oh God, Hen, that must have been awful. Who does that?"

There's so much anguish in his next sentence, I feel my heart break. "I tried, Stor. I tried to make it work, but she wasn't interested in anything more than money—"

I believe every word. It's one of the reasons I left so abruptly. I know he would have moved heaven and earth to raise his child with two parents.

I think back to what I was doing while he was being a single parent—surfing, traveling around Australia, drinking—all the things someone in their early twenties is supposed to do.

"What was Max like when he was little?" I ask, more to add levity to the mood, though I can't deny I'm not curious. But missing out on the last six years comes with a heavy amount of guilt.

A smile grows on Hendricks's face, one I've not seen for years. Warm, broad, contagious.

"So cute. Whip smart, and sassy. Walked before he was one, obsessed with horses. When he was teething, the only way to stop him crying was to get him out to the stables. Had everyone wrapped around his finger, still does . . ." He leans back, chuckling.

"I can imagine. He's the same at school."

"Yes." He huffs, amused. "That's what happens when you grow up with five adults and a nanny who all answer to your beck and call."

Leaning in, I whisper, "Don't tell him this, but he's my favorite."

Hendricks turns his head. It's the closest I've been to him since the night we almost kissed over a week ago, and then it was dark. I can see every detail in his face—his blue eyes delicately ringed in navy, the slight bump across the bridge of his nose, the dip in his top lip usually hidden by his beard now quivering in amusement.

"I think he knows."

"Impossible, I'm very discreet." I laugh. "But either way, he's amazing. Though every so often he gets a look I *know* came from Miles."

"You mean this one?" Hendricks's brows draw down and his mouth pulls into a pout. It's uncanny.

I shove him playfully. "*Stop*. You're giving me the creeps."

He laughs loudly before it fades away, and he's quiet again. "It was so fucking hard sometimes. I don't know how I got through it."

"I'm so sorry, Hen. I'm so sorry I wasn't here."

Both our hands are down by our thighs and less than thirty centimeters separates us. My fingers find his, and for a second they flex against mine before he snatches his hand back and smooths it down his thigh. "I got Max. It's all that matters."

I want to say more, but I don't know where to start. God, I'm such a dick. The assumptions I've made . . .

Both our heads shoot up as James Winters, the Burlington family's chief of staff, walks in. A former army major general who used to command thousands of troops, yet has always said his hardest job was corralling the five Burlington children. The last time I saw him, I was nineteen, drunk, and trying to climb up the centuries old wisteria outside Hendricks's bedroom at three in the morning. For some reason, we thought it was a better idea than walking up the stairs.

His eyes land on me before Hendricks, and he doesn't flinch. It could be his army training not to react, but something tells me he already knew I'd be here.

"Hello, Story," he booms, and I realize I'm now fully resigned to being Story again. Sophie was fun while she lasted.

I wave. "Hi, James, how's it going?"

"Very well, thank you." He nods and holds out a toolbox.

Hendricks jumps to his feet and takes it. "You could have sent someone else."

"Your mother wanted me to check you hadn't done any damage."

I snort, grateful for the opportunity to ease the tension. "Only to his ego."

"Do you need help?"

"No," Hendricks snaps as I laugh, "Yes."

"No. We're *fine*," he presses.

James raises an eyebrow, but aside from that, his expression remains as stoic as ever. One summer, I made it my mission to see if I could get him to smile, even the tiniest twitch of his mouth, but nothing. "You know where I am if you need anything."

"Thanks, but we'll be fine."

I raise my beer to James and watch his face. "Pray for us."

But he nods again and walks away.

"Bollocks. Zero for one," I mutter.

Hendricks is riffling through the toolbox, pulling out an electric screwdriver, a hammer, a small bag of . . . nails, maybe. Screws? He lays them all on the floor to the side. "What is?"

"James. He never ever smiles."

He buzzes the hand drill a couple of times. "He does. You're just not funny."

My tone is borderline amused, borderline insulted at the incredibly false accusation. "I'm hilarious. I've been told that many, many times."

"By whom? *Australians*?"

Putting my beer down, I stand to join him. "Um . . . yes."

"That doesn't count."

"Why not?"

He spins his cap around. "Australians aren't funny either."

I frown, arms crossed firmly over my chest, and watch as he picks up plywood A and drills a hole into its edge. I look down at the instruction paper, which he's not bothered to consult. This is *not* going to end well.

"There are plenty of funny Australians . . . Kylie Minogue."

"Singer, not funny." The drill screeches through the wood.

"Russell Crowe."

"Never seen him do comedy. Pass me the screwdriver, will you?" He holds his hand out. "The Phillips head."

I find it the first time, which, for a non-screwdriver aficionado, is impressive. I slap it in his open palm. "Hugh Jackman, Rebel Wilson, Chris Hemsworth—"

"Is that Thor?" He reaches for plywood B.

"Yes."

"A screw, please."

I empty the bag and pass them to him one by one as he needs. "And Nicole Kidman, Cate Blanchett, Margot Robbie—"

"What about them?"

"They're funny."

"You're just naming actors."

"*Funny* ones."

He stands back. "Potato, pota-*toh*."

I've been too busy arguing with him that I barely noticed he's attached three sides of the booth. Enough that it actually *looks* like a booth, with its pre-painted red-and-pink stripes.

"Hey, you've done it."

His eyes slice to mine, narrowed. "I told you I wasn't completely useless at flatpack furniture."

"I never said you were." I nudge him hard enough that he *oofs*. "It's not quite the same as the one Miles destroyed, is it?"

Hendricks shakes his head and laughs. "No."

"Shame. He deserves a little PTSD from that day."

Now that the sides are on, it takes no time to attach the roof, a scalloped-edge design that makes it look like we've built a life-sized—if not cartoony—pink-and-red-striped shop front. It's very kitsch and fifties, and we discover what the red fabric is for. Mrs. Winston, being Mrs. Winston, added drapes.

There's also a packet of self-adhesive decals, including a sign to go across the top, plus a whole bunch of hearts in red and different shades of pink—and applying them is where I make my usefulness known. Hendricks is only too happy to let me.

When we're done, I stand back, hands on my hips, and admire our collective handiwork.

"Not bad at all. Cute, actually."

"I'd go as far as beautiful—"

"Yes." I nod. "Beautiful." But when I look over,

expecting to see Hendricks admiring the stand, he's spun his hat back around and is looking at me. "What?"

"Nothing." He reaches down to the cool box of beer and pulls out two, then hands one over. "Good teamwork for one day."

"Even if the start was rocky."

"As well as the dubious claim about your comedic skills."

"Hey!" I gently nudge my leg against his. "I am funny."

"Okay, we can agree to disagree." He brings the bottle to his lips. "What else were you doing in Australia? Wrestling crocodiles? Barbecuing?"

"Barby at the weekends, no crocs, but . . . I learned to surf." My voice is quieter because I miss it. And it begs the question, do I miss it as much as I would miss Valentine Nook again? "I got pretty good at it. Went every morning before work, in fact."

His eyes skate over me, assessing, appraising. I don't know if he's trying to picture me on a surfboard because it feels more than that. It's slow, deliberate, holding for a beat too long around my hips, and back up. By the time his eyes finally meet mine, there's heat emanating from beneath my skin, and my cheeks are flushed.

If I'm not mistaken, for the first time ever that I'm aware of, Hendricks Burlington has checked me out.

"I'm impressed," he says eventually, raising his bottle to me. "What was the school like?"

"Like Valentine Prep, but bigger." I smile, and the memories of the children running around in the sunshine help me hold my composure. I imagine them breaking from school and heading straight to the beach for a surf. It's still the height of summer there, and here it's dark at four. "I liked it a lot."

"I'm glad you did." His smile pulls up, but it's more pensive than happy. "You worked hard to find a good school."

He looks away again, back at the stand, and tosses the screwdriver he's still holding over and over. The energy between us feels like it's on the verge of turning tense again, or maybe we're already there.

"So secret valentine, huh?"

Hendricks looks at me, bemused. The screwdriver stills. Yes, that's much better.

"What?"

"I believe your son outed you." I waggle my brows, for no reason at all. "Who is it? Annabel Stenson, Lauren MacCauley—or was she just Miles's? Maybe Polly—"

"Stop it, Stor. Don't do that."

I shrug, wishing it hadn't been niggling at me since Max brought it up.

Hendricks sips his beer again. "What about you, anyway?" It's casual, too casual. "Any blasts from the past? Old-school buddies who've recently shown their face?"

I peer at him over the rim of my bottle and shake my head. "Nope."

"None?"

I shake my head.

"Oh," he replies, which is enough for me.

It doesn't take a Mensa membership to know he's talking about Sam Pelling.

I have no intention of letting him know that Sam messaged me on Facebook to say he'd heard I'd returned and asked me to meet, because I never replied. If there's even the slightest chance that Hendricks and I might move into something more than friends, I'm not going to jeopardize it.

But the fact he's brought it up adds to the warmth still circling deep inside my belly.

"Yeah, going to Australia really helped me cull my friendship group," I quip. The ones from Valentine Nook anyway. I still kept up with some uni friends now and again. "I'd been waiting for the right time to do it, and the opportunity presented itself."

He's laughing as he pulls his phone from his pocket. Whoever's name is on the screen wipes all amusement from his face, and before he answers, he turns his back.

"Sienna?"

19

Hendricks

"Don't normally see you in this early."

I smile sheepishly at Claudia. "Couldn't sleep."

She raises an eyebrow in response. She's not buying the bullshit I'm selling this morning.

It's not bullshit, though. Not totally anyway. I woke up exceptionally early after a fitful night. The quality of my sleep has gradually worsened since Saturday, since Sienna called and the countdown to seeing her again after years of no contact began. Because I still don't know what she wants.

But I'll find out today.

The other reason I'm here this early, the one I suspect Claudia has already guessed for herself is the date. February 5th. Story's birthday.

"Nothing to do with my other early morning customer then, I s'pose?"

Yup. She knows.

I pull my best confused expression and peer around, there's not a soul in here. The pre-commute rush hasn't started yet, but once the church clock chimes seven a.m. and The Beanery officially opens, there'll be a queue out the door.

"Don't know what you mean, Claud." I shake my head. "I'll take the two coffees to go, please. And can you put the flapjacks in separate bags . . . on second thought, put two in one bag and one in the other."

As I'm out this early, I may as well take a flapjack home for Max while I'm at it.

Claudia turns to the coffee machine and the familiar whirr and chug of the beans grinding, followed by the drip and scent of brewing coffee fills the air.

"Am I putting six sugars in one of these?" This time, both brows shoot up and she knows she's got me.

I don't know why I'm so reluctant to admit I'm in the coffee shop before the sun's risen buying flapjacks and coffee for Story and me. It's probably got something to do with all the meddlers—Claudia included—who give me a look every time they see us together. A look that says "six years apart and we want to know what's going on."

Because they saw us grow up together, they're as invested in our relationship as I am.

The other reason—one I'm never going to admit—is that I only know Story will be here because I overheard her talking to Claudia at the meeting on Monday.

Apparently, she runs every morning and picks up a coffee from The Beanery on the way home.

This morning, however, I've taken care of the coffees and will be intercepting her regular schedule.

"Yes, please."

She continues in silence, virtually unheard of for Claudia. Every so often she opens her mouth, only to close it again when one of her staff rushes in with a tray of croissants fresh from the oven. By the time she's done with the coffees and bagged up the flapjack, a small queue has formed behind me.

"Wish Story many happy returns." She calls after me as I exit the shop, loud enough that every single person hears.

Not telling Claudia was my first mistake. My second is that I don't actually know which direction Story will come in. It's still dark enough the streetlamps are lit, casting a warm glow over the cobblestones. Down near the Valentine archway, I spot a few people rushing toward the station for the 07.07 train to London, but I don't see anyone who looks like Story.

Deciding that she's more likely to come from the direction of the fountain, I hedge my bets and walk toward it. I'm not halfway there before my chance pays off.

I wait while she sprints past The One True Love, along the pavement, legs powering her forward at an impressive speed.

Tight Lycra hugs her body—every curve, every dip and swell—leaving nothing to the imagination. I've lost count of the number of times I've thought about her like this since we rescued Churchill. It's what's been haunting my dreams during the very little sleep I've had.

That, and the almost kiss.

She's passing Agatha's when she spots me, surprise flashes in her eyes before it's replaced with a little twinkle as she slows to a stop. Pulling out her AirPods, she swipes away the sheen of sweat on her forehead and grips her waist.

"Hey, what are you doing here?" she puffs.

I give her the excuse I gave Claudia. "Couldn't sleep."

I don't want to admit that I'm here especially for her birthday. We might be trying this friends thing on for size, but it doesn't have the same fit it once did—even after spending Saturday together building the kissing booth.

"Is today the day?"

I nod. "Yes."

Her head tilts a fraction, studying me, but her eyes fall onto the coffee cups and the paper bags with The Beanery stamped on the side. "Can I smell flapjack?"

"Nothing gets past you." I grin and hold one out to her. "Happy Birthday, Stor."

She stares, incredulous, then snatches it out of my hand like she's worried I'm going to change my mind about giving her a flapjack. "You remembered?"

"Of course I did." Even when she was in Australia I always remembered. I pass over the coffee. "To dunk it in."

She takes it, eases off the plastic and sticks her nose so close she comes away with a tiny spot of frothy milk. "Mmm. And you put—"

"Six sugars."

Her smile rivals the sunrise. "Thanks, Hen. This is the best birthday present I've ever had."

"You're welcome."

She takes a long sip, followed by another. "So what happens today?"

I shrug. "I don't know, we're meeting at my solicitor's offices as per Sienna's request. We're as prepared as we can be for all eventualities."

"It's going to be okay, Hen," she says, wrapping her free arm around me, squeezing me tight.

My chin drops onto her head, allowing myself to settle against her.

Because this, the hug, breathing her in—even sweaty—until my nervous system relaxes, is exactly what I'm doing in Valentine Nook before the sun's fully risen.

"Are you sure you don't want me to come with you?"

I shake my head. On one hand, no, I'm not sure. On the other, I know bringing Miles with me to Arthur's office to meet Sienna could make things worse.

Or better. It's impossible to decide.

"Let me drive you at least," he pleads. "You're not exactly thinking straight, and you need someone to talk it through with."

"Mum's coming with me because she's got a meeting with the estate anyway. James is driving." I place my hands on Miles's shoulders. He's as tense as I am. "But could you please collect Max from school? Maybe take him to Foxleigh after?"

My twin nods, and even if worry wasn't written all over his face, I'd feel it. It's one of the reasons I don't want him with me. He's much more explosive than I am, and I can't have it jeopardizing anything if Sienna acts like the bitch we all know her to be. The PTSD from two years of dealing with her is real, and I know how to stay calm amid her excessive demands and bullish solicitors.

The quicker this meeting is over, the better. I've barely slept in the four nights since she called and asked for it.

The first night, I didn't go to bed at all. I just sat up all night in the library working through game plans A, B, C, and D while reruns of *The Simpsons* played on the TV. The second night, Miles joined me. The third, I took a sleeping tablet, which didn't work until halfway through the morning of the fourth day. Which is why I didn't sleep that night.

My body clock is fucked. I'm currently eight hours behind. If I were in California for the meeting, I'd be golden.

"Sure, we can do that. He can take Chester for a ride. That'll stop him from asking too many questions. He might even think I'm you." He winks, and I admit it raises a small smile.

"Thanks, Milo. I love you."

"I love you. Remember elbows in, bump hard, and you'll be fine. Especially if the duchess is there channeling her best Rottweiler."

"What's that?"

We both turn as our mother walks in, pulling on a pair of black leather gloves.

"See, she's come prepared for murder. Everything will be fine."

"Miles, what are you talking about? Who's been murdered?"

"Just talking about your gloves, Mother."

She holds her hands up, turning them back and forth. A dignified wave. "These? They're Hermès, why?"

"Don't worry about it, Mum." He slings an arm around her and kisses her cheek. "Just let us know where to bury the body later. James can help. I'm sure he's had plenty of experience with that in his time."

My mother rolls her eyes, though her lips twitch in amusement. "I'm sure it won't come down to that."

"I'm just saying, I'll provide you an alibi."

"Miles, shut up," I snap, though it's more weary than annoyed. "Mum, can we go?"

"Yes, darling. James is bringing the car around." She nods and walks out of the kitchen.

Miles and I follow down the corridor, accompanied by Dolly, Maud, and Hamish the Labradors, because they always have to know what's happening.

I stare out of the huge mullioned windows that line each side to the wide lawns below. Beyond that, fields stretch as far as the eye can see, some dotted with cows, others with horses. Ironically, it's a stunning day, where thunderous clouds would be more suitable. The skies are clear, and the air is crisp. The best kind of day.

But then my eyes catch Max's fire engine on the veranda, and the rage bubbling under my skin becomes too much.

"Fuck." My fingers press into my temples before a migraine sets in.

Miles's hand clamps around my neck, and he pulls me in. "It's going to be okay. This is Max's home."

"Where's Clem?"

"In the gym, but I'll take her on the school run later. Auntie and Uncle to the rescue." Miles victory pumps his fist.

"Thanks. Sorry it's all happening on Birgitta's day

off." I open the front door to where the car is waiting, and my mother is already in the back seat. I slide in next to her. "I'll text you when it's over."

"Ready?" asks James.

I nod and debate asking him to play Ice Cube for good luck, but in the end, we drive in silence. At least until we get to the end of the driveway.

"James said Story MacIntosh was helping you with the Valentine committee."

I glance at him, expecting him to meet my eye through the mirror, but his focus stays straight on the road. He's excellent at pretending not to hear anything, which is why half the time we forget he's there and how one hundred percent of the time our mother knows everything. Because he's told her.

"She was. She's part of the school representation. The choir is singing."

"And I hear she helped you with Churchill the other week?"

I nod. "She found him and called the surgery."

"How is he?"

"Back to normal. I saw him in Alex's garden this morning on the way back from dropping Max."

She chuckles as she looks out the window. "But she's back for good now?"

I sigh. "I don't know, Mum. Why?"

She turns her body toward me, reaching over the center console to take my hand. "Hendricks, Max is six this year. In that time, I've never seen you even remotely interested in meeting a woman—"

"Mum—"

"Don't interrupt. I know the past few years have been a lot, that you haven't wanted to bring someone into your life for Max's sake, and I respect that. I think it's the right thing to do. But . . ."

Of course there's a but.

"I think you've been waiting for Story. And now she's here."

"I—"

"You know I always suspected the two of you would end up together, and truth be told, it made me very nervous. You were so young when you met, and you spent all your time together whenever Miles was off with polo. I can't say I wasn't happy you seemed to drift apart when you went to university. Her mother told me she had a boyfriend in Australia, but she broke it off—"

I frown. "She had a boyfriend?"

"He wasn't the one, apparently. I suspect for reasons similar to why you haven't made the slightest effort to meet someone."

"Mum, c'mon. That's not fair."

Her mouth purses, then she shrugs and goes back to looking out the window. It's her way of saying I'm right and you know it. Maybe it's true. Maybe there are reasons I've stayed single beyond dedicating my time to raising my son.

"All I'm saying is that once we're done with today's mess, maybe this is your chance to be more than Max's father."

We pull up to the law offices with their black

doors, iron railings, and double-sided stone steps.

One of the junior associates is waiting, opening the door for my mother once the car stops. He's equal parts intimidated and sycophantic, a reaction she elicits from most people. Lando receives the same treatment, Alex sometimes, whereas Miles, Clemmie, and I are too far down the pecking order to have any real effect.

"Lord Burlington"—he nods deeply, though it's aimed at my mother—"your Grace." I know that had she not been here, he would have stayed waiting inside, perhaps wouldn't even have bothered coming to greet me until I'd checked in. "It's wonderful to see you again, if not for some unusual circumstances."

"Edward." She smiles, pulling out her uncanny knack for remembering every single person's name, and he simpers underneath it while following close on her heel as she marches inside. "Good to see you again. Now, shall we get on with it? Where's Arthur?"

I glance at the clock. Sienna is scheduled to arrive in five minutes. For the past thirty, we've been going over my legal team's strategy—somewhat tricky, seeing as we don't know what she wants.

"Again," Arthur says, "these are the possible scenarios we've come up with. One, she wants more money. Two, she wants to meet Max. Or three, she's decided she wants a relationship with him, including visitation rights and custody."

"She can fuck off if she thinks she's getting two or three."

My face drops to my hands, fingers digging into my skull. I sit there trying to block everything out while my mother and half a dozen solicitors debate my fate.

It's so hard.

It's so fucking hard to figure out what's right for my son. Whether denying him access to the woman who gave birth to him is for his benefit or mine. What will happen when he's eighteen and discovers I'm the one who blocked a relationship with her because I thought it was for the best?

Is five years old too young for him to decide for himself? If that's even what she wants.

And so we go around and around. The boardroom becomes a pressure cooker as the clock ticks toward the hour and beyond.

"Where is she?" my mother snaps. "She's half an hour late, for goodness' sake. This isn't the sign of a person responsible enough to look after a child."

"Try her again. Where are her solicitors?"

Edward leans across the table and hits redial. Ringing sounds out over the speakerphone until it cuts out. No voicemail, nothing. We leave another message with her legal team.

"She's got fifteen minutes, and then we're leaving. We're not wasting time sitting here for someone we don't want to see in the first place."

We don't need fifteen minutes because in five, my phone beeps with a message.

SIENNA: Sorry, Hendricks. I'm not coming.

20

Story

"Miss MacIntosh, what are you doing?"

At the sound of the voice, my head jerks up, startled, and I hit the drooping branch. "Ouch."

"Are you okay?"

Scooching around on my hands and knees, careful not to knock myself out, I find Max bent at the hip, hands on his knees, and peering at me curiously.

"Hello, Max, what are you doing?"

"I'm wondering what you're doing?"

Nodding, I sit back on my bottom, and the cold, damp ground seeps into me. I already know I don't have anything spare to change into. At least my trousers are black.

"Miss MacIntosh, what are you doing?"

"Right. Yes. Good question, good question. I'm looking for something I lost a long time ago." Lost. Left here on purpose.

"Hmm," he ponders, finger tapping his chin. It's something he does a lot, I've noticed, and it always makes me smile. I get to relive all the little mannerisms

Hendricks had. "Do you want some help?"

"That's very kind, thank you. But I think break time is almost over, so perhaps another day."

There won't be another day because the tree is coming down tomorrow. It was a long shot anyway, and it's not like they were Roman artifacts, but I kind of wanted to see if they'd survived even though I can't remember what we left except the map.

"Okay then." He stands up and holds his hand out. "Do you need help to get up?"

"Oh no, thank you." I don't think he notices me struggling to hold in the laugh as I pull on the branch to get my balance, and it's not that I can't stand, it's that when I'm at my full height of five feet five inches, I hit my head. It's why I crawled in. There was definitely more space in here when we planted the map. But his comment has set off the usual paranoia I have about getting one year older. "Out of curiosity, how old do you think I am?"

He shrugs in that way five-year-olds do when posed a question they've never given any thought to before replying. "Fifty?"

"Do you know how old your daddy is? Or Uncle Miles?"

He shrugs again, shifting around a low-lying branch that I have to fully bend to avoid. "Fifty?"

I cancel the list of anti-wrinkle products I'm mentally compiling. "No, Daddy and I are a little younger than that. Miles is fifty, though."

Max nods, and I almost feel bad, but then I think about Miles's face of objection, and it warms my heart. Childish, yes, but also funny.

The bell rings as we make it out from under the giant

horse chestnut, and play gradually stops, and everyone starts making their way back into school.

"Break time's over, Max, if you want to hurry and change," I say, brushing myself down and freeing all manner of twigs and leaves from my hair.

Crawling along the ground during school hours wasn't the best idea I've ever had, but I've been meaning to do it since Mrs. Benson announced the trees were coming down, and seeing Hendricks this morning reminded me.

Instead of him running off, a little hand slips into mine. "That's okay. I'll walk with you."

"Oh," I say, "thank you."

"Then you're not alone," he adds, moving himself up into the top spot of my favorite children I teach.

In all seriousness, Maxwell Burlington is one of the sweetest, kindest children I've ever had in my classroom. Friends with everyone, conscientious, thoughtful. An old soul trapped in a five-year-old's body.

Whatever Hendricks is doing, he's doing it right, and it's hard to begrudge his reasoning for putting Max first. Especially after everything they've been through. It's what makes the fresh bruises around my heart hurt a little bit less.

"Do you have a dog?" he asks.

I smile. "Yes, I have a golden retriever called Oxford. Do you?"

"We have three. Dolly, Hamish, and Maud. And all the farm dogs, but I don't have any that are just my own."

"Dogs need a lot of looking after," I reply only for Max to nod solemnly in agreement.

"You know that tree you were looking under?"

"Yes."

"I found a treasure map there once."

I stop walking, and Max stops with me, peering up. "Did you?"

"Mm-hmm. Harry and I found it together. It wasn't a real map, though."

"How d'you know?"

"We never found anything."

"What happened to it?"

"It was in a bag with a bunch of boring stuff. Harry kept everything, and I got the bag. I keep my snails in it."

"Snails?"

He nods solemnly. "Yes, Uncle Lando won't let me have them in the house. I keep them in the bag, so he doesn't notice."

It's a struggle to keep a straight face. "That sounds like a good idea."

We start walking again. "Do you know my daddy?"

"I do, yes." I stick to facts because I have no idea what Hendricks has told Max about me, if anything. Max only knows me as Miss MacIntosh, and I'm not about to change that without Hendricks's approval.

"*How* do you know him?"

"Has he ever told you?"

Max shakes his head. "No."

"Did you know your daddy used to go to this school, just like you?"

"Yes, with Uncle Miles."

"That's right, and I was also at this school."

"Oh," he replies, as we reach the main doors along

with the stragglers, reluctant to leave the playing fields. "Do we have singing now?"

I ease my hand from his. "We do."

His head flops back. "Urgh. I *hate* singing."

"Do you think we should double the practice sessions?"

Celeste, for all her eternal optimism, constant smiling and generally cheerful demeanor, looks truly beaten.

"If you think it'll help."

"Nothing will help," she groans, and it's so pitiful that I dissolve into laughter. "It's not funny."

"It is. They're five- and six-year-olds, not King's College Choir."

"Henry tried to stick his triangle baton up Maria's nose," she wails.

"Kids do stupid things," I counter, handing over a cup of tea. "It's a cute choir. They don't need to be perfect, and it would be weird if they were. Everyone's going to love it, especially when they're all dressed up."

She stays slumped in her chair. Even the sip of tea doesn't perk her up.

"Come on, it's nearly the final bell. I'm going back to class to finish getting them ready."

Sixteen pupils sitting at their desks, blazers and caps on, greet me, waiting for the moment they're allowed out. "Thank you," I mouth to Katie, my classroom assistant.

As a last form of order before they're unleashed on their parents, the class lines up in alphabetical order and files out one at a time to wait by the gates. They're not allowed to leave the area until a parent has come to collect them. The usual early-bird parents sweep off with their charges, and the rest congregate and make plans for playdates, coffees, and yoga.

I don't realize how eagerly I'm waiting for Hendricks until Miles walks around the corner with Clementine. Disappointment knocks the wind out of me. Outside of the Valentine meetings and the day we erected the stand, we don't talk much except on drop-offs and pickups. Easing into our new friendship.

"Uncle Miles. Auntie Clem," he cries, taking off before remembering the rules, at which point he grinds to a halt and turns around, yelling, "Miss MacIntosh, Uncle Miles and Auntie Clem are here. I'm going."

Miles catches him at full pelt and swings him in the air. "Hi, buddy, let's go and get in the car."

"Where's Daddy?"

"He went to London with Granny. But guess what, we're going to Foxleigh—"

"CHESTER," Max screams, wriggling until his feet are firmly on the ground again so he can run off.

"Hang on, Maxy." Clementine pulls him back. "I want to say hello to Miss MacIntosh."

Clementine steps toward me, and I wonder if I'm about to be on the receiving end of the same treatment Miles usually aims my way. I was close to Clemmie, but only in the way you're close to your best friend's siblings. When I left Hendricks, she was at university, and our ties were cut. So the hug she yanks me into takes me by surprise.

"It's great to see you, Story."

The tension I'm carrying softens against her. "Good to see you too, Clem. You look really well."

"Thanks, so do you. Let's go for a drink and have a proper catch-up, though. I want to hear all about Australia."

I glance at Miles, who's seconds away from tapping his foot. "Yes, I'd like that."

"Clem, let's go."

She frowns at Miles, who's yet to acknowledge me. "I'll catch you up."

He huffs, like it's my fault Clementine is standing here, but doesn't move away.

"Do you want to take my number, or I can get yours? I can ask Hendricks if he has it."

Miles tuts. It's followed by another long huff.

"Calm down, Milo. No one's stopping you from going to the car. Why are you in such a mood all of a sudden?"

"It's me." I force my voice to stay calm, but honestly, he's such a dick it's amazing to me he shared the same egg with Hendricks. "He's still annoyed he got punched in the face."

I'm facing Clementine, but the words are directed at Miles, and he knows it. The starter pistol goes off.

"You think *that's* why I don't like you? Typical. You're so fucking conceited, Story."

"Uncle Miles, you said a bad word again."

He peers at his nephew. "Sorry, Maxy. Cover your ears."

Clementine gasps, but I'm reeling. "*I'm* conceited?

Miles, there's literally no one on this planet more arrogant than you."

"The difference between you and me is, I own it. I don't pretend I'm Little Miss Perfect, then go around destroying people's lives."

"Miles—" Clementine warns.

"No, Clem, this has to be said—"

She shakes her head, mouths, "Sorry," to me, and holds her hands out to Max. "Max, come on, come and hang with me. Let's go and see if any crocuses are coming up yet."

He dutifully takes it and asks, "Auntie Clemmie, are you fifty?" as they walk away.

Miles steps in closer, enough so that the parents still collecting their children can't hear. He's thoughtful that way. "I was the one who had to pick up the pieces when you left. *Me*."

"You don't get to blame me for everything that happened, Miles. Hendricks was just as complicit. And you can include yourself while you're at it—"

"He was never cruel. He doesn't have a cruel bone in his body, and he would *never*"—his hand slashes through the air—"have cut you out of his life as callously as you did to him. Never."

Guilt bubbles under the surface of my skin. "Why are you telling me all this?"

"Because I want to know what your plan is."

"My plan?"

He stares at me like I'm supposed to know what he's talking about. "Yes, your plan. For being here. For leaving. Your contract is until July, yes?"

My arms cross tight over my chest, and I clench my

teeth. God, this fucking place where everyone knows everything.

"And then what are you doing?" he continues, like he has every right to know.

"Why do you care?"

He scoffs, and his entire face screws up, making it clear he thinks I'm an idiot, and I'm *this* close to punching him. "You're so naive, Story. I *don't* care. I just want to be prepared—"

"Prepared for what?"

"You leaving again. I want to know when it's happening. Your contract is until July, but Hendricks thinks you're leaving at Easter. So which one is it?"

"I'm sorry—" My hip pops, arms tighten, lips roll. "What?"

"Which one. Is. It?" he enunciates, like I'm hard of hearing. I'm hard of something, that's for sure.

"Who says I'm leaving at Easter?"

"Hendricks heard you tell Benson—"

It takes a significant amount of brain-racking to recall the specific conversation I had with Mrs. Benson because I've had many conversations with her over the weeks. And then I remember the first, how Hendricks interrupted us. The day Churchill was stuck, the day we almost kissed, two days before he decided we'd be better off as friends.

Hendricks was right. We are fucked up.

"All my stuff is in Australia. I was only planning to visit here for two weeks. If I'm staying, I need to pack it up, don't I? Unlike you, I don't have lackeys to do the grunt work for me. Us peasants have to do it ourselves."

Only the twitch in his jaw—the same one Hendricks

gets when he's stressed—makes this entire interaction bearable. Being wrong isn't an experience Miles used to enjoy, and it doesn't seem he's gotten any better at it.

"You're *staying*?" he grits out, and the more annoyed he is with himself, the bigger my smile.

"I'm leaving at Easter to pack my things up."

"That's not a yes to my question," he shoots back, like he's caught me in a lie.

"I'm *staying*."

If I hadn't already decided to stay, it would be worth doing so simply to annoy the fuck out of Miles *and* prove him wrong. But I have. It's something I've mulled over since Churchill's accident, and now that I know the reason for Hendricks's abrupt one-eighty, I think I may be able to prove *him* wrong too.

We *can* be more than friends.

"Then I'll leave it up to you to tell Hendricks," he says finally, "but do it soon."

"I'll do it in my own time, Miles."

Eyes narrow, he glares at me, and I glare back. Parents walk past us. A few of them stare because obviously a teacher having a standoff with a parent is weird and, unless they looked closely at Miles's Foxleigh Park jacket with his name embroidered on it, they wouldn't be able to tell who I'm glaring at.

"Don't make me regret telling you this, Story." Miles breaks eventually, and I'm tempted to do a little jig on the spot. Winner. "But for what it's worth, it's only ever been you for him."

He turns on his heel and sprints over to where Clementine and Max are playing, and I stand there watching as the three of them head to the car together,

Miles's words still ringing in my ears.

For what it's worth, it's only ever been you for him.

I can't be sure, but I *think* for the first time ever, in his own weird way, Miles just gave me his approval.

21

Story

Age 21

"Beers: tick, pizzas: one spicy pepperoni—excellent, one pineapple—wrong. Tick."

I'm mid-inhale, breathing in the delicious aroma of cheese, herbs, and carbs courtesy of Tony's, the best pizza place in Valentine Nook, but it morphs into a squeal when Hendricks digs his finger deep into my ribs.

"Watch it. Don't diss my pineapple."

I glance down at his choice, which hasn't changed since he first discovered it ten years ago, wondering if I can force my mind to change. I like pineapple. Even pineapple with cheese. But hot pineapple, with tomato sauce? Nope. Bleugh.

"Who knows, maybe today's the day I'll finally get you to try it."

"I'd rather make out with Miles," I shoot back, and immediately the air stills.

Hendricks's laugh is tight as he tries to brush off the visual or whatever it is I've put in his mind. Our history of him and Miles swapping places doesn't have the best memories.

"I pray hard that day never *ever* happens."

"It won't if I have anything to do with it. And thank God I can tell the difference between you, eh?" I slap a hand against his chest.

"It's a gift I'm thankful for every day," he drawls, and only the sound of my stomach rumbling loud enough to set off an avalanche moves us out of the last weirdly awkward thirty seconds.

Hendricks's brows disappear into the curls flopping onto his forehead. "Okay, impatience. We can eat."

Gathering up the pizza boxes and a couple of beers, we take them through to the living room, where he places them on the sofa. Before then, though, I take in the room, the two candles he's lit, the bowl of popcorn on the coffee table, the blankets piled up on one side.

Because he and Miles have only lived in this cottage for a couple of months, this is the first time I've been here. Now that Miles is playing polo professionally, his mother let them move into it, probably more to save her own sanity from the revolving door of women than anything else. I can't imagine the duchess being too happy about arriving at breakfast only to be greeted by a different girl every day.

I've always wondered what Hendricks would be like living on his own, because during term time in London he's at their family place, staffed twenty-four seven. It's a stark contrast to the boys who live off campus at my university. I wonder daily how they haven't brought back dysentery or the bubonic plague based on the state of their accommodation.

But this? I'm liking what I see, especially when my

eyes drop on a framed photo of the two of us, lying on a picnic blanket trying to shield our eyes from the sun.

It was taken on the hill at Honeysuckle Lane last summer, we'd sat there all day, me with a book to read, him with a book to revise from—Vets 101—or something. We barely spoke except to say things like "pass the crisps" or "want another drink?" It was quiet and perfect, and one of my favorite days of the year.

"Aw, look at us. Hen, you're such a cutie—"

He glances up, confused, until he sees what I'm looking at. "Yeah, I know."

Placing it back on the coffee table, I slide next to him. "I have to be honest, I thought this place was going to be such a mess."

He doesn't even bother to look offended or pretend to. He just shrugs and grins. "Miles is away."

It's believable, it really is. Except I know that Hendricks is equally as messy, so I stand there and wait.

"Okay, fine, the housekeeper was here today. But"—he holds a finger up—"with only me around to mess it up, it takes a little longer to get messy. And I have very little time to do anything right now except revise."

"Literally the only twenty-one-year-old I know with a housekeeper."

"Hey, I'm not turning down the offer just because I'm young. That's ageist."

I hold my hands out, weighing options. "Ageist and lazy. Who's to know?"

"Not all of us are neat freaks." Hendricks takes on a stern expression, or what he thinks is stern. "Do you want to watch your choice of movie or not? Because I'm good with *Die Hard*."

"What movie are we watching?"

"I thought you wanted that new Netflix romcom?" He says it with such disdain, but it's all show. The last time we watched a movie that I picked, he cried like a baby and blamed it on allergies.

"For that"—I smile over at him—"I'll let you have a slice of my pepperoni."

"Planned to anyway." He winks, grabs the one I have in my hand, and takes an enormous bite.

We eat and talk, eat and talk. We go over the exams he's got between now and the end of the term. I tell him about the teaching English abroad program I applied for and haven't heard back from. As the pizza boxes empty and get put to one side, we become a tangle of legs under the blanket. I lean into his side only to slide into the spot he creates when he lifts his arm, and I swear I feel his lips brushing my hair as he takes a deep breath.

Popcorn balances precariously between us, and when Hendricks moves to reach the remote, I have to grab it before it spills.

"Ouch, you're on my hair." I wince when he sits back.

Releasing the end of my ponytail from where it was trapped, he curls it around his fingers, flicking the ends between his fingertips. "It's so long now."

"I know, I'm trying to see how long I can get it."

"Think you'll be able to sit on it?"

"We'll have to see."

He nods, satisfied, and picks up the remote. "Let's start this thing, shall we? I want to see how love develops when you're stuck in the middle of the rainforest . . ." He smirks, reading the synopsis. "Not very practical, is it? Bugs, bug spray. All the creepy-crawlies—"

"Stop ruining it already and start the movie."

He presses play, we get through the familiar bong of the Netflix logo, and then it stops.

"What are you doing?"

He shifts his body around, hands gripping my thighs so I don't move away from him. He stares at me long enough that I'm about to ask if he's having an aneurysm. "I miss you, Stor. I've missed *us*."

Miss you. It's words we say to each other all the time, and they're the truth. We mean it when we say it to each other. But this feels different. This time, they feel heavier, more resolute.

"I miss you too." My head drops to the side. "What's going on?"

"It feels like there's always been something coming up lately that's kept us apart. We haven't spent more than a day together all year. I've been away, you've been away, exams, *boyfriends* . . ." He nudges me with a grin. It's teasing but *not*. He has no proof that I've had a boyfriend, because I've never told him. He's fishing.

I've known Hendricks a long time, and the tic under his eye is his tell. A loaded question disguised by the casual, breezy tone.

I know he won't ask, just as I won't ask him, because we don't talk about other people. If we pretend they don't exist, then they don't.

But he wants to know if I'm single.

The ugly truth, the one I only admit to myself in the dark of the night, is that any boyfriend I've had has only been fleeting, *casual*. Because deep in my soul, I've been waiting for Hendricks, and as harsh as it might sound, even if I wasn't single, I would end things in a heartbeat if it meant we finally got our chance.

"I don't have a boyfriend," I volunteer. "Haven't in a long time."

His head bobs, his mouth rolls, and his brain ticks. In that order. "Oh yeah? No Pelling hanging around lately?"

I sigh, frustrated. How does he not know it's only ever been him for me? Sam Pelling has never and will never hold a candle to the guy in front of me. My best friend. The only boy I've loved for as long as I can remember.

"Hendricks, c'mon." I shift around, scooching onto my knees, changing the subject. "How long's it been since we did this?"

"A couple of months, maybe. It was Easter, after Miles and I got back from skiing? We spent the weekend in the farmyard with the new calves."

I shrug, even though I absolutely know that it was then. "My point is, we've barely seen each other. I know we talk every day, but it's going to be summer break soon." I hold my hand out to him. "Let's make a deal right now that we spend as much time as possible together this summer. Waterfall, fields . . ." I wink. "Rolling down the hill on Honeysuckle Lane—"

Quick as lightning, his fingers reach out. This time, he digs right into the spot he knows will have me crying, laughing, and waving a white flag of defeat within seconds. "I'm *not* rolling down that fucking hill."

"Okay . . . okay . . . *stop*. No hill. But the rest?"

He settles back, grin wide on his face, dimples on show as he pulls my legs across his lap again. "The rest we can do. Still got that blue bikini for the waterfall?"

My internal temperature kicks up a few degrees. "I'm sure I can dig it out of a drawer somewhere."

I hold my hand back out. "Let's make this our summer, deal?"

He takes my hand and shakes it. "Deal. Nothing's getting in our way."

22

Hendricks

"We could have literally chosen any other shade of pink—"

"Al, stop complaining. It brings out the blue in your eyes—"

"It's the color of my face—"

"All I see is a face of blood, sweat, and tears. But here . . ." Miles tosses a bottle of water to Alex. "Now, can you please pay attention to what I'm saying so we can win this fucking match? You're dragging down my level of play."

To anyone passing, they might think Miles is joking, but we know better.

There's nothing that Miles takes more seriously than winning and how he plays. When we watch him during the regular polo season, we pay such close attention to the match, not because we can't bear to miss a second, but because it's better for our mental health not to miss a second of Miles. Which was his best goal? What did we think of his defensive play? How did he stack against his opposing number?

A pop quiz at the end of each match isn't unheard

of.

"Miles, I don't need to remind you that this is a charity match."

"No, Lan, you don't. But that doesn't mean I've dressed my ponies in head-to-toe pink and plaited their tails with little red hearts for nothing. I expect to win."

Alex gives up looking at himself in the mirror and scoffs. "Your grooms plaited, you mean."

"Actually," Miles snaps, "I did Chester. Now, for the *third fucking time*, can we please get back to discussing what's important?"

Alex smirks behind a sip of water. Lando's trying to hide his by dropping his head, and wipes his hands across his muddy jodhpurs, and I just sit back and grin. I don't see the point in hiding anything. We all know how Miles gets, and as much as Alex and Lando love winding him up as the worst loser in our group, they also hate losing. So I don't know why they woke up this morning and chose violence.

"Thank you. Now . . ." Miles's jaw ticks, and he exhales loudly through his nose. "Alex, why is your hand up?"

Alex lowers it and shrugs. "I thought it was the correct etiquette for this situation—"

"Al—"

"Just wanted to check you know that the other team is objectively, not to mention, *statistically*, better than ours."

"Yes. I know that—"

"But it seems like you *don't*—"

"I do. They have four international players, all ranked between seven and ten goals. We have you three and me. None of you has played since our last charity match."

If Miles were the type of person to go red, he would be rivaling a tomato right now, but instead, his jaw is clenched so hard that he's in danger of breaking a couple of molars. Lando dissolves into braying laughter.

I reach out a reassuring hand to Miles and squeeze his shoulder.

"C'mon, Milo, it's only halftime. We've got three more chukkas to go. We can easily level the score, given we're only four goals down."

He takes a deep breath. It's one of those breaths therapists advise you try while counting to ten.

"We won't do anything if you don't. Fucking. Listen."

I stare at our older brothers. "You two, shut the fuck up. Let Miles speak."

Lando and Alex sit up straight. Alex takes a second to compose himself. I catch Lando rolling his eyes, but they thankfully stay silent.

"Miles, please go ahead."

"Thank you, Hen. As I was trying to say, we need to change our play. Hen, you ride Chester this chukka, and I'm taking Clover. Alex, you have Owl, and Lando can take Lemondrop. She'll help you score with your eyes closed. And we're switching positions." He stands up, gesturing Lando to do the same, and tugs his shirt over his head. "Give me yours."

Lando, who I'm certain wasn't even listening to a word Miles said, visibly recoils at the suggestion. "Do I have to?"

He tosses the shirt onto Lando's lap. "Yes. Otherwise, we'll have the wrong numbers. I'm playing four now, you're one."

"Can't we just tell people?"

"No."

"Lan—" I warn.

With a heavy eye roll and a grumble about being very sweaty, Lando whips his shirt off.

I don't know if it's going to help our game, because wherever Miles isn't on the field is where we're going to be weakest. On the other hand, it might be the strategy change we need. Number one, where Miles usually plays, is the most offensive player, the attacker, the goal scorer. Number four, where Lando's been playing, is the defender, the guardian of the goal.

Unfortunately for him, his guarding skills are no match for someone who's paid to score. It might be for charity, but since we rode onto the field, it was clear only Alex, Lando, and I came for fun. The rest came to win.

While they change, I check my phone again. I can't help it. A fresh wave of anxiety pushes aside all the adrenaline from the first two chukkas. Just like it has been for the past week, the screen is blank.

Sienna hasn't returned any of my calls.

She hasn't returned the solicitor's calls.

Her legal team is nonresponsive. It's become a waiting game that's making me increasingly nervous with each passing day. More than I care to admit.

In fact, the only time it hasn't been in the back of my mind is when I was being chased by half a ton of Argentinian pony with a very determined rider on his back.

Alex slides along the bench to me. "Still nothing?"

I shake my head. "No, and I don't understand. She

called so frequently, but it's been crickets since the meeting she didn't turn up to."

"Hang in there. It'll be okay."

I wish I shared his enthusiasm, but I don't. And I don't want to voice the nightmares I'm having every night, when I wake up drenched in sweat from boiling rage and panic at the idea of losing Max.

"What about Story? Is she here today?"

I nod, a smile appearing on my face.

Two days ago, at drop-off, she handed me a paper bag with a "Good morning" and no further explanation. When I got back to the car, I opened it to find a freshly baked flapjack. After a night filled with dreams I don't want to become reality, it kept me going through a busy morning checking the pregnant heifers.

Yesterday, it was a jam donut, which I swapped for a chocolate croissant I'd brought her.

Knowing Story's stance on polo—too fast, too shouty, too *Miles*—I hadn't expected her to come and watch, but as we galloped onto the field for the second chukka, I spotted her, and she wasn't alone. Beside her, her mum, and Oxford, the golden retriever, were my sister, Holiday, and Max. It was a foursome I didn't know I needed to see—them laughing together while Max swung his mallet around.

I'm convinced the look on Story's face when she spotted me is the sole reason I scored two goals. The only two goals of the match so far.

"Oh, bud, I know that look . . ."

I focus back on Alex. "What?"

"I'm here when you want to talk," he says, patting me on the knee.

"Right." Miles snaps our attention. "Everyone clear on what they have to do?"

Lando's too busy fidgeting in Miles's sweaty shirt to respond. But I nod, and Alex resumes his role as Miles's tormentor.

"Remind me which one's our goal again?"

"Alex, if we lose this match, I'm holding you entirely responsible." He fumes, jabbing a finger in Alex's direction before storming out to the stables where our four ponies are waiting patiently and yelling, "Pull your fucking finger out."

"Why d'you keep winding him up today?"

Alex shrugs. "Because it's funny. He seems edgier today, and I thought it would loosen him up."

"C'mon, you know how badly he wants to win. This is the first match since he went up to nine. He's putting so much pressure on himself to get back to ten in the summer." I take Clover's reins from the groom and check Miles isn't in earshot. "Plus, I heard someone say Santiago Torres is here."

Alex stops, his foot halfway to Owl's stirrup. "*What*?"

"I don't know, I haven't seen him, and I don't know if Miles knows," I spit out before Alex can bombard me with questions. "One of the grooms said they saw him."

"Who let him in?"

"An international polo player at a polo ground? They probably opened the front door."

"I thought Miles had banned him from here."

"Evidently not." I vault onto Clover without thinking and it takes all my strength to keep her calm. "But I can't believe he'd dare show his face here. He knows Foxleigh is Burlington property."

It's a testament to Miles's skills that he makes riding her look easy.

Clover is the equine equivalent of a Formula One race car, revving up for the moment she's allowed to gallop onto the field. I can feel her adrenaline pumping through her while I try to avoid being reared off before we get out there.

She's also Miles's favorite pony, and he never lets anyone ride Clover. That's how much he wants to lift the cup later.

Alex waits patiently on Owl, a deceptively cunning and brave little pony who never shies away from getting involved in the scrum, until Clover is standing still. "Okay, fine, but only until I find out if Torres is really here."

"I can live with that."

Miles's strategy works.

By the fifth chukka, we even the score, and Miles's mood drastically improves. It's helped by Alex and Owl, powering down the pitch ten seconds before the bell, hooking the opposing number three, a guy called Billy Walsh, who plays with Miles on the England team, and smashing the ball between the goal posts from the thirty-yard line.

For the final chukka, Miles swaps us all out again. I move onto Messiah, a gallant Welsh cob, and Miles takes Clover, who barely worked up a sweat in the fourth. Seeing him on her back, I almost feel bad for riding her, like a Sunday school driver behind the wheel of an eight-hundred-and-nineteen-horsepower, twelve-cylinder Ferrari Spider.

With Miles, she unleashes her full potential, thundering up and down the field, bumping any pony in her way until she can bring Miles in front of the goal, where, courtesy of his left hand, they score. And we move into the lead, where we stay until the final bell is rung.

The Foxleigh Park crowds go wild, even more than usual, when a home game is won.

Confetti cannons explode, showering everyone in pink and red hearts. The slight breeze in the air blows them over the pitch and beyond.

"He's going to be unbearable." Alex shakes his head after we witness Miles galloping around on Clover, taking her over to the crowds and his fan base, screaming and hanging over the boards, who never miss a chance to see him play.

He's still signing autographs and taking selfies, all of which include Clover, by the time Lando, Alex, and I have handed our reins over to the waiting grooms. For February, it's unusually mild, the clear skies and bright sunshine giving a deceptive impression that it's warm, but we grab our body warmers anyway and make our way out.

"Don't forget we have the trophy ceremony in twenty minutes. Lando, where's Holiday?" Miles barks after extracting himself from the autograph hunters.

"I don't know, Miles. I just came off the field." Lando yawns.

"Right . . . well, don't forget. See you over there."

Grabbing Alex's shirt before he starts baiting Miles again, something that will end up lasting all weekend, I tug him out of the stables. Lando takes off in the direction of the podium, though I suspect he's going to find Holiday rather than ensure he's not late for presentation.

I turn to Alex, dodging a particularly loud group of women outside the stable area wearing pink shirts with Miles's face on the front. "Where's Haven?"

"She said she'd be with Mum in the stands. I'm going to head over there."

"I'll come. It seems the most likely place to start looking for my son."

Once I've found Max, then I can look for Story.

As fast as the second half was, whenever we reset, I found myself drifting to the boards searching for her, but she'd moved. I haven't seen her since the halftime break, and now that I don't have polo to distract me, I'm getting restless. Alex pushes through the crowds ahead of me, shaking hands with everyone who stops us, while I'm peering around for any resemblance.

By the time I make it up to the Burlington stands, I still haven't spotted her through the sea of pink and red.

"DADDY."

I catch Max a split second before he pummels into me, somehow managing to avoid the polo mallet he's still swinging when I lift him into my arms.

"Hi, bud." I kiss him, a grin instantly appearing on my face as I take in his obvious excitement. "Did you enjoy the game?"

"Yes. Clover played so good in the fourth chukka. And Uncle Miles. And Uncle Alex . . . um . . ." Max peers at him, head tilted in sympathy. "It's not easy to play polo, is it?"

He's so sincere with his question and encouragement

of Alex's skills on the field, it's impossible not to smile. "No, Maxy, it isn't. But I still scored."

He nods gravely. "Yes, Owl is very steady and reliable."

Alex's eyes flick to mine. "Where is he getting this from?"

"Hey, he tells it how it is." I laugh. "Max, where's Granny?"

He jabs a finger toward nothing particular. Usually only used by members of the family and guests, it's much quieter and private, so it only takes a quick scan to know Story's not up here either. I do find my mother, though, half obscured by a pillar and talking to one of her friends while holding Everly.

"Ah, that's my daughter. Now I need to find my fiancée."

"Hello, darlings," our mother croons. "Well played, all of you. Max and I were cheering along. Exciting to have a win today."

"Where's Haven?" asks Alex, kissing Mum's cheek and relieving her of Everly.

"And Clemmie?" I add.

"They went down to the podium to see Holiday. And yes, Story was with them before you ask."

If my mother high-fived, Alex would be meeting her halfway. I wait until they're done with their gleeful chuckles.

"Al, you coming? Don't want to be late."

"Daddy, can I come?"

"Of course, bud. We're all going. Even Granny."

Like wasps around a honey jar, the crowds have

swarmed away from the field toward the podium by the champagne tent. Aside from seeing our team—*Miles*—crowned as the winners, most people are hoping to spot Holiday, Lando's girlfriend, presenting the trophy. While the matches during the summer attract a host of A-list celebrities, we don't normally have anyone of her caliber at the Valentine charity match.

"There's Miss MacIntosh," screams Max.

I don't even notice the direction he's pointing before my entire body spins around, and I spot her five feet away smiling at us. She's wrapped up in a thick, high-neck jacket, and since halftime, seems to have acquired a pink Foxleigh Park cap that's pulled low on her forehead. It's no wonder I didn't spot her, camouflaging herself among the hordes.

All at once, the noise quietens, and everything calms, except my heartbeat.

I wish I could say I was immune to her, but now I know what Alex meant earlier. After six years of no contact, it's astounding how quickly my heart has remembered her, and keeping my distance becomes more impossible every day.

"Hey," she breathes out, landing a playful punch on my shoulder. "Congratulations, champ. What a match. I'm regretting never watching you play before."

Her smile is so broad, and I stare into the warmth of her eyes. "Can't be right all the time."

"Eh . . ." She laughs, turning to Max. "How's it going? Having fun?"

"Where's Oxford?" Max asks, though it's more of a demand.

"He's gone home now. It's a long day for him to be out in the cold."

"I could bring him a blanket next time if you like?" He smiles, and my heart grows ten times in the process. Especially when Story looks at me, her face screwing up to say "He's the sweetest" and I'm so fucking proud to be his father.

"That's so kind. I'm sure he'd love that."

A big arm falls around my shoulder. "Hen, ready to come and meet your fans?" drawls Miles, turning to Story. "Hello, Story. It's good to see you here. Thank you for coming to support us today."

I'm not sure who's more surprised, me or . . .

"You're welcome, Miles. Happy to be here. Well played today. Excellent polo skills and all that."

"Thank you, Story. I appreciate it."

Maybe Miles is already drunk. Perhaps they both are, because I'm the only one who's finding this interaction both weird and rare.

"Hen . . . coming?"

I nod, bemused. "Hey Maxy, can you stay with Miss MacIntosh while I'm awarded our trophy?"

Max takes her outstretched hand, and we walk up to the platform where Holiday, Lando, and Alex are waiting.

"What was that?" I whisper to Miles as we step up.

"What?"

"You know what."

"Just being friendly to our supporters."

Cameras flash violently the moment Holiday joins us, handing over the trophy to Miles, the captain of our team. We stand against the press boards and pose for pictures. We laugh. We pop the champagne, and most of Alex's bottle sprays onto Miles. And then, before everyone departs, Miles announces that we've raised over fifty thousand pounds for our local hospice, the chosen recipient of the match this year.

Alex grabs Miles's neck, pulls him in, and plants a kiss on his cheek. "Well done, Milo. Good work today. Proud of you, mate."

I'm giving it until supper for their truce to last, and decide to leave them to their love fest, and return to Max and Story. I'm now free. I have the whole afternoon to do exactly what I want. And what I want is to spend it with Story.

"Shall we go get a drink?"

Story nods and smiles. "I'd love to."

I hold my hand out to Max, who's charging around in front of us, riding his polo mallet. "Come on, polo player, let's go."

Max is less enthused about going to the bar. "Where's Granny? She said we could go to the stables."

"I'm not sure."

Max tugs on my arm. "Let's find her. Please. I want to see Chester."

I turn to Story and grimace. "Sorry, he'll only go on and on *and on* about it. Why don't you go to the bar and order? I won't be long. I'll have whatever you're having. Put them on my tab."

"I'm drinking a banana daiquiri with a little straw." She smiles evilly.

"Delicious. One of my five a day," I shout behind me as Max pulls me away.

With Max tugging me along, it takes five minutes to find my mother, and another ten to head back to the path on the way to the drinks tent. I don't know why I didn't suggest going to the box, away from the crowds, where Story and I could have a perfectly *friendly* catch-up, but I wanted us to spend time together without the gawking eyes of my family.

A week ago, we—*I*—assembled the booth, and now I'm spending another afternoon in her company. I'm seriously wondering how I can turn Saturdays with Story into a "thing" when I stop dead and focus on two people a couple of meters ahead of me.

There's no way I'm looking at what I think I'm looking at.

They're so deep in conversation with barely an inch between them that they don't even notice me approaching until I'm two feet away and yelling in their ears.

"What the hell is going on?"

Clementine gasps, lets go of Santiago Torres, and jumps back. Though, as she's already against the wall, she doesn't get too far.

"Clem, what the fuck are you doing?" I don't wait for a response. Instead, I pull her out of the way, shielding her with my body as much as I possibly can. "You know who this is?"

Not waiting for a response, I turn to the other member of this cozy little party. "Torres, I don't know what you're playing at, but stay the hell away from my sister."

I'm so incensed that it doesn't occur to me that Clementine didn't seem to be resisting him. Quite the opposite.

"Burlington," he drawls, in his distinct, thick American accent, "I have no beef with you, but if you touch Clementine again, you and me are gonna have a problem."

My eyes widen. I'm being glared at by a guy who looks like I've just slept with his mother and embezzled his life savings, and I don't think I've ever been so confused in my entire life.

"*Beef*? What are you, the fucking Mafia?" I do my best to glare back, but truthfully, I'm no match. This guy nails the Goodfellas vibes. "Get the fuck out of here. You too, Clementine. You're lucky it was me who walked into whatever the fuck this is . . ."

From behind me, where I'm still trying to shield her, my sister yells loud enough that my ears ring, "Stay out of my life, Hendricks. I didn't ask for your opinion."

"*Didn't ask my*—have you gone insane?" I stare into her bright blue eyes. "Are you high?"

She spins around, freeing herself. "Who knows, Hen? Maybe I am." And as I watch my sister storm away, she flips me off.

I might have no idea what's going on, but I know I don't like the way Torres's gaze follows Clementine's departure. Don't like it one bit. When they come back to mine, my fists ball. Miles is right. He's dangerous.

"I mean it, Torres. You have no business being here. Stay the hell away from Clementine and stay the hell away from Miles. In fact, while we're at it, stay the hell away from my entire family. And Foxleigh."

He nods, contrite, almost as his hands rub together. Hands covered in tattoos. "One thing you'll learn about me, Burlington, is that I don't make promises I can't keep."

It's taking all my patience to remain calm. "Is that so? Well, neither do I." I smile, one that doesn't even come close to reaching my eyes. "After what you did to Miles, I *promise* that if I see you again, I will return the favor."

I wait. And wait some more until Santiago Torres eventually does the sensible thing and decides to walk away. The moment he's out of sight, I sprint off. Clementine's vanished, but I track down two of the Foxleigh Park security and instruct them to escort Torres off the premises.

I'm still reeling when I return to the bar, my brain trying to reason with what I *know* I saw with what I'm hoping I *didn't* see, but I can't shake the feeling I've just witnessed infidelity. Not a one-night stand either, the twenty-five years with a secret lover type.

"Hendricks. Hen—"

I follow the sound of Story's voice, her hand waving in the air until she comes into view, and find her laughing along with the guy standing next to her.

Fuck my life.

"Great match today, Hendricks."

"Thanks, Pelling. Appreciate you coming to support."

Story holds a beer out. "They were all out of banana daiquiris."

"Damn." I manage a grin, though I suddenly feel incredibly tired.

The adrenaline from the match has worn off, and teenage jealousy rears its ugly head to mingle with whatever the fuck's going on with Clemmie. Not to mention Sienna. I've officially reached my capacity for tolerance, and I don't have the energy for a fight, nor the inclination to stand here and pretend to tolerate Sam Pelling and Story joking together.

I hated it ten years ago. I hate it now.

I put the beer down. "I'm sorry, guys, I need to go. Have a fun afternoon, Stor. Good to see you again, Sam."

I've barely moved through six feet of people swarming the bar before she catches up to me.

"What's the matter with you?"

"I'm sorry, I really am. I can't do this right now. I'm not going to tell you who to hang out with, I'm not going to tell you who to be friends with, but . . ." I tug on my neck, trying to keep my tone neutral, and I fucking hate that I'm this person when I have no right. I know I have no right, but I can't help myself. "Why does it have to be with him? There are plenty of other people we were at school with. What about the girl you teach with? Anyone but him, Stor. Please."

"He was passing by and said hello. I'm not going to be rude, Hen. He's done nothing wrong."

I sigh. "Honestly, I don't care. I don't like him. I've never liked him—"

She pops a hip, and I know I'm in for it. "You're a hypocrite, you know."

"Oh yes, how so?"

"You don't want me, but you don't want anyone else to have me."

"I never said I didn't want you, Stor." Gently tucking my finger under her chin, I push her mouth—open with indignation—closed, then I lean down and kiss the top of her head. Breathing in the soft floral notes of her perfume until I'm lightheaded, it takes all my self-discipline not to throw her over my shoulder and carry her out with me like the Neanderthal I clearly am. "I never said I didn't want you."

23

Story

It's bittersweet to watch Hendricks walk away.

Bittersweet and fucking frustrating.

Sam's still standing exactly where I left him. Of course he is, because where else would he be?

"Everything okay?" He takes a long draw of his beer.

"It will be." I punch him playfully on the arm, the way friends do, the way he could infer no other meaning from. "Sorry to do this too, but I need to leave—"

"I figured." He nods, his mouth pulling downward. "I never could compete. It was good to bump into you, anyway, Story. Let me know if you're ever in London."

I don't bother with a protracted goodbye because Hendricks already has a minute head start on me. "Thanks, Sam. See you around."

I rush out of the drinks tent, figuring he can't have gotten too far, except I fail to account for the second match of the day ending. It's the Foxleigh Park under 21s, and the grounds are flooded with late teens, big poofy hair tumbling down their backs, wearing too-tight *everything*.

"Fuck."

I make a snap decision to head to the Burlington stand, though in hindsight, it's the most likely place he'll be.

Dodging around several groups of girls that bring back all forms of nostalgia, I rush past the presentation podium where the winning team is accepting their trophy. Deciding to take a shortcut via the car park, I'm too busy wondering if this is a good idea to pay much attention to a first glance of a solitary figure sitting in the doorway of a fire exit, face blotchy and swollen.

Only a double take has me grinding to a halt.

"Clemmie?" She looks like she's having a hard time focusing through the tears to realize who's talking to her. "It's me, Story."

"I know." She hiccups.

"What are you doing?"

"Hiding."

Opening my purse, I pull out the pack of wet wipes I always carry with me. They've been in there such a long time that the packet is curled at the edges, the prints worn off, and they're no longer wet, but I shove them toward her anyway. "Here."

She's skeptical, but phlegmy beggars can't be choosers when it comes to nose-blowing paraphernalia. "Thanks."

The doorway she's sitting in is so small I debate squeezing in next to her, but I do it anyway. Sure enough, it's tight.

"Who're you hiding from?" I ask, freeing my elbow.

She pulls out a dry wet wipe and blows hard. "My horrid brother. Men in general, take your pick."

Doesn't exactly narrow it down. Though we can

start with the four she's related to. My money's on Miles. "Miles?"

To my surprise, she shakes her head. "His evil twin."

Given her state, I have to admit it takes me a second. "Hendricks? *Hendricks*?"

More surprisingly, she nods her confirmation. "Hey, d'you want to get out of here? I've had enough of polo players for one day."

If we weren't rammed in so tight to this tiny doorway, I'd slump. Who knows where Hendricks is, but getting out of here and away from polo players doesn't sound like a bad idea at all.

"Yes. I'd love to."

After some very unladylike maneuvering, wiggling ourselves from side to side before one of us frees, we find Clementine's car and leave.

"Where shall we go?"

"The pub?" Clementine suggests. "Everyone's at the polo anyway, so The One True Love will be quiet, and we can sit by the fire."

She's exactly right, and when we walk in, Eddie takes one look at Clementine—whose face is less wet than it was twenty minutes ago, but no less blotchy—and jerks his head toward the back room. We're seated two minutes before he brings over two glasses of water, a bottle of wine, and glasses.

"You two look like you're up to no good."

"Yet you choose to fuel us with alcohol?" I quip.

"I can take it back." He reaches for the bottle, but I snatch it out of the way before he can.

"No, no, we want it. We love you, Eddie. Thank you, thank you."

"Hmm." He peers over his bifocals at us. "I trust when you're done, you'll tell me who I need to ban from my pub?"

"Count on it. Thanks, Eddie."

He heads back behind the bar, though I know he'll be keeping an eye on us for as long as we're in here. Picking up the bottle, I pour out two glasses, slide one toward Clementine, and take a too large sip from mine.

"Do you want to talk about it?"

Her lips roll and unroll. Her fingertips run up and down the stem of the glass.

"I'm a virgin."

Sitting back in the booth, I stare at Clementine, who's still focused on the glass of wine. I must have misheard her, so I lean forward and ask, "Could you repeat that?"

"Never would have guessed, right?" She laughs, without humor. "Shocked?"

"No," I reply truthfully. "But that's not why I'm *surprised* it's your answer. I'm just not understanding why that's what's got you this upset." I gesture to her face, usually so stunning, perfectly clear, bouncy skin, bright blue eyes the same as all the Burlingtons. Honestly, it might be the worst I've ever seen her look. "Also, I'm not clear what that has to do with Hendricks."

"How long have you got?"

"Clem, I've just returned to a place I ran away from six years ago. All my things are in Australia, I have no friends left here, and the only guy I've ever loved doesn't want to know me. I have all the time in the world." I try to brush it off with a dry, merciless laugh, but it's all true, and my throat tightens.

God, my life sounds bleak.

Clementine reaches across the table, placing her hand over mine. "I'm your friend, Story."

I swallow down the surge of emotion from my brief pity party speech. "Thank you, but let's get back to you."

She downs her glass of wine and immediately pours another. It's going to be that kind of night.

"A few years ago, during the summer after my first year of university, I went traveling with a couple of girlfriends. We went all the way through Central America together before I left them and went to meet Miles in Florida. He was playing polo there, and I was getting a ride home with him. He flies all his ponies private, so it was easy for me to jump on the plane too."

I nod and sip.

"I watched the finals of the tournament, which he won, and afterward waited for Miles to get his shit together." She takes a big sniff and a deep breath before her tears start up again. "He was ages—like *hours*—but I had a book, so it didn't matter. But then this guy walked into the lounge where I was and sat down next to me. It started small, what was I reading, did I watch the polo etcetera, etcetera, but then we moved onto wider subjects—traveling, school. And we talked, and talked, and *talked*. I totally lost track of time until one of Miles's grooms came to find me. So I said goodbye, and he asked for my number. I thought I'd never hear from him because *obviously* we live in different countries, but he already texted me before I'd gotten on the plane."

My chin rests in my palm, and I let out a dreamy sigh. "Wow."

"The texting turned to phone calls and FaceTime. We talked about everything. He grew up in New York, but he's half American, half Argentinian. His dad left when he was young, and his mum raised him, so we have that in common. When I returned to university, the biggest bunch of flowers I've ever seen in my life was waiting for me."

"Then what happened?"

"It went on for months, and even though we were talking every night, we'd only met that one time. I was stuck revising, so we decided he'd come to England for the weekend. It was clear things between us were going to progress to sex, and I told him I hadn't done that before—"

"Okay—"

"The weekend he was due to come to England, Miles was playing in a friendly tournament in Palm Springs between England and America, as part of the preseason selection. He was involved in a terrible accident and placed in a coma. Hendricks and my mum flew out. The doctors weren't sure he would ever be able to play again—"

My hand flies to my mouth as Clementine wipes away her tears. "I never realized. That must have been so scary. Fuck, poor Miles. Poor Hendricks."

She nods, her jaw flexing as she tenses. "The other rider, the one that caused it, had been on a mission to get Miles after he got him fined for an illegal bump the summer before. This time, he was given a two-year suspension."

"Shit. I never realized." Not that I ever give Miles any thought at all, but he's clearly been through a rough few years too. "Anyway, carry on with the dream guy—"

"Have you heard of a player called Santiago Torres?"

I shake my head. "I missed a lot in Australia."

"When Mum and Hendricks flew to Miles, I went back to Burlington to be with Lando, Alex, and Max. He was only two, and Hendricks had only just been awarded full custody, but Miles is his twin, you know. They hurt together."

I nod, knowing only too well of their connection.

"Lando and Alex were distraught, so was I. We did everything we could to keep Max's life normal without his dad . . ." Her eyes close. "Among all the early chaos, being kept up to date by the doctors while Hendricks and Mum were flying over, I didn't ask details. But later we were having dinner . . . and that's when Lando and Alex told me what happened. Santiago Torres had been crossing the line all match, which is illegal, but it was his foul hook that brought Miles down. His pony tripped, Miles was thrown off, and his leg got tangled. He was dragged up the sideline until his teammate caught him . . ."

Again, my empathy for what Miles has been through, what Hendricks has been through, what they've all been through, spills over, and I'm wiping away the tears just like Clementine. "I'm so sorry, Clem . . . what a fucking arsehole this Torres guy is. I hope he's rotting somewhere cold and damp."

"He's not." It's so quiet I barely hear it, and she takes another glug of wine.

"Fuck. How d'you know?"

"I saw him—"

"I'm so sorry. And what happened to the sexy guy? Did he still come over?"

She shakes her head. "No, I blocked him from everything—social media, my phone, everything."

I frown, maybe I've had too much wine, because I

feel like I've missed a key part of the story. "Clem, I'm not following—"

"The guy I met in Palm Beach, the man I had fallen in love with through our calls every night, is Santiago Torres, the player who nearly killed Miles."

It's a plot twist I don't see coming. My jaw nearly unhinges it drops so quickly. Clementine's eyes shoot up when I gasp.

I reach out and grab her hand because, above everything, it's clear how distressed she is. "Does anyone know?"

She shakes her head. "I've never told a soul. I've tried to forget him, I've tried to sleep with other guys, but I can't bring myself to. I can't do it, Story. I still love him. We shared things we never shared with anyone."

I'll say one thing, Clementine's story is putting my marginally fucked-up situation with Hendricks into a much more flattering light. I also wrote the book on men you shouldn't be in love with.

"Clem. I . . . um . . ." I'm actually lost for words.

Picking up the bottle, she tops up our glasses, emptying it. We're definitely going to need another one.

"I saw him today."

"Who?"

"Santi, he was at the match—"

I blink, not sure I heard correctly. Because this Torres guy being at Foxleigh Park where Miles plays isn't just crazy, it's a death wish.

"Sorry, *what*?"

"His letters, flowers, emails . . . I can ignore them, but since his suspension ended last summer, he's popped up at tournaments when I'm least expecting. Always when Miles is playing."

"He's still contacting you?"

"All the time. Begging me to speak to him."

"Jesus, Clem."

"I finally gave in today, said I'd listen if he agreed to leave me alone after, but then Hendricks caught us. He was so mad, and I don't blame him—"

"This was this afternoon?"

She nods. I could likely time it down to the minute. Directly before he came to find me in the champagne tent. I knew something wasn't right with him, even considering his dislike for Sam Pelling.

Poor Hendricks. Poor Clementine. Poor *me*.

"Do you think he'll tell anyone?"

She shrugs. "I don't know. He and Miles share everything, but this . . . might do more damage."

"We're in uncharted territory."

The pair of us look up to find Eddie with a new bottle of wine. "How're things going? Working on the list of who's caused this?"

Clementine grins at him through bloodshot eyes. "Sure are."

"Good, good," he gruffs, and trudges back to the bar with the empty bottle.

Clementine tops up our glasses and wipes a hand under her nose. "Anyway, tell me what's happening with you and Hendricks? Are things better?"

I shake my head and follow it with a shrug. It's hard to find the words.

"Not really . . . I don't know . . . I thought it was okay, then it wasn't . . . I was looking for him when I found you."

"Shit, I'm sorry. We can go—"

"No. I'm glad we're here."

"What are you going to do?"

I shake my head. "I don't know. He wants us to be 'friends,' he says that's all he can offer. I know he thinks I'm returning to Australia, I was going to tell him I'm not . . ." I glance down at my handbag, casually placed next to me. Clementine is totally unaware that it's carrying around a ticking time bomb. "You want to hear something stupid?"

"Hey," Clementine scoffs, "I think I have the monopoly on stupid."

"We'll see." Reaching into my handbag, I pull out an old phone and place it on the table. "That's six years old."

Clementine's brows slowly raise. "Happy Birthday?"

I huff a humorless laugh. "A couple of weeks ago, Hendricks said he'd messaged me, and I never replied. I never replied because I never got them. I racked my brain, trying to figure it out until I realized he sent them to my old UK phone. That one."

"Hendricks's messages are on there?"

"Maybe, I don't know. I've charged it, but I'm too scared to turn it on. I don't want to be reminded of how badly I fucked things up when I already know."

"Story. You were both young, and young people do stupid stuff, so give yourself a break—"

"Are you including yourself in that?"

"Touché."

Picking up the phone, I run it between my fingers,

turning it over and over. The alcohol is making me brave but not brave enough.

"Will you read them with me?"

Her hands reach across the table and take mine. "I'd be honored." It might be the wine talking, but I'm taking it.

"Do you want me to turn it on?"

I slide it across to her. She presses the button, then pushes it back to the center of the table, and we wait.

The first thing that comes up is my lock screen, a picture of Hendricks and me taken on Honeysuckle Hill one summer.

"Shall I go and get Eddie's Wi-Fi code?" she asks, just as the first *ping* sounds out.

It's followed by another, and another. *Ping. Ping. Ping. Ping.*

My stomach drops a little further with each one.

"Shit."

Clementine tops up our glasses again and holds hers out. "Come on, it's going to be okay."

Gingerly, I pick up the phone and open it. The messages are still coming through thick and fast, making it harder to get back up to the beginning.

Then I find the top.

HENDRICKS: You're in Australia? What the fuck, Story?

HENDRICKS: Call me.

HENDRICKS: This isn't funny. Are you seriously in Australia?

HENDRICKS: AUSTRALIA?

HENDRICKS: I can't believe you've gone without a word.

HENDRICKS: What did I do?

HENDRICKS: Whatever I've done, I'm sorry, Story.

What's left of my belly churns. This is worse than I thought it would be. I glance up at Clementine, and her eyes are as wide as mine.

"It's okay, keep going."

HENDRICKS: It's official.

HENDRICKS: The paternity test came back today, and I'm going to be a dad.

HENDRICKS: Fuck.

HENDRICKS: I'm scared.

HENDRICKS: I miss you, please call me back. Please let me know you're okay.

HENDRICKS: I saw your dad today, he says you're settling in and you have a job teaching.

HENDRICKS: Proud of you, Stor.

HENDRICKS: So Miles hates Sienna.

It's weak, but for the first time, I laugh because of course Miles does. Clementine leans over to read the screen better and scoffs when she gets to the message.

"Yeah, he really did, and he tried to like her, which is *so* not Miles. But she was awful. I only met her a couple of times too, which tells you everything you need to know."

I don't know why, but the fact Miles tried to like her makes me really sad.

HENDRICKS: Apparently, the weather in Sydney has been a scorcher today. It's getting cold here.

HENDRICKS: I saw Eddie today, and he told me to say hi. So, hi. Claudia said flapjack takings are down ha ha. As I don't actually know, I said you were lying on the beach every day, wrestling crocodiles and kangaroos. Whatever you're doing, I hope it's fun.

HENDRICKS: I went to the ultrasound appointment today. We're having a boy. I'm going to be a dad. I miss you. I wish you were here. Please call me, Story, please. I'm begging.

HENDRICKS: I fucked things up so badly. I'm so sorry, Stor.

HENDRICKS: Happy Birthday, Storyteller.

HENDRICKS: I don't want to be a shit dad. I'm so scared I'm going to fuck up. I wish my dad was here.

HENDRICKS: I don't think it's going to work out with Sienna.

HENDRICKS: *photo*

HENDRICKS: Story, meet my son, Max. He's perfect. I'm so in love with him. I wish you were here. I wish he could meet my best friend.

HENDRICKS: You're still my best friend, Stor.

All the emotions I've tried to keep at bay pour out in a loud, chesty sob. He's so cute and tiny. It's followed by pictures of Hendricks holding Max, Miles and Clementine holding Max, Max and the dogs. And it hurts, the pain of seeing everything I missed is more acute than I expected it to be.

Clementine's hand covers mine. "I'm sorry, Story. It must be hard seeing all this."

"I tried to block it all out, you know—" I ease a dry wet wipe from the packet and blow my nose.

"It doesn't work," she finishes for me.

HENDRICKS: Happy Birthday, Storyteller.

HENDRICKS: Max is teething, it's brutal. On the plus side, I seem to have moved my sleep schedule to match your time zone.

HENDRICKS: Max started walking. We got eight steps. I feel very strongly he's going to be an athlete.

HENDRICKS: Miles has introduced Max to polo. He can barely walk, but he swings the mallet like a pro. But we had to move all the priceless china before Lando's head exploded ha ha.

HENDRICKS: *photo*

HENDRICKS: My boy is one. Can you believe it?

Clementine grabs my phone. "Oh, he was so cute. He wore that birthday hat all day."

I nod. It's all I can manage without crying. But then I catch sight of the next message, and holding it in is impossible. Tears spill down my cheeks and splash on the screen.

HENDRICKS: Sienna and I are done. I tried, Stor. I tried so fucking hard, but I have to put Max first.

HENDRICKS: I have meetings with the solicitors today, and they think I can get full custody. I wish you were here. I wish you could tell me what to do.

HENDRICKS: Happy Birthday, Storyteller.

The timestamps between the messages become increasingly far apart. Until the last message.

HENDRICKS: Happy Birthday, Storyteller.

That was three years ago. They stopped, just like he said.

Clementine picks up the dry wet wipes and silently passes them over.

"What are you going to do?"

I blow my nose, pick up my water, and drink half in one go. "I love Hendricks, and I always have. And he loves me. I just need to show him that we're better together than apart."

Clementine picks up her wine. "I'll drink to that."

Picking up the bottle, I fill my glass. "Now I need to figure out how to do that. I need to stop him seeing me as the teenage Story."

"Seduce him." She laughs, and it's followed by a dramatic shudder. "Bleugh. Not that I want to think about my brother having sex—"

"If it makes you feel better, I think about him having sex all the time." I snort, before dissolving into giggles, and when Clementine joins in, it turns into full belly laughter.

We laugh and laugh and laugh. Every time we think we're stopping, we catch each other's eye, and it starts all over again until Eddie comes over with more water.

"Looks like things are improving."

We both know he's trying to be nice, but it silences us into realizing our shared desolation. Eddie runs off the moment our faces crumble.

"Clem, what are you going to do about Santiago Torres?" I ask after using the last dry wet wipe to blow my nose.

"Honestly"—she grins, but there's a sadness behind it—"I have no fucking clue, and I'm not going to figure it out tonight."

And so, we finish the wine and order another bottle.

We each come up with a plan on how to tackle our respective problems. Eddie brings us huge plates of steak pie and mash. We laugh, we cry, and eventually, after debating whether a fourth bottle of wine would be a step too far, we decide it's perhaps time to go home.

Which is when Hendricks storms into the pub.

24

Hendricks

I take one look at Story propped up against my sister, the pair of them howling with laughter, and turn to Eddie.

"What the hell? How did you let them get so drunk?"

"I called you. What'd you want me to do?" His shoulder jerks, but I swear I see his mustache twitching. "I'm not getting between a pair of girls and their need to set the world right with a bottle of wine."

"I see three bottles."

"There was a lot of setting."

"Is that so?"

He solemnly nods once. "And I feel like it's my duty to warn you that your name came up more than anyone else's."

My eyes roll to the heavens, and I scrub a hand through my hair. Fucking hell. Spending my evening taking care of my very drunk sister and equally drunk best friend / ex-best friend / childhood love was nowhere close to what I had planned.

Not that I had plans per se, because I'd only just managed to get Max to sleep after the fifteenth story about a pirate boy and his pet sea-dragon. Miles is out with his polo buddies, my mother has gone up to London for a dinner party, Lando and Holiday were watching a movie, and after an exhausting morning playing polo followed by an equally exhausting afternoon panicking about handling the Clementine / Torres situation, I would have been more than happy with a beer and an early night.

"How long have they been here?"

"Five hours, give or take."

"*Five*?"

"I'd say so. Maybe six."

I can see Eddie's going to be no help whatsoever. I don't know if it's the publican in him, upholding the trust of his patrons as sincerely as a doctor / patient relationship, or because he saw all of us through our formative years, and feels he has a duty to oversee our rites of passage too—namely passing out drunk in the pub.

I've done it, Lando's done it, Alex has done it, and Miles has *definitely* done it.

"Okay, fine."

My approach is ginger. The table is strewn with tissues and half-drunk glasses of water. Their cheeks are pink from the fire and far too much wine, and they're laughing at whatever's on their phone screen. It's what makes me take my time, slow down, and observe.

Story's hair is flopped onto her face, and from this angle, I can only see the curve of her nose peeking through from the curtain. Her full lips, open wide as she barks a laugh out at Clementine's commentary, curve up, creasing her cheekbones and adding the hint of a dimple. Her lashes flutter as she tips her head back in amusement and, as her hair falls away, I'm treated to the rest of her silhouette—the graceful bow of her neck, rounded breasts under her thick woolen jumper, and the delicate arch in her back as she pushes away from the chair.

It gives me an all-too-real idea of how she'd look straddling me.

It's not the first time I'm slack-jawed around Story, and it won't be the last.

"Hey . . . it's my *brother*."

The pair is now staring at me, and I realize the extent of the situation. Blackish-gray streaks line the tops of their cheeks, eyes puffy and bloodshot. It's debatable, but I *think* my sister comes off worse.

"Jesus. You two smell like a distillery."

"You mean vineyard," Clementine snaps back. At least I think that's what she says. It's more of a slur. She points her finger at me. "And before you think about judging us—"

"Don't," adds Story.

"*And* when you boil it down"—Clemmie's arm swings around, and I duck just in time—"this is all your fault anyway."

"Yeah? How so?"

In front of me, the determination on Clementine's face morphs and crumbles, her eyes lose their furious sparkle, the glare aimed my way vanishes, and her mouth, set hard only seconds ago, droops. Before I know what's happening, tears fall down her cheeks.

"Because you're so *mean*." She sobs loudly enough that the tables on the other side of the pub turn around. They can hear her over all the other raucous commotion you'd normally associate with a pub on a Saturday night.

Oh dear God.

"Clem. . ." I pull her out of her seat and into a hug, partly to comfort her, partly to muffle her. "Let's talk about it when we get home, okay?"

"What about Story? You're mean to her too."

Releasing half my body from my sister's grip, I look around and find Story also on the verge of a meltdown, completing this alcohol-soaked double act.

I'm living my worst nightmare.

A guy, who I dearly hope I don't know, subtly pumps his fist at me. I appreciate the solidarity, but I want nothing more than to get out of here.

"Okay, you two, let's go." I pick up two jackets, two bags, and one really old phone. "The car's outside."

Without any help from Eddie, who's watching on in amusement, I grab one girl with each hand, while making sure I don't drop anything, and guide them gently but quickly out of the pub.

"Eddie, we'll bring you the list in the morning," my sister calls behind her before the door closes.

I might be busy trying to ferry two drunken girls, but my ears perk up nonetheless, because as a parent I have a sixth sense for when things sound suspect. "What list?"

"None of your"—Clemmie's finger spins toward me until she presses it against my nose—"beeswax."

It takes just as long to wrestle them into the car as it did to get them out of the pub. I no sooner get into the driver's seat when Clemmie's head pops through from the back seat.

"Are you mad at me, Hen?"

"No."

Then Story decides to join in, pulling Clementine back to make room for her head. "Are you mad at *me*?"

"What? No."

"You know what?" shoots drunk number one. "I don't even care if you are. I've done nothing wrong. Arsehole."

"And *you* know what?"

"What, Stor?"

"Me either."

"Kill me now," I mutter to myself as they dissolve into giggles in the back seat and congratulate themselves for who-the-fuck-knows-what.

I hit speed dial for Lando, who has the audacity to send me to voicemail. So I try again.

"I'm kind of busy right now, Hen."

"I don't fucking care. I'll be outside the front doors in five minutes, and I need your help."

To his credit, he's waiting next to Holiday. I jump out as quickly as I can because if I'm not mistaken, Clementine's on the verge of being sick. I'm proven correct when I yank the door open, and she leans out to vomit in spectacular fashion.

"Fucking hell," grunts Lando, jumping back, as Holiday surges forward to take her from my arms.

"Oh God, Clemmie, what's happened?"

"They've been in the pub all afternoon."

"*They*?"

Rushing around, I open the other passenger door, where Story is much more graceful and less pukey in her exit from the car. On closer inspection, she seems marginally less drunk too.

Even though Holiday is guiding Clementine up the steps to the front door, her brows shoot up at the sight of my arm around Story. Lando sports a similar expression as we watch her teeter toward the front door and into the house.

"Does Story need to go home?"

I nod. "But I'm not taking her back to her parents' place in this state."

Grabbing on to one of the stone pillars in the hallway, she spins around. "Whoa, Burlington Hall. Long time no see." Her arms spread around the circumference. "I missed you. Thought I'd never be invited back."

"Okay, Story, let's get you to bed."

She gasps and giggles behind her hand. "Why, Lord Burlington, I thought you'd never ask."

I shoot a glare at Lando as he snorts loudly behind me, then another one for being absolutely no help whatsoever.

"I'll be waiting downstairs for a beer. Are you hungry? Shall I see if Pierre can rustle up some pizzas?"

"Yes," I say, begrudgingly, and guide Story up the stairs. Holiday and Clementine are way ahead of us. I debate putting Story in the spare room in the east wing near me, but it's *near me* and so is Max. I don't want him asking questions about why his teacher is staying over.

Therefore, we turn left at the top of the staircase toward the west wing instead.

"Did the corridor always used to be blue?" Story muses, trailing her fingertips along the wall. There's a whimsical, dreamy quality about the way she's moving, slow and preoccupied that any other time I might find cute, but right now, I don't have the patience for.

I nod. "Yes."

"Could have sworn it was yellow."

"Nope, blue. Remember, you always said it could do with having clouds painted on it."

"Oh yes. I remember now." She grins. It turns into another giggle, followed by a pirouette. "I used to love having sleepovers. Remember when we used to have sleepovers, Hen?"

I hum in response, but my only recollection of the sleepovers is how they stopped around the time we were thirteen. Right before sleeping in the same bed all night would come with a set of challenges, and sneaking down the corridor to each other's rooms was too risky.

"Okay, Stor, you can sleep in here." I open the door to the bedroom farthest away from mine.

Following me in, she stands by the bed and watches me walk around the room, switching on the bedside light, drawing the curtains, and checking the warmth of the radiators. In the bathroom, I find spare toothbrushes and toothpaste, face cloths and towels, and a little basket with anything a guest could need.

She hasn't moved by the time I return. "Story, I'm going to fetch you some water and painkillers for the morning. In the meantime, you can brush your teeth and go to sleep."

"Hendricks, are you going to stay with me?"

I lean in and kiss her cheek, my body tensing in refusal to betray how much I want to stay. "Make sure you call your mum and let her know you're okay."

Softly, her fingers link with mine. "Do you promise

you're not mad at me?"

She's drunk, so she doesn't get it. "I could never be mad at you, Stor." Not anymore, anyway. Not ever really. It was me I was mad at.

Her smile is heartbreaking, offset only by her slightly unfocused eyes. "You're a terrible liar."

"Go to sleep. You'll feel better in the morning."

"Wait." She pulls me back. "Tell me you love me again."

Standing in front of her, I pretend she's not swaying. I pretend my words don't come with restrictions, and that she's not leaving again.

I want them to hit her with the full force of their meaning.

"I love you, Story MacIntosh."

This time, I walk out and don't turn around. The second the latch clicks on the door, I sprint down the corridor, avoiding all the creaky floorboards, and rush down the stairs.

I haven't thought through this plan at all. Story sleeping under the same roof as me. Maybe I should lock her door, maybe I should ask Lando to lock *mine*.

"Didn't think I'd see you until the morning." Lando grins as I walk into the kitchen, slightly out of breath.

I pause mid-stride. "You said you were organizing pizza."

"Yes, but I figured you'd stay with Story."

"No. Nooo. *No*." *No*, I add to myself for the fourth time, hoping it'll sink in.

I will not be staying with Story. I'll see her in the morning, as per any regular overnight guest.

"Okay." He slides a beer across the kitchen island to me. "What happened, then?"

Closing my eyes, I take a long draw from the bottle and finish half. "Eddie called, said it would be a good idea for me to collect Clementine and Story. They've been in there all afternoon."

"They certainly looked like they had." He chuckles. "Why was Clementine so upset?"

Finishing the beer in two gulps, I remove another one from the fridge, though honestly, I could do with something much stronger, like a triple scotch. While I don't know the ins and outs of why Clementine was so upset, I know *enough*. Telling him about Clementine and Torres is something I've been debating all afternoon, because I need to talk to *someone*.

But it's a situation so farfetched that I can't even wrap my head around it to tell him. I also don't want to unleash the shitstorm I know will happen. Although the thought briefly occurs to me that he already knows, because if Clementine had confided in Holiday, Holiday would have told Lando.

"Hen?"

"Oh, drunk girls, who knows?" I shrug it off, hoping it's convincing enough. "But . . . hypothetically speaking, has Holiday ever mentioned anything to you about Clem dating?"

He shakes his head. "Why? Is she?"

"No fucking clue."

And that is all we touch on the subject because Pierre brings up enough pizzas that we can have leftovers cold for breakfast. I'm so hungry that the pineapple on mine has me salivating before I've taken a bite. Holiday joins us, having seen Clementine to sleep, and it's not long after that before I decide to turn in myself.

A hot shower later and I've almost rinsed the day off me, until I realize I forgot to take water and painkillers to Story. Pulling on a pair of pajamas and a shirt, I run back downstairs to fetch them.

It takes one hundred and twenty-seven seconds for me to walk from the top of the stairs to Story's room. That's one hundred and twenty-seven opportunities for me to turn around and ask Holiday to deliver her water instead.

Avoiding all the floorboards again, including the one outside her room, I lean against the door. Only when I'm certain I don't hear a peep do I slowly open it.

The light is still on, and her bed is empty.

I'm cursing to myself as I cross the room and leave the water and painkillers on the bedside table. There aren't that many places she could be, and my first stop will be my sister's room.

Turning to leave, the sound of the bathroom door opening catches my attention, and I look around just in time to get an eyeful of Story walking out, backlit by dim light.

My brain short-circuits, my mouth dries up, and all my blood rushes to my dick.

Every teenage fantasy, hell, every adult fantasy, I had about Story is way off base. The reality exceeds every expectation.

Reminiscent of the Matisse hanging in the library downstairs, her curves are a work of art. Soft in all the right places. Satiny knickers hug her hips, riding high enough up her thigh that they make her legs look ten feet long. The matching bra makes me want to put my face between her breasts until I can't breathe.

I can't breathe *now*. She's stolen all the oxygen.

Her lips pop, but she stands statue-still, save for the rise and fall of her chest. As she stares, her expression changes until I *know* I'm in trouble. All sense of propriety and "doing the right thing" vanishes. I need to leave, but I couldn't if I tried.

"I didn't want to sleep in the clothes I was wearing all day." Her mouth tilts on one side, lopsided but challenging. "I don't have anything else."

"I can get you some." My voice pitches, my eyes traveling slowly up her body, taking in every line, every dip and hollow, thinking what a shame it would be to cover her up.

"Thank you, but there's no need."

I'm still standing trapped by the edge of the bed when she slowly pads toward me. She doesn't look like the same Story I left here an hour ago. Her face is fresh and clean, eyes focused and determined, darting between me, my face, and what's going on below my hips. I should be scared because *that look* is the one she gets when someone's told her she can't do something.

"Story," I warn, but it's futile. A pathetic, weak effort at putting up a fight.

"You know," she begins, trailing a finger down my shirt, stepping so close my erection brushes against her belly. "I've been thinking . . ."

"Oh?"

"Thinking about us being friends. I know you want it, Hendricks, but I've decided that doesn't work for me anymore. And I'm taking matters into my own hands."

"Story," I croak, only for her to push into me, my dick nestled between us, and my words vanish with a low groan.

"And this doesn't feel very friendly." She presses again. "Or the way you're looking at me."

She's got me there. I know my eyes are on stalks. "No?"

"No," she replies, pushing me until I tip back and I'm sitting on the end of the bed.

I don't know what's going on, but I do know I'm not strong enough to stop it. When she straddles me, her tits are centimeters from my face, and I might get my wish after all. I'm so thankful I jerked off in the shower because that tiny movement creates enough friction that I would have blown in my pants.

"Put your hands on me, Hendricks—"

"Stor—"

"Put. Your. Hands. On. Me."

When I do, they're not steady. I can't even find it in myself to be embarrassed. I'm shaking as I take hold of her hips, my fingers digging into the supple flesh of her arse, creeping under the thin satin elastic of her knickers, touching her how I always dreamed of touching her. My heart is working overtime, pumping harder than it did the day I lost my virginity.

"I'm real, Hen."

Even though I'm not entirely sure any of this is real, I reply, "I know you are."

"But you don't treat me as real. You've never *seen* me as real."

"I have." *Fuck*, of course I have.

"You never looked at me like I wanted you to."

She slowly flexes her hips, gently rolling herself over my thighs until she's positioned right *there*, on the tip of my throbbing dick. The only thing separating me from her pussy is the flimsiest strip of lilac fabric and a pair of cotton pajamas.

"Well, I'm fucking looking at you right now," I grit, holding her still before I explode. "Story, what are we doing? What are *you* doing?"

"Showing you what you're missing."

"You're drunk—"

"I'm not."

"Story." It's a plea, all I can manage, because as much as I want this, I know there's a cognitive imbalance between the two of us right now. "We're not doing this until you're sober."

"Hendricks." She draws out my name, and I can smell mint on her breath. "I don't believe you. You'll brush me aside again." She grinds so hard in my lap, my pulse roars in my ears. "Haven't you ever wanted to know how good we could be together? How it would feel being inside me?"

The sounds I let out as her lips reach my neck are part prayer of thanks, part frustrated garbled moan.

I'm so fucking hard.

Her fingertips dig so deeply into the muscle on my shoulders that I wince. "I know you have, Hen. I have too, and it gets me *sooo wet*."

Who the fuck is this person on my lap, punctuating each sentence with the slow drive of her hips?

I'm on the brink of snapping, an elastic band pulled so tight it's see-through, and it's a whispered *please show me* that finally breaks me.

"Fuck it."

My fist thrusts into her hair, and I pull her back. Puffy lips, pupils blown wide, and full, rounded breasts pushed into my face. She's absolutely glorious. Everything I've ever dreamed of. I'm lightheaded looking at her.

Leaning forward, I trail my lips across her chest, tasting the faint traces of her perfume. "Is this what you want?" My tongue follows the swell of her breast, across the delicate hem of her bra to the point of her nipple. Air sucks through her teeth, sharply. "Is this?" I ask, grinding my pelvis into her, my dick slipping between her soaked thighs.

"*Yes.*" Her eyelids flutter closed, and her back arches as she takes another pass. "Oh yeah."

Her voice is gruff and so fucking sexy it takes me closer to my breaking point. I want to do nothing more than sink inside her. The patience I'm exhibiting is nothing short of saintly, but I can't do it. When she attempts to move my hand between her legs, I grip her hips tighter.

"I'm not touching you, Stor. Not doing anything you'll regret when you sober up. If you want it, you take it." Her lips are inches from mine. I'm sucking in her carbon dioxide, waiting for her to make a move.

She leans away from me, and I immediately miss the heat from her body. Her breath matches mine, shallow and sharp, but she raises an eyebrow to me nonetheless, accepting a challenge I didn't realize I'd set.

Her hands trail up, nails scraping through my nape and into my hair. It's a sensation I feel *everywhere.*

Her hips tilt, and she grinds harder, doing exactly as I instructed and taking what she needs—the alcohol making her brave. In the process, she gives me exactly what *I* need.

Satin knickers bunch in my fist. "*Fuck.*"

The friction, the pressure and precision of each movement. My lap is soaked in her. My *dick* is soaked in her.

"Jesus, Stor."

"Tell me how good this feels."

It's a struggle to get words out. "So. Fucking. Good."

Arching back, she shifts forward, searching for more friction. Her breathing turns ragged, and so does mine. Our eyes lock in a silent confirmation that we're both so close.

She grinds so torturously slowly, it's fucking mind-blowing. "Tell me more."

I imagine her clit, swollen and wet, her tight pussy spread open and desperate for my cock. The feel of her clenching around me, squeezing me.

I grip her hips, positioning her so my dick hits exactly where she needs it. "I remember the first time I made myself come thinking of you."

Her pupils flare, and her breath catches. Her nipples harden further, twisting to viciously sharp tips.

"We'd been swimming in the waterfall, my teenage hormones were out of control. I only had to think about you and I'd get hard"—I drag her slowly up my dick, and her jaw slackens—"but we were friends, and I wasn't ready to admit to myself that I loved you more than that . . ."

Her pelvis jerks, and it sets off a series of sparks twisting my balls.

". . . but holding my cock and thinking about you naked . . . kissing you . . ." I flick my tongue on her lower lip. "Fucking you . . ."

It happens out of the blue.

"*Hendricks*," she cries, and then she explodes on my lap.

Watching her shuddering orgasm, and riding out her pleasure with a series of uncoordinated thrusts, is all it takes. I come harder than I ever have before, white lights blinding me. It's a painful punch to the gut that would double me over if I were standing.

Story becomes a rag doll in my arms, head resting on my shoulder until her breath settles down. I'm not convinced she hasn't fallen asleep.

"Stor?" It takes all my strength to push to standing so I can twist her around and put her back into bed, trying not to stare at the dark, damp patch between her legs.

Her eyes are wide open, looking at me when I stand. "Don't go, Hen. Don't ruin this by leaving."

I look away, her face, her eyes, they're what got me into this in the first place. "Stor, I can't stay."

But she pulls back the covers on the other side of the bed and pats the white cotton sheet. "Just for a little while."

A deep sigh escapes me because I really don't want to stay.

I can't risk having Max wandering about in the night, looking for me and finding us. I need to clean up. I need to sleep in my own bed, with my own thoughts, and figure out what the hell I'm going to do now.

Because, like it or not, our lives just changed.

But because I've never been able to say no to Story MacIntosh, I slip inside, slide down next to her, and pull the covers over us.

25

Story

I wake thirstier than I've ever been and guzzle the bottle of water by the bed. Padding as quietly as I can to the bathroom, I pee, brush my teeth again, and take a long, hard look in the mirror.

Seducing Hendricks last night wasn't my plan, but when opportunities present themselves, you have to take them. And seducing him was way better than anything I've already come up with. But now comes the hard part—seeing it through.

"Stand firm, Story," I mouth to myself, then wash my hands and open the door.

The bedside light is on, and as predicted, Hendricks is sitting up in bed, staring at . . . something? Anything but me, that's for sure.

"Hendricks?"

His eyes find mine, bright blue even in the dim light. "I couldn't leave until you'd woken up."

"Are you already having regrets?"

"I regret nothing," he replies.

"Then what are you thinking about?"

He sighs deeply, his head falls back against the headboard, and he looks genuinely anguished. Crossing over the room, I get back into bed and kneel next to him.

"Hendricks?"

"I don't know how to be around you and not be in love with you. I can't say no to you, Stor—"

"And that's a problem, why?" I laugh, hoping to release some tension with humor.

"Because when you leave again . . ." His head shakes.

I haven't seen Hendricks enough this week to tell him about the job offer and what I've decided. I would have mentioned it yesterday at polo, but he left before I could. Now is as good a time as any.

"I'm not going anywhere."

He rubs across his brow. "What do you mean?"

"I know you overheard me talking to Mrs. Benson. Miles told me. But you heard wrong. I'm only going back to Sydney to pack up my things. That's all."

He sits up, his body turning toward mine, and I'm pinned with an intense stare. "You're staying in Valentine Nook?"

"I'm staying."

He inches close enough that I can feel the heat rising from his body. "You're *staying*?"

"I'm staying."

My eyes drop to his lips, full and soft. My tongue darts out, wetting mine. My body vibrates, waiting for his touch because I'm certain it's coming. Last night / a few hours ago / whenever it was, was all me. My orchestration. I got what I wanted at that moment, but I crave more.

We've always been a game of chess, and it's his move now.

I don't have to wait long.

I've barely got out my confirmation for the second time when his hands surround my face. Then his lips are on mine, crushing me, and twenty years of missed opportunities, of being too scared, of wondering what this moment would be like, are brought to a head.

Everything finally slots into place.

The faint scent of soap drifts between us with each inhale, breathing through my nose so I don't have to disconnect from Hendricks's mouth, and the best kiss I've ever had in my life. I always knew he would be a good kisser, but his tongue slipping across mine, exploring, soft yet firm, tastes like our life together is beginning.

Hendricks and Story.

Long fingers dig into my nape, hands gripping either side of my head like he's scared I might leave again. I cling to him with equal desperation, finding it impossible to get closer.

Hendricks's fist tangles in my hair, pulling me back. His face, so close to mine, looking at me like it's the first time he's seen me. Checking I'm real.

"You're here," he whispers, more to himself than me. "Not leaving."

I'm about to nod the affirmative, *again*, but then he whips his shirt off.

"Holy shit." I've seen cheese graters less impressive. Reaching out, I run my fingers over the hard, deep ridges of his abs. I was right, Hendricks is an absolute rig. "You got ripped."

He laughs, dry and humorless. "Celibacy will do

that to you. I needed to channel it somewhere."

My brows shoot up, his response taking me by surprise. "There's been no one?"

He looks away and shrugs. "There has been the odd night or two when Miles has dragged me out, but no one regular. No one I wanted to bring into Max's life."

His words hang in the air unspoken. Because Max is the priority, and I know that navigating a relationship with Hendricks will require time and patience.

"Well," I say, watching his breath catch as I take a second pass, ghosting my fingers over each deeply defined muscle and down to the crevices on either side of his hips. "I approve."

My hand skates lower to the impressive tent in his pajama bottoms, the one that caused me to orgasm so hard I nearly blacked out.

His hand darts, and fingers wrap around my wrist. "Not yet."

"Hen—" It's a desperate, childish plea.

He chuckles, and this time, I hear the amusement. "I know it's not your strong suit, but have patience, Story."

It really isn't. Even watching him reach out, using his thumb to gently push aside my bra straps when I want to rip them off my body and rub against his, is driving me crazy. So I'm unprepared when he yanks me closer and onto his lap.

His mouth drags across my chest, hands roaming my curves, palms flat on my back. I'm so distracted by his tongue licking the length of my neck that I don't register he's unsnapped my bra until it falls away.

Huge, strong hands, so used to dealing with unruly animals, gently cup my breasts. He studies me, like one would a piece of art, with consideration and reverence.

"Story, *fuck*. They're perfect," he says before burying his face between my breasts, mumbling words I cannot hear.

Wetness floods between my legs. His lips find a nipple and close around it. Using his tongue, he teases the bud like it's a challenge to see how rock-hard he can get it. I'm convinced they can already cut glass. On my other breast, his thumb moves in circles between pinches and swipes. The mixed sensation of the two is enough to have my head explode.

My ability to hold on becomes a tenuous thread when his hand slips between my legs, and he groans.

His solid thighs widen, splaying me open, and the expression forming as he peers between my legs is nothing short of wolfish while he runs a finger back and forth across the satin strip of my knickers.

"Is this how wet you were last night, Stor? Riding my lap? Getting yourself off?" he asks, pushing the fabric aside. I drip onto his palm.

My response is a gasp when one thick finger slides inside me.

His finger twists. "Tell me."

"Ohhh, *yes*." I exhale.

"How long have you been waiting?"

With lips on my neck, his thumb finds my clit. I writhe against his palm, needing to increase the pressure. His legs spread farther, opening me up, the movement forcing my hips forward.

It feels like forever, literally and figuratively.

I buck against a second finger pushing inside me up to the knuckle, a delicious sensation hurtling me nearer to detonation. They work together, scissoring and stretching me, curling up to hit that perfect spot. Whether he's been celibate or not, there's no doubt I'm in the hands of a master.

I open my mouth to tell him, but all that comes out of me is a deep groan, a cry, and a prayer.

"Want to hear a secret?"

My head is barely attached to my neck, but I nod.

"I've never come in my pants before, Stor, and *fuck me*, I nearly blacked out."

I'm trying to concentrate on his words, but all I can focus on is the torturous *in / out* of his fingers, and the weight of his throbbing cock against my hip.

"Seeing you come . . . *feeling* you come . . ." His thumb swipes my clit. "You're so wet, Stor . . . so ready for me to fuck you."

My orgasm shoots down my spine, the force ripping any solidity I have in my bones. I'm a jellied mess slumped against a chest of rock-hard muscle.

Hendricks's breath is as jagged as mine, but I'm not anywhere near done. He's lit the match of my fuse.

I gently release the elastic of his pajamas, and his dick frees itself.

Taking it in my hand, I understand why he was attempting to stretch me wider. He is big. *Thick.* I can barely fit my fingers around the circumference *thick*. I'm equal parts nervous and excited about the power I hold in my hands.

When I run my thumb over the slick precum, I'm rewarded with a tight hiss of air through his teeth.

"Nice growing, Hen."

The smile is wiped off my face, however, as my legs

are ripped from under me, and in my next breath, I'm staring at the ceiling. Blue eyes and a wide grin come into focus.

"None of your smart mouth right now." His voice is two octaves lower, like it's been dragged over coals and barrel-smoked for six months. "I won't last."

He leaves my field of vision. The bed dips, and I hear the soft padding of footsteps across the bedroom floorboards. Thirty seconds later, he returns, resuming his position of kneeling between my legs. Easing up on my elbows, I spot a foil packet ripped open.

There's something so arousing about watching a man roll on a condom, gripping himself with both strength and tenderness. When he's done, his hands wrap around my calves, slowly rubbing along the back, behind my knees, and the sensitive spot hidden in the crook.

My skin crackles as his hands take free rein. Fingers knead my thighs, but his eyes? They never stray from the spot between my legs.

He takes hold of his dick, running the blunt end through my slit and up to my clit. It's torturously slow, mind melding with each pressured swipe, until the tip stops and presses into my entrance.

I let out a sharp gasp and I'm squirming even before he begins his impalement, writhing against him as my body struggles to adapt to his size.

"Stay still, Story. Wriggling's only going to make it worse," he rasps, his jaw clenched. "I promise, I'll fit."

I barely manage a breath before he pushes in another inch.

"Fuuuck"—his tongue drags over his lips—"look at you taking me. So good, Stor. Such a good girl."

My hips rise to meet him, adjusting, and he watches himself fill me while I watch him. He's barely halfway in, while I'm too full to breathe.

I never thought Hendricks Burlington could get hotter. I was wrong.

The concentration on his face, nostrils flaring while he mutters "*a little more . . . yes, so tight. . . good girl*", showing me he's a band ready to snap, is so fucking hot. My body sizzles more with each inch he takes from me, until he's finally buried inside me and I can feel his balls snug against my arse.

We fit together perfectly, like I always knew we would.

His forehead is damp when it drops to mine, resting as he catches his breath and regains control. "*Fuck.* Fuck. This is . . . it's better than . . ."

He doesn't need to finish his sentence because I know. I *know*. Better than anything either of us could have imagined.

Breathing through my nose, I wait out the stinging of being stretched so wide.

And then, sensing my body has settled into his size before I do, Hendricks unleashes himself.

Stroke after long, deep stroke, his eyes never leave mine. He memorizes every expression my face makes, adjusting his moves until I make them again. He murmurs sweet nothings in my ear, only to follow them up with, "You're so fucking desperate for my cock, Story. Look at you."

It's those words, growled into the crook of my neck, that really get me wet. They make my skin hum. And he knows. He can read my body like a map. Tweaked nipple here, grind of my clit there, and I'm clawing his back.

"I've imagined you like this since I knew what it meant, what we could be together."

Kneeling up, he props one leg around his hip, gaining purchase. My fists bunch the sheets, desperate to stop myself from being pummeled up the mattress.

"But it's so. Much. Better." He punctuates each word with a thrust that has me spinning.

I can barely catch my breath, let alone form words to respond. My back bows like I was a contortionist in a previous life, meeting each punishing drive forward. Those powerful hips and thighs I watched control six different horses yesterday now control me.

His eyes meet mine with an intensity I've never seen in Hendricks before, his irises almost completely swallowed. It's carnal. It's possessive. And I fucking love it.

He's mine. I'm his. I've *always* been his.

It's our undoing.

My pussy spasms around him, and his fingers bruise my thighs as he fucks me relentlessly until he empties himself inside me with such force, I swear I taste him in the back of my throat.

He collapses to the side with a hoarse, "Fuck."

I've barely caught my breath before I sense him moving next to me, and I wait to see if he leaves. Instead, he shifts closer, wraps himself around me, and after a whispered good night, the bristle of his stubble brushing against my cheek with a kiss, I fall into a dreamless sleep.

When I wake, Hendricks is gone, but next to the bed is a fresh bottle of water, electrolytes, more painkillers, and a note.

Drink this.

26

Hendricks

"Hey, I've been looking for you everywhere."

I turn in the direction of Miles's voice. "Well, you found me."

He leans over the metal gate and peers into the stall where I'm checking on one of our pregnant heifers. I don't need to see him to know he's staring at me, wondering why I haven't answered his messages this morning.

Peeling off the protective gloves, I toss them into the rubbish bin and give Daisy a hard pat. "Good girl. Baby is looking on track. He'll be here soon."

"A boy, eh?"

I nod, dropping my stethoscope into my vet bag. "Yup."

He frowns, leaning so far on the gate he's practically swinging. "What's wrong?"

"Nothing."

"Something is . . ." His head tilts, and I know he's trying to figure it out. He once convinced himself we could read each other's minds, but thankfully, while we can communicate silently, our abilities don't stretch that far.

My mind is not the place for him to be right now.

"And, I'm guessing, our drunk overnight guest?"

I stifle a smile because he's half correct.

Boy, that was a fun morning.

Watching Clementine grapple her steaming hangover while Max was being extra himself was the best part of my day. Was the second croissant and hot chocolate I allowed Max to have as a Sunday treat necessary? No. But she puked on the doorstep *and* called me an arsehole. Not to mention the position I'm in now with her secret, whether she wanted me to know it or not.

Therefore, her punishment was dealing with a sugared-up Max while she mainlined black coffee and bacon sandwiches like they were a newly discovered hangover cure.

The worst part of my morning was dropping Story off at home before Max saw her. I still can't believe I get to kiss her, but the lingering one I planted on her halfway down her parents' driveway didn't curb the feeling that I was hiding a dirty little secret. I arrived back home ready to burst with all the information I'm holding.

I have new empathy for Miles and his intolerance for keeping anything to himself.

But he's the one I'd normally share everything with, which is making things a thousand times harder. I can't tell anyone until I know what it is I'm dealing with, and catching our baby sister and his sworn enemy in a compromising situation isn't something you bring up in casual conversation.

No. I need to speak to Clementine once she's

hangover-free. Though it did occur to me that a three-day recovery was more of an avoidance issue so I'd leave her alone.

"Have you seen Clemmie?"

He shakes his head. "Lando and Holiday caught me up on what happened. Did anyone get a photo?"

"No, Milo." I laugh, knowing exactly why he wants it. "You already used her for last year's Christmas card, two years in a row, and you're asking for serious trouble."

"Hmm."

I can tell he's thinking about it. Every December, Miles, because he clearly hasn't done enough shit stirring throughout the year, sends out a personal Christmas card to everyone he knows with an—let's just say—unflattering photo of one of us on it. I usually come out fairly unscathed, but that's only because Miles and I are identical.

It briefly occurred to me that's why Clementine is conversing with Torres, before dismissing it as an extreme reaction. I know she was mad about the Christmas card Miles sent this past year featuring her, but going after Miles's arch nemesis is not Clementine's style.

Moving past my twin, I fetch a bucket of grass for Daisy and leave it in the stall for her to enjoy before she's taken back to the fields with all the other cows.

"So . . ."

I pick up my equipment and walk out. "So what?"

He frowns again, annoyed. It's an emotion Miles very rarely feels. "Hendricks, what's going on with you? Is it Story? Because I think you should go for it. Fuck everything else, it will sort itself out."

I weigh my answer. I never hide anything from Miles. My developing relationship with Story is definitely something I would have talked about with him. But I just don't know whether I'll pull it off so that he thinks that's *all* I'm concerned about. Lying isn't a skill I was blessed with.

In the end, I swallow hard and spill. I do it while washing my hands in the big outdoor trough. If I'm not looking at him, he can't see that it's not all that's bothering me.

"Things progressed with Story over the weekend."

He leans back against the wall, arms crossed. "How so?"

I go into detail without going into *too much* detail, starting with collecting Story and Clementine from the pub, and ending with taking her home.

"So she told you she was staying? Good, I was worried she'd drag it out."

I look at him, confused. "You knew?"

"She told Clem and me when I went to collect Max the day you went into London."

I shake my hands dry, not caring in the slightest that I get Miles with the drips. "I can't believe you knew. Why didn't you tell me?"

"I would have, but she said she wanted to tell you, and it was better coming from her anyway."

Huffing, I pick up my bag and walk toward my car. He's right. It was better coming from her, but call me a hypocrite because I'm annoyed he didn't tell me.

"Fucking Clementine," I grumble to myself, deciding right there that she needs to tell Miles. Or I will.

"What?"

"Nothing."

"So . . ."

"So *what*?" I snap again.

"Hen, I'm asking what happened with Story," he replies, slowly and deliberately. "Are you two together now, or what?"

I shake my head because we're not. Not even close. "It's something we need to figure out." I push my cap up and give my head a good scratch, which is followed by a yawn. "It's hard, though."

Maybe the reason I'm in such a bad mood is because I haven't properly slept in days. Too many complications are going through my head at once. The exact reason I wanted to wait with Story. She deserves more than a half-present and distracted partner.

Miles stays silent, probably so I don't snap at whatever he suggests. He waits for me to speak.

"As much as I wanted it, I thought it would be weird with Story and change our relationship so drastically. But it felt so normal, like it was always meant to be this way. However, I still need to take my time with her because of Max."

Miles nods gravely, like he knows what it's like to be in a relationship, the concept of which has me grinning.

"You don't want to introduce Miss MacIntosh as Daddy's new girlfriend just yet."

"Exactly, he's never seen me with anyone."

"*But* . . . you still want the sex, and Story lives with her parents. You can't have her sleep over at Burlington because of Max, so you're a bit fucked. Or not—" He snorts.

I watch my brother and the gears turning in his

head. The moment sex is involved in any problem, he becomes a savant.

"It's not solely about the sex, but also yes," I admit, even if I'm loath to.

I haven't had sex for months. I haven't had *good* sex for . . . well, compared to the experience with Story . . . maybe I've never had good sex. Mind-blowing, toe-curling sex. Something between us clicked that night, and ninety-five percent of my thoughts over the past two days have been about when we can do it again.

"What was it like?" Miles holds his hands up, right before I tell him to mind his own fucking business. "Actually, you know what? I don't want to know."

"I wasn't going to tell you."

His mouth drops, and his brows shoot up. "That good?" His hands wave again. "Nope. Please don't answer." He lets out an exaggerated shudder. "*Bleugh*."

I am *not* going to ask what that's about.

"But"—he snaps his fingers—"you need a hookup venue."

"Milo—"

"I'm serious. Otherwise, how are you going to get down to it? It's not healthy to be celibate at our age, Hen. Sex adds years to your life, and I really don't want you to die before me. No one else puts up with my crap like you do."

Staring at Miles, at how serious he is, a smile stretches across my face, and then I burst out laughing. I don't know why I find it funny because it's not, but I can't help it. I'm barreled over, wheezing so hard I can't breathe. It's the first time I've laughed all day. It's the first time I've laughed like *this* in weeks.

I wipe the moisture from my eyes. "So I'm doing this to live longer and to put up with your crap?"

"Yup." He nods. "I have it. Use Bluebell."

"What?"

"It's empty. Holiday doesn't live there anymore since she's at Burlington. No one uses it."

I clap a hand on Miles's shoulder and pull him in for a hug. It's rare, but sometimes my brother is a genius. "You're right."

"When it comes to sex, I'm never wrong."

Opening the Land Rover boot, I toss in my bag. "D'you want a lift somewhere? I'm heading over to the stable yard."

He pulls a pleading face and puts his hands together. "You can't take me to Foxleigh, can you? I left my car there the other day."

"Sure, jump in." It's in the opposite direction, and I don't really have time, but since Miles has helped me with one of my problems, I can help him. "Give me one second."

Pulling out my phone, I shoot off a message to Story.

HENDRICKS: Meet me at Bluebell at 10? Clothing optional, door will be open.

STORY: Why, Lord Burlington, is this a booty call?

HENDRICKS: Call it what you want, but for clarification purposes, we're fucking tonight.

STORY:

I'm still grinning by the time we drive out of the farmyard gates when he turns to me. "You didn't hear anything about Torres at the charity game on Saturday, did you?"

Fuck. My grin dies, and my fists tighten a fraction on the steering wheel. Guilt and anxiety turn up the volume on the party they've been having in my belly since Saturday.

"I overheard Lydia talking about it. But I don't know what it was based on." There, facts, and I didn't lie.

Yeah, keep telling yourself that.

"That fucker. How dare he? What the fuck does he think he's playing at?"

Here I *can* tell the truth. "No fucking idea. I think he wants to be as destructive as possible."

Miles sits in silence, his eyes on the country lane in front of us. "I found out that groom is working the summer season in Aspen. I've decided I'm going over there."

"To do what?"

He shrugs. "Not sure yet. At the very least, get some intel I can use against Torres. I bought a new pony last week after I discovered it was one he had an eye on. Best-case scenario, I ruin his career like he almost ruined mine. I'm not stopping until he's barred from the circuit and resorts to teaching American rich kids with daddy issues how to ride a horse."

The venom in Miles's voice grates on me exactly how nails on a chalkboard would. I don't blame him one bit, either. In fact, I'll join his thirst for blood. But I have a lot to do before I get to that point on my list of shit I have to deal with.

Pulling through the Foxleigh gates, I spot Miles's

red Ferrari in his usual space and stop next to it.

"Thanks, Hen." He moves to slam the door, then opens it again. "I forgot to ask, have you heard from Sienna yet?"

I shake my head.

One fucking problem at a time.

I get through the rest of my day thinking about nothing except seeing Story.

I don't hear from Sienna, and I don't see Clementine beyond a rushed passing of each other when I get home from collecting Max. It only confirms she's definitely avoiding me.

I take my time reading Max his bedtime stories, and I follow with a long shower. The clock strikes ten o'clock, and the house is quiet when I walk down the main stairs and leave without telling a single soul I'm going out. Except Birgitta, in case Max wakes.

It takes seven minutes to arrive at Bluebell and another thirty seconds to walk up the path. My dick throbs with every step.

And then Story opens the door wearing absolutely nothing.

My heart stalls. My jeans become painfully tight. Without giving her the chance to say a word before my mouth is on hers, I kick the door shut behind me and scoop her into my arms.

Her nails scrape through my hair, legs locking around my hips as I pin her against the wall. Her groan tumbles down my throat, chased by the words, "fuck, yes."

Once more I'm wondering what happened to the girl I used to run through the fields and roll down the hill with. But then I remember I've spent the day fantasizing about her riding my cock.

My palms grip her ass as I press into her, fingers digging into her soft flesh.

She's pinned by my body, but I'm crushed by hers. The heat of her bare skin seeps through my shirt, while her tongue greedily pushes past my lips. Carnal, indelicate. The chemistry between us the other night was incredible – but this is another level.

It's incendiary.

We kiss like we're the last people on earth after a lifetime of wandering alone.

Story's bare pussy spreads against the crotch of my jeans. The denim offering the friction she needs, writhing against my dick. The sensation wreaks havoc on my ability to think, because all I want to do is lose myself in her.

Her thighs squeeze my hips. My cock throbs.

This is going to be over far too quickly.

Wrapping my palm around the delicate column of her throat, fingers cupping her jaw, I have to prize her away from my mouth.

Air passes staccato through her puffy, swollen lips. Chest heaving. Her cheeks have that rosy glow travelling down to her chest, her pupils blown so wide that I can barely see any of the pale brown I love so much. She's so close I'd only have to rock my hips once against her clit. But I have other plans.

"You're not coming like this again, Stor." I growl and

drop to my knees.

Arousal drips down her thighs, a silvery patch glowing like moonlight and lighting my way.

Glancing up I'm treated to the sight of her watching me, breasts cupped and squeezed together, as she pinches her tight nipples. I've never wanted to fuck someone more.

Spreading her with my thumbs, I take a moment to revel in her soaked pussy then get to work. Slow. Firm. Deep.

She tastes like soap, she smells like heat and all I hear are the muffled "yeah... right there" and "just like that" of encouragement, one hand thrown over her face, the other digging into my shoulder.

When my tongue pulls firm and flat along her slit, flicking her clit, my name falls off her lips as though it's been dragged from the depths of her soul.

Like she owns it.

Like I'm hers.

I eat her like my last meal. Lips suction on her clit, and she grinds against me, breathlessly begging me not to stop.

When she finally gives in, Story's knees buckle and I grip her trembling thighs as tightly as her fists clutch my hair, until she slumps against the wall on a massive, shuddering orgasm. "Hen, fuck, yes . . . *HEN*!"

Her pussy clamps hard on my tongue, and I keep going determined to draw out every drop of pleasure. Lap after lap, until her palms are pushing against my forehead and she's gasping for breath.

"Oh . . . no more . . . I can't . . . take it . . ."

I stand, pressing my lips to her, and scoop her limp

body up. My cock twitches at the moan she lets out, tasting herself on my tongue.

"Oh, yes you can. I'm not nearly done with you yet."

I don't point out I will never be done with her.

27

Story

When I walk to school the following morning, I do so bow-legged.

I'm both exhausted and exhilarated.

Every time I yawn, I think about another position Hendricks had me in, once more bringing out my inner contortionist. We fucked all over the house, moving from room to room until it was time to wave the white flag and fall asleep.

My limbs, still soft and gelatinous, are working out how to function. So when I turn the corner toward the school gates and a woman walking in the opposite direction bumps into me before I can dodge her, I have neither the dexterity nor the reflexes to hold the folder I'm carrying, along with a tote bag filled with pink and red cards. Today, we're making valentines.

"Oh crap." I watch as papers float around me and drift to the ground.

I catch exactly none, which is all the more annoying when half of them land in a puddle.

"I'm sorry. I wasn't looking where I was going."

As I delicately try to pick up soaking wet sheets

of paper and pile them up before they turn to pulp, I glance up from my position of scrambling into the eyes of a very pretty woman.

"Don't worry," I grumble, though there's no irritation in my tone.

Not as much as there should be. I am a little annoyed she's just staring at me, however, and not making the slightest attempt to assist me in the collection of soggy silhouettes the children will be decorating and cutting out later for their Valentine's cards.

Gathering the last of them, I push to standing. Except my thighs are so sore I can't get myself into position without looking like I'm either drunk or standing is a skill I only recently learned.

"They look cute." She points at the pile. "I'm sure Valentine's is a busy time for you in school."

I nod and smile, trying to figure out why this woman seems so familiar to me. "Are you a parent here?"

Her eyes drop, and her head bobs, but in an almost timid, coy way. "Yes."

Great. I stand straighter to appear a little more professional. "Lovely, what year? I teach reception, if you can't tell."

Her eyes widen, and she reaches into her bag to pull out her phone. "I'm so sorry. I have to take this. Nice to meet you."

"You too." I wave as she hurries off out of sight.

My eyes are still trained on the spot where she disappeared because I can't decide if the whole interaction was bizarre. Who doesn't help someone pick up all the stuff they were complicit in dropping?

It becomes my second biggest problem of the day,

however. When I walk into my classroom a few minutes later, I attempt to separate the soggy papers and hang them over the radiator. It's a disaster. The ink on the wettest ones has diluted, and several have ripped.

My leisurely morning becomes a race to get new ones printed before the bells ring and pupils arrive.

"Good morning, Miss MacIntosh."

"Good morning, Miss MacIntosh."

"Good morning, Miss MacIntosh."

The third voice greeting me is decidedly deeper and more delicious.

It's a voice I recognize most recently from whispering in my ear that my pussy was made for his cock. It sets off a flutter of excitement radiating from my belly outward, and a flurry of memories from my evening floods my synapses.

Me bent over the hallway table while Hendricks filled me.

Me sitting on the stairs, thighs wide, Hendricks eating me out like a man possessed.

Me on my knees with Hendricks's cock down my throat.

Me caged against the wall, arms pinned above my head, Hendricks tormenting me for hours before dragging my fourth orgasm out of me.

Waking up before the sun, wrapped up in the warmth of Hendricks's huge biceps and solid thighs.

A night I will never forget.

I bite back an incriminatory smile. "Good morning, Lord Burlington. Good morning, Max."

"Morning," Max replies in his usual dulcet tone. "Are we singing today?"

I nod. "We are."

He turns to Hendricks, who peers down amused. "Daddy, I hate singing."

"Max, remember what we talked about?"

He puffs out an exasperated, "Don't say hate?"

Hendricks nods. "Good job, bud. Any other word is fine."

"Then I really, really, *really* don't like singing."

It's hard to stop myself from laughing or catching Hendricks's eye when he replies, "Sometimes we've got to do things we don't like. But you know what? I'll like watching your concert. So will Granny."

Skepticism flashes in his eyes before he decides to be satisfied with his father's response, then tugs him forward toward his classroom.

"See you later?" Hendricks whispers so quietly that only I hear it.

I nod, turning my attention to more parents who've arrived for drop-off and need me, but I'm also incredibly aware of Hendricks.

Fingertips brush mine as he passes. He's focused straight ahead, giving nothing away. I forget that we've known each other for a lifetime, that us talking and laughing like the best friends we've always been is nothing out of the norm. But the adrenaline rush that we're being intimate in broad daylight, in front of witnesses, is more thrilling than I thought possible.

The morning passes relatively quickly, and even

though I've barely had two hours of sleep, I feel incredible. Much to Max's chagrin, along with a few others in the rabble that he's incited, we practice the Valentine's concert while we craft. I figure it kills two birds with one stone.

"Pink and red cards are on the front desk, which you can help yourself to if you want them," I point out. "On the side tables, you'll find everything you need to decorate your card. Please remember our sharing skills."

There's a scramble to get to the desk, so I step out of the way and gather up the bottles of glitter glue to hand out. When I do, my eyes catch a movement across the path outside the classroom and over to the road in front of the school. It's not unusual to see people walking up and down it, but it's a country lane, so outside of drop-off / pickup hours, it tends to be farmers, or horse and rider, or the Burlington Estate teams mending the hedgerows.

So a woman walking back and forth feels a bit out of context, especially when I look a little closer and realize it's the woman who knocked into me. If she hadn't caused a mountain of extra work, I probably would have forgotten all about it. But it brings back the feeling that I know who she is.

"Miss MacIntosh, Miss MacIntosh? Are these real diamonds?"

Leaving the window, I walk over to Alice, who's turning a plastic jewel over and over in her hand.

"They aren't, but they look real, don't they? Very sparkly." I hold out a bottle of glitter. "You can use this to stick it on your card, and the glitter will add to the sparkle."

It's followed by more demand for glitter, and I hand them out as quickly as possible. For the next hour, I hurry between desks—helping to cut out shapes, unstick the globs of glue, and wipe up spillages—but I can't shake my thoughts about the woman who's still outside.

The children are too focused on making their valentines and who's using feathers on their card, which means everyone wants to use feathers on their card, to notice me opening the classroom door. Rushing across the hall to Celeste, I knock and pop my head around the doorframe.

"Could I borrow you for a minute?"

She turns to her class, motioning to Katie, our shared classroom assistant, that she's leaving, but like mine, everyone is too deep in their craft projects to notice.

The moment we're out of earshot, she grunts loudly, "God, I could use a cup of tea. Henry's already stuck four hearts to Sabine's school skirt with Gorilla Glue. *Gorilla Glue*! I have no idea where it came from, but that child is a menace." Her cheeks blow out as she exhales. "Anyway, what's up?"

"I want to show you something, then I'll go and make you a cup of tea."

"Oh, you absolute angel. Two sugars? Thank you."

She follows me through to my classroom, where the children are too busy to acknowledge her. I point out the window, where the woman is still standing there.

"Who's that?"

She pulls down the glasses from where they're resting on her head and squints. "No idea. Why?"

"You've never seen her before? She's not a parent?"

Celeste shakes her head. "No, I've never seen her before."

"Are you sure?"

She looks again, hard. "Yes, positive. I've done enough morning duties by now to know all the parents by sight." She points to where the woman is standing. "I've never seen her before in my life."

"Shit."

"Why?"

I shake my head. "Something's not right. I bumped into her this morning, and she said she was a parent. But it just dawned on me she didn't have a child with her, and it was too early for drop-off. She's been sitting there for over an hour."

"That does seem a little odd." Celeste pushes her glasses back onto her head. "But who knows why people do things. Now, would you like a cup of tea? I know you said you'd make it, but I'm out now and would like to stay out for another few minutes before I return to the chaos of my classroom."

I nod, distracted. Maybe I should report her to Mrs. Benson. "Sure. Thank you."

Once I've partaken in the soothing properties of English Breakfast, I feel better. The children tidy up their workstations, and unlike Celeste's room, we don't have any major accidents to deal with.

"Would everyone like to share their Valentine's cards?"

Several hands shoot up. "Me, me, me."

Alice is leaning so far over her desk, one hand pushing her other arm up, that it looks like she's in danger of dislocating it at any moment.

"Yes, Alice—"

Her Valentine's card shoots in the air, a red and pink chaotic jumble of pompoms and hearts, with more bling than the Crown Jewels. "This is for my mummy because she's always doing nice things for me, and she's my valentine."

"That's very sweet, Alice. Well done." I smile encouragingly. "Who's next?"

All hands shoot in the air again, and we speed around the class. Everyone is showing off their artistic skills.

"Thank you, Felicity. Very good," I say to a Valentine that's more glue than card. It's so wet and heavy that it sinks in the middle. "Who's left?"

"Me," says Max, standing up with a simple red card with stenciled animals and swirls of pink. When he holds it to the light, I catch hints of glitter because after Felicity, there probably wasn't much to go around. "This is for my daddy because he doesn't have a valentine."

I don't know what it is about Max's sentence, but my sixth sense perks up and smacks me right between the eyes.

I know who that woman is.

28

Hendricks

I stare at the message one more time.

STORY: This sounds super weird, but I think Sienna is standing outside the school gates.

STORY: Obvs if you already know this, pls ignore.

That was eight minutes ago. I was in the car when the message came through, so I turned around, hit the accelerator, and I've been parked in the car park since.

I haven't seen her in a couple of years, and she's twenty meters away, but it's definitely Sienna.

And I confirm as much to my solicitor.

"It's her. What do I do?"

"It's not going to hurt to speak to her. Maybe you'll find out once and for all what's going on. She's obviously there for a reason."

"Yeah, to take Max," I reply.

"You don't know that."

"You're certain you haven't heard from her solicitors?"

His reply is frustrated. "I haven't heard from them, Hendricks."

"Okay, thanks. I'll call you back," I say, and hang up.

Fuck, fuck, fuck.

I run through the list of things she could be wanting, of why she could be *here* outside Max's school. There's only one thing I can come up with, like I said to Arthur, and it's Max.

It's every fear I've had since he was born come to life.

I'm nothing but a ball of anxiety and nausea. The pressure building inside me is giving me a splitting headache, and I can't decide whether I'm going to be sick. I do know, however, that sitting in the car watching Sienna isn't going to make any of it go away.

Better get this over with. Face the dragon.

I open the car door, get out, and close the door without slamming it. I don't want to alert her or startle her only for her to run off before I reach her.

Sienna's staring straight ahead as I walk out of the school gates. I expect her to sense movement and look up at some point, but she's in a trance. I get closer and spot a manila envelope in her hand, the type they use for legal documents.

Legal documents, legal documents. *Fuck.*

For what has to be the thousandth time today, I take a deep breath.

Not until I'm crossing the road directly in front of her does she register that she's not alone. There's not a flicker of surprise on her face either. She's been waiting for me. She knew I'd come here.

Immediately, I flare up, feeling like I've been caught in a trap. "Sienna? What the fuck are you doing here?"

"Hello to you too." She smiles, and I'm stalled briefly. In my years of hating her, I'd forgotten how pretty she is. Her nose, the same one Max inherited, squashes up as her smile gets wider. Faint creases I don't remember her having fan around her eyes.

It makes me angrier and more suspicious. "Answer my question."

"I came to see you."

"Why? Why here? Why now and not at the offices like you requested?" I snarl. "I waited for two hours, Sienna, and I haven't heard from you since. What game is this, because I'm not fucking playing. Tell me what you want."

"It's not a game," she replies, and looks genuinely repentant that I'm taken aback for a second. "I'm sorry, I wasn't ready to see you, but you should have been told earlier I wasn't coming. I didn't realize my solicitors hadn't informed you."

"Solicitors I fucking pay for."

She nods. "Yes. You're right."

I don't know what's going on here, but the Sienna in front of me isn't the Sienna I know. The one I'm used to is abrasive, bristly, gearing for a fight over anything and everything.

The best word I can use to describe her mood today is passive, and I honestly don't know how to take it. It's making me fucking edgy, that's for sure.

She's a barn cat playing with her food before she devours it in one bite, and it takes all my patience not to shake the answer out of her. "Sienna, I'm asking you one more time. What are you doing here?"

She runs her fingers along the edges of the manila envelope, turning it over in her hand, her gaze fixed once more on the school. I wonder if she knows that Max's classroom is visible from where we are. Or if she'd know which child was Max if she could see them all lined up.

"I tried, you know."

"Tried what?"

"To be a mother. To *want* to be a mother, a good one."

I don't know what to say. Not a single memory I have would prove this, only the exact opposite. Even throughout her pregnancy, she tried to pretend it didn't exist, and it only got worse once Max was born.

"Did you?"

The glare she shoots my way is exactly the woman I remember.

It's also the look Max gets when he has to do something he doesn't want, and while it doesn't quite make me laugh, it does help ease some of the tension running through me.

It's hard to remember that another person made up half of him with me. That Max's DNA is connected to someone who barely knows him. She has no idea he hates bananas, or that he always ties his shoelaces with the left foot first because he's right-handed and thinks it balances things out.

She'll never have the memory of waking up next to him, face smooshed into the pillow, or watching his first time on a pony. She'll never see the way the dogs follow him around religiously in case he's got biscuits in his pocket.

She'll never know about his passion for snails, which is what's usually in his pocket.

"I guess you won't let me see him."

I hold in the scoff. "You guess correctly."

"Then tell me about him, please. I deserve that."

I bite my tongue. *Do you?* I want to say. *Do you really believe you deserve to know anything about the child you didn't want?*

But I relent, though I keep it to the bare minimum. "He's sweet, funny. Getting taller every day. He loves reading, and his current favorite is about a pirate boy. Miles has been teaching him how to play polo—"

She holds her hand up. She's had enough, whereas I could go on and on *and on.* I'm almost disappointed she hasn't proven herself to be different from the person I thought she was.

Her eyes flick from me to the school, then drop to where her hands are in her lap. "I came because I wanted to make sure I was making the right decision. One I've been weighing for a long time. I thought maybe if I caught a glimpse of him, that my mind would be swayed in one direction or another—"

My stomach drops to the floor, and my jaw is clenched so tight I can barely get the words out. "Swayed about what?"

She turns her whole body to me. "I'm moving away. I've spent the past twelve months in India building a community over there. I opened up a yoga retreat, and it's really turning into something." She smiles, peacefully, proudly, but I have no idea what to do with this information. Am I supposed to congratulate her, or is she about to drop the bomb that she wants Max to move to India with her, because . . .? "And I've decided that's where my heart is. I don't want to be in England anymore."

"Okay." My eyes narrow, and I get the distinct impression she's enjoying my misery.

"Relax, Hendricks. I've instructed my solicitor to hand over the deed for the London flat to you. And to request your solicitors stop the monthly payments."

I stare at her, wondering if I've heard correctly. I watch her lips move, but the words coming out don't make any sense. "Sienna—"

"I don't need or want anything from you, Hendricks. I have to do this by myself."

Once more, I bite my tongue, declining to mention that opening a yoga studio "by yourself" hardly counts when someone else has funded the entire thing because I assume that's where all my money went. But, fuck it, if she wants to live in India forever, then I'll drive her to the airport myself.

"Congratulations."

Sienna bows her head. "Thank you, it means a lot. Here." She presses the envelope to my chest and, before I can stop her, leans in to kiss my cheek. "Bye, Hendricks."

I'm speechless. Tongue stuck to the roof of my mouth as I watch her walk away. I hope it's for good. I *pray* it's for good. It's different from any interaction we've ever had before, that's for sure. I want to latch on to the little bubble of hope growing in my belly, and I'm tempted to go into the school just so I can see Max, to hold him and kiss him.

It's only caution that stops me because he'd know something was up, beyond me being a weird dad. And I never ever want Max to know anything about what happened until he's old enough to understand.

So I walk back to my car, much less angry than I left it. Once my heart has settled into a steadier beat, I call Arthur back.

"What happened?"

"She's moving to India," I reply and reiterate the financial aspect.

"That's . . . um, unusual."

"She also gave me an envelope, but I haven't opened it." I'm too scared.

"Go ahead, we can deal with it."

Twisting open the fastening at the top, there's a single sheet of paper inside, and I pull it out.

It's an official government document, but I scan the words so quickly that it's hard to take in what they say, let alone what they mean. I'm reading it again for the third time when Arthur reminds me he's on speakerphone.

"Hendricks, are you still there?"

"Yes, sorry . . . the top of the page says it's an adoption order . . . I *think* . . . Arthur, she's signing away all rights to Max as being her son. Can that be right?" I scan it again in disbelief.

I'm certain that's what it says, but it's also too good to be true. And sad, so desperately sad.

"Can you read the page to me?" he asks, so I do, starting from the top and without skipping anything in case it's vital. "Okay, I'm going to send a courier to you right now to collect this in person, but can you get home and scan it to me so I can read it before the original arrives? Then I'll contact her team. He'll be with you in two hours."

I nod. I don't even realize tears are streaming down

my face until they fall onto my lap in big wet globs.

"Hendricks?"

"Sorry . . . yes, give me ten minutes, and I'll send it. Thanks, Arthur."

"Congratulations. This is a good day for you all."

Carefully slipping the paper back into the envelope, I turn the engine on and head home.

Beyond a couple of the housekeeping staff, Burlington Hall is quiet when I arrive, and I don't stop until I reach my study. I'm on autopilot, hands shaking, as I scan the paper and email it over.

I read it again. Words like *rescind* and *withdraw* swim before my eyes. I've no doubt this isn't the end yet because the solicitors will need to go over everything with a fine-tooth comb, but it's a start. A beginning.

When I walk out of my study, I feel ten stone lighter. My shoulders are softer, there's a spring in my step that the dogs notice, and sensing weakness, they walk me straight up to the treats cupboard.

On the way, I notice things that usually blend into the background. Max's framed finger-paintings from his kindergarten days hanging along the wall, the Spider-Man costume slung onto the kitchen stool after he removed it this morning before we left for school, a ratty drawstring bag he keeps his snails in inexplicably filled with glitter. All of it.

Handing over the treats, I sit on the floor with Dolly, Maud, and Hamish in the middle of the kitchen, soaking it all in. This place has been home to Max. The only home he's ever known and will continue to know. The home I knew as a child.

I hadn't realized how tightly I was gripping our reality until it was almost taken away, and the relief is too great for me to hold on to any longer. Tears stream down my face quicker than Maud and Dolly can lick them away.

I've been living with a constant niggle of worry that one day Max would be taken from me. He'd be gone as Story was gone. As my dad was gone.

But we survived.

I turn at the sound of footsteps walking down the hallway, only to see Clementine clock me, pause mid-stride, and turn away.

"Not so fast." Drying my eyes, I run after her in time to see her dart into Lando's study. "Clementine, don't be so fucking childish."

The door rebounds against the wall from the force of her pushing it open, and I catch it just before it slams into my face. As calmly as I can, I close it behind me and prop myself against it. If she wants to bolt, she'll have to push past me first.

She's leaning against Lando's desk, arms crossed defiantly over her chest like she's ready for battle.

"We need to talk."

Her chin juts. "I don't have anything to say."

"Then I'll talk . . ." I summon the will to stay calm, which comes quicker than I expected. Perhaps as I've already dealt with one evil today, the second will come easier. "Are you in a relationship with Santiago Torres?"

Her mouth purses tight. "No."

"Have you ever had—"

"You're a vet, Hendricks. Not a fucking solicitor."

My eyes roll heavily at the dramatics, but she's right. I am a vet. And I know a scared, defensive animal when I see one. Any doubt I had about her and Torres vanishes.

"What's going on? Can you explain what I saw?"

Her mouth rolls tight.

"Are you the reason Torres has been turning up to all Miles's games?"

Her jaw pops.

"Clem, I know what I saw, and I haven't told anyone. But fuck me, I have enough shit to deal with without holding on to this secret too. D'you know how hard it is for me to keep a secret from Miles?"

She stays silent, but this time, her eyes lose their wariness and drop down.

"Miles is out for blood, you know. He's going to pay him back for nearly killing him."

That gets her attention. "What's he going to do?"

"I don't know." I shrug. "Have you forgotten that Miles nearly died?"

"Of course, I haven't."

"Then I'm asking again, what are you doing? You know how fucked up this is?"

"Nothing's happening, Hendricks."

I shake my head. I can see in her eyes that she's lying, but I just don't know why. "I'm not keeping this secret for you, Clementine. It's too big. Either you tell Miles or I will."

"Hen, please don't. Miles will never speak to me again. Nothing is going on, I promise. I promise. You don't understand."

"Then help me to understand."

Her head drops again, and she wipes away a tear. I wait for a response, *anything*, but she's gone back to being silent.

I know why she thinks I'll be a soft touch to her begging, because I am with Max, but this is different. Miles is the most loyal of all of us, and Clemmie's behavior won't make him angry. It'll break his heart.

"Explain to him, Clem. That's all you have to do."

I leave her to her thoughts and walk back to the kitchen. Adrenaline is pumping through me, and I'm tempted to burn it off with a run, but I need to wait and hand over Sienna's document to the courier.

So I order some lunch, pour myself a beer, and ruminate on everything that's happened since the beginning of the year, starting with Story and ending with my son.

It's been a whirlwind, to put it lightly. My past and everything I thought I'd buried have returned with vigor and smacked me in the face. But I see it clearer.

My life is slowly slotting into place. My brain has space to figure out what I want for my future, where I want it to be, and who I want it with.

My mum was right. I now have the chance to be more than Max's father, and I know exactly where to start.

29

Story

The first thing Hendricks does when I open the door is pull me into his arms and kiss me.

Really kiss me.

It's different from our other kisses. I might be pushed hard against the wall, but there's no urgency to rip my clothes off. His hands stay locked around my waist, and he holds me like he has no intention of ever letting me go.

I love it.

He tastes fresh and delicately minty. I can sense his smile growing at whatever's going through his mind while his tongue strokes against mine. Hard, soft, firm. After a minute, he pulls back, enough to search my face, and I guess he finds whatever he was looking for, because he goes back in. Soft nips at my lips, and then his mouth surrounds mine again.

And I melt.

It's the kiss I dreamed about as a teenager, lying in bed at night after a romcom marathon. It's Peter Kavinsky and Lara Jean, Noah Calhoun and Allie, and all the couples I fantasized about at fifteen who had what I wanted.

The perfect movie kiss.

And when it ends, he doesn't pull away but rests his head against mine. "I still can't believe that I can finally do that. It almost doesn't feel real."

My hands find his face, resting against the soft stubble covering his cheeks. "It is real, Hen."

Bending down, he picks up the most enormous bunch of pale lilacs I've ever seen. I'd been so focused on him when he arrived that I hadn't even noticed them.

I breathe them in, and their sweet almondy scent takes me straight back to our childhood.

"Thank you."

"You're welcome." He presses his lips to mine, then leads me through to the sofa and asks me to sit.

I haven't heard from him since this morning, except for his request to meet here. After that kiss, the flowers, and the fact he's still holding my hand, I'm positive he's not going to pull his usual trick of changing his mind, but the way he's staring at me has me curious.

"Is everything okay?"

His dimples pull in, his eyes sparkle as he leans toward me for another kiss, and he kneels in front of me. "Yes, actually, they are. For the first time in a really long time."

"That's great—"

"Sienna has given up any right to Max and her title as a mother."

Hendricks's voice breaks, and my heart cracks. My Hendricks. The pillar of strength for everyone—his son, animals he cares for, Miles, *me*—it's always been the same. All the years I've known him. He looks out for those around him so fiercely you'd never guess the levels of pain he was carrying too.

The emotional toll it's taken is all the more obvious when contrasted with the strength he usually radiates.

Meeting him on the floor, I wrap my arms around his thick shoulders and let his head drop to mine while he sobs quietly.

My palm rests between his shoulders. "Hen, this is amazing. He's finally all yours."

"I know, he's finally mine. But it's more than that. When I read the document, I realized I've been holding my breath, waiting for the day when she'd claim rights and take him away." He sniffs loudly and sits back. I wait while he dries his tears on the sleeve of his jumper. "I've blocked out everything in my life to concentrate on being the best dad I can be. To give Max a life he deserves, but it means I've neglected everything else."

Taking my hand, he curls his fist around it. One fitting inside the other. Lifting it to his mouth, he runs my fingertips along his lips. It's so slight, but I feel the softness.

"I love you, Story MacIntosh. Since we were six years old, I've loved you. Before I even knew what it meant. The past few days have made me realize I should have come after you in Australia. I shouldn't have let you go . . ." He pushes a hand through the curls flopping on his face. "Sometimes I wonder if we were inevitable. That we were always supposed to be together."

My mouth quirks. "You sound like Agatha."

"Maybe I'm just coming around to her way of thinking." He chuckles back. "Do you believe we were always supposed to be together?"

I think he's expecting me to agree with him, but I

shake my head. "I prefer to have a little more control over my decisions . . ." I pause as Hendricks rolls his eyes. "And by that, I mean I don't want any credit taken away from me for choosing you. I chose you, Hendricks. I chose you for me. Maybe I did it a little too young, but I still did it. It was my decision . . ." I lean forward and kiss him, my choice. "And I'm glad you didn't come and find me. We needed time. We needed the time apart to find our way back to each other. I loved you so, so much, Hen, enough that it almost became my identity. It wasn't right or healthy. I was so consumed in waiting for you that I also never gave you the opportunity to *choose* me."

"I'll always choose you, Stor." He's so sincere that the sting of tears twitches behind my eyes. "Something that's gone around and around for me is that we never got each other's firsts. We missed every opportunity. First kiss . . . first time we had sex . . . first everything. But lately, I've been wondering if perhaps firsts aren't what we should be aiming for. I never got your firsts, but if you'll let me, I'll give you all my lasts."

I launch myself at him, mouth hitting his all at the wrong angle, nothing smooth or sexy about it. Too much teeth, not enough lips. But it's real. It's passionate as I cling to him, clutching the front of his shirt so tight that he can't get away. He doesn't want to, though. His grin tells me that much as he maneuvers us so we're lined up perfectly again.

I will never get tired of kissing him, *ever.*

Hendricks Burlington, the first boy I've ever loved. The *last* one I will ever love.

Gently gripping my shoulders to pull me away, he holds my gaze, but there's a knowing curve on his mouth. "We still need to take things slow. I have Max to consider, and he's going to need time adjusting to Miss

MacIntosh as his dad's girlfriend."

"Is that what I am now?"

"It's what I'd like you to be."

I bite my top lip, trying and failing to stem the flow of tears. I feel like I have everything I've ever wanted. Today at least. "I would be honored to be your girlfriend."

"Which means we need to plan our first date." Hendricks shifts onto his knee, and my heart drops to the floor. There's no way, not *this* soon. "I'd like to ask you to meet me on Saturday morning at nine o'clock at The Beanery. Our first date. And I'm bringing my son."

I snort so hard at what a dick I am that air gets lodged in my throat. I attempt to laugh through it, but it turns into more of a wheezy cough.

Hendricks watches on, brow raised, but not once do I see any flicker that would suggest he was having second thoughts, only amusement.

"It's the Valentine Fair on Saturday," I say eventually, once I can speak again.

"I know. It's high time we were there together."

30

Hendricks

"Daddy?"

"Yes, bud?"

"I think I'm going to have a cinnamon bun today."

I peer down at Max, whose fingers are splayed on the glass wall that separates tiny hands from the freshly baked goods. When he steps back from the screen, he leaves a smeary little circle where he pressed his nose against it.

"That's a great idea. How about we get two cinnamon buns? And two hot chocolates."

His eyes find mine, always so curious. "I can have both?"

I nod. "I think today's a special occasion, don't you?"

He turns slowly around the coffee shop, taking in all the red and pink and the hearts falling from the ceiling. Each table is covered in a red or pink tablecloth, with pink croissants, sugar hearts sprinkled over the flapjacks, brownies, and custard tarts.

It's a lot, and Max's expression says as much.

"Because it's Valentine's?"

"Exactly." I don't add that there's an element of

bribery in my offer. "Would you like to find a table before it gets too busy?"

He rushes off almost before I finish my sentence, narrowly avoiding a collision with Matt, one of the baristas. I watch him settle into a seat toward the back of the bakery. It's a table we sit at a lot because Max likes to stare out the window at everyone walking past.

After putting our order in, I join him and find he's building a house from the sugar cubes. I stack two together and add them to the top.

"Chimney." I wink.

Sitting across from him, I'm weirdly nervous about our conversation. It's a subject I've never touched on with Max. Thanks to Miles, he believes girlfriends are gross. He's not wild about the fact that his cousin is a girl either. So it's anyone's guess how this conversation will go.

For five years, it's just been the two of us.

I've reveled in every single moment, every tradition we've created. Even the not-so-great ones have been a rite of passage instead of something to endure, like the time he had chickenpox and I stayed up for three days straight to stop him from scratching in his sleep, having to leave him with Sienna before I was awarded full custody, or any tantrum because he's inherited Miles's dramatic side.

He's my sweet, funny boy, and I am so lucky to have him.

For five years, he's had all my attention. Everything I've done I've done for him, and I'll continue to do so for as long as I can.

But things are going to change.

"Are you excited about the fair?"

He places his latest sugar cubes down and taps a chubby finger to his chin, as he gives it some real consideration.

"Hmm. I'm not excited about the singing. But I *am* excited about seeing Honey at the kissing booth. As long as no one takes her." His mouth turns down, just like Miles taught him.

That would be Honey the puppy.

Earlier in the week, Max accompanied me to the local animal rehoming center to run through a last-minute check of the dogs being brought in today. Thanks to the public service announcement running from the tannoy, he's been parroting commentary all week about the importance of giving dogs a good home.

He visited all of them, but one in particular caught his eye—Honey, a three-month-old golden retriever/dachshund mix who'd been abandoned.

She was so tiny, clearly the runt, and Max carried her under his arm and almost out into the car for the journey home before I noticed. It's not the first time Max has tried to sneak a small creature home with him, and I doubt it'll be the last. Normally, it's a farmyard animal, like the pygmy goats we rescued at Christmas, and were definitely not allowed in the house.

Each time it happens, it's met with a discussion about where their real beds are.

Honey doesn't come with that restriction. Max already knows she's allowed in the house with the other dogs, an argument he's put forth many times.

Normally, it doesn't take long for him to get distracted with a new subject, but it's been a week, and he's still talking about her. So yesterday I called the center and said I'd take her in return for a sizeable donation.

By the end of the day, we'll be a four-dog household.

Reaching out, I ruffle his hair. "No one will have taken her," I reassure him.

He smiles, his eyes open wide, and I assume it's because he's happy with my answer, but it's Claudia arriving with hot chocolate and the cinnamon buns. Pink whipped cream tops Max's hot chocolate, and the buns have been sprinkled with glitter and pink hearts.

He gets the exact same expression he had in the queue earlier.

"Thanks, Claudia." I smile up at her.

"You're welcome, and Happy Valentine's Day, Maxy."

His brows drop low as he looks suspiciously at his hot chocolate. "It's very pink."

"Yeah, that's love for you," she replies, droll as ever. "Tastes the same, though."

He stares at me over the top of the whirl of cream, silently demanding that I offer an opinion too.

"Happy Valentine's," I call after her as she walks away while Max picks the pink hearts off his cinnamon bun. "I'm sure they taste okay."

He shrugs. "I just want to taste cinnamon."

"Fair enough, bud . . . but as it's Valentine's Day, I wanted to talk to you about something."

"Okay."

Out of the window, the queues are already forming for Agatha's. Teenagers, couples, and adults who should know better are all waiting patiently for her store to open and to get their hands on a new love potion or spell to take home.

"Do you remember when you asked me about

having a valentine?"

He shakes off a heart stuck to his finger and takes an enormous bite of the bun. After wiping the sugar from around his lips, he mumbles, "It's a secret?"

I nod. "Right. And now you've been at school learning about Valentine's Day."

"I made my card for you."

He's so proud of himself, I can't help but grin back, forgetting that I received it at a little after five o'clock this morning when Max burst into my room. "I know you did, bud. I love it. Thank you."

"That makes you my valentine." He smiles, though he's more focused on licking the cinnamon sugar off his fingers. "I wanted to put more glitter, but Felicity used it all." His eyes roll.

"I think it's perfect. And what did your friends make?"

He shrugs. "I dunno."

Removing the blob of pink cream from both our cups, I sip at my hot chocolate. "If I wanted to give a valentine to someone, what would you think about that?"

"You mean someone you love?"

"Yes—"

"Like Granny?"

I suppress a smile. "Not quite like Granny. But a lady. A woman."

He's thinking about his answer when he points out the window. "Look. There's Miss MacIntosh."

Following the line of his finger, I see what he sees. Sure enough, Story is crossing the street. After years of having no contact, seeing her walk toward me again with her beaming smile is something I will never tire of. It's the smile I pictured on my darkest of days.

"She's waving at us." He delights, waving back. "D'you think she's coming in here?"

"It looks that way."

When Max turns away and faces me, his expression is curious. "Daddy, I think she's by herself."

I spin around to check. "I believe you're correct again, Maxy."

"Maybe she'd like to join us?" Max's shoulders lift so high they brush his ears.

"Would that be okay with you if she did?"

Max nods. "Yes."

"Then why don't you go ask her?"

He jumps up, bold and determined, and my heart swells three sizes. Story coming to meet us was planned, but I had nothing to do with my son's reaction to seeing her. I can't lie and say it doesn't make me inordinately happy. It gives me a shred of hope that the process of changing his relationship with her from teacher to personal will be much easier.

I've already ordered *all* the books from Amazon about single dads and dating. *Too* many, probably, but I refuse to believe that you can be overprepared.

"Good morning," greets Story, arriving at the table she's being dragged to.

"Good morning." I grin, standing to pull her chair out, fighting the urge to kiss her like I want to. When she flicks her hair behind her ear, the faint floral scent it leaves behind makes my heart judder. "Thank you for joining us. You look very pretty."

"Why, thank you." She tips her head and smiles at me, and her cheeks turn as pink as the hair band she's wearing. "Max invited me to join you both, though he's already warned me everything's covered in pink."

"Even the hot chocolate," he grumbles. "Chocolate is supposed to be brown."

Story peers around. "You're right, Max. It's very pink. *Very* pink. But I don't mind because it's my second favorite color."

Max's eyes meet hers over the hot chocolate he's still not touched. "What's your first favorite color?"

"It's light purple."

His reply is immediate. "Did you know light purple is called lilac?"

My hand drops to my side. Under the table, I reach for Story's hand and squeeze it. She squeezes it back, gentle and affirming.

Fuck, I love her. I always have, and sitting here listening to her have a conversation with my son is something I never realized I needed.

"Actually, I did know."

"That's my favorite color too. And it's my daddy's."

Story turns to me, eyes sparkling bright. Miles isn't the only one I can have silent communication with because I hear everything she says with that look. We're transported back to the day we first met two decades ago.

"What other things are your favorites?"

His lips roll and purse as he thinks about it. "I love flapjacks, and polo, and snails, and dogs . . ." His eyes flick to me, and he continues in the same breath. "Daddy, can we go see Honey?"

"I don't think she's here yet, bud. They're not coming until later."

Story turns to me. "Who's Honey?"

"Can we go check? Pleeeeeaase?" Max drags out the vowels, an expert in negotiation. "Miss MacIntosh can come too."

I turn to Story, lips quirking. "Shall we go and see if the dogs have arrived at the kissing booth? Max would like to show you a puppy he met. Her name is Honey."

"I'd love to." She chuckles.

Max pushes his chair back so quickly that it hits the man in the chair behind hard enough that he jerks forward. "Sorry," he shoots out before the stranger reprimands him.

I glance at the table of his untouched hot chocolate and half-eaten cinnamon bun, which he normally devours. "Maxy, are you done?"

"It's too pink." That's his only explanation, and next to me, I feel Story's shoulder shaking with laughter. "Please, Daddy, can we go now?"

My brow arches at Story. "This is what a Saturday morning looks like, just so you know."

Her hand brushes along the back of my arm, and she leans in. "Seems pretty idyllic to me, but we might need more coffee."

Glancing at the queue, which is now snaking out of the door and looping around the corner with Agatha's, we come to the same decision.

"Coffee cart outside."

"Lead the way." I sweep my hand in front of me. "Max, remember it's busy, so you have to stick close. And please walk, not run," I add quickly.

He turns to the door, then to Story, and thrusts his hand at her. "Would you like to hold my hand?"

"Of course." She grins down at him. "I haven't forgotten you're my favorite hand holder."

Max and I have been in The Beanery for less than an hour, but in that time, the number of visitors to Valentine High Street has tripled. It's quite a sight.

Groups of people are clustered at the top and bottom of the street, where they've walked around the corner and seen the festivities for the first time. Phones are out, and everyone's taking pictures of the decorations threaded from lamppost to lamppost, or of the light-up heart installations, perfect for selfies. Actors stand on strategically placed boxes hosting impromptu poetry sessions, and halfway down is a poet who'll write you a sonnet on the spot based on any set of words or subject you give them.

It's the busiest time of year for Valentine Nook, and the season it thrives in. And you can't help but be swept up in the joy and cheer, the infectious happiness that love brings you.

Therefore, we take our time to ease through the crowds, soaking in everything around us. Halfway down, Max's free hand slips into mine, and from then on, Story and I walk with Max between us. I try to concentrate on where I'm going, but my attention frequently drifts to them. Max is chatting away while Story listens intently, and it's hard to believe I'm not in a dream.

It's everything I ever wanted.

Up ahead, I see the stripes of the kissing booth roof before the rest comes into view. Big pink hearts, the curtains scooped to the side, and the heart-shaped cutout window designed for visitors to have their photo taken. Eddie's currently manning it. He should be taking the pictures, but I suspect the couple took one look at him, his deep frown lines and drooping mustache, and decided they could do a better job.

"Where are the dogs?" Max demands before saying hello. "Are they here?"

"Not here yet, little man. Come back after lunch." Eddie ruffles his hair, then his attention lands on Story and me. His finger points back and forth between us. "What's going on here, then?"

Story shrugs, but when she looks up at me, her eyes flash knowingly. "Just enjoying Valentine's together."

"Oh yeah?" Eddie's eyes narrow, and he stares, waiting for us to say more. But while that might have worked on us when we were ten, it doesn't any longer. And our official line, until we're ready to tell Max, is that we're spending time together. "Better than seeing you arguing, I s'pose."

"Our thoughts exactly," I add, only to find my son frowning at me like it's my fault the dogs aren't here. "I told you, but we'll come back later. By the time you've finished your concert, the dogs will have arrived. Then you'll see Honey."

"But what are we going to do until then?" he huffs.

"I have an idea," Story says, pointing at the booth. "Did you know your daddy and I built this?"

Max looks so skeptical it's almost insulting.

"I can build things, I'll have you know," I grumble in jest, but poke his ribs, which is guaranteed to make him laugh. Pulling my phone out, I hand it to Eddie. "If I could trouble you . . . I want a photo with my son and his teacher."

"Make it a good one, Eddie, because we're not

leaving until you do," Story adds, slapping him on the shoulder, only to follow up with a kiss on his cheek.

The window is designed to keep the subjects close together, which is fine by me, as the three of us squash into the space. Max, being Max, almost puts his head into the hole, while Story and I stay a little farther back.

I find Story's hand again, lacing our fingers together while I have the opportunity.

"Are you okay?" she whispers.

"I'm perfect," I reply. "Are you?"

She doesn't speak, only leans in as gently as possible and angles her cheek toward me, to which I oblige.

And that's the photo we get—Max between us in the foreground while I'm kissing Story.

There's so much to see, and the morning passes quickly, especially with Max dragging us from stall to stall.

We manage to avoid being targeted by the overly enthusiastic Cupids, and Max requests a poem about butts, which sets him off giggling for the rest of the day. On our second trip past Agatha's shop, she rushes out and, before we can stop her, hugs us tight.

"Wonderful. So wonderful. The reunion we've all been waiting for." Her hand cups Story's cheek, and it takes all my willpower not to laugh at the expression on her face. "I told you that spell would work. All you needed was a little faith and trust in magic."

"Sure." Story smiles sheepishly. "Thanks, Agatha."

Agatha takes my hand along with Story's and squeezes hard. "You're welcome, you're welcome, my darlings. Come back this week, and we can make a little potion to set your journey off with success."

She rushes back into the store as quickly as she left. She's not out of sight before I spin around to Story, who's already wincing.

"What spell?"

"Nothing." She waves me off, but unlucky for her, I know when she's lying.

"Story MacIntosh, *what spell*?"

She rolls her eyes. "What? Agatha gave me a spell to summon what my heart desired most. It's not a big deal because it didn't work."

"Um . . . yes, it is. And Agatha seems to think it worked. When did you do this spell? Am I under it right now?"

"I never said it was about you." Brown eyes narrow at me.

I waggle my eyebrows, enjoying the annoyance on Story's face. "But it was, though, wasn't it?"

She's on the verge of stomping her foot. "It was ten years ago, Hendricks. It didn't work."

Barking out a laugh, I sling my arm around her shoulders and pull her in close enough that I can drop a kiss on her temple. "I've always been under your spell, Story MacIntosh."

Her body softens into my side. "You're so cheesy."

"But you love it," I whisper.

She doesn't reply, but as she starts to walk ahead,

I hear her chuckling. I wait, and watch, and when she spins around, I'm hit with the full weight of her smile. It's spectacular, and for a second, I can't breathe. I survived too many years without it, and in this moment, I honestly don't know how.

"Max"—she holds her hand out—"it's time to go to the concert. Come with me, and Daddy can watch in front of the stage."

He glances up at me, eyes begging to get him out of it. "We're all going to be watching and cheering, Maxy. I'll be standing next to Granny and Uncle Lando."

"All right," he grumbles and takes Story's hand.

She leads him off, and I head for the stage, wondering how the hell I'm going to find the rest of my family in the crowds. But Lando is the first person I see, arm around Holiday, who's wearing the biggest pair of sunglasses, a beanie, and a thick winter coat with the neck pulled high. Locals are getting used to having a Hollywood star around the village, but there are so many people here today that she's decided to come in disguise.

"Where's Story?" he asks, after pulling me into a hug, followed by Holiday.

I point at the stage. "Directing the rabble. Where's Mum?"

"Front row, obviously."

"*Obviously*." I laugh with him.

Lando and Holiday push through the crowd ahead of me, and it takes us no time to find our mother. Clementine is with her and acknowledges me with nothing more than a tight smile, which I'd imagine has something to do with Miles standing on her other side. Haven and Alex, who's carrying a very wrapped up Everly, are next to him.

"How long does this thing last?" Miles asks me.

"I don't know, twenty minutes? Why?"

"I'm flying out later."

"Where?"

He looks straight ahead when he replies, "Aspen," because he knows *I* know why he's going, and that I think it's a fundamentally bad idea.

I don't get the chance to object verbally because Story and her colleague, Celeste, march onto the stage. Everyone in earshot falls silent.

"Thank you, everyone, for coming to watch the Valentine Nook Valentine's concert, put on by the pupils of Valentine Prep . . ." begins Celeste, before Story takes over.

"Our reception classes have been working very hard over the past month, learning and preparing for this moment, so please cheer loudly and put your hands together . . ." Her hand sweeps to the side as the first pupil walks on.

Miles's whistle deafens everyone within a two-foot radius, and when Max arrives, it's even louder.

Whatever nerves or reticence he had about the concert seem to vanish the moment he spots us all in the front row, along with the size of the crowd behind us.

His hand shoots in the air. "Daddy. Hello . . . Hello, Daddy . . . Uncle Miles, Granny . . ."

"Hello, darling." She waves back.

Max isn't the only one waving at family members. The whole class is doing it, which, admittedly, makes everyone in the audience laugh, especially at the kid who shouts, "*Look at me, I'm singing.*" Celeste and

Story work on getting the class settled, but once the background music begins, their shoulders straighten, and they stand still and quiet.

"You should try that in the mornings before school," mutters Miles.

What follows is a fifteen-minute demonstration of cuteness.

The first song is "LOVE" by Nat King Cole, which has all the children running around and spelling the word every time it's sung, which is highly amusing. The performance is peppered with loud sighs and *awws*. It's kitschy and adorable, especially when two of them appear on stage with a large basket and throw love hearts into the crowd.

For someone who complained about it every time the concert was brought up, Max is remarkably enthusiastic. We're close enough that I can hear his loud, tuneless singing, and my favorite part is him waving at us every time a song ends.

By the time it finishes, my cheeks ache from smiling. The cheer and applause from the audience is loud enough to be heard over at Foxleigh Park, and it doesn't stop until each child races off the stage into the arms of proud family members.

Max runs straight into my mother, who makes a huge fuss over how delighted she is. But predictably, Max immediately asks, "Can we go see Honey now?"

Scooping him up into my arms, I plant a big kiss on his cheek. "You were brilliant, Maxy."

"I *know*, but can we go and see Honey?"

I nod and spot Story walking over. "Yes, and Miss MacIntosh is coming too."

"Let's go, then."

Turning to the rest of my family, I tell them where we're going and grab Story's hand before my son tugs me away.

The puppies are there. Five meters out, Max recognizes the shelter manager, lets go of my hand, and runs straight up to him.

"Is Honey here?"

"Max has been talking about her all week," I add, reaching the desk behind the booth where the rescue is set up.

"What a coincidence." She peers at Max. "Because Honey has been talking about you too."

I don't think I've ever seen Max as excited as he is right now, watching the manager step into the rescue bus and reappear with tiny Honey. Max trembles as he takes her in his arms, allowing her to lick his face as he cuddles her.

"She remembers me," he says in a quiet voice that almost breaks me. If I wasn't already planning to take Honey home with us, that would have sealed the deal. "Please let me keep her. Pleeeease."

But he's five, and I can't be seen to be a complete pushover. "Maxy, you know how much care and love she needs?"

"I know, Daddy," he replies solemnly.

"She needs feeding and walks—"

"Dolly, Maud, and Hamish will show her. She can join them."

"And she can't sleep in your room. She has to sleep in her own bed."

"Stop being such a hard-arse," mumbles Story, reaching out to stroke Honey's silky ears.

Ignoring her, I hide the smile at my flash forward to the future where she's the pushover to *our* children, and turn to the manager, "I'll sign the paperwork."

Max looks at me, and I should truly be given a medal for any time I say no to him. "She's mine?"

I nod and bend down to stroke her. She's already fallen asleep in the comfort of Max's arms. "Welcome home, Honey Burlington."

I sign, and we're given a booklet of instructions and a little blanket.

"Can we go now? I want to show Honey her new home."

"We can, but after one more stop." I grin, holding my hand out for Story. "Maxy, do you want me to carry Honey through the crowd?"

He shakes his head and yawns wide. "Can you carry me while I carry Honey?"

"I think I can manage that," I say, lifting him carefully into my arms. Honey doesn't even stir.

"Where are we going?"

"The car."

Max is occupied with watching Honey, but next to me, I can tell Story is wondering about the destination. She doesn't say a word as we reach the Defender parked outside Miles's and get in. Only when we turn left at the end of the road, instead of right, and head up the hill does she turn to me.

"Hen, where are we going?"

Glancing in the rearview mirror, I see Max is totally focused on Honey and use the opportunity to lift Story's hand to my lips. "I wanted to show Max my favorite place with my favorite people."

The farm gate has been purposely left open for me, and I drive straight into the field. It's bumpy and steep, but the car is heavy and powerful enough that we barely jostle, and when we reach the top, Story's jaw drops.

A blanket is laid out on the flat ledge of the hill, with hot chocolate waiting for us in big Yeti flasks.

Max looks up from Honey and out the window. "Where are we?"

"We're in the field above Honeysuckle Lane."

"Why?"

"Because I wanted to show you something. Unbuckle, and we can get out."

"Can Honey come?" he asks, a question I predict I'll get a dozen times a day.

"Of course. Keep her on the lead, though." I peer at Story, who still hasn't said anything. "Come on, let's go."

I jump out and open the door for Max, helping him to step out carefully. He takes one glance at the picnic blanket and ignores it to play with Honey.

"How did you do this?" Story asks quietly.

"James organized it for me. I told him what time we'd be here." I drop down on the blanket and pat the space. "Join me."

Twisting off the cap from the hot chocolate, I pour out a mug for her. She takes it and joins me while I pour out another. "I haven't been here since the last time we were here together."

"Me either," she replies.

We sip, quietly watching Max run around with Honey. A million thoughts run through my brain, most of which have to do with the girl next to me, who I've known forever. I watch her watching Max, her face expressionless, and for the first time, I can't read it.

"Still with me, Stor? Because this is my life. Hot chocolate, a five-year-old, and a puppy."

Her gaze sweeps around the space, the hill, our hill, and finally lands back on me. "I've always been with you, Hendricks. Even when you haven't realized. I don't want a life of anything else."

The weight of her stare hits me. The weight of her love warms me from the inside out, and I know now that this moment right here is worth everything we've been through separately and together.

Our future starts today, with a five-year-old sprinting toward us.

"Daddy, can Honey be my valentine?"

I laugh, deliriously happy. "Of course."

"Actually"—his mouth twists, like it always does when he has a particularly deep thought—"if I'm Honey's, then who is going to be your valentine?"

I glance at Story, then back at my son. "I was thinking that perhaps Miss MacIntosh could be, if that would be okay with you. What do you think?"

His nose curls up, and his eyes dart back and forth between us. "Sure. I guess," he says eventually, only to be distracted again when Honey stretches onto her belly.

Story giggles quietly, reaches out to stroke Honey, then settles back into my side. I pour a hot chocolate for Max and pull him into my lap along with Honey.

We stay there on the picnic blanket until the sun begins its descent. We don't move until long after it's gone to bed, and it's too cold to stay any longer. Quietly, we pack up. Max jumps into the car, and I carefully place a sleeping Honey on his lap.

"Daddy, d'you want to know something?"

I turn around to see him in the back. "Tell me, Maxy."

"Today is the best day of my life," he declares with his whole heart, and I'm inclined to agree.

"D'you know what, Maxy? Me too." I look at Story, but she's smiling at Max, radiantly happy and so fucking beautiful.

Then her hand reaches across, fingers slipping between mine. "Me three."

Epilogue

Hendricks

Six weeks later

"Daddy, can we get a koala at home?"

I shake my head, which has become a habit at this point in the day. "No, bud, they belong here, in their home."

"A zoo isn't a home."

"You're right, a zoo isn't. But I meant Australia. Koalas belong here, and this particular koala is here because of a special program to prevent them from becoming extinct. He's here because he's protected."

"I think Honey would really love a koala friend."

"Well, perhaps we can send her a postcard. Story can help you pick one out."

My son makes it clear he's not particularly happy with that response, but if he had his way, we'd be living in an animal sanctuary along with every breed under the sun. And all to keep Honey company, of course.

Honey Burlington has settled into family life like a duck to water. Even though she's a quarter the size of Maud, Dolly, and Hamish, she's quickly become the leader of the pack, and they follow her around wherever she goes. When Max is at school, I often spot her trotting around the gardens, followed by her posse, assessing their domain while she waits for him to return home.

She's become a fixture on the morning drop-off and afternoon pick-up, Max seems more upset about leaving her than he does me. I spent the week before we left for Australia reminding him she couldn't come with us.

We've discovered she loves broccoli, but only because Max was sneaking it off the table for her. It was the week I boasted he'd been doing so well with his vegetables. She loves balls, though she's still too small to carry a large one. And she loves cheese, which is the only thing we can use to tempt her away from Max at bedtime without howling because, out of everything she's seen and done, Max is who she loves the most.

And the feeling is mutual, which is why he's on a mission to persuade me to take home any animal from Sydney's Taronga Zoo, so Honey isn't lonely. Before we had lunch, he wanted a kangaroo.

"Maxy"—Story holds her hands out to him—"how about we go to the zoo shop and pick out a stuffed koala for Honey, then she can take him wherever she goes, and we don't have to worry about feeding it?"

If I wasn't already deeply in love her, I would be now. Especially when Max looks at her like it's the best idea he's ever heard. He takes her hand and follows her in the direction of the shop.

I don't even care about the smug grin she shoots my way as they walk off. Her and Max have bonded hard. Outside of school it's them against me, especially on our Saturday morning trips to the Beanery where she insists on flapjacks *and* hot chocolate. Story's sugar cravings are a bad influence on my son, and while I pretend to put up a fight, I really don't care.

The three of us together is all I've ever dreamed of.

"I'll catch you up," I call out because however short it might be, I like to give them time by themselves.

A wave of jet lag washes over me, and I take a seat on the nearest bench I find. We've been in Australia for four days, and I still have no idea what time it is. A few weeks ago, Story reminded me she was returning to Sydney to pack up her apartment, so Max and I decided to accompany her. We spent two days putting things into boxes, and today is our first day visiting the city.

Since we decided to take the leap and give our relationship a go, it's been slow. It's been for Max's sake, as well as ours, though he's been surprisingly nonchalant about the whole thing, because Honey is all he cares about right now.

My family, however, has not.

Our first Friday family dinner Story was invited to, my mother held on to her hand all evening like she was scared she'd bolt at some point. Clementine sat on her other side and monopolized the entire conversation to the point where I moved up to sit with Alex and Lando because I couldn't get a word in edgewise. By the end of the evening, it was men on one end, women on the other, and I'd barely spoken to her all night.

The next morning, my mother's questions began, much to my older brothers' amusement. Most of the time, I tried to zone out, but I caught the gist. When are Story and I going to settle down?

It's a question I don't yet have an answer for.

Truth be told, I could marry Story this afternoon and be happy for the rest of my life. But we're in no rush. We both know this is endgame, and right now we're making up for the six years we lost.

We've settled into a routine, which consists of date nights a couple of times a week, followed by a sleepover at Bluebell, because it's easier for me to leave from there than for her to sneak out of Burlington. It works for us, and seeing her at the school gates after I left her in bed only hours before has become our new favorite thing. It feels sneaky and illicit, brushing fingertips or touching hands while everyone goes about their mornings.

The only thing we really care about is Max. All that matters to us is that he's comfortable, and thankfully nothing has indicated to us otherwise.

I'm watching him now through the window of the gift shop and can see we're taking home more than one koala. Deciding I've had enough on the bench, I stand up to join them, and that's when my phone rings.

"D'you want a stuffed koala?" I ask Miles.

"Sure, why not. But I need a favor first."

I step aside to let a couple walk past me carrying half a dozen bags each. "Okay."

"Are you done in Australia?"

"Done? What do you mean?"

"I need you here."

"Where's here?"

"Aspen."

I groan loudly, tug my baseball cap off, and scrub a hand through my hair. Miles has been going back and forth to Aspen over the past month and has been uncharacteristically mysterious about it. I know it has to do with this girl. And I know it has to do with Santiago Torres, but that's all.

Miles is a big boy, but after meeting Torres, I can't

deny it makes me nervous, because Miles is also the biggest shit stirrer.

"Hendricks—"

"Yes, I'm here."

"But I need you *here*."

"In Aspen?"

"Yes, the day after tomorrow. You have to be here, Hen."

"Why, what's so important?"

I don't like the tension in his voice or the silence that follows.

And I *definitely* don't like his answer.

"Because I'm getting married, and I need you to be my best man."

Read on for an excerpt from Foxleigh Park

Miles

Four months ago

Rage boils my blood with every step I take, my feet crunching the remains of the snow shovelled off the path.

The stables are a hive of activity when I storm through. Grooms readying ponies for the next chukka, teams strategizing for the later matches, the sweet scent of hay and manure fills the air.

It's something that usually calms me, but not today.

Peering into each stall, stopping briefly to say hello to any pony inside, I'm no closer to finding my wannabe assassin until the noise of water spray hitting the concrete floor drags my attention to what I'm looking for. *Who* I'm looking for.

Admittedly I'm not entirely sure.

All I have to go off is the shock of thick auburn hair plaited down her back as she galloped past, screaming at me to get out of the way on a path she had no business being on.

The fucking cheek.

The same plait, now flops over her shoulder while she cools her pony's legs down.

"Found you." I spit, "You nearly killed me back there. Do you want to explain what the fuck you're playing at? The sign clearly said no ponies."

I wait for the apology she owes me. Then I'll decide how much she needs to grovel, but she's yet to turn around.

It takes her so long to answer, I'm about to repeat myself at a much *much* louder volume. If she's trying to rile me, it's worked. The reputation I've built on being icy cool is dangerously close to cracking.

"Did I?" she drawls eventually.

"Yes-"

"And the sign said no ponies?"

"Yes!"

"Oh. My bad."

What the fuck? "Your *bad*?"

She shifts and moves the hose to her pony's hind quarters, and his nostrils flare. He doesn't like it. My fists clench. If I saw a groom hosing their pony like this at *my* yard, I'd lose my shit, not to mention it's too cold and she shouldn't be hosing him down at all.

"Yup. My bad."

My jaw clenches. "Your *bad*."

She spins. A pair of bright green eyes glare at me, and for the first time I get a look at her. A *good* look. Dressed in all black, standing against the stark white walls of the shower she's a nineties Herb Ritts ad. Long limbs, tight curves, full lips. Stunning.

Lust stirs in me, but only until she opens her mouth again.

"Do you need me to clean your ears? I'm about to do Muffin's here, so I can do yours too if you want."

Whatever the hell is going on right now, I don't like

it. I might not be based full time at Aspen Polo Club, but I'm a nine-goal player. I've spent thousands of hours on polo pitches around the world, scoring goals, winning matches.

I've earned the respect she should be paying me a hundred times over, and she's asking me if I want my ears cleaned.

"No. I fucking don't."

She shrugs, and goes back to hosing poor Muffin who would rather be anywhere else. If she gets kicked, it'll be her own fault.

"You shoudn't be hosing him-"

"You'd better not be telling me how to look after my own horse-"

"You clearly don't know how to do it."

Normally my reflexes are much quicker, but I'm jet lagged and not entirely sober. So when she turns the hose on me, I don't jump out of the way in time.

"What the fuck is the matter with you?"

Her head falls back with a laugh. Loud, animated, and annoyingly infectious. But I'm too soaked through to find anything amusing. Too soaked to appreciate she's the most beautiful woman I've ever seen.

It's obvious she's also a lunatic who will not be reasoned with.

"My bad." She calls behind me as I storm off, leaving a trail of wet footsteps behind me. "There's towels in the locker room."

She has no idea who she's messed with.

I'm already plotting my revenge before I reach the outside. I can't decide if I want to fuck her or kill her.

But I do know this isn't over.

Foxleigh Park releases on July 10 and the preorder is open on Amazon.

ACKNOWLEDGMENTS

This is the first book of 2026. I promised it was going to be a big one and I feel we're starting with a bang. I can't wait for everything happening this year, they're all so different and exciting in equal measure.

But there's no way I can do it alone.

The Valentine Nook Chronicles would be what they are without my wonderful team of editors - Marion, Jenny and Julia. I'm so grateful for your continued patience with me. I'm so lucky to have your time and expertise working with me on this series.

To the Jupiter Reeves Fan Club, OG members and newbies. We grow in size every day, and I'm delighted to welcome every single one of you to the Luluverse. I always say my readers are the best readers in the world, and I'll die on that hill.

As always, for Sam at Ink and Laurel, and Cleo at Devoted Designs for creating a beautiful book for me. Glav for all the hours you put into socials for me, and Jamie, my PA for managing my newsletter and website so seamlessly.

And finally, to all my wonderful friends - you know who you are and how much you mean to me. Thank you for you continued and unwavering support, where IRL or virtually. I see it all.

For everyone joining me on this ride, buckle up.

ABOUT THE AUTHOR

Lulu started writing by accident, and somehow found herself stuck in a fictional world of ice hockey, baseball and billionaires. A world she has no plans to leave.

More recently she's ventured across the Atlantic to where her latest novel is set - the beautiful cities of Oxford and Cambridge, and the annual rowing showdown on the River Thames.

She's a big fan of strong heroines, because those fierce alphas need someone to keep them in check. You'll find her navigating her way through Romance Land one HEA at a time, and trying to figure out the latest social media platform she needs to post to.

She'd love to hear from you, loves hearing your opinions and thoughts, so please message her on any of the social platforms @lulumoorebooks and she'd love you to come and join her reader group on Facebook - aptly named The Jupiter Reeves Fan Club.

But if you don't want to do any of that, there's always her website - lulumoorebooks.com

ALSO BY LULU MOORE

The New York Players

Jasper

Cooper

Drew: The Vegas Edition (extended prologue)

Drew

Felix

Huck

The Tuesday Club

The Secret

The Suit

The Show

The New York Lions

The Third Baseman

The Shake Off

The Baller

The Strike Zone

Home Run

The Valentine Nook Chronicles

Once Upon A Christmas Tree - OUT NOW

Valentine Nook - OUT NOW

Wylder Ranch

Honeysuckle Lane

Foxleigh Park

Burlington Hall

The Oxbridge Series - published by Penguin

Oar With Friends

You Float My Boat

Printed in Dunstable, United Kingdom

79842087R00221